倍斯特出版事業有限公司
Best Publishing Ltd.

NEW

全新制 新多益 金色證書 聽力

一次滿足所有師生需求
集三種動物特長
一舉奪「金」

莊琬君、韋爾◎著

MP3

應考＋備考　　獵豹

像獵豹一樣反應快，能即刻
秒殺試題。

教學解說　　貓頭鷹

貓頭鷹的特長，能查覺問題、
到問題癥結。

解題＋靈活運用　　浣熊

浣熊一樣思考靈活，能應對
題變化。

作者序・1

　　首先，感謝倍斯特出版事業有限公司從 2016 年給予個人機會，讓筆者陸續出版《iBT 新托福寫作：獨立＋整合題型拿高分》、《與國際接軌必備的中英展場口譯》及合著《一次就考到雅思閱讀 6.5+》、《全新制新多益閱讀：金色證書》、《全新制新多益聽力：金色證書》。在近十四年的英語教學生涯中，這的確是段美妙的插曲，讓我有機會將教學經驗轉化成文字，與更多人分享。

　　特別感謝陳韋佑編輯提出以三種動物特性搭配不同解題模式的企劃書，並在撰寫過程中，提供許多建議。當初看到企劃書時，立刻有耳目一新的感覺，三個層次的解析方式，適合各種英文程度的考生，就像在教學過程中，需要針對程度不一的學生，不斷調整教學方式及解析講法。

　　在寫書過程中，筆者盡力融入教學時常常提醒學生要注意的重點及解題技巧，因此，這本書要獻給以往有緣相遇的學生，感謝他們給我淬鍊教學的舞台，而淬鍊的結果，濃縮在此書，希望對讀者有所助益，順利考取

理想的多益證書。

莊琬君 敬上

作者序・2

　　一位外籍老師於課堂中詢問學生們對於剛才聽的一長段聽力內容是否都理解了。老師用對於聽力訊息理解的百分比數 90%、80%、70%、60% 等等，詢問學生並要求學生舉手。有些對自己英文感到自信且本身英文不錯的學生，在老師詢問「理解了 90%」的同學請舉手時，舉了手。分別有部分的同學在 80%、70% 時也舉了手。還有些搞不太清楚狀況的學生或尚未舉手的學生，趕緊在老師詢問 60% 時舉了手，或許是因為對於沒有理解 60% 感到丟臉、或是大多數學生都舉了手、或是覺得不想被老師詢問原因，例如是哪部分沒有理解到呢？

　　其實不管學生舉手的原因或背後影響的其他因素，很重要的一點是，學生是否是理解了相對應的百分比數呢？或是自己認為自己理解了但是其

實實際上並未理解到某個程度。

　　如果外籍老師進一步於播放一長段聽力訊息後，請同學寫一份聽力試題，卻發現實際上學生並未理解到自己所認為的理解百分比數。認為自己理解了 90% 聽力內容的學生，在寫試題後察覺自己僅答對 80% 的聽力內容。其他學生也於寫完試題後察覺到自己高估了自己本身認為理解的程度。雖然當中也有少數學生評估自己理解程度與實際考試後的百分比相近或相同，但大部分的學生都開始察覺自己本身的問題。這也使得我們不經去思考著，影響「學習」和「實際表現」在考試等上面的因素為何。

　　這一切其實要回歸到聽力的兩個很重要的一環。聽力要獲取高分或聽力能力要進步到某個分數段，其實很重要的兩個基石（也卻常被忽略的是）「聽力理解力」和「聽力專注力」。正確的學習方式跟相對應的英文實力才是能讓自己獲取理想成績的關鍵。例如：題海策略（即購買大量試

題好了）僅能提升對考題的熟悉度和適應程度，寫完大量試題就能於下次考試立刻提升到自己欲獲得的分數段是不太可能的。像是前次新多益考試 800 分的考生在寫完試題後，再報考下次考試前，寫了 10 回試題後希望自己能於下次考試考到金色證書，但是下次報考時聽力成績可能落在 780-820 或仍維持 800 分，因為聽力跟閱讀中，理解力的提升才能使分數提升到相對應的程度。而聽力理解力的實際理解才能達到那樣的分數段。

實際的聽力理解是等同於我們聽一段中文訊息，我們不需要先看題本上題目和選項，預測可能問的部分是什麼就能答對中文問題。而新多益聽力太多的方式是要求學生或考生「眼走在耳前」先趕快看可能問的是什麼協助答題。真的做到聽力實際理解的就等同不需要「眼走在耳前」，就如同上課不抄筆記卻每科都考高分的學習者是一樣的，實際理解數學和化學概念後，其實就能在腦海中推演那些概念，不需要抄筆記來協助記憶。

「理解力」遠比「答題技巧」和「記筆記」能力等重要，但這也是許多學習者不願意改變或不想承認的部分，會認為多看答題技巧的書或寫大量試題就能相對應的獲取高分。所以要於考試中提升相對應的分數其實重點該放在「**聽力理解力**」。

另一部分的影響因素是「聽力專注力」，除了聽力良好的學習者有可能因為分心考到於聽力能力稍差者相同的分數外，聽力專注力能協助考生在聽完一段訊息後腦海中有剛才的每句聽力訊息，進而修正聽力理解力，不受到題型變化和干擾選項影響答題，而過於專注於看題本題目和選項，聽力沒這麼專注的考生就有可能比聽力時都非常專注且聽力理解力都有到位的考生答對較少的題目。而這次書籍中規劃三個學習方式，修正考生的學習，使學習者能有效突破分數關卡獲取高分。

❶ 寫試題：傳統的寫試題、對答案和看解析並知道自己錯在哪。
❷ 影子跟讀：重新播放試題音檔，在寫完每份試題後，做數次或數

十次的聽力跟讀練習，修正「聽力專注力」。

❸ 加碼題：重新播放同樣的音檔，寫「加碼題」，有效檢視自己同份聽力內容換了題目後是否自己也能答對。

　　影子跟讀的部分，讀者可以依自己的程度依音檔的同步語速、唸完第一句、唸完第二句、唸完數句後進行跟讀，能拉的越長對自己能聽一段話後聽力訊息的掌握和 recall 的能力越佳。此外，音檔對話或獨白的內容與題目是拆開的，便於考生做影子跟讀練習，考生也能於播放音檔後接續做完音檔後的試題和浣熊試題（例如：part 3 第一單元播放 MP3 036 即對話內容，接著播放對話內容的試題 MP3 037，翻閱到浣熊圖示頁面播放 MP3 038，考生可以自由搭配練習或單獨播放 MP3 036+MP3038 寫浣熊試題，寫完試題後用 MP3 036 做影子跟讀練習等等）。然後要感謝倍斯特出版社和合著作者，讓這本書能更完備的呈現出給讀者。最後祝所有考生都能獲取理想成績。

韋爾 敬上

使用說明
INSTRUCTIONS

播放音檔選出最合適的選項。

超強解析，獵豹解析迅速應對考題。貓頭鷹深入剖析各選項，浣熊解析含「加碼題」，照片改變其他問法也能答對。

聽力原文和中譯對照，便於寫試題後立刻觀看。

Part 2 浣熊解析，包含兩個題目改寫句，能立刻達到舉一反三的功效。

涵蓋三個主要學習法，❶ 完成試題並觀看解析、❷ 重新播放音檔，並使用中譯與聽力原文處的設計做「跟述」練習，有效修正聽力專注力。（建議在寫試題後，至少做數次跟讀練習）、❸ 播放音檔並寫浣熊解析所設計的另外兩題加碼題，檢視同篇題目改成其他問法，是否自己也能答對。

（p.s. 務必確實實行這三步驟，三重檢視聽力學習，聽力分數才能實質提升）

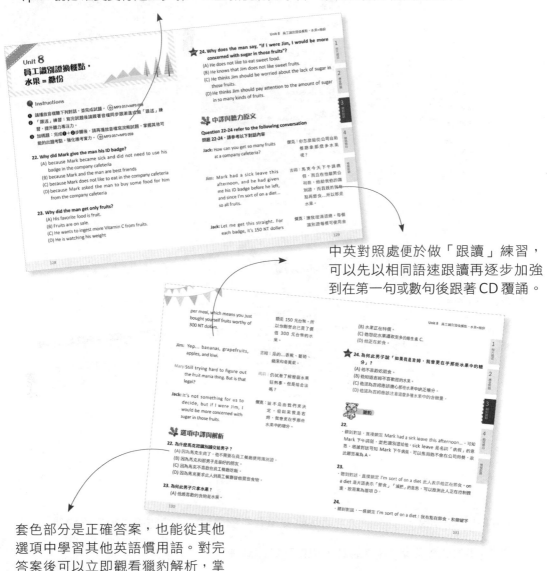

中英對照處便於做「跟讀」練習，可以先以相同語速跟讀再逐步加強到在第一句或數句後跟著 CD 覆誦。

套色部分是正確答案，也能從其他選項中學習其他英語慣用語。對完答案後可以立即觀看獵豹解析，掌握聽力關鍵。

星號圖示為新題型。

看完「獵豹」解析後，請觀看「貓頭鷹」的深入剖析。

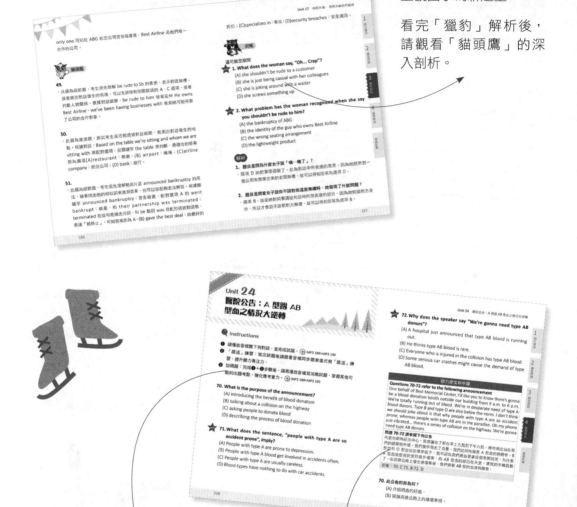

Part 4 也設計了三個學習法，請也確實照著步驟學習，三道防線檢視自己學習。

下表的聽力原文和中譯處設計，更便於做跟讀練習。

重覆播放音檔並寫「浣熊加碼題」，同篇文章改個問法也要確保自己都答對。

浣熊解析包含更多你需要知道的進階關鍵考點，包含聽力原文未明講直航航班但題目卻詢問直航航班等較不容易答的問題。

模擬試題。一次掌握題型變化，提升對新制「暗示性」題型的應對和推測能力，靈活應答。

對話表達道地且融入更多慣用語，能實質強化生活和工作中口語表達。

話題涵蓋更多新穎題型，包含 fuzzy, techie, a hiring freeze, kissing cam, kissing booth, black Friday, ugly wall 等等。

聽力原文和選項均中英對照，便於閱讀。

聽力原文也可以同前面 part 3 or 4 設計，做更多的影子跟讀練習。

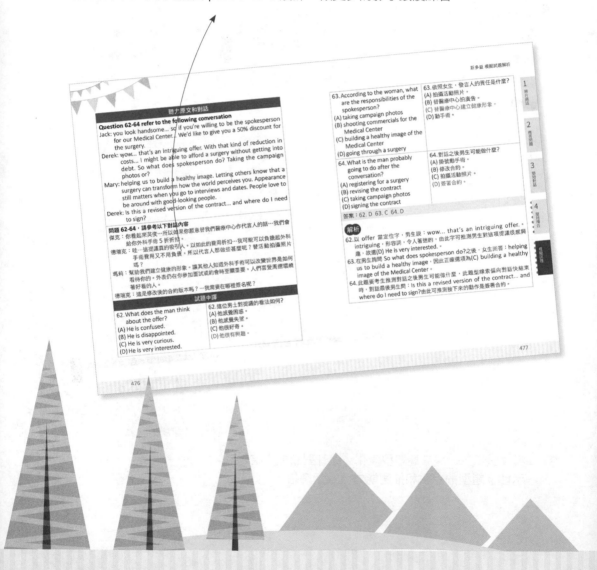

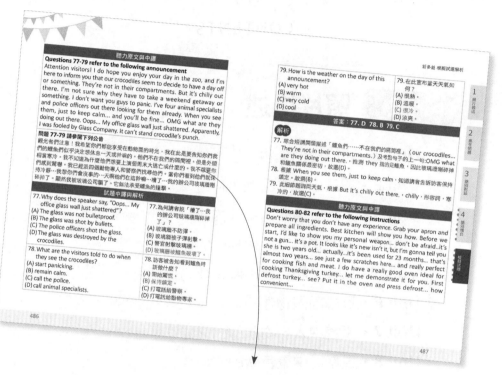

聽力原文與中譯

Questions 77-79 refer to the following announcement

Attention visitors! I do hope you enjoy your day in the zoo, and I'm here to inform you that our crocodiles seem to decide to have a day off or something. They're not in their compartments. But it's chilly out there. I'm not sure why they have to take a weekend getaway or something. I don't want you guys to panic. I've four animal specialists and police officers out there looking for them already. When you see them, just to keep calm... and you'll be fine... OMG what are they doing out there. Oops... My office glass wall just shattered. Apparently, I was fooled by Glass Company. It can't stand crocodile's punch.

問題 77-79 請參閱下列公告

觀光客們注意！我希望你們都能享受在動物園的時光，我在此是要告知你們我們的鱷魚們似乎決定想要休息一天或幹嘛的。他們不在我們的隔間裡。但是外頭相當寒冷。我不知道為什麼他們想要上演個周末大逃亡或做什麼的。我不想要你們感到驚慌。我已經派四個動物專人和警察們在那找尋他們。當你們看到他們的就保持冷靜...我想你們會沒事的...天啊他們在這幹嘛...糟了...我的辦公司玻璃牆剛碎掉了。顯然我被玻璃公司騙了。它無法承受鱷魚的揮擊。

試題中譯與解析

77. Why does the speaker say, "Oops... My office glass wall just shattered"?	77. 為何講者說「糟了...我的辦公司玻璃牆剛碎掉了」？
(A) The glass was bulletproof.	(A) 玻璃牆不防彈。
(B) The glass was shot by bullets.	(B) 玻璃牆被子彈射擊。
(C) The police officers shot the glass.	(C) 警官射擊玻璃牆。
(D) The glass was destroyed by the crocodiles.	(D) 玻璃牆遭鱷魚破壞了。

78. What are the visitors told to do when they see the crocodiles?	78. 訪客被告知看到鱷魚時該做什麼？
(A) start panicking.	(A) 開始驚慌。
(B) remain calm.	(B) 保持鎮定。
(C) call the police.	(C) 打電話給警察。
(D) call animal specialists.	(D) 打電話給動物專家。

79. How is the weather on the day of this announcement?	79. 在此宣布當天天氣如何？
(A) very hot	(A) 很熱
(B) warm	(B) 溫暖
(C) very cold	(C) 很冷
(D) cool	(D) 涼爽

答案：**77. D 78. B 79. C**

解析

77. 綜合短講開頭描述「鱷魚們......不在我們的隔間裡」（our crocodiles... They're not in their compartments.）及考點句子的上一句: OMG what are they doing out there.，推測 they 指的是鱷魚，因此玻璃遭撞碎掉和鱷魚關係最密切，故選(D)。

78. 根據 When you see them, just to keep calm，知道講者告訴訪客保持鎮定，故選(B)。

79. 此細節題詢問天氣，根據 But it's chilly out there.，chilly，形容詞，寒冷的，故選(C)。

聽力原文與中譯

Questions 80-82 refer to the following instructions

Don't worry that you don't have any experience. Grab your apron and prepare all ingredients. Best kitchen will show you how. Before we start, I'd like to show you my personal weapon... don't be afraid...it's not a gun... it's a pot. It looks like it's new isn't it, but I'm gonna tell you she is two years old... actually...it's been used for 23 months... that's almost two years... see just a few scratches here... and really perfect for cooking fish and meat. I do have a really good oven ideal for defrost turkey... let me demonstrate it for you. First convenient...

天氣預報等均與實際國外氣象播報表達相同且許多公告等內容富含趣味性，包含動物園鱷魚大逃亡、整形手術、籃球簽約、訂電影票等等。

除了學每篇 talk or announcement 的道地表達外，也要做更多的影子跟讀練習喔！

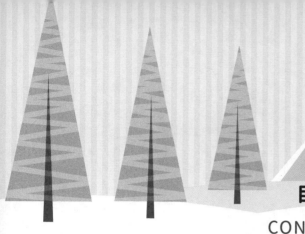

目次
CONTENTS

Part 1 照片描述

Part 2 應答問題

Part 3 簡短對話

Part 4　簡短獨白

模擬試題

PART 1

PART 2

PART 3

- 日本奈良：鹿的粉紅迷戀和 photo credit
- 日本嵐山：躁動的猴子讓導遊的話破功
- 尋找精子捐贈者：⋯可是最優質的居然要等到 2025 年了
- 球星簽約：跳脫框架思考就能在法律規範下也簽成功高檔球星
- 建築提案票選：各有優弊，但一切交由董事會決定
- 富商遺產拍賣會：誰料想的到舊椅子這麼重要呢？
- 訂購電影票：四部片，四個電影級別，攜帶小朋友就要避開某幾個級別
- 討論加班：工作狂就是希望有多些 overtime 啊！
- 史丹佛的分類：你是 techie 還是 fussy 呢？
- 模特兒表現評價：不只是 high fashion 和 commercial 之爭
- 整形代言：外貌姣好者有五折折扣只要願意代言即可
- 總機代接：藥品的銷售業務代表致電
- 食安出狀況：樣本受到汙染了

PART 4

- 黑色購物節廣告：有 personal shopper 就不用感到迷失
- 新聞報導：電腦小故障，但健身天氣播報男用海報代替
- 動物園公告：鱷魚上演了大逃亡，但講者顯然把重點放在別地方了XDD
- 廚房教學廣告：向您展示如何使用廚房器具，烤箱的去凍鍵就是好用啊
- 新聞報導：遊樂園慈善親吻亭…連播報員都要失守啦！
- 購物網站廣告：家庭用品能魔法般出現在家門口喔！
- 學院招生廣告：快來看看 go beyond that 指的是什麼呢？
- 談話：導遊在法國地窖的小小解說，可以嚐嚐白酒，但就別酒駕了
- 百貨公司廣告：四個口紅口味，買超過還有精緻手提袋可以拿喔！
- 談話：遊樂園內部消息透漏將有鬼屋的新增

照片描述包含各類型的圖片，其實搭配不同
簡單的表達句，同張圖片就能變化出許多描
述句子，浣熊的表達句能強化應對這類的題
型。

Part

1

照片描述

Unit 1
街道中的人物、景色的狀態描述

1. 🎧 MP3 001

(A) (B) (C) (D)

聽力原文和中譯	
1. (A) There are two vending machines. (B) Some people are wearing backpacks. (C) There is no gate. (D) It is raining.	1. (A) 有兩台販賣機。 (B) 有些人正揹著背包。 (C) 沒有大門。 (D) 正在下雨。
答案：(B)	

· 注意聽力訊息中動詞及名詞的描述。圖片中可看到三個人有揹背包，故可知道答案為(B)。

(A) 圖片中只看到左側有一台販賣機，two vending machines，兩台販賣機是錯誤的描述。

(B) 三個人有揹背包，複數主詞 Some people 是正確的，並以現在進行式 are wearing 描述動作，是正確答案。

(C) 圖片中央稍微偏右有一日式大門，因此沒有大門是錯誤的描述。

(D) 由圖片中的人物打扮可推測沒有下雨，因此正在下雨是錯誤的描述。

加碼題－還可能怎麼描述

· A woman is pushing a stroller. 一位女生正推著娃娃推車。

描述圖片中人物的動作通常用現在進行式：beV.+現在分詞 Ving，重點放在現在分詞 Ving 和之後的受詞，此句的現在分詞是 pushing，原型動詞 push 推，受詞是 stroller 折疊式推車。

飯店中的物品擺設描述

2.  MP3 002

(A) (B) (C) (D)

聽力原文和中譯	
2. (A) This is a study. (B) There are two pillows. (C) The bed is neatly made up. (D) The wall is decorated with paintings.	2. (A) 這是一間書房。 (B) 有兩個枕頭。 (C) 床鋪鋪得整齊。 (D) 牆壁以繪畫裝飾。
答案：(C)	

 獵豹

· 注意聽力訊息中名詞的描述。圖片中可看到一個整齊的床鋪，neatly <adv.> 整齊地，故可知道答案為(C)。

 貓頭鷹

(A) study 在此是名詞，意思是書房，明顯與圖片主題不符合，是錯誤的描述。

(B) 由圖片可見只有一個枕頭，所以有兩個枕頭是錯誤的描述。

(C) 「整理床鋪」的片語是 make up the bed，此句以動詞的被動語態描述，副詞 neatly，整齊地，修飾 made up，是正確答案。

(D) 圖片左側的牆壁幾乎是一片空白，沒有任何裝飾物，所以(D)牆壁以繪畫裝飾，是錯誤的描述。

 浣熊

加碼題－還可能怎麼描述

· There is a trash can at the corner of the bedroom. 臥房角落有一個垃圾桶。

There is... 的句型描述某個空間裡的人物或物品，重點放在名詞及單複數是否符合圖片物品，如 a trash can，也要注意介係詞引導的副詞片語，這種片語描述物品的位置，如 at the corner of the bedroom。

3.  MP3 003

(A) (B) (C) (D)

聽力原文和中譯	
3. (A) The hallway is empty. (B) There is no advertisement banner in the hallway. (C) The hallway is lined with flowers on both sides. (D) This is a department store.	3. (A) 走道是空的。 (B) 走道沒有廣告旗幟。 (C) 走道兩邊有花朵裝飾。 (D) 這是百貨公司。
答案：(A)	

 獵豹

· 注意聽力訊息中形容詞及名詞的描述。圖片主要場景是空蕩的走廊，故可知道答案為(A)。

 貓頭鷹

(A) 注意主要場景幾乎沒有人物，此時很可能重點要放在形容詞及名詞，走廊或走道的名詞：hallway，此選項的形容詞：empty，是正確選項。

(B) 名詞 banner 指「廣告橫幅或旗幟」，走道兩側各有一個廣告橫幅，所以是錯誤的描述。

(C) 走道兩側只有矮樹叢，沒有花朵，所以是錯誤的描述。

(D) 從主要場景，只能確定是空蕩的走廊，沒有線索能斷定是百貨公司，所以是錯誤的描述。

 浣熊

加碼題－還可能怎麼描述

· There are bushes on both sides of the hallway. 走道兩側有矮樹叢。

There are... 的句型描述某個空間裡的人物或物品，重點放在名詞及單複數是否符合圖片物品，如矮樹叢的名詞 bush 是可數名詞，因為走道兩側都有，所以此時該用複數 bushes 表達。on both sides of the hallway 是副詞片語，描述物品的方位。

4.  MP3 004

(A) (B) (C) (D)

聽力原文和中譯	
4. (A) This is a western style building. (B) The sign of a store is over a rooftop. (C) People are taking pictures. (D) People are drinking coffee.	4. (A) 這是西方風格的建築。 (B) 一間商店的標誌在屋頂上方。 (C) 人們正在拍照。 (D) 人們正在喝咖啡。
答案：(B)	

 獵豹

· 因為圖片沒有人物，所以注意聽力訊息中形容詞、名詞及物品方位的描述。(B) The sign of a store 主詞是正確的，over a rooftop 也是正確的位置，故可知道答案為(B)。

 貓頭鷹

(A) 形容詞 western，西方的，但圖片的建築物不是西方風格的。

(B) 注意場景幾乎沒有人物，此時重點要放在形容詞及名詞，並注意介係詞，如 over 在上方。介係詞引導的副詞片語描述物品間的對應方位，The sign of a store is over a rooftop 是正確的。

(C) 聽到主詞 People 即可排除此選項，因為圖片幾乎沒有人物。

(D) 聽到主詞 People 即可排除此選項。

 浣熊

加碼題－還可能怎麼描述

· This is an oriental building. 這是一棟東方風格的建築物。
此句重點放在形容詞及名詞，oriental <adj.>，東方的、亞洲風格的，building <n.>，建築物，同義字是 architecture。

Unit

旅遊景點街道周圍物件的描述

5. 🎧 MP3 005

(A) (B) (C) (D)

聽力原文和中譯	
5. (A) There are no pedestrians on the street. (B) A giant octopus decoration is hung from the building. (C) There is a truck in the middle of the street. (D) A tower is in the background.	5. (A) 路上沒有行人。 (B) 一個巨大的章魚裝飾從建築物垂吊。 (C) 馬路中央有一輛卡車。 (D) 背景有一座高塔。
答案：(D)	

獵豹

· 注意聽力訊息中物品或建築物的描述。圖片中央背景處有一座高塔。高塔的名詞：tower，確定答案為(D)。

貓頭鷹

(A) pedestrian <n.>，行人。但 There is no... 是否定句，是錯誤的描述。

(B) octopus <n.>，章魚，圖片裡沒有看到任何章魚圖案的裝飾，所以是錯誤的描述。

(C) 按照選項描述的位置 in the middle of the street，在馬路中央，並沒有卡車，所以是錯誤的描述。

(D) 聽到主詞 A tower，高塔，是正確的，再確定位置：in the background，在背景，也正確，所以選(D)。

浣熊

加碼題－還可能怎麼描述

· A giant fish decoration is hung from a building. 一個巨大的魚形裝飾從建築物垂吊。

此句重點放在名詞及其修飾詞，主詞 A fish decoration，一個魚形裝飾，以形容詞 giant，巨大的，修飾。另外的修飾詞是 hung from a building.，從建築物被垂吊。hung 是原型動詞 hang 的過去分詞，前面搭配 be 動詞 is 形成被動語態，即 is hung，被垂吊。

1 照片描述

2 應答問題

3 簡短對話

4 簡短獨白

模擬試題

Unit 6

遊樂園內物件的描述

6.  MP3 006

(A) (B) (C) (D)

聽力原文和中譯	
6. (A) People are celebrating Christmas indoors. (B) There is no tower. (C) There is a Ferris wheel. (D) People are in a church.	6. (A) 人們在室內慶祝聖誕節。 (B) 沒有高塔。 (C) 有一座摩天輪。 (D) 人們在教堂內。
答案：(C)	

 獵豹

· 注意聽力訊息中名詞及地點的描述。(C) There is a Ferris wheel，有一座摩天輪。是正確的。

 貓頭鷹

(A) 圖片右側雖然有一棵聖誕樹，但 indoors <adv.>，室內地，是錯誤的描述。

(B) 摩天輪及聖誕樹後方的建築物屋頂上有三座塔，因此沒有高塔是錯誤的描述。

(C) There is... 的句型描述某個空間裡的人物或物品，注意名詞及其單複數，一座摩天輪，a Ferris wheel，在此是主詞，是正確選項。

(D) 由圖片場景判斷是戶外，也無法斷定建築物是否是教堂，所以人們在教堂內是錯誤的描述。

 浣熊

加碼題－還可能怎麼描述

· The Christmas tree is decorated with a big star on top. 聖誕樹頂端以一個大星星裝飾。

將重點放在主詞及其修飾詞，主詞 Christmas tree 無誤，be 動詞 is 搭配過去分詞 decorated 形成被動語態，is decorated，被裝飾。副詞片語 with a big star on top 描述的也是正確的細節。

Unit 7

街道中人、物狀態的描述

7. 🎧 MP3 007

(A) (B) (C) (D)

聽力原文和中譯	
7. (A) Five people are sitting on a bench by the road. (B) None of the pedestrians are carrying backpacks. (C) There is a box on the trolley. (D) A man is pushing a trolley.	7. (A) 五個人坐在路邊的椅凳上。 (B) 沒有路人揹背包。 (C) 推車上有一個盒子。 (D) 一個男士正在推手推車。
答案：(D)	

 獵豹

· 注意聽力訊息中動詞及名詞的敘述，畫面左側有位男士推著推車，依照動詞 push 及名詞 trolley，所以正確選項是(D)。

 貓頭鷹

(A) 圖片右側有兩個人坐在路邊，(A)的主詞五個人是錯誤的。

(B) 注意主詞: None 是「沒有人或物」，圖片左側有三個人揹背包，因此是錯誤的描述。

(C) 注意名詞: a box 和 trolley，trolley 指兩輪或四輪，運送重物的手推車。手推車上至少有三個盒子，因此 a box 是錯誤的。

(D) 以現在進行式敘述動作，是正確答案。

 浣熊

加碼題－還可能怎麼描述

· Some houses are two-story high. 有些房子是兩層樓高。

畫面左側可見到一排房子，大部份是兩層樓高，樓層的名詞是 story 或 floor。

1 照片描述

2 應答問題

3 簡短對話

4 簡短獨白

模擬試題

風景區中景色狀態的描述

8.  MP3 008

(A) (B) (C) (D)

聽力原文和中譯	
8. (A) The lake is surrounded by trees. (B) Two houses are located by the lake. (C) There is no tree in the middle of the lake. (D) A snowstorm is hitting the lake area.	8. (A) 湖泊周圍被樹環繞。 (B) 兩間房子在湖泊旁邊。 (C) 湖泊中央沒有樹。 (D) 一場暴風雪正襲擊湖區。
答案：(A)	

　獵豹

· 注意聽力訊息中景色的描述。圖片中可看到湖泊周圍都是樹，「被環繞」以 be 動詞+ surrounded by 表達，因此知道答案是(A)。

　貓頭鷹

(A) 以被動語態 is surrounded by 表達「被環繞或在周圍」，是正確選項。

(B) 圖片中只看到一棟房子，因此主詞 Two houses 是錯誤的。

(C) 是否定句，但圖片中可看到湖泊中央有樹，是錯誤選項。

(D) 湖面看來是平靜的，因此由主詞 A snowstorm 即可判斷是錯誤選項。

　浣熊

加碼題－還可能怎麼描述

· The architecture and trees are reflected by the lake. 建築物和樹被湖泊反射。

將重點放在主詞和動詞。主詞 The architecture and trees 符合圖片中的細節，主要動詞以被動語態表達: are reflected，被反射。原型動詞 reflect，反射，反映。此圖清楚地看到湖面反射出樹及房子。

Unit 9

橋周圍物件的描述

9.  MP3 009

(A) (B) (C) (D)

聽力原文和中譯	
9. (A) People are playing in the river. (B) A bridge spans the river. (C) Only a few people are on the bridge. (D) There is no vehicle on the bridge.	9. (A) 人們在河裡玩。 (B) 一座橋橫跨河上。 (C) 橋上只有幾個人。 (D) 橋上沒有交通工具。
答案：(B)	

 獵豹

· 注意聽力訊息中動詞及名詞的描述。圖片中可看到一座橋橫跨河上，橫跨的動詞是 span，因此知道答案是(B)。

 貓頭鷹

(A) 河面上沒有任何人物，是錯誤的描述。

(B) 主詞 A bridge 及動詞 spans 都正確。

(C) 仔細觀察，可看到橋上幾乎站滿人，所以 Only a few people 是錯誤描述。

(D) 橋上有一台汽車及公車，所以 no vehicle 錯誤的描述。

 浣熊

加碼題－還可能怎麼描述

· Some buildings are located at the foot of the mountain. 一些建築物坐落在山腳下。

此句將重點放在主詞和動詞。「位於某處」的片語是 beV. located at/in，或 beV. situated at/in，「山腳下」的片語是 at the foot of the mountain。圖片背景處可見一些建築物位於山腳下。是正確敘述。

Unit 10
街道中人物狀態的描述

10.  MP3 010

(A) (B) (C) (D)

聽力原文和中譯	
10. (A) There is no traffic light. (B) There is no car. (C) A man is pulling a rickshaw. (D) There are at least four traffic lights at the intersection of the streets.	10. (A) 沒有紅綠燈。 (B) 沒有汽車。 (C) 一個男生正拉著人力車。 (D) 馬路交叉處至少有四個紅綠燈。
答案：(C)	

獵豹

·注意聽力訊息中動詞及名詞的描述。人力車是 rickshaw。可知道答案為(C)。

貓頭鷹

(A) 可看到有兩個紅綠燈,所以沒有紅綠燈是錯誤描述。

(B) 圖片右側看到一台汽車,是錯誤描述。

(C) 以現在進行式 is pulling 描述動作,畫面左側可見一個男生正拉著人力車,是正確描述。

(D) intersection,交叉處。至少有四個紅綠燈是錯誤描述。

浣熊

加碼題-還可能怎麼描述

·A man is walking with his headphones. 一個男生戴著頭戴式耳機走路。

將重點放在名詞和動詞。圖片右側看到一個男生正在走路。仔細觀察可看到他戴著頭戴式耳機,headphones。所以此句是正確敘述。

1 照片描述
2 應答問題
3 簡短對話
4 簡短獨白
模擬試題

Unit 11
風景區中遊客和動物的描述

11.  MP3 011

(A)　(B)　(C)　(D)

聽力原文和中譯	
11. (A) Many tourists are looking at the monkeys. (B) All of the monkeys are in the cage. (C) People are petting the monkeys. (D) Five monkeys are on the ground.	11. (A) 許多觀光客正在看猴子。 (B) 所有的猴子都在籠子裡。 (C) 人們正在摸猴子。 (D) 地面上有五隻猴子。
答案：(D)	

· 注意聽力訊息中動詞及名詞的描述。圖片中可看到地面上有五隻猴子，地面上的片語是 on the ground。因此知道答案是(D)。

(A) 聽到主詞 Many tourists，許多觀光客，即可排除，因為只有兩個人物。

(B) 籠子是 cage，地面上有猴子，所以猴子都在籠子裡是錯誤描述。

(C) pet 當動詞是「撫摸」，人們正在摸猴子與細節不符合，是錯誤描述。

(D) 主詞 Five monkeys 是正確的，修飾詞 on the ground 也正確。

加碼題－還可能怎麼描述

· Two people are taking photos. 兩個人正在拍照。
將重點放在主詞和動詞。畫面左側可見兩個人正在拍照，拍照的動詞片語是 take photos 或 take pictures。

12. 🎧 MP3 012

(A)   (B)   (C)   (D)

聽力原文和中譯	
12. (A) The city view can be seen. (B) The sky is very clear. (C) There is no chair. (D) No one is taking photos	12. (A) 可看到城市的風景。 (B) 天空很晴朗。 (C) 沒有椅子。 (D) 沒有人在拍照。
答案：(A)	

獵豹

· 注意聽力訊息中名詞及其修飾詞的描述。圖片看來是從高處拍攝，可看到遠方有許多建築物，可推測是城市風景，所以(A) The city view can be seen.是正確選項。

貓頭鷹

(A) 主詞是 The city view，以被動語態 be seen 表達「被看到」，是正確選項。

(B) 圖片中看到天空大部份被雲遮蔽，因此修飾詞 very clear 是錯誤的。

(C) 圖片中有數張椅子，所以是錯誤選項。

(D) 畫面左側有兩個人正在拍照，所以是錯誤選項。

浣熊

加碼題－還可能怎麼描述

· The sky is gloomy. 天空是陰暗的。

將重點放在主詞和其修飾詞。gloomy <adj.>，陰暗的。天空被大片雲朵遮蔽，所以此描述是正確的。

家庭後院中人、物的描述

13. 🎧 MP3 013

(A) (B) (C) (D)

聽力原文和中譯	
13. (A) Two people are standing. (B) Everyone is playing with the facility. (C) No one is on the swing. (D) Two men are sitting and talking.	13. (A) 兩個人正站著。 (B) 每個人都在玩設施。 (C) 鞦韆上沒有人。 (D) 兩個男生正坐著聊天。
答案：(C)	

 獵豹

· 注意聽力訊息中動詞及名詞的描述。圖片中可看到空蕩的鞦韆，所以答案是(C)。

 貓頭鷹

(A) 可看到一共四個人站著，因此兩個人站著是錯誤描述。

(B) 圖片中雖然有遊戲設施，但沒有人在玩耍，所以是錯誤描述。

(C) 鞦韆的單字是 swing，搭配主詞 No one，是正確描述。

(D) 可看到只有一個人坐著，聽到 Two men are sitting 即可排除此選項。

 浣熊

加碼題－還可能怎麼描述

· There are five people on the playground. 五個人在遊樂場上。

There is/are +名詞的句型描述某個空間裡的人物或物品，注意 be 動詞之後的名詞才是主詞，也要注意主詞的單複數是否符合圖片細節，此句的主詞 five people 是正確的。

Unit 14

交通運輸系統的描述

14.  MP3 014

(A) (B) (C) (D)

聽力原文和中譯	
14. (A) There is a roof over the platform. (B) The platform is empty. (C) The train is leaving the station. (D) People are getting off the train.	14. (A) 月台上有屋頂。 (B) 月台上沒有人。 (C) 火車正離開車站。 (D) 人們正離開火車。
答案：(A)	

Unit 14　交通運輸系統的描述

1 照片描述

2 應答問題

3 簡短對話

4 簡短獨白

模擬試題

獵豹

· 馬上辨認圖片主題是車站月台，注意名詞的描述，屋頂是 roof，月台是 platform，因此知道答案是(A)。

貓頭鷹

(A) 注意名詞和名詞間的相對關係，相對關係以介係詞表達，在上方的介係詞是 over，所以是正確選項。

(B) 圖片中看到幾個人物，因此形容詞 empty 是錯誤描述。

(C) 圖片中看到火車是靜止的，因此 leaving the station 是錯誤描述。

(D) 沒有人在下車，因此 getting off the train 是錯誤描述。

浣熊

加碼題－還可能怎麼描述

· Some chairs and signs are on the platform. 月台上有一些椅子和標誌。

將重點放在主詞。主詞 chairs and signs 符合圖片中的細節。

Unit 15
餐桌上食物和餐具擺設的描述

15. 🎧 MP3 015

(A) (B) (C) (D)

聽力原文和中譯	
15. (A) There is a tray on the table. (B) There are a fork and a spoon on the plate. (C) There are four cups on the table (D) There are a knife and a dessert on the plate.	(A) 餐桌上有一個托盤。 (B) 盤子上有一個叉子和湯匙。 (C) 餐桌上有四個杯子。 (D) 盤子上有一把刀和一個甜點。
答案：(D)	

 獵豹

· 注意聽力訊息中名詞和介系詞片語的描述。根據 knife、dessert 和 plate，知道答案是(D)。

 貓頭鷹

(A) tray 是托盤，餐桌上沒有托盤，所以是錯誤描述。

(B) 聽到 a fork and a spoon，一個叉子和湯匙，即可排除此選項。

(C) 圖片中看到兩個杯子，所以 four cups 是錯誤描述。

(D) 除了確認名詞 knife、dessert 和 plate 符合圖片物品，數量各為單數也是正確的。

 浣熊

加碼題－還可能怎麼描述

· Some ice cubes are in one of the cups. 其中一個杯子有冰塊。

當圖片中只有物體時，將重點放在名詞。圖片右側的杯子可看到一些冰塊，冰塊是 ice cubes。

這部分的聽力問題，分數比起 part 3 和 part 4 相對好拿分，其實只要掌握各式的問句其就能答對這個 part 的題目，考生可以多做這部分的練習。另外，也要注意別因為 part 2 太容易答就分心或粗心錯了幾題喔！

Part

2

應答問題

Unit 1
Do 開頭的疑問句

You will hear a question or statement and three answers. Choose the best answer to the statement or question. MP3 016

1. Mark your answer on your answer sheet. (A) (B) (C)

聽力原文與中譯	
1. Excuse me, do you have the time? (A) Sorry, I'm occupied. (B) Yes, it's ten to five. (C) I know. We're running out of time.	1. 不好意思，你知道現在幾點嗎？ (A) 抱歉，我在忙。 (B) 是的，現在是四點五十分。 (C) 我知道。我們時間快不夠了。
答案：(B)	

獵豹

　　注意疑問詞是助動詞 do，屬於 Yes/No 疑問句，故(B)第一個字 Yes 是線索，另外要注意 have the time 是慣用語，意思是「知道幾點了」。

 貓頭鷹

　　首先注意助動詞 do 是現在式助動詞，Do you have the time? 不是問對方有沒有時間，而是問「你知道現在幾點嗎?」，只有(B)提到時間點，ten to five 指的是 ten minutes to five，再十分鐘就五點，即四點五十分。(A)及(C)與時間點完全無關。

 浣熊

❶ 若原題目改成 Are you available? 你現在有空嗎? 此時要選(A)。
　　・Available **adj**，有空的，可行的。(A) Sorry, I'm occupied 暗示他沒空。Occupied **adj** 類似 busy，忙碌的。

❷ 若原題目改成 You should hurry up!你要快一點!此時要選(C)。此時題目是肯定句，句意的目的是催促對方，對方表示贊同他們的時間快不夠了。run out of Sth. 是固定動詞片語，表示「用完，耗盡」，注意(C)時態是現在進行式，beV. running out of Sth. 意思則是「快用完某物」。

Which 開頭的疑問句

You will hear a question or statement and three answers. Choose the best answer to the statement or question. 🎧 MP3 017

2. Mark your answer on your answer sheet. (A) (B) (C)

聽力原文與中譯	
2. Which candidate is more competitive? (A) the Harvard graduate (B) They need to compete again. (C) They were competing with one another.	2. 哪一位人選比較有競爭性？ (A) 那位哈佛畢業生。 (B) 他們需要再競爭一次。 (C) 他們正和彼此競爭。
答案：(A)	

 獵豹

　　將耳力鎖定在疑問字 which，which 用在從數個選項挑選的疑問句，which candidate 指「哪一位人選」，注意 candidate 在此是單數，因此答案一定會明確描述某位人士的特色。故選(A)。

貓頭鷹

　　Which 疑問字及單數 candidate 是主要解題線索。形容詞 competitive，強調「具備競爭優勢的」，因此可推測答案提及的人選應具備正面特質。不難判斷(A)是最切題的回應。(B)及(C)都使用競爭的動詞: compete，以不同時態表達競爭的動作，與題目的 competitive 意義不同。

浣熊

❶ 若原題目改成 What do they need to do? 他們需要做什麼? 此時要選(B)。What 疑問字詢問什麼事，do 是簡單現在式的助動詞，此時答案的主要動詞通常是簡單現在式的普通動詞，如(B)的 need。

❷ 若原題目改成 What were they doing yesterday afternoon? 他們昨天下午正在做什麼?此時要選(C)。疑問句的時態是過去進行式: was/were+現在分詞 Ving，此時答案的主要動詞通常也以過去進行式表達，如(C)的 were competing。

You will hear a question or statement and three answers. Choose the best answer to the statement or question. MP3 018

3. Mark your answer on your answer sheet. (A) (B) (C)

聽力原文與中譯	
3. What the CEO said in the convention is inspiring. (A) Yes, he needs to be encouraged. (B) I couldn't agree with you more. (C) The convention is at a great location.	3. 總裁在大會裡說的話是激勵人心的。 (A) 是的，他需要被鼓勵。 (B) 我不能同意你更多了。 (C) 大會位於一個很棒的地點。
答案：(B)	

獵豹

　　將耳力鎖定在 What... is inspiring.，由主詞 the CEO 和 be 動詞 is 的位置，判斷此句不是疑問句，是肯定句。通常題目若是肯定句，答案常表達贊同。(B)的句意是表示非常贊同。

 貓頭鷹

　　此題由 inspiring **adj**，鼓勵的，激勵的，這一正向意義的形容詞，可推測答案是認同題目句意。注意 I couldn't agree with you more 是慣用語，雖然是否定句，卻是強調「非常贊成」。注意句首的 What 不是疑問字，而是導引名詞子句: What the CEO said。(A)不可選，因為 Yes 開頭的選項是回應 Be 動詞或助動詞導引的疑問句，且句意與題目毫無關聯，(C)評論大會地點也和總裁説的話無關。

 浣熊

❶ 若原題目改成 Does he need more motivation? 他需要更多動力嗎？此時要選(A)。聽到助動詞 does 導引的疑問句，可能答案以 Yes/No 開頭，且疑問句和(A)動詞都是 need，另外 motivation 和 encourage 雖然詞性不同，但意義近似。motivation<n.>，動力，激勵，類似 inspiration，encouragement。(A)以被動語態的 to be encouraged 表達贊成提問者的看法。

❷ 若原題目改成 What do you think about the convention?你覺得大會如何?此時要選(C)。題目詢問對大會的看法，(C)表示地點很棒，是切題的回應。

Unit 4
現在完成式的助動詞 have 開頭的問句

You will hear a question or statement and three answers. Choose the best answer to the statement or question. 🎧 MP3 019

4. Mark your answer on your answer sheet. (A) (B) (C)

聽力原文與中譯	
4. Have you cut the deal with the buyer? (A) No, we haven't. (B) Just deal with the problem. (C) The buyer might want more discount.	4. 你和買家達成協議了嗎? (A) 不,還沒。 (B) 去處理問題。 (C) 買家可能想要更多折扣。
答案:(A)	

獵豹

　　將耳力鎖定在 Have you...,由現在完成式的助動詞 have 導引的 Yes/No 疑問句,判斷答案可能以 Yes/No 開頭,再確定(A)以助動詞 have 簡答。

貓頭鷹

　　Yes/No 疑問句的答案除了可能以 Yes/No 開頭，也常使用和題目一樣的時態，故選(A)。確定(A)以助動詞 have 簡答。注意 cut the deal 是慣用語，表「達成協議」。(B)是祈使句，要求對方處理問題，與題目所問無關。(C)「買家可能想要更多折扣」不如(A)明確切題，故不可選。

浣熊

❶ 若原題目改成 What should I do next? 我接下來該做什麼？此時要選(B)。疑問字 What 搭配助動詞 should 和動詞 do，詢問「要做什麼」，(B)以祈使句交代該做的事：deal with the problem.，處理問題。

❷ 若原題目改成 What does the buyer want?買家想要什麼？此時要選(C)。疑問字 What 搭配動詞 want，詢問「想要做什麼」，(C)主詞同疑問句的主詞 buyer，且明確回答「買家可能想要更多折扣」。

Unit 5
Do 開頭的疑問句

You will hear a question or statement and three answers. Choose the best answer to the statement or question. 🎧 MP3 020

5. Mark your answer on your answer sheet. (A) (B) (C)

聽力原文與中譯	
5. Do you think he will pitch in with an offer of help? (A) Sure, he has been very generous. (B) I don't like that pitcher. (C) She might pitch in.	5. 你認為他會投入提供協助嗎？ (A) 當然，他一直很慷慨。 (B) 我不喜歡那個投手。 (C) 她可能會投入。
答案：(A)	

獵豹

　　將耳力鎖定在 Do you think...，由現在式的助動詞 do 導引的 Yes/No 疑問句，判斷答案可能以 Yes/No 或表示贊成或否定的類似字開頭，(A)以 sure 開頭表示贊成。

貓頭鷹

　　題目以 Do you think 詢問對方看法，名詞子句：(that) he will pitch in with an offer of help 是 think 的受詞，整個完整句是包含一個名詞子句的間接引述疑問句。注意動詞片語 pitch in 是「投入，參與（協助）」。(B) pitcher，投手，是發音與 pitch 類似的陷阱字，整句答非所問。(C)不可選，因為主詞 She 是錯誤的。

浣熊

❶ 若原題目改成 Do you like the pitcher?你喜歡那個投手嗎？此時要選(B)。由現在式的助動詞 do 導引的 Yes/No 疑問句，(B)清楚地表示「我不喜歡那個投手」，是非常切題的回答。雖然題目是 Yes/No 疑問句，不一定每次的答案都會以 Yes 或 No 開頭，只要句意明確表示贊同或否定，仍是合理回答。

❷ 若原題目改成 Do you think she might give us a hand?你認為她會協助我們嗎？此時要選(C)。先確定疑問句的主詞和(C)的名詞子句裡的主詞一致：she，再確定 give us a hand 和 pitch in 意義類似，此時可選(C)。

Unit 6
Could 開頭的疑問句

You will hear a question or statement and three answers. Choose the best answer to the statement or question. 🎧 MP3 021

6. Mark your answer on your answer sheet. (A) (B) (C)

聽力原文與中譯	
6. Could you hand me that notebook? (A) Sure, here it is. (B) The notebook is expensive. (C) Yes, you may borrow my laptop.	6. 你可以把那本筆記本拿給我嗎？ (A) 當然，在這。 (B) 那本筆記本是昂貴的。 (C) 是的，你可以借我的筆電。
答案：(A)	

 獵豹

　　將耳力鎖定在 Could you...，因為 Could 是助動詞，導引 Yes/No 疑問句，得知答案傾向贊同或否定，搭配動詞 hand，遞給……，判斷 (A)是最佳選項。

 貓頭鷹

　　注意 Could 導引的疑問句在此表示客氣詢問或要求，不是詢問能力。因為 Yes/No 疑問句的字序是:助動詞+主詞+動詞，可依照字序判斷 hand 在此題目是動詞，不是名詞。遞東西時，常用的慣用語是 Here it is。(B)形容筆記本是貴的，答非所問。(C)由動詞 borrow，借，判斷不可選。

 浣熊

❶ 若原題目改成 What do you think about the notebook? 你覺得這本筆記本如何？此時要選(B)。What do you think about Sth.?詢問對方對某事或某物的看法，(B)以形容詞 expensive 表達看法。

❷ 若原題目改成 May I borrow your laptop? 我可以借你的筆電嗎？此時要選(C)。疑問句以助動詞 may 導引，表示客氣要求准許。(C)清楚地准許對方。

What 開頭的疑問句

You will hear a question or statement and three answers. Choose the best answer to the statement or question. MP3 022

7. Mark your answer on your answer sheet. (A) (B) (C)

聽力原文與中譯	
7. What's wrong with Jim? (A) Why don't you take some rest? (B) He just got laid off. (C) I don't know anyone by that name.	7. 吉姆怎麼了？ (A) 你為何不休息一下？ (B) 他剛被裁員了。 (C) 我不認識任何叫那個名字的人。
答案：(B)	

 獵豹

　　將耳力鎖定在 What's wrong...，因為 What's wrong...? 通常用來問「有什麼不對勁？」，因此(B) 他剛被裁員了，合理呼應題目。

Unit 7 What 開頭的疑問句

1 照片描述

2 應答問題

3 簡短對話

4 簡短獨白

模擬試題

貓頭鷹

　　What's wrong with Sb./Sth.?是口語表達關切常用的疑問句，合理答案應該描述負面事件，如(B) 他剛被裁員了。動詞片語 lay off，裁員。(A)聽到 Why don't you 馬上排除，因為主詞 you 與題目的 Jim 不符合。(C) I don't know anyone by that name.，我不認識任何叫那個名字的人，沒有針對「Jim 哪裡不對勁？」回答，不如(B)切題，也不可選。

浣熊

❶ 若原題目改成 I feel exhausted. 我覺得好疲倦。此時要選(A)。此題目是肯定句，關鍵字是形容詞 exhausted，另一方回答「你為何不休息一下？」，是合乎邏輯的應答，(A) Why don't you... 在此不是詢問原因，而是提出建議。

❷ 若原題目改成 Do you know Jim? 你認識吉姆嗎？此時要選(C)。題目和(C)的動詞都是 know，是解題線索，另外注意 by that name 的意思是「以……為名」。

How 開頭的疑問句

You will hear a question or statement and three answers. Choose the best answer to the statement or question. 🎧 MP3 023

8. Mark your answer on your answer sheet. (A) (B) (C)

聽力原文與中譯	
8. How was your skiing trip? (A) Yep, that skit was really funny. (B) No, I did not go on the trip. (C) It went pretty well. I had lots of fun.	8. 你的滑雪旅行如何？ (A) 是啊，那場幽默短劇確實很好笑。 (B) 不，我沒有去旅行。 (C) 蠻順利的。我玩得很高興。
答案：(C)	

獵豹

　　將耳力鎖定在 How was...? 得知是詢問狀況的疑問句，再由 trip 的字義:旅行，判斷(C)是最合理的答案。

貓頭鷹

　　疑問字 How 表「如何」，(C) It went pretty well. I had lots of fun.，「蠻順利的。我玩得很高興。」針對旅行發表個人看法，非常切題。It 指的是 trip。(A)的主詞 skit 意思是「幽默短劇」，是發音類似 ski 的陷阱字。(B)聽到 No 即可排除，因為題目不是 Yes/No 疑問句。

浣熊

❶ 若原題目改成 Did you enjoy the skit? 你喜歡那個幽默短劇嗎？此時要選(A)。疑問句是過去式助動詞 did 導引的 Yes/No 疑問句，(A) Yep 常在口語代替 Yes。

❷ 若原題目改成 Did you go on the trip? 你有去那趟旅行嗎？此時要選(B)。疑問句是過去式助動詞 did 導引的 Yes/No 疑問句，(B)開門見山地否定: 我沒有去旅行。

You will hear a question or statement and three answers. Choose the best answer to the statement or question. MP3 024

9. Mark your answer on your answer sheet. (A) (B) (C)

聽力原文與中譯	
9. Where should we hold the luncheon? (A) the tourist information center (B) A restaurant in a five-star hotel would be a good choice. (C) I'd like to have lunch with you.	9. 我們應該在哪裡舉辦午宴？ (A) 觀光客資訊中心。 (B) 在五星級旅館的餐廳是不錯的選擇。 (C) 我樂意和你一起午餐。
答案：(B)	

獵豹

　　將耳力鎖定在 Where，where 導引的疑問句，答案通常有地點方面的名詞，如(B) A restaurant。

貓頭鷹

　　luncheon 指「正式的午宴」，因此適合舉辦宴會的五星級旅館的餐廳是切題的地點。(A)觀光客資訊中心，答非所問。(C)提及的 lunch 是發音類似 luncheon 的陷阱字。

浣熊

❶ 若原題目改成 Where can we get the information on the festival? 我們哪裡可以取得關於節慶的資訊？ 此時要選(A)。根據 information 及 festival，判斷此時(A) the tourist information center 較切題，且 festival，節慶，常是觀光客感興趣的主題。

❷ 若原題目改成 Would you like to have lunch together?你想一起吃午餐嗎?此時要選(C)。疑問句以助動詞 would 導引，Would you like to V.?表達以禮貌的語氣邀請對方，(C) I'd like to V.表示接受邀請。

1 照片描述

2 應答問題

3 簡短對話

4 簡短獨白

模擬試題

Unit 10
Who 開頭的疑問句

You will hear a question or statement and three answers. Choose the best answer to the statement or question. MP3 025

10. Mark your answer on your answer sheet. (A) (B) (C)

聽力原文與中譯	
10. Who is in charge of the department? (A) They charged us 50 dollars. (B) I'm getting used to working in this department. (C) Kelly is.	10. 誰負責這個部門? (A) 他們向我們索價五十元。 (B) 我正漸漸習慣在這個部門工作。 (C) 是凱莉。
答案：(C)	

獵豹

　　將耳力鎖定在 Who，Who 導引的疑問句，答案通常有人名，所以選(C) Kelly is.。

貓頭鷹

　　注意題目使用慣用語 beV. in charge of Sth.，「負責/掌控」之意。
(C) Kelly is.有人名，be 動詞 is 的時態是簡單現在式，也符合題目的時態。(A)的動詞 charge 在此句是「索價」。(B)聽到 I'm getting used to...，「我漸漸習慣……」，馬上排除，因為與題目所問的「誰負責……」毫無關聯。

浣熊

❶ 若原題目改成 How much did you pay to the vendors? 你（們）付了多少錢給那些小販？ 此時要選(A)。How much?，多少錢？，did 是過去式助動詞，合理回答應該使用過去式動詞，故(A) They charged us 50 dollars.的過去式動詞 charged 是重要線索。主詞是複數代名詞 they，指疑問句的 vendors，也是線索。

❷ 若原題目改成 How are you doing with your work? 你的工作進展地如何？此時要選(B)。疑問字 How 表「如何」，注意動詞時態是現在進行式: beV.+ Ving。(B) I'm getting used to working in this department.也使用現在進行式，且針對工作情況回答。

You will hear a question or statement and three answers. Choose the best answer to the statement or question. MP3 026

11. Mark your answer on your answer sheet. (A) (B) (C)

聽力原文與中譯	
11. The sales figure isn't pretty, is it? (A) She has a nice figure. (B) No, we don't need to figure out the problem. (C) No, it isn't.	11. 這銷售數據不漂亮，是嗎？ (A) 她有不錯的身材。 (B) 不，我們不需要想出來問題之處。 (C) 不，不漂亮。
答案：(C)	

獵豹

　　將耳力鎖定在句尾的 is it?，由句尾的 is it?判斷是類似 Yes/No 疑問句的附加疑問句，因此回答方式類似 Yes/No 疑問句的應答，故選(C)。

貓頭鷹

　　此題考附加疑問句及 figure 的多重意義。附加疑問句的應答通常類似 Yes/No 疑問句的應答，也要注意主詞是單數或複數，及主要動詞的時態，題目的主詞 The sales figure 是單數，由此判斷(C) No, it isn't.的 it 是正確的，isn't 的時態也和題目的動詞時態一致。(A)由主詞 She 馬上排除。(B)聽到 don't need to figure out 馬上排除，因為 figure out 是「想出來」之意，整句句意也不如(C)切題。

浣熊

❶ 若原題目改成 What do you think about the model? 你對那位模特兒看法怎樣？ 此時要選(A)。題目以 What do you think... 詢問對方看法，(A) She has a nice figure.考慮 She has 及題目的 model，figure 在此是指「身材」。

❷ 若原題目改成 Should we identify the problem? 我們應該把問題辨識出來嗎？此時要選(B)。此疑問句是以助動詞 Should 導引的 Yes/No 疑問句，動詞 identify 有「辨識」之意，類似(B)的 figure out。

Unit 12
Did 開頭的疑問句

You will hear a question or statement and three answers. Choose the best answer to the statement or question. 🎧 MP3 027

12. Mark your answer on your answer sheet. (A) (B) (C)

聽力原文與中譯	
12. Did the bulk order account for 30% of the annual order? (A) Mary is the one to account for the order. (B) That's right! (C) 30% is not enough.	12. 這筆大量訂單佔了年度訂單的 30%嗎？ (A) 瑪莉是負責訂單的人。 (B) 沒錯！ (C) 30%不夠。
答案：(B)	

 獵豹

　　將耳力鎖定在 Did，馬上判斷清楚表明贊成或否定的選項是最佳答案，故選(B)。

貓頭鷹

　　此題考過去式助動詞 did 導引的 Yes/No 疑問句及動詞片語 account for 的多重意義。由 account for 搭配 30%，得知 account for 在此是「佔據」，同義字有 occupy，take up。(A)聽到 Mary is the one 馬上排除，因為答非所問，且 account for 在此是「負責」之意。(C)聽到 not enough 馬上排除，因為題目不是詢問對訂單數據的看法。

浣熊

❶ 若原題目改成 Who is responsible for the order? 誰負責這筆訂單？此時要選(A)。Who 導引的疑問句，答案通常有人名，(A) Mary 是第一個線索，又 account for 和 is responsible for 在此同義，都是「負責」。

❷ 若原題目改成 Is 30% enough for our target? 30%對我們的目標而言是足夠的嗎？此時要選(C)。疑問句是 be 動詞簡單現在式 is 導引的 Yes/No 疑問句，(C)明確表示「不足夠」。

現在完成式的助動詞 has 開頭的問句

You will hear a question or statement and three answers. Choose the best answer to the statement or question. 🎧 MP3 028

13. Mark your answer on your answer sheet. (A) (B) (C)

聽力原文與中譯	
13. Has your assistant made the reservation? (A) Yes, she had. (B) Yes, she has. (C) Unfortunately, I don't have any assistant.	13. 你的助理已經做好預訂了嗎？ (A) 是的，她有。 (B) 是的，她有。 (C) 不幸地，我沒有任何助理。
答案：(B)	

獵豹

　　將耳力鎖定在 Has... made，馬上判斷是現在完成式的助動詞 has 引導的 Yes/No 疑問句，(B) Yes, she has. 時態相同。

 貓頭鷹

　　現在完成式的格式是:助動詞 have/has+過去分詞。題目的主詞 assistant 是單數,搭配助動詞 has,過去分詞是 made,只要注意時態,不難判斷答案是(B)。(A)不可選,因為 Yes, she had.的 had 在此是過去完成式的助動詞。(C) 我沒有任何助理,與題目所問的「預訂」毫無關聯。

 浣熊

❶ 若原題目改成 Had she informed the client before she left the office?她在離開辦公室前有告知客戶嗎？此時要選(A)。此疑問句以過去完成式的助動詞 had 引導,(A) Yes, she had.主詞 she 也符合題目的主詞。

❷ 若原題目改成 Do you have an assistant?你有助理嗎？此時要選(C)。(C) Unfortunately, I don't have any assistant.的時態和疑問句的時態都是簡單現在式,副詞 unfortunately 也是傾向否定答案的線索字。

When 開頭的疑問句

You will hear a question or statement and three answers. Choose the best answer to the statement or question. MP3 029

14. Mark your answer on your answer sheet. (A) (B) (C)

聽力原文與中譯	
14. When is the flight to New York? (A) eight o'clock sharp (B) The flight will last 3 hours. (C) We're going to fly to New York	14. 往紐約的班機幾點？ (A) 八點整。 (B) 飛行時間將持續三小時。 (C) 我們將飛往紐約。
答案：(A)	

 獵豹

　　將耳力鎖定在 When，立刻選擇有準確時間點的(A) eight o'clock sharp。

貓頭鷹

　　When 導引的疑問句通常以時間點回答。(A) eight o'clock sharp 的 sharp 在此是副詞，表「準時地」。(B)及(C)都沒有針對 When 回應。

浣熊

❶ 若原題目改成 How long will the flight last? 飛行將持續多久？此時要選(B)。How long，多久，此疑問句和(B) The flight will last 3 hours.都使用未來式的助動詞 will，時態都是簡單未來式。

❷ 若原題目改成 What are you going to do on the third day of your trip?你們旅程的第三天要做什麼？此時要選(C)。此疑問句和(C) We're going to fly to New York 都以「beV. going to+原型動詞」表未來式。

Unit 15
Why 開頭的疑問句

You will hear a question or statement and three answers. Choose the best answer to the statement or question. MP3 030

15. Mark your answer on your answer sheet. (A) (B) (C)

聽力原文與中譯	
15. Why was the flight delayed? (A) Yes, that's exactly the reason. (B) He enjoyed the flight. (C) because of the blizzard	15. 班機為何延遲了? (A) 是的,正是因為這原因。 (B) 他享受這趟飛行。 (C) 因為暴風雪。
答案:(C)	

 獵豹

　　將耳力鎖定在 Why,為何,及 was delayed,被延遲,「because of+名詞」表達原因,blizzard 指暴風雪,是延遲的合理原因。

 貓頭鷹

Why 詢問原因，常用來表達原因的片語有 because of，owing to，due to，因為 of 和 to 都是介系詞，以上片語之後都只能接名詞。(A)只是重複延遲的事實，沒有說明原因。(B)聽到 He enjoyed 馬上排除，答非所問。

 浣熊

❶ 若原題目改成 Was the flight delayed because of more security checks?因為更多安檢，所以這班機才延遲嗎?此時要選(A)。疑問句是 be 動詞過去式 was 引導的 Yes/No 疑問句，以 because of 帶出原因，(A)直接肯定原因。

❷ 若原題目改成 How was his trip to Taipei?他到台北的旅行如何?此時要選(B)。疑問句的所有格是 his，能呼應(B)的主詞 He，(B) He enjoyed the flight.，他享受這趟飛行，是針對他的旅行狀況切題的回答。

You will hear a question or statement and three answers. Choose the best answer to the question or statement. MP3 031

16. Mark your answer on your answer sheet. (A) (B) (C)

聽力原文與中譯	
16. They had to take a detour due to the road construction. (A) The road construction is way over the budget. (B) No wonder they were late. (C) The tour session usually lasts for 1 hour.	16. 因為道路建設他們必須繞道。 (A) 道路建設超出預算太多了。 (B) 怪不得他們遲到。 (C) 這場導覽行程通常持續一小時。
答案：(B)	

 獵豹

將耳力鎖定在 take a detour，繞道，(B) 怪不得他們遲到，合理暗示繞道是遲到的原因。

Unit 16　肯定句

1
照片描述

2
應答問題

3
簡短對話

4
簡短獨白

模擬試題

　　題目是肯定句，描述因為道路建設他們必須繞道。take a detour 是常考慣用語，解題關鍵主要依賴考生是否知道 take a detour 的意思。(A)聽到 over the budget 即可排除，沒有針對題目的主詞 they 和「繞道」回應，不如(B)切題。(C)的 tour 是和 detour 發音類似的陷阱字，(C)整句大意和題目的重點詞 take a detour 毫無關聯。

❶ 若原題目改成 What's the problem with the road construction?道路建設的問題是什麼？此時要選(A)。聽到 What's the problem，判斷答案傾向有負面意義的句意，(A) The road construction is way over the budget.，道路建設超出預算太多了，清楚敘述是預算超支的問題。

❷ 若原題目改成 How long does the tour session last?這場導覽行程持續多久？此時要選(C)。How long，多久，此疑問句和(C) The tour session usually lasts for 1 hour.的時態都是簡單現在式。以 for 1 hour 針對 how long 回答。

Why 開頭的疑問句

You will hear a question or statement and three answers. Choose the best answer to the statement or question. 🎧 MP3 032

17. Mark your answer on your answer sheet. (A) (B) (C)

聽力原文與中譯	
17. Why was Nancy not in the office yesterday? (A) She was under the weather. (B) Yea, she just walked in. (C) We'd better purchase more office supplies.	17. 南西為何昨天不在辦公室? (A) 她身體不舒服。 (B) 是的,她剛剛走進來。 (C) 我們最好購買更多辦公用品。
答案:(A)	

獵豹

　　將耳力鎖定在 Why 及 not in the office,因為 beV. under the weather 這個慣用語的意思是「身體不適」,故選(A)。

　　此題主要測試考生是否理解慣用語 beV. under the weather，「身體不適」。搭配題目所問:為何不在辦公室，(A)説出切題的原因。(B)聽到 Yes 馬上排除，因為題目不是 Yes/No 疑問句。(C)不可選，聽到 purchase 或 office supplies，就能判斷與「為何昨天不在辦公室」是文不對題的。

❶ 若原題目改成 Did you see Nancy?你有看到南西嗎？此時要選(B)。先判斷疑問句是過去式助動詞 did 導引的 Yes/No 疑問句，並確定 Nancy 是女生名字，(B)主詞 She 是正確的。

❷ 若原題目改成 We are running out of paper, ink, and toner.我們快用完紙，墨水和碳粉了。此時要選(C)。paper，ink，toner 都是辦公用品，呼應(C) We'd better purchase more office supplies 提及的 office supplies。(C)的動詞 purchase，購買，也呼應題目的動詞片語 are running out of，快用完。

Unit 18
Why 開頭的否定疑問句

You will hear a question or statement and three answers. Choose the best answer to the statement or question. 🎧 MP3 033

18. Mark your answer on your answer sheet. (A) (B) (C)

聽力原文與中譯	
18. Why don't you try to think outside the box? (A) Maybe it's in that box. (B) She just jumped into the box. (C) That's a good suggestion.	18. 你為何不跳脫框架思考？ (A) 它可能在那個盒子裡。 (B) 她剛跳進盒子裡。 (C) 那是個好建議。
答案：(C)	

獵豹

　　將耳力鎖定在 think outside the box，是常考慣用語，意思是「更有創意地思考，跳脫框架思考」，偏向建議。故選(C)。

貓頭鷹

Why don't you... 在此不是詢問原因，而是提出建議。(A)也使用 box 一字，是陷阱字，且聽到 it's 馬上排除，因為主詞 it 和題目的 you 不同，也可運用類似解題技巧將(B)刪去。

浣熊

❶ 若原題目改成 Where is my book?我的書在哪裡？此時要選(A)。根據疑問字 Where，且 book 的代名詞是 it，因此(A)的 it 及位置 in that box 都是解題線索。

❷ 若原題目改成 Have you seen my cat?你有看到我的貓嗎？此時要選(B)。(B) She just jumped into the box.，她剛跳進盒子裡，雖然沒有直接回答 Yes/No，但言下之意就是: 我有看到你的貓。

Will 開頭的疑問句

You will hear a question or statement and three answers. Choose the best answer to the statement or question. MP3 034

19. Mark your answer on your answer sheet. (A) (B) (C)

聽力原文與中譯	
19. Will the plan work out as predicted? (A) Probably (B) We should work out three times a week. (C) It's pretty accurate.	19. 計劃是否將如預測的進展呢？ (A) 可能會。 (B) 我們應該一星期運動三次。 (C) 它蠻準確的。
答案：(A)	

　獵豹

　　將耳力鎖定在 Will，判斷是未來式的助動詞 will 引導的 Yes/No 疑問句，(A) Probably，有可能，是傾向肯定的副詞。未來式的助動詞 will，時態都是簡單未來式。

 貓頭鷹

　　Yes/No 疑問句的答案傾向肯定或否定，probably 是可能性偏高時使用的副詞。注意動詞片語 work out 的意思會依照情境變化，題目的主詞是 plan，這時搭配 work out，work out 的意思是「進展」。在別的情境，work out 的意思是「健身」，例如在(B)的情境，這也是不可選(B)的原因。(C)聽到 accurate，正確的，即可刪除，與「是否將……進展呢？」文不對題。

 浣熊

❶ 若原題目改成 How often should we exercise?我們應該多常運動？此時要選(B)。How often 疑問句詢問頻率，多久一次，(B)...three times a week. 一星期三次，針對 How often 回應。也要注意 exercise 的類似字是 work out。

❷ 若原題目改成 What's your take on the prediction?你對這個預測的看法是什麼？此時要選(C)。在口語常用 take 當名詞，像在此疑問句，take 的意思是「看法」，類似字是 opinion。(C) It's pretty accurate.以形容詞 accurate 表達看法，it 即代替 prediction。

What 開頭的疑問句

You will hear a question or statement and three answers. Choose the best answer to the statement or question. MP3 035

20. Mark your answer on your answer sheet. (A) (B) (C)

聽力原文與中譯	
20. What is the book the professor assigned us to read? (A) Geez, I forgot the title. (B) Yes, we have done that. (C) The book is a bestseller.	20. 教授規定我們唸的書是什麼？ (A) 哎，我忘了書名。 (B) 是的，我們已經做了那件事。 (C) 這本書是暢銷書。
答案：(A)	

獵豹

　　將耳力鎖定在 What is the book，判斷答案可能跟書名有關。(A)雖然沒說出書名，title 是線索字，仍是合乎邏輯的答案。

貓頭鷹

　　What 引導的疑問句題型屬於較開放式的問答，像(A) Geez, I forgot the title.是比較靈活的答案。Geez 是口語常用的感嘆字。(B)不可選，因為題目不是 Yes/No 疑問句。(C)... a bestseller，暢銷書，與題目所問的書名無關。

浣熊

❶ 若原題目改成 Have you signed up for the study group?你們已經報名讀書小組了嗎？此時要選(B)。此時是現在完成式的助動詞 have 導引的 Yes/No 疑問句，(B)也以現在完成式表示肯定的回答。

❷ 若原題目改成 What's special about the book?這本書有什麼特別的?此時要選(C)。聽到 What's special，判斷答案通常會敘述某種特色，例如(C)提及的 bestseller，暢銷書。

　　書中的對話幾乎都是三人的對話，能有效強化考生面對聽力對話由兩人變成三人對話的應對能力。此外，更重要的是使用音檔（扣除題目的部分）做影子跟讀練習數次或數十次，訓練耳朵聽三人對話的能力和聽力專注力，養成聽完對話時就能接續劃答案卡三題的能力。

Part

3

簡短對話

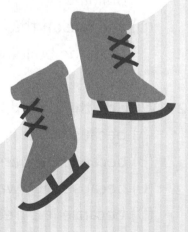

Unit 1
停車場看出職場地位

Instructions

❶ 請播放音檔聽下列對話，並完成試題。 🅟 MP3 036+MP3 037

❷ 「跟述」練習：寫完試題後請跟著音檔同步跟漸進式做「跟述」練習，提升聽力專注力。

❸ 加碼題：完成❶＋❷步驟後，請再播放音檔寫浣熊試題，掌握其他可能的出題考點，強化應考實力。 🅟 MP3 036+MP3 038

1. **What are the three people talking about?**
   (A) how to walk to the parking lot
   (B) walking a lot is good for health
   (C) the reason that they need to park far away from the building
   (D) the reason that someone in a higher position parks farther from the building

2. **Why do they need to park at D lot?**
   (A) because D lot is closer to the company
   (B) because they are assistants
   (C) because they want to walk a lot
   (D) because it is free to park at D lot

3. Why does the man say, "I'm feeling a little better"?

(A) because those in higher positions need to walk the same distance to the parking lot as he does

(B) because he feels walking to the parking lot makes him more energetic

(C) because he enjoys the conversation with the woman

(D) because those in higher positions decided to give him a promotion

 中譯與聽力原文

Questions 1-3 refer to the following conversation
問題 **1-3**，請參考以下對話內容

James: Why do we have to park at D lot? It's five blocks away from the entrance building.

詹姆士：為什麼我們要停在 D 停車場呢？離建築物入口要走五個街區。

Mary: Assistants park at D lot. That's the rule, unless you get promoted.

瑪莉：助理停在 D 停車場。這是規定，除非你獲得升遷。

James: Right, managers can park at B lot, two blocks away, and of course CEOs and clients, A lot.

詹姆士：對，經理能停在 B 停車場，距離兩個街區遠，然後當然 CEO 和客戶停在 A 停車場。

Linda: You know what... what makes me feel better is that C lot and D lot are all five blocks away from the building, but they are on the opposite of the company.

琳達：你知道嗎？...使我感到好多了的是 C 停車場和 D 停車場同樣都離建築物五個街區，只是他們在公司不同方位。

James: I'm feeling a little better, knowing someone who is in a superior position has to walk the same miles.

詹姆士：我覺得好些了，知道有些位階優於我們的工作者要走相同的路程。

選項中譯與解析

1. 兩人正在談論什麼？

(A) 如何走到停車場。

(B) 多走路有益健康。

(C) 他們需停離大樓很遠之處的原因。

(D) 某些高層人員，停在離大樓更遠處的原因。

2. 為何他們需要停在 D 停車場呢？

(A) 因為 D 停車場離公司更近。

(B) 因為他們是助理。

(C) 因為他們想要多走路。

(D) 因為停在 D 停車場是免費的。

3. 男子說「我覺得好些了」代表什麼意思？

(A) 因為那些位階優於他們的人，需要像他走相同的路程。

(B) 因為他覺得走到停車場讓他精力更充沛。

(C) 因為他喜歡和女子聊天。

(D) 因為那些位階較高的人決定讓他升遷。

1.

· 聽到對話，直接鎖定首句 Why do we have to park at D lot? 主角討論把車停在 D 停車場的原因。根據對話，it's five blocks away from the entrance building，可知答案即為 C：討論把車停在離入口較遠的停車場的原因。

2.

· 聽到題目，馬上鎖定 Assistants park at D lot，推測答案跟職位有關。根據對話，公司規定助理的車必須停在 D 停車場，故答案為 B：因為他們是助理。

3.

· 聽到對話，直接鎖定 knowing someone who is in a superior position has to walk the same miles，直接解釋 I'm feeling a little better 的原因。根據對話 C lot and D lot are all five blocks away from the building，可知 C、D 停車場到公司的距離相同，停在 C 停車場的職位較高者和停在 D 停車場的助理是走相同的距離到公司；故此題答案為 A。

1.

· 此題屬於情境題，題目詢問對話主要的討論內容，測試考生是否能理解對話內容。

· 根據首句，我們可以得知對話內容是 Why do we have to park at D lot?的延伸。因為 D 停車場距離入口較遠，而延伸出公司位階和升遷等討論。可以先刪除對話內容沒有提及的 A、B 選項，接著從 C、D 選項選出最符合答案的 C 選項：討論由於職位而必須停在 D 停車場的理由。

2.

· 此題屬於推測題，題目詢問他們停在 D 停車場的原因；關鍵字 Assistant 是助理的意思。

· 根據對話，助理停在 D 停車場、經理停在 B 停車場、執行長和客戶停在 A 停車場；雖然主角沒有直接表明：we're assistants，但仍可以依此推測：他們停在 D 停車場的原因是因為職位。

3.

· 此題屬於推測題，測試考生是否能理解對話內容所提及的公司規定。

· 根據對話，助理停在 D 停車場、經理停在 B 停車場、執行長和客戶停在 A 停車場；雖然沒有明確指出什麼職位的人停在 C 停車場，但我們可以推測 C 停車場的職位介於經理和助理的中間，也就是高於助理的職位。並且，C、D 停車場距離公司都是五個街區遠，所以他才會說 someone who is in a superior position has to walk the same miles：某些職位較高的人和他們走相同的路程。

浣熊　MP3 036+MP3 038

還可能怎麼問

1. **Who gets to park at A lot?**

   (A) CEOs

   (B) managers

   (C) assistants

   (D) secretaries

2. **What is the distance between the office building and A lot?**

   (A) 2 blocks

   (B) 5 blocks

   (C) 10 blocks

   (D) none of the above

解析

1. **題目是問誰能停在 A 停車場？**

   ・選項 A 執行長，對話中有提到「然後當然 CEO 和客戶停在 A 停車場。」，故可以得知答案為選項 A。

2. **題目是問 A 停車場跟辦公室大樓之間的距離是？**

   ・對話中有提到街區距離的敘述「為什麼我們要停在 D 停車場呢？離建築物入口要走五個街區。」、「對，經理能停在 B 停車場，兩個街區遠」、「…C 停車場和 D 停車場都是離建築物五個街區。」，但沒有明確說明 A 停車場跟辦公室大樓之間的距離是多少，所以可以得知答案為選項 D。

停 A 停車場，羨煞旁人

Instructions

❶ 請播放音檔聽下列對話，並完成試題。 🎧 MP3 039+MP3 040

❷ 「跟述」練習：寫完試題後請跟著音檔同步跟漸進式做「跟述」練習，提升聽力專注力。

❸ 加碼題：完成❶＋❷步驟後，請再播放音檔寫浣熊試題，掌握其他可能的出題考點，強化應考實力。 🎧 MP3 039+MP3 041

4. Why does the man say, "from now on I've got to work extra hard"?

(A) because he wants to make more money

(B) because the woman pushes him to work harder

(C) because he wants to get promoted

(D) because he wants to work out more

5. Why does the woman say, "Think of this as a transition"?

(A) Her company is experiencing a transitional period.

(B) She thinks their current status is temporary.

(C) She understands the man is going through some transitions.

(D) She sees that the man is experiencing personal transformation

6. Why does the man say, "I'm jealous"?

(A) He is jealous that some co-workers can park at Lot A.

(B) He is jealous that the woman has more clients.

(C) He envies the woman for her working capabilities

(D) He envies the woman because she walks faster than he does.

 ## 中譯與聽力原文

Questions 4-6 refer to the following conversation
問題 **4-6**，請參考以下對話內容

Mary: It's just temporary. We are all going to get promoted after three to five years. Think of this as a transition. Then you won't carry a negative mood into the work.

瑪莉：這只是暫時的。我們總會在三到五年後升遷。想像一下這只是過渡期。然後你就不用在工作時帶著負面情緒。

Linda: I parked at A lot once. It was a great feeling, walking directly to the entrance. Five seconds. You can even do it in slow motion, still faster than anybody.

琳達：我有次停在 A 停車場。感覺很棒，直接走到路口。五秒。你甚至可以慢動作走到公司入口，卻仍然比誰都快。

James: You've gotta to be kidding

詹姆士：你在開玩笑對吧！

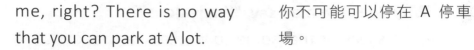

| me, right? There is no way that you can park at A lot. | 你不可能可以停在 A 停車場。 |

Linda: Not if you're with managers and major clients.

琳達：如果你是跟著經理和主要客戶就不在此限。

James: I'm jealous. It means from now on I've got to work extra hard.

詹姆士：我忌妒了。這意味著從現在起我必須更努力工作。

 ## 選項中譯與解析

 4. 男子說「從現在起我必須更努力工作」，代表何意？

(A) 因為他想賺更多的錢。

(B) 因為女子督促他更努力工作。

(C) 因為他想升遷。

(D) 因為他想多做運動。

5. 為何女子說「想像一下這只是過渡期」？

(A) 她公司正在經歷過渡期。

(B) 她認為目前的情況是暫時的。

(C) 她明白此人正在經歷某些轉變。

(D) 她看到此人正經歷個人轉變。

6. 為何男子說「我忌妒了」？

(A) 他忌妒一些同事可在 A 停車場停車。

(B) 他忌妒女子有更多的客戶。

(C) 他羨慕女子的工作能力。

(D) 他因為女子走得比他快而羨慕她。

獵豹

4.

· 聽到對話，直接鎖定(C) ...get promoted；promote 是升遷的意思。根據對話，推測 work extra hard 的目的是為了 get promoted，並藉由升遷，得到可以停在距離公司較近的停車場的資格。

5.

· 看到題目，回想對話首句 It's just temporary.，temporary 是形容詞：暫時的。Transition 是名詞：過渡期的意思，搭配對話內容的 temporary，可知現狀是暫時性的故答案為 B。

6.

· 聽到對話，馬上鎖定 I parked at A lot once.；A lot 是此題的關鍵字。根據對話，It was a great feeling, walking directly to the entrance. .... 可以推測停在 A 停車場是讓人羨慕的。

貓頭鷹

4.

· 此題屬於推測題，需推測 work extra hard 的目的和結果，同時測驗考生是否理解 get promoted 的意思。

· 根據對話，男士表示羨慕，是因為能停在距離公司較近的 A 停車場，而根據公司規定，除非升遷，否則助理必須停在 D 停車場；我們可以依此推測，男士表示要更努力工作是為了得到升遷，然後有機會可以停在距離公司較近的 A、B 停車場。

5.

· 此題屬於情境題，測驗考生是否理解對話內容語意，同時測試考生關鍵字 transition 的字意。

· 根據對話 We are all going to get promoted after three to five years. 可知女士認為他們三五年後遲早會升遷，現狀只是暫時的過渡期。Transitional 是形容詞：過渡的；transformation 是名詞：轉型。我們可以先刪除錯誤的 A、D 選項，然後選出較符合敘述的 B 選項；C 選項「她理解男士將會面臨一些過渡期」是一個干擾選項，並不是女士主要想表達的語意。

6.

· 此題屬於推測題，若無法推測答案，也可以將選項對照對話內容作刪去法。

· 根據對話內容，沒有提到女士擁有較多客戶或是較高的工作能力，故 B、C 選項可以先做刪去；而女士之所以可以走得比別人快，是因為停在距離公司較近的 A 停車場；故 A 選項是最適合的答案。

浣熊 MP3 039+MP3 041

還可能怎麼問

1. **According to the woman, how long does it take for a person to walk from A lot to the main building?**

(A) 10 seconds

(B) 5 seconds

(C) 20 seconds

(D) 60 minutes

2. **Why did Linda get to part at A lot?**

(A) she was just too lucky.

(B) she got the promotion.

(C) she carried a positive mood.

(D) she was with cilents.

解析

1. 題目是問根據女子，從 **A** 停車場走到主要大樓需要花費多久的時間呢？

· 這題可以綜合一起看，對話中有提到「我有次停在 A 停車場。感覺很棒，直接走到路口。五秒。」，選項 B，5 秒，故可以得知答案為選項 B。

2. 題目是問為什麼琳達能停在 **A** 停車場？

· 選項 **D**，對話中有提到「如果你是跟著經理和主要客戶就不在此限。」，此訊息與選項敘述一致，跟客戶在一起是能停在該停車場的原因，所以可以得知答案為選項 D。

Unit 3
病房省思人生

Instructions

❶ 請播放音檔聽下列對話，並完成試題。 🎧 MP3 042+MP3 043

❷ 「跟述」練習：寫完試題後請跟著音檔同步跟漸進式做「跟述」練習，提升聽力專注力。

❸ 加碼題：完❶＋❷步驟後，請再播放音檔寫浣熊試題，掌握其他可能的出題考點，強化應考實力。 🎧 MP3 042+MP3 044

7. Where might these speakers be?
    (A) in their office
    (B) in a hospital
    (C) in an insurance company
    (D) in the cafeteria

8. What are they talking about?
    (A) the costs of various hospital wards
    (B) the importance of privacy
    (C) how ill Ken has become
    (D) the costs of health insurance

9. What does "quite a sum of money" mean?
    (A) a little bit money

(B) the total amount of medical treatment

(C) a small amount of money

(D) a large amount of money

中譯與聽力原文

Questions 7-9 refer to the following conversation
問題 7-9，請參考以下對話內容

Mary: I still can't figure out why Ken chose a semi-private room. He always says he values privacy a lot.

瑪莉：我仍無法理解肯為什選擇半私人房。他總是說他極重視隱私。

James: I can't believe it, either. Perhaps it's because of prices. I remember one of my relatives lives in a quad room when he is that sick.

詹姆士：我也不敢相信。或許是因為價格。我記得我其中一個親戚住在四人房，當他病得很重的時候。

Jimmy: I bet an individual room at a hospital certainly costs lots of money.

吉米：我打賭這間醫院的單人病房要花很多錢。

James: even if it's not costly, from a long-term perspective, it

詹姆士：即使要花很多錢，從長遠的角度來

ends up being quite a sum of money.

看，最終是要花費相當多錢。

Jimmy: That sounds pretty reasonable.

吉米：這聽起來相當合理。

Mary: Good news is that he still has health insurance to cover it. I just can't imagine living our lives without health insurance.

瑪莉：好消息是他仍有健康保險可以支付。我真不敢想像活著卻沒健康保險。

選項中譯與解析

7. 談話者可能身處哪裡？
(A) 在他們辦公室。
(B) 在醫院。
(C) 在保險公司。
(D) 在自助餐廳。

8. 他們正在談論什麼？
(A) 醫院各種病房的費用。
(B) 隱私的重要性。
(C) 肯病得多嚴重。
(D) 健保的費用。

9.「相當多錢」是什麼意思？

(A) 一點點錢。

(B) 醫療總額。

(C) 小錢。

(D) 相當多錢。

7.

· 聽到對話，直接鎖定 semi-private room、quad room、an individual room at a hospital 等關鍵字，由其中的 hospital 可以確定以上所指的是病房的種類。根據對話中出現的病房種類，推測對話發生在醫院，故此題答案為 B。

8.

· 聽到對話，直接鎖定 Perhaps it's because of prices，推測答案和價格有關。除了病房的種類，對話內容大多圍繞著花費：costs lots of money、ends up being quite a sum of money，所以選項 A 是最適合的答案。

9.

· 聽到對話，直接鎖定 I bet an individual room at a hospital certainly costs lots of money.，可知此處 ...it ends up being quite a sum of money 的主詞 it 指的是 an individual room at a hospital。由 lots of money 這個線索及推測語意：醫院裡的個人病房儘管不貴，但長時間下來會是一筆可觀的費用，故答案為 D。

貓頭鷹

7.

· 此題屬於細節題，測試考生是否能從對話中抓出關鍵字，並依此推測談話地點。對話中的 semi-private room、quad room、individual room 在沒有特定所指的時候，可以指的是雙人房、四人房和單人房；在對話裡直接指出 at a hospital，所以可以判斷分別指的是醫院裡的雙人病房、四人病房和個人病房，由此推測對話最有可能發生在醫院。

8.

· 此題屬於情境題，透過情境測試考生是否理解對話的主要內容，也可以藉由選項的刪去法來作答。Ward 是名詞「病房」的意思。對話內容由 Ken 入住的 semi-private room 引發討論，猜測可能是因為價格而沒有選擇最有隱私的 individual room，但並沒有提到隱私的重要性以及 Ken 的病情，所以可以先將 B、C 選項刪除。對話最後談到還好有健保可以分擔醫療費用，但沒有談論到健保費用，所以 D 選項也不正確。

9.

· 此題屬於細節題，考生必須先找到 it ends up being quite a sum of money 的主語並依此判斷說話者的語意。承接上句「醫院的個人病房肯定很貴」，從轉折連接詞 even if 引導的 it's not costly 和 from a long-term perspective 來判斷，「就算不貴」的病房「長遠來看」最終累積的花費應該不少，所以 quite a sum of money 應指的是相當多錢。

浣熊　 MP3 042+MP3 044

還可能怎麼問

1. How many patients can a quad room accommodate?

(A) 1

(B) 2

(C) 3

(D) 4

2. Why does the woman say, "can't figure out why Ken chose a semi-private room"?

(A) because Ken needs more privacy.

(B) because privacy is the best policy

(C) because privacy is very important

(D) none of the above

解析

1. 題目是問四人房可以容納多少病人呢？

‧這題可以綜合一起看，其實單純考對單字的理解，a quad room 是指 4 人房，所以可以得知病房可以容納 4 人，故可以得知答案為選項 D。

2. 題目是問為什麼女子說「我仍無法理解肯為什選擇半私人房」？

‧選項 A，從對話中可以推斷出她知道以她對肯的了解肯其實很重隱私，所以才很意外他沒選單人房，故可以得知答案為選項 A。

走錯醫院，經理找不到人

 Instructions

❶ 請 播放音檔聽下列對話，並完成試題。 ⊚ MP3 045+MP3 046

❷ 「跟述」練習：寫完試題後請跟著音檔同步跟漸進式做「跟述」練習，提升聽力專注力。

❸ 加碼題：完成❶＋❷步驟後，請再播放音檔寫浣熊試題，掌握其他可能的出題考點，強化應考實力。 ⊚ MP3 045+MP3 047

10. Why does the woman say, "It's just too luxurious"?

(A) She loves luxury.

(B) The medical equipment is expensive.

(C) The things in the room look very expensive.

(D) She thinks it's wasteful to use luxurious things.

11. What is the speakers' problem?

(A) They forgot to call their manager.

(B) They did not answer the manager's phone call.

(C) They went to the wrong hospital ward.

(D) They went to the wrong hospital.

12. Why does the woman mention a five-star hotel?

(A) in order to show she could afford a five-star hotel room

(B) in order to compare how luxurious the room is with a five-star hotel

(C) because they should have gone to a five-star hotel

(D) because staying in the hospital room is more expensive than in a five-star hotel

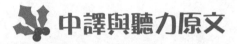 中譯與聽力原文

Questions 10-12 refer to the following conversation
問題 **10-12**，請參考以下對話內容

Mary: Wow! It's just too luxurious. I don't think we can afford a room at this hospital even if our insurance covers part of it, right?

瑪莉：哇！這太奢侈了。我不認為我們能負擔得起這間飯店的旅館，即使我們的保險包含這部分，對吧！

Jimmy: Probably not... look at those oxygen tanks, wheelchairs, and pillows.

吉米：可能不是…看著這些氧氣瓶、輪椅和枕頭。

James: Seriously? Pillows?

詹姆士：真的嗎？枕頭？

Jimmy: I've never seen pillows like that. Everything seems so fancy... and expensive.

吉米：我從未看過像這樣的枕頭。每樣東西似乎都如此豪華…和昂貴。

Mary: It's even better than a five star hotel I just checked into last month.

瑪莉：這比我上個月登記入住的五星級飯店更高級。

James: My phone just rang... It's from our manager.

詹姆士：我的手機剛響...是我們經理打來的。

Jimmy: So what did he say?

吉米：他說了什麼？

James: We are totally in the wrong hospital, no wonder he couldn't find us, giving him the wrong impression that we're somewhere else.

詹姆士：我們全然在錯的飯店，難怪他找不到我們，讓他有錯誤印象我們還在其他地方。

Mary: Oh! God... hope we don't have to write a report on where we went.

瑪莉：嘔！天啊...希望我們不會要寫我們到哪去了的報告。

 ## 選項中譯與解析

10. 本篇對話中的女子為何說「這太奢侈了」？

(A) 她喜歡奢侈。

(B) 醫療設備很貴。

(C) 房間裡的物品看起來很貴。

(D) 她認為使用奢侈品很浪費。

11. 談話者的問題為何？

(A) 他們忘了打電話給他們經理。

(B) 他們沒有回答經理電話。

(C) 他們去錯病房了。

(D) 他們去錯醫院了。

12. 為什麼女子會提到五星級飯店？

(A) 為了表示她住得起五星級飯店的房間。

(B) 為了和五星級飯店比較這間房間的豪華程度。

(C) 因為他們本來應該要去五星級飯店。

(D) 因為住在病房比住五星級飯店貴。

 獵豹

10.

• 聽到對話，直接鎖定關鍵字 luxurious，luxurious 是形容詞：奢華、豪華的意思。根據對話 I don't think we can afford a room at this hospital... 和 Everything seems so fancy... and expensive.，可以推測她認為這間豪華病房是很昂貴的，故答案為 C。

11.

• 聽到對話，馬上鎖定 We are totally in the wrong hospital...... 可知說話者面臨的問題是因為他們走錯了醫院。根據對話，說話者接到經理的電話，因為 he couldn't find us 並得知他們走錯了醫院，故此題答案為 D。

12.

· 聽到對話，馬上鎖定關鍵字 five star hotel 找出題目問題點。根據對話可知此處用五星級飯店來對比病房，故 B 是較適合的答案。

貓頭鷹

10.

· 此題屬於細節題，考生須由對話細節推測語意，同時測試考生 luxurious 的字意。根據對話，就算有健保部分給付她也負擔不起這間病房，可以推測他認為病房費用是非常昂貴的。將敘述的重點擺在費用上，即可以先刪除較無關的 A、D 選項，從對話內容可知，除了醫療設備、病房裡像是枕頭這類的一般用品也看起來十分奢華，所以 C 是最符合答案的選項。

11.

· 此題屬於情境題，根據對話情境，原本談論的內容在接了經理電話後開始改變，所以我們可以先刪除錯誤的 A、B 選項；接著，he couldn't find us 也就是問題的所在，(C) They went to the wrong hospital ward 是陷阱選項，對話裡明確指出 We are totally in the wrong hospital 可知他們跑錯了醫院而不是單純跑錯病房，所以 D 選項最符合答案。

12.

· 此題屬於細節題，也可用刪去法快速答題。先刪去無關的 C、D 選項。從 It's even better than a five star hotel I just checked in last month. 可知，此處利用了比較句型將五星級飯店和病房做對比，凸顯

了病房的奢華，相較之下 A 選項並不符合語意，所以 B 即是最佳解答。

 浣熊 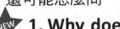 MP3 045+MP3 047

還可能怎麼問

★NEW **1. Why does the man mention, "oxygen tanks, wheelchairs, and pillows"?**

(A) to inform their colleagues that their insurance covers it.

(B) to valid his viewpoints

(C) to negate his colleagues' argument

(D) to symbolize it's costly

2.　Why is the woman concerned?

(A) They're letting the manager down

(B) They could be punished for writing a report.

(C) The manager has a short temper

(D) The manager is hard to get along with

解析

1.　題目是問為什麼男子提到「氧氣瓶、輪椅和枕頭」？

‧選項 D，此為對話中所表達的意思，所以男子才會說「可能不是...看著這些氧氣瓶、輪椅和枕頭。」，故可以得知答案為選項 D。

2.　題目是問女子為什麼覺得擔心？

‧選項 B，對話中有提到「嘔！天啊...希望我們不要寫我們到哪去了的報告。」，此為同義表達，所以可以得知答案為選項 B。

Unit 5
提案會議

🔍 **Instructions**

❶ 請播放音檔聽下列對話，並完成試題。 🎧 MP3 048+MP3 049

❷ 「跟述」練習：寫完試題後請跟著音檔同步跟漸進式做「跟述」練習，提升聽力專注力。

❸ 加碼題：完成❶＋❷步驟後，請再播放音檔寫浣熊試題，掌握其他可能的出題考點，強化應考實力。 🎧 MP3 048+MP3 050

13. Where might the speakers be?

(A) on the beach

(B) in a zoo

(C) in a meeting room

(D) in an aquarium

14. What are they talking about?

(A) the environmentalists

(B) marine creatures

(C) their favorite stories

(D) the topic of a project

15. Why does the man say, "we will upload videos on Facebook"?

(A) The hits on the videos on Facebook will bring revenues.

(B) The hits on the videos will make him famous.

(C) He likes to make friends on Facebook by sharing videos.

(D) He believes sharing videos can raise the awareness of protecting dolphins.

 ## 中譯與聽力原文

Questions 13-15 refer to the following conversation
問題 13-15，請參考以下對話內容

Jane:	OK... Let's begin out pitch meeting as usual... Best circus needs a feature story to rebuild its brand images, and the deadline is tomorrow... what do you have for me, team D?	簡：	好的…讓我們像往常一樣開始我們的提案會議…倍斯特馬戲團需要一則能重建它們品牌形象的專題故事，截止日期是明天…D 團隊你們準備了什麼給我呢？
Mary:	We're thinking about using dolphins as our feature story.	瑪莉：	我們正考慮使用海豚當我們的專題故事。
Jimmy:	You know how environmentalists love marine creatures. Dolphins are a good way for	吉米：	你知道環境保護人士有多愛海洋生物。海豚是很容易讓觀看者

viewers to relate. Videos with interactions between visitors and dolphins can dilute the harm it has done before. Plus, we will upload videos on Facebook. Sharing videos can create hits, which will bring ad revenues.

有共鳴的生物。參觀者和海豚互動的視頻能夠減低先前所造成的傷害。再者，我們會上傳視頻到臉書。分享視頻能創造點擊率，這也會帶來廣告收益。

Jane: I think they are gonna love it.

簡：我覺得他們會很喜愛這個。

選項中譯與解析

13. 談話者目前身處哪裡？
　　(A) 在海灘。
　　(B) 在動物園。
　　(C) 在會議室。
　　(D) 在水族館。

14. 他們談論內容為何？
　　(A) 環保主義者。
　　(B) 海洋生物。
　　(C) 他們最喜愛的故事。
　　(D) 提案主題。

15. 為何男子說「我們會上傳影片到臉書」？

(A) 臉書上視頻的點擊率將帶來收益。

(B) 視頻的點擊率將使他成名。

(C) 他喜歡透過在臉書分享視頻來交友。

(D) 他認為分享視頻能提高保護海豚的意識。

獵豹

13.

・聽到對話，直接鎖定 pitch meeting，pitch 在此作名詞有「提案」的意思。根據對話內容，主要是一個環保相關的提案討論，可以推論討論人應處於會議中，故答案為 C 會議室。

14.

・聽到對話，馬上鎖定關鍵字 pitch meeting：提案會議。根據對話，討論內容由 pitch meeting 做延伸，圍繞著海洋環境保護做主題，可以推測討論內容為提案的主題，故選項 D 為最適合的答案。

15.

・聽到對話，馬上鎖定 we will upload videos on Facebook 來定位問題點。根據對話，Sharing videos can create hits, which will bring ads revenues.可知影片透過網路分享可以達到宣傳效益，故此題答案為 A。

13.

・此題屬於細節題,考生須從對話細節找出關鍵字,並依此推論答案。根據對話的關鍵字 pitch meeting 來延伸,team D 以海豚為主軸設定了專案,可以推測討論應該是發生在會議室裡,除了 D 小組也還可能有其他組別和提案,但無法確定其他提案主題都跟環保或海洋生態有關,所以會議室是最適合的答案。

14.

・此題屬於情境題,測驗考生是否理解對話情境和對話內容,並依此推論答案。我們可以將 14 題視為 13 題的延伸,先確定了對話是會議中的提案討論,就可以直接確定選項 D:企劃的主題是正確答案。A、B 選項的環保人士和海洋生物在對話中都有出現,是誘答選項但不是討論的中心,要特別小心。

15.

・此題屬於細節題,可以先鎖定題目句來定位問題點,再用刪去法找出答案。根據對話,Sharing videos can create hits, which will bring ads revenues.可知答案即為選項 A;revenue 是名詞「收入」,在此有「廣告效益」的意思。我們也可以先刪除對話未提及的 B、C 選項,接著從 A、D 選項選出最佳答案;由 D 選項的「sharing videos」來看,語意偏向「分享影片」這個動作,可以提高保護海豚的意識,但是沒有專指「分享提案的影片」,所以是一個有瑕疵的選項,不是最好的答案。

浣熊  MP3 048+MP3 050

還可能怎麼問

1. Why does team D choose dolphins as their feature story?

(A) because it is the easiest thing to do at the moment.

(B) because they know their boss would love it.

(C) because it can raise the awareness.

(D) because it can create hits.

2. What will team D probably do next?

(A) choose another topic and wait for the next pitch meeting.

(B) contact advertising companies

(C) help environmentalists clean the beach

(D) start their search probably filming the video of dolphins

1. 題目是問為什麼 D 團隊選擇海豚當他們的專題故事？

· 對話中有提到「你知道環境保護人士重視海洋生物。藉由做這個故事，
我們可以提高對保護海豚的意識和海灘的乾淨。」，故可以得知答案為
選項 C。

2. 題目是問 D 團隊接下來可能會做什麼呢？

· 選項 D，從對話末可以推測出他們提案通過了，所以可能著手進行他們
的計劃，所以他們可能會進行視頻的拍攝，所以可以得知答案為選項 D。

Unit **6**
不厚臉皮可能就要丟飯碗了

Instructions

❶ 請播放音檔聽下列對話，並完成試題。 🎧 MP3 051+MP3 052

❷ 「跟述」練習：寫完試題後請跟著音檔同步跟漸進式做「跟述」練習，提升聽力專注力。

❸ 加碼題：完成❶＋❷步驟後，請再播放音檔寫浣熊試題，掌握其他可能的出題考點，強化應考實力。 🎧 MP3 051+MP3 053

16. Who are these men?

(A) car mechanics

(B) car salesmen

(C) car manufacturers

(D) car marketing specialists

17. Why did the man become Mary's assistant?

(A) Mary asked him to be her assistant.

(B) He volunteered to be Mary's assistant.

(C) He needs to learn from Mary's working performance.

(D) He likes to assist his co-workers.

18. Which of the following is the best description of Mary?

(A) Mary is the most experienced worker in this company.

(B) Mary always has the most clients.

(C) Mary is a new employee.

(D) Mary is good at selling cars.

🌿 中譯與聽力原文

Questions 16-18 refer to the following conversation
問題 16-18，請參考以下對話內容

Jack: How many times do I have to tell you that you really need to develop a thick skin. You just have to let go of that rejection. I can't run those reports. It's zero.

Jim: I totally understand. I'm working on it. Pretty soon it'll turn out to be ok.

Jack: OK? You have been here for like... three months, but you haven't sold a car.

Jack: From now on, I'm assigning you to watch how other people perform. You're now an

傑克：有多少次我告訴你你真的需要厚臉皮。你只需要放掉被拒絕的感覺。我無法看那些報告。銷售數字是零。

吉姆：我能理解。我正努力了。很快事情都會沒問題的。

傑克：沒問題？你已經來這裡有...三個月了，但你尚未賣掉一台車。

傑克：從現在開始，我將你分派到觀看其他人如何執行。你現在是瑪

assistant to Mary. She just won Employee of the Month Award. I'm sure she will tell you what to do. She always knows what she is doing.

莉的助理。她剛贏得每月最佳員工獎。我相信她會告訴你怎麼做。她總是知道自己在做什麼。

選項中譯與解析

16. 這些人的職業為何？

(A) 汽車修理員。

(B) 汽車業務。

(C) 汽車製造商。

(D) 汽車經銷專家。

17. 男子成為瑪麗助理的原因為何？

(A) 瑪麗讓他當助理。

(B) 他自願成為瑪麗的助理。

(C) 他需要向瑪麗學習工作方面的表現。

(D) 他喜歡幫助同事。

18. 下列關於瑪麗的描述，何者最佳？

(A) 瑪麗是這間公司最有經驗的員工。

(B) 瑪麗擁有的客戶一直最多。

(C) 瑪麗是一名新進員工。

(D) 瑪麗擅長賣車。

獵豹

16.

・聽到對話，馬上鎖定關鍵字 sold a car：車輛銷售。Salesmen 是名詞：銷售員，最符合銷售車輛的工作內容，所以此題答案為 B。

17.

・聽到對話，先由 You're now an assistant to Mary 來定位問題點。根據對話前後句，watch how other people perform、she will tell you what to do，可知他擔任 Mary 的助理是為了學習銷售技巧。

18.

・聽到對話，直接鎖定 She just won Employee of the Month Award. 可知 Mary 是本月的最佳員工。根據對話 watch how other people perform，來推測 Mary 是很有銷售技巧並值得學習的，所以選項 D 是最適合的答案。

貓頭鷹

16.

・此題屬於情境題，測試考生是否能抓出對話中的關鍵字，並理解對話情境。根據對話，從 develop a thick skin、let go of that rejection 還有最關鍵的 you haven't sold a car，可以推測他們的工作跟銷售、推銷最有關係。(A)car mechanics 指的是負責維修保養的汽車機械師；(C)car manufacturers 指的是汽車製造廠商；(D)car marketing specialists 指的是負責市場評估、定位等等的汽車營銷專家。

17.

· 此題屬於推測題，考生須根據對話情境和內容推測答案，也可搭配刪去法解題。17 題可以作為 16 題的延伸，先確定了此人的身分是汽車的銷售員，接著由題目 you haven't sold a car.、I'm assigning you to watch how other people perform.可以推測此人是因為銷售成績太差，所以先被任命為 Mary 的助理，進而從旁觀察和學習別人的銷售技巧，故此題答案為選項 C。

18.

· 此題屬於細節題，考生須根據選項一一回推比照對話細節，選出最正確的選項。根據對話，She just won Employee of the Month Award.、She always knows what she is doing.可知 Mary 剛獲選為本月的最佳員工、她的工作表現很好；我們可以先刪除無法由對話判斷是否正確的 A、C 選項，再從 B、D 選項選出答案。根據對話，我們可以推測 Mary 是很有銷售技巧並值得學習的，但是無法確定她總是有最多的顧客，所以 B 也是一個有瑕疵的選項，故此題答案為 D。

 浣熊　🎧 MP3 051+MP3 053

還可能怎麼問

1. Why does the man say, "develop a thick skin"?

    (A) because it's good for one's health

    (B) because it's about having the ability to withstand a criticism

    (C) because it has something to do with those reports

(D) because it can increase confidence

2.　**What problem has the boss identified?**

(A) The sales rep needs to win the Employee of the Month Award

(B) The sales rep needs to run those reports

(C) The sales rep needs to learn how to sell from someone who surely knows how.

(D) The sales rep needs to assign his work to other colleagues.

解析

1.　題目是問為什麼男子說「培養厚臉皮」？

・選項 B 因為這關於承受批評的能力，這與對話中敘述為同義表達，develop thick skin 其實就是要對方能承受壓力和批評不怕被拒絕，才能銷售成功，故可以得知答案為選項 B。

2.　題目是問老闆指出了什麼問題？

・選項 C，對話中有提到「從現在開始，我將你分派到觀看其他人如何執行。你現在是瑪莉的助理。她剛贏得每月最佳員工獎。我相信她會告訴你怎麼做。她總是知道自己在做什麼。」，可以推斷此為同義表達，且為老闆指出的問題，所以可以得知答案為選項 C。

Unit 7
漏了要做員工識別證

Instructions

❶ 請播放音檔聽下列對話，並完成試題。 🎧 MP3 054+MP3 055

❷ 「跟述」練習：寫完試題後請跟著音檔同步跟漸進式做「跟述」練習，提升聽力專注力。

❸ 加碼題：完成❶＋❸步驟後，請再播放音檔寫浣熊試題，掌握其他可能的出題考點，強化應考實力。 🎧 MP3 054+MP3 056

19. How many new badges do they need to make?

(A) 10

(B) 20

(C) 5

(D) 15

20. What does the woman mean by saying, "I have no errands to run?

(A) She needs to move faster to deal with some business.

(B) She is bored with running errands.

(C) Running can boost her working performance.

(D) She has no business to attend to at this moment.

21. Who are these speakers?

(A) colleagues

(B) new employees

(C) new recruits

(D) Cindy's friends

🌿 中譯與聽力原文

Questions 19-21 refer to the following conversation
問題 19-21，請參考以下對話內容

Linda: Cindy forgot to prepare new ID badges for our new hires. I can't believe this is happening.

Jane: How many? I thought she did this yesterday.

Linda: Ten to be exact, but I have to prepare documents for the HR managers; there is no way that I can make the new ID badges now.

Jack: I saw her at the gate, leading new recruits to the hall.

Jane: Yesterday was so chaotic.

琳達：辛蒂忘了替我們新人們準備新的識別證。我不敢相信這件事發生了。

簡：多少？我以為他昨天完成了。

琳達：準確來說是十個，但是我必須準備給人事經理們的文件，我現在不可能有時間做新的識別證。

傑克：我在大門看到她，帶領新人們到大廳。

135

Perhaps I can make new ID badges for her. I have no errands to run. If they're ten new badges short, this can be done by noon. Ten new ID badges usually take around two hours.

Jack: I was just on the phone with an HR manager. It's twenty.

簡：昨天太忙亂了。或許我可以幫她做新的識別證。我沒有差事。如果短少 10 個新的識別證，那中午前我可以完成。十個新的識別證通常要花費兩小時。

傑克：我剛跟人事部經理在電話中確認過了。是 20 個。

 ## 選項中譯與解析

19. 他們需要多少新的識別證？

(A) 10

(B) 20

(C) 5

(D) 15

20. 女子說「我沒有差事」，這句話意思為何？

(A) 她需趕快去處理業務。

(B) 她厭倦了差事。

(C) 跑步可以提高她的工作表現。

(D) 她現在沒什麼需要處理的事。

21. 這些談話者是誰？

(A) 同事。

(B) 新員工。

(C) 新成員。

(D) 辛蒂的朋友。

獵豹

19.

· 聽到對話，直接鎖定關鍵字 ID badges；badge 是名詞徽章、證章的意思，此處的 ID badges 指的是員工的識別證。根據對話 I was just on the phone with an HR manager. It's twenty.可知正確數量是 20 個，故此題答案為 B。

20.

· 聽到對話，馬上鎖定 I have no errands to run.找出題目問題點。Errand 是名詞：差事、雜事的意思，一般搭配動詞 run 使用，所以 have no errands to run 就是沒有差事要忙，故此題答案為 D。

21.

· 聽到對話，馬上鎖定關鍵字 our new hires：我們的新進員工。根據對話，從 new hires、new recruits 和 HR manager 彼此的關係來推測，說話者最有可能是公司同事，負責處理新進人員的人事資料。

19.

- 此題屬於細節題，考生須透過對話細節了解對話情境，並推測答案。根據對話，Cindy forgot to prepare new ID badges for our new hires.可知目前所需的識別證數量是新進員工的數量，從 Ten to be exact 到 It's twenty.，可知 A 選項是一個誘答選項，正確數字為 20 個。

20.

- 此題屬於細節題及推測題，考生須先理解動詞片語 have no errands to run 的意思，對照選項找出意思類似的片語，並推測出答案。
- 根據對話，have no errands to run 和 D 選項 has no business to attend to 意思相近，attend to 是動詞片語，處理之意，搭配對話 Perhaps I can make new ID badges for her，可以推測此人目前沒有事情要忙，所以可以幫忙，故 D 選項是最符合的答案。

21.

- 此題屬於情境題，測試考生是否理解對話情境並判斷人物關係。根據對話 prepare new ID badges for our new hires 可知說話者並不是新進員工，即可先刪除錯誤的 B、C 選項。由於無法從對話明確得知說話只和 Cindy 是不是朋友，所以 A 選項「同事」是最適合的答案。

浣熊 MP3 054+MP3 056

還可能怎麼問

1. **How long does it take to make 20 new badges?**

   (A) 2 hours

   (B) 4 hours

   (C) 6 hours

   (D) 8 hours

2. **What does the woman say she can do for Cindy?**

   (A) she can lead new recruits for her.

   (B) she can make new ID badges for her.

   (C) she can run errands for her.

   (D) she can prepare documents for her.

解析

1. **題目是問製作 20 個新識別證需要花費多少時間？**

   · 這題可以綜合一起看，女子有提到「十個新的識別證通常要花費兩小時。」，所以可以計算出 20 個識別證需要 4 小時，選項 B，4 小時，故可以得知答案為選項 B。

2. **題目是問女子說她可以替辛蒂做什麼？**

   · 選項 B，對話中有提到「昨天太忙亂了。或許我可以幫她做新的識別證。」，故可以得知答案為選項 B。

1 照片描述

2 應答問題

3 簡短對話

4 簡短獨白

模擬試題

Unit 8

員工識別證換餐點，水果＝糖份

Instructions

❶ 請播放音檔聽下列對話，並完成試題。 🎧 MP3 057+MP3 058

❷ 「跟述」練習：寫完試題後請跟著音檔同步跟漸進式做「跟述」練習，提升聽力專注力。

❸ 加碼題：完成❶＋❷步驟後，請再播放音檔寫浣熊試題，掌握其他可能的出題考點，強化應考實力。 🎧 MP3 057+MP3 059

22. Why did Mark give the man his ID badge?

(A) because Mark became sick and did not need to use his badge in the company cafeteria

(B) because Mark and the man are best friends

(C) because Mark does not like to eat in the company cafeteria

(D) because Mark asked the man to buy some food for him from the company cafeteria

23. Why did the man get only fruits?

(A) His favorite food is fruit.

(B) Fruits are on sale.

(C) He wants to ingest more Vitamin C from fruits.

(D) He is watching his weight

24. Why does the man say, "if I were Jim, I would be more concerned with sugar in those fruits"?

(A) He does not like to eat sweet food.

(B) He knows that Jim does not like sweet fruits.

(C) He thinks Jim should be worried about the lack of sugar in those fruits.

(D) He thinks Jim should pay attention to the amount of sugar in so many kinds of fruits.

 中譯與聽力原文

Questions 22-24 refer to the following conversation
問題 22-24，請參考以下對話內容

Jack: How can you get so many fruits at a company cafeteria?

傑克：你怎麼能從公司自助餐廳拿那麼多水果呢？

Jim: Mark had a sick leave this afternoon, and he had given me his ID badge before he left, and since I'm sort of on a diet... so all fruits.

吉姆：馬克今天下午請病假，而且在他離開公司前，他給我他的識別證，而且既然我有點再節食…所以都是水果。

Jack: Let me get this straight. For each badge, it's 150 NT dollars

傑克：讓我理清頭緒。每個識別證每餐可使用金

per meal, which means you just bought yourself fruits worthy of 300 NT dollars.

額是 150 元台幣。所以你剛替自己買了價值 300 元台幣的水果。

Jim: Yep... bananas, grapefruits, apples, and kiwi.

吉姆：是的...香蕉、葡萄、蘋果和奇異果。

Mary: Still trying hard to figure out the fruit mania thing. But is that legal?

瑪莉：仍試著了解整個水果狂熱事。但是這合法嗎？

Jack: It's not something for us to decide, but if I were Jim, I would be more concerned with sugar in those fruits.

傑克：這不是由我們來決定，但如果我是吉姆，我會更在乎那些水果中的糖分。

選項中譯與解析

22. 為什麼馬克把識別證交給男子？
(A) 因為馬克生病了，他不需要在員工餐廳使用識別證。
(B) 因為馬克和那男子是最好的朋友。
(C) 因為馬克不喜歡在員工餐廳吃飯。
(D) 因為馬克要求此人到員工餐廳替他買些食物。

23. 為何此男子只拿水果？
(A) 他最喜歡的食物是水果。

(B) 水果正在特價。

(C) 他想從水果攝取更多的維生素 C.

(D) 他正在節食。

 24. 為何此男子說「如果我是吉姆，我會更在乎那些水果中的糖分」？

(A) 他不喜歡吃甜食。

(B) 他知道吉姆不喜歡甜的水果。

(C) 他認為吉姆應該擔心那些水果中缺乏糖分。

(D) 他認為吉姆應該注意這麼多種水果中的含糖量。

 獵豹

22.

‧ 聽到對話，直接鎖定 Mark had a sick leave this afternoon...，可知 Mark 下午病假，並把識別證給他。sick leave 是名詞「病假」的意思，根據對話可知 Mark 下午病假，可以推測他不會在公司用餐，故此題答案為 A。

23.

‧ 聽到對話，直接鎖定 I'm sort of on a diet 此人表示他正在節食。on a diet 是片語表示「節食」「減肥」的意思，可以推測此人正在控制體重，故答案為選項 D。

24.

‧ 聽到對話，一樣鎖定 I'm sort of on a diet：我有點在節食，和關鍵字

sugar。根據對話，you just bought yourself fruits worthy of 300 NT dollars.可知他的午餐是大量的水果，對於在節食的人來説，也可能會攝取過多的糖分。

22.

· 此題屬於細節題，此處的 ID badge，指的是身分的識別證。可以先鎖定關鍵字 sick leave 來推測 Mark 今天由於生病請假，不會在員工餐廳用餐所以不需要他的識別證；接著用刪去法，刪除對話內容無法得知的 B、C、D 選項，確定 A 選項為最適合的答案。

23.

· 此題屬於細節題，考生須先了解動詞片語 be on a diet 的用法，然後推測此人只選擇水果的原因。從 be on a diet 找到他的類似用法「watch one's weight」，兩者都有控制體重的意思。根據對話，此人將重點放在節食，並沒有提及喜歡水果或是水果的其他好處，也可以用刪去法得到正解。

24.

· 此題屬於推測題，根據對話細節推測語意，可以搭配刪去法解題。根據對話關鍵字「on a diet」，可知正在節食的 Jim 企圖以大量的水果取代正餐，我們可以推測説話者認為 sugar in those fruits 將無益於正在節食的 Jim，所以需要特別留意水果中的糖分。對話中的 be concerned with「關心」、「關注於」是 D 選項 pay attention to 的同義詞。

浣熊  MP3 057+MP3 059

還可能怎麼問

 1. Why does the man say, "let me get this straight"?

(A) he needs more ID badges to get more fruits

(B) he is tired of being so indirect.

(C) he wants to be direct with other colleagues.

(D) he is trying to figure out the whole thing.

 2. Why does the woman mean when she says "fruit mania thing"?

(A) one's craziness toward sugar

(B) one's preference of choosing fruits as a meal

(C) one's goal of saving more money

(D) one's diet plan

 解析

1. 題目是問為什麼男子說「讓我理清頭緒」？

· 選項 D 他正試著了解整件事情，此為對話中所表達的意思，他正試著了解是怎麼回事，故可以得知答案為選項 D。

2. 題目是問當她說「水果狂熱事」，女子指的是什麼？

· 選項 B 一個人選擇水果當餐點的偏好，此為同義表達，所以可以得知答案為選項 B。

Unit 9
情人節：巧克力盒看人生

Instructions

❶ 請播放音檔聽下列對話，並完成試題。 🎧 MP3 060+MP3 061

❷ 「跟述」練習：寫完試題後請跟著音檔同步跟漸進式做「跟述」練習，提升聽力專注力。

❸ 加碼題：完成❶+❷步驟後，請再播放音檔寫浣熊試題，掌握其他可能的出題考點，強化應考實力。 🎧 MP3 060+MP3 062

25. What holiday are they talking about?
　　(A) Christmas
　　(B) Thanksgiving
　　(C) Valentine's Day
　　(D) Easter

26. How do the speakers feel about getting bouquets and chocolates?
　　(A) sad
　　(B) frustrated
　　(C) cheerful
　　(D) uncertain

27. What does the sentence "Life is like a box of chocolates" imply?

(A) We cannot predict what will happen to us.

(B) We should eat more chocolates.

(C) Chocolates are good for our health.

(D) Life is bitter sweet, just like chocolate.

中譯與聽力原文

Questions 25-27 refer to the following conversation
問題 25-27，請參考以下對話內容

Cindy: So considerate. Everyone gets a bouquet and a box of chocolate on Valentine's Day. The box totally makes my day, so fancy.

辛蒂：真是體貼入微。在情人節，每個人都收到花束和一盒巧克力。今天全然因為這盒而讓人感到美好，很豪華。

Mandy: Yep, kind of sweet. I love this company. You won't have a feeling that you are desperately lonely. There is no way that your colleague gets a boutique from an admirer, but you don't.

曼蒂：是的，有點體貼。我喜愛這間公司。你不會覺得太寂寞。也不會有你同事收到愛慕者的花束，但你卻沒收到。

照片描述　1

應答問題　2

簡短對話　3

簡短獨白　4

模擬試題

Cindy: Those feelings... even if it sounds like so tiny, it actually affects how we're going to perform at work.

辛蒂：那些感覺…即使看起來很些微，實際上卻影響我們在工作如何表現。

Mandy: I'm gonna go with the strawberry flavor... Eww it tastes bitter.

曼蒂：我要先嚐草莓口味的…哎喲…嚐起來苦。

Jim: It's like life. Life is like a box of chocolates; you don't know what it is until you experience it.

吉姆：就像生命一樣。人生像是一盒巧克力，除非你親身體驗，否則你不會知道你會遇到什麼事。

選項中譯與解析

25. 他們在談論什麼節日？
    (A) 聖誕節。
    (B) 感恩節。
    (C) 情人節。
    (D) 復活節。

26. 說話者對花束和巧克力看法如何？
    (A) 難過的。
    (B) 挫折的。
    (C) 開心的。
    (D) 不確定的。

27.「人生像是一盒巧克力」，這句話含意為何？

(A) 我們無法預測我們會發生什麼事。

(B) 我們應該多吃巧克力。

(C) 巧克力有益健康。

(D) 生活苦樂參半，就像巧克力一樣。

 獵豹

25.

‧ 聽到對話，馬上鎖定關鍵字 Valentine's Day，可知對話談論的是情人節。配合對話 gets a bouquet and a box of chocolate 等內容，最符合情人節的送禮項目，故此題答案為 C。

26.

‧ 聽到對話，直接鎖定 The box totally makes my day, so fancy，可知說話者對於收到花束和巧克力感到很開心。根據對話，How sweet is that、makes my day、so fancy 等感嘆語和形容詞，可知收到花束和巧克力是讓人感到十分貼心和雀躍的。

27.

‧ 聽到對話，馬上鎖定 Life is like a box of chocolates 來定位題目的問題點。需特別留意結論句 you don't know what it is until you experience it. 由此可知，人生像一盒巧克力，是因為必須品嚐了才知道滋味，故此題答案為 A。

貓頭鷹

25.

‧ 此題屬於情境題，可以直接鎖定對話關鍵字 Valentine's Day，接著透過對話中的 bouquet、a box of chocolate 和 gets a boutique from an admirer 等細節來驗證，最符合這樣的節日就是情人節，所以答案即為 C。

26.

‧ 此題屬於細節題及推測題，考生須先理解慣用語 make one's day 的意思，接著推測與 make one's day 相關的情緒形容詞。片語 make one's day 有讓人非常開心的意思，就像讓人的一天都因此而美好，搭配對話中提到的 sweet、fancy，都有很正向的意思，所以與其最相近的就是選項(C)cheerful 快樂的。

27.

‧ 此題屬於推測題，考生須根據題目細節推測答案，可以搭配選項的刪去法來解答。Life is like a box of chocolate，是比喻的句型。又根據對話關鍵句：you don't know what it is until you experience it「必須經歷才能理解」來對照選項，可知選項 A 的內容「人生是無法預測的」和題目意義最為相近。也可先刪除錯誤的 B、C 選項；而 D 選項「人生有苦有甜」是一個誘答選項要特別小心。

浣熊　MP3 060+MP3 062

還可能怎麼問

NEW **1. What does the woman say "Yep, kind of sweet"?**

(A) because the move of an admirer makes her feel that way.

(B) because the company cares about their feelings.

(C) because the chocolate is sweet.

(D) because she needs to sugarcoat whatever she says.

NEW **2. What does the woman mean when she say "makes my day"?**

(A) because it's Valentine's Day

(B) because receiving gifts makes her really happy

(C) because she needs take control of her day

(D) because she wants to cherish the moment.

 解析

1. 題目是問為什麼女子說「是的，有點體貼」？

・選項 B，從對話內容中可以推斷出此為對話中人物的感受，覺得公司在乎自己，故可以得知答案為選項 B。

2. 題目是問當女子說「讓人感到美好」，她指的是什麼？

・選項 B 因為收到禮物讓她真的感到快樂，此為女子講這句話的原因，故可以得知答案為選項 B。

（右側標籤）

1 照片描述

2 應答問題

3 簡短對話

4 簡短獨白

模擬試題

Unit 10
慶幸自己是會計部門的人

Instructions

❶ 請播放音檔聽下列對話，並完成試題。 🎧 MP3 063+MP3 064

❷ 「跟述」練習：寫完試題後請跟著音檔同步跟漸進式做「跟述」練習，提升聽力專注力。

❸ 加碼題：完成❶+❷步驟後，請再播放音檔寫浣熊試題，掌握其他可能的出題考點，強化應考實力。 🎧 MP3 063+MP3 065

28. What are the speakers discussing?
(A) the issue at the pitch meeting
(B) the issue of reducing expenses in the company
(C) how to make the boss satisfied
(D) working in the accounting department

29. How might the woman feel at the pitch meeting?
(A) frustrated
(B) pleased
(C) excited
(D) sad

30. Which of the following is the closest in meaning to the word "pitch" in this conversation?

(A) the level of something
(B) a proposal that attempts to persuade someone
(C) a throw in a baseball game
(D) the tone of a voice

🍀 中譯與聽力原文

Questions 28-30 refer to the following conversation
問題 28-30，請參考以下對話內容

Mary: I just don't understand what our CFO said at the budget meeting. Are we short of money?

瑪莉：我只是不了解我們財務長在預算會議説的話。我們資金短缺嗎？

Jack: I think we are. They're cutting expenses on almost everything.

傑克：我想我們是。他們幾乎每件事都在砍支出。

Jane: No wonder, I'm having a feeling that I'm having a hard time at the pitch meeting as well. For the past two months, none. The boss is never gonna be satisfied with any pitch.

簡：難怪，我有種感覺，我在提案會議時感到很難通過。過去兩個月，通過 0 個。老闆幾乎不滿意任何提案。

Mary: Thank God! I'm from the Accounting Department.

瑪莉：謝天謝地！我是會計部門的。

Jack: Why don't you go with the "it's gonna save lots of money", or "cost cutting", instead of focusing on the idea?

傑克：為什麼我們要專注在想新點子，而不專心在「節省金費」和「減少支出」上呢？

Mary: Perhaps, they're looking for a pitch that will cost the least money, but can earn lots of money in the long run. They don't care about which topic you pitch as long as they are feeling it's costly.

瑪莉：或許，他們正找尋會花費最少錢的提案，但是最終卻能賺許多錢。他們不再乎你所提的提案，只要他們覺得很花錢。

選項中譯與解析

28. 提案者正在討論什麼？

    (A) 銷售會議上的問題。

    (B) 公司減少開支的問題。

    (C) 如何讓老闆滿意。

    (D) 在會計部門工作。

29. 女子在開提案會議時可能的感覺為何？

    (A) 沮喪的。

    (B) 高興的。

    (C) 興奮的。

    (D) 難過的。

30. 本篇談話中，下列何者和 **pitch** 的意思最接近？

　(A) 事情程度。

　(B) 試圖説服某人的提案。

　(C) 棒球比賽的投球。

　(D) 音調。

28.

・聽到對話，馬上鎖定關鍵字 budget meeting 推測討論主題和預算有關。根據對話，short of money 跟 cutting expenses，可知討論主題是關於公司的預算縮減，故此題答案為 B。

29.

・聽到對話，馬上鎖定關鍵字 pitch meeting 來定位問題點。根據對話 I'm having a hard time at the pitch meeting、The boss is never gonna be satisfied with any pitch.可以推測此人在提案會議中感到挫折。

30.

・聽到對話，一樣鎖定關鍵字 pitch meeting。此處的 pitch 指的是提案，pitch meeting 也就是提案會議。根據關鍵字的相關敘述，satisfied with any pitch、focusing on the idea 和 which topic you pitch 等來推測，pitch 指的是想法、主題的提案。

 貓頭鷹

28.

・此題為情境題，根據對話，從 Are we short of money?開啟話題，接著提到 They're cutting expenses on almost everything.，可知對話主題圍繞著公司預算縮減的事件，與 B 選項 reducing expenses 意思最相近，故答案為 B。

29.

・此題為細節題，考生須先了解關鍵的動詞片語 have a hard time 的意思，對照選項找出意思最相近的詞。have a hard time 是「有一段艱難的時光」的意思，根據對話 The boss is never gonna be satisfied with any pitch.可以推測選項(A) frustrated「挫折的」是最相近的詞，故此題答案為 A。

30.

・此題為細節題，可以根據對話 satisfied with any pitch.、focusing on the idea、looking for a pitch 和 which topic you pitch 等細節，推測 pitch 和 B 選項的 proposal 最為相近，故此題答案為 B：嘗試説服某人的提案。

 浣熊 🎧 MP3 063+MP3 065

★NEW 還可能怎麼問
1. Why does the woman say "Thank God! I'm from the

Unit 10　慶幸自己是會計部門的人

1 照片描述

2 應答問題

3 簡短對話

4 簡短獨白

模擬試題

Accounting Department.”?

(A) Accounting Department is cutting all expenses

(B) the boss is not satisfied with any pitch.

(C) she feels relieved that she doesn't have to pitch.

(D) the CFO is on the Accounting Department's side

 2. What does the woman suggest about making a pitch?

(A) a pitch that costs the most money, but can earn less money

(B) a pitch that costs the least money, but can earn less of money

(C) a pitch that costs the most money, but can earn lots of money

(D) a pitch that costs the least money, but can earn lots of money

1. 題目是問為什麼女子說「謝天謝地！我是會計部門的」？

· 選項 C，此為女子講這句話的原因，因為她不用為此事苦惱，慶幸自己 是別的部門的人，故可以得知答案為選項 C。

2. 題目是問關於提一個提案，女子建議了什麼？這題要很細心地看，且 要注意比較級和最高級的使用，才不會選錯。

· 選項 D 花費較少錢的提案，但能賺許多錢，對話中有提到「或許，他 們正找尋會花費最少錢的提案，但是最終卻能賺許多錢。他們不再乎你 所提的提案，只要他們覺得很花錢。」但能賺許多錢，此為選項的同義 表達，所以可以得知答案為選項 D。

Unit 11
不靠大量訂單也談成某個折扣

Instructions

❶ 請播放音檔聽下列對話，並完成試題。 MP3 066+MP3 067

❷ 「跟述」練習：寫完試題後請跟著音檔同步跟漸進式做「跟述」練習，提升聽力專注力

❸ 加碼題：完成❶＋❷步驟後，請再播放音檔寫浣熊試題，掌握其他可能的出題考點，強化應考實力。 MP3 066+MP3 068

31. What does the woman mean by saying "Isn't that wild"?

(A) Mr. Smith is a wild person.

(B) A huge discount is pretty amazing.

(C) Talking on the phone about the order makes her angry.

(D) It is not reasonable to place a bulk order.

32. How would they receive a discount under normal circumstances?

(A) by placing a bulk order

(B) by negotiating with Mr. Smith

(C) by doing something under the table

(D) by bargaining with Mr. Smith

33. Why does the woman say, "I guess that will be my little secret"?

(A) She is good at keeping secrets.

(B) The order is confidential information.

(C) Mr. Smith asked her to keep a secret.

(D) She does not want to reveal how she received the discount.

 中譯與聽力原文

Questions 31-33 refer to the following conversation
問題 **31-33**，請參考以下對話內容

Jane: I was just on the phone with Mr. Smith, and he said that he could give us a huge discount at our CY10008 order. Isn't that wild?

簡：我剛才與史密斯先生通話，他說 CY10008 的訂單他會給我大量折扣。是不是很瘋狂？

Jack: Congratulations. Normally, he won't give us a discount, unless it's a bulk order.

傑克：恭喜。通常，他不會給我們折扣，除非這是大量訂單。

Mark: Meaning we have to order a certain amount to have a discount?

馬克：意思是我們必須訂購到特定的量才能享有折扣嗎？

Jack: Yep. Just a little bit curious how you can pull that off.

159

Mark: How? I'm curious about that, too.

Jane: I guess that will be my little secret. Oh... the boss wants to see me. I'm gonna see you guys later.

傑克：是的。只是有點好奇你怎麼能成功做到。

馬克：怎麼辦到的呢？我也蠻好奇的。

簡：我想那就成了我的小秘密了。喔...老闆想要見我。我稍後再與你們見面。

選項中譯與解析

31. 女子說「是不是很瘋狂」含意為何？

(A) 史密斯先生是個狂人。

(B) 大量的折扣相當驚喜的。

(C) 在電話中談論訂單讓她生氣。

(D) 大量訂單是不合理的。

32. 在正常情況下，他們想獲得折扣該如何做呢？

(A) 透過大量訂購。

(B) 與史密斯先生協商。

(C) 私下交易。

(D) 與史密斯先生討價還價。

33. 為何女子說「我想那就成了我的小秘密」？

(A) 她善於保密。

(B) 訂單是機密資訊。

(C) 史密斯先生要求她保守秘密。

(D) 她不想透露如何得到折扣。

 獵豹

31.

· 聽到對話，直接鎖定 Isn't that wild 定位問題點，找出關鍵字 discount。根據對話，he said that he could give us a huge discount，可知此人感到 wild 的原因跟得到大量折扣有關，故此題答案為 B。

32.

· 聽到對話，馬上鎖定 discount 來定位問題點，找出關鍵字 a bulk order。根據對話，Normally, he won't give us a discount, unless it's a bulk order.，可知通常是透過大量訂單取得折扣的，故此題答案為 A。

33.

· 聽到對話，直接鎖定 I guess that will be my little secret.來定位問題點；secret，名詞「秘密」。根據對話，I guess that will be my little secret.表示說話者對於取得折扣的方法想要保密，故此題答案為 D。

 貓頭鷹

31.

· 此題屬於情境題，根據對話，Normally, he won't give us a discount, unless it's a bulk order.「可知除非是大量訂單，否則一般很難有辦法拿到折扣」，由此推測此處的 Isn't that wild 是想表達對於拿到大量折扣感到驚喜，所以最適合的答案為 B。

32.

· 此題為細節題，題目關鍵在 under normal circumstances，考生可以從題目回推到對話，對照對話中的「Normally」找到關鍵字 bulk order。根據對話 Normally, he won't give us a discount, unless it's a bulk order.很明確的表示通常常是透過大量訂單拿到折扣，底下也解釋必須 order a certain amount to have a discount，故此題答案為 A。

33.

· 此題屬於推測題，根據對話，Normally, he won't give us a discount, unless it's a bulk order.，可知這次能取得大量折扣，有別於一般狀況，而從 I guess that will be my little secret.來推測說話者並不想公開方法，故答案為(D)She does not want to reveal how she received the discount.。

 浣熊 🎧 MP3 066+MP3 068

還可能怎麼問

1. Why was the woman on the phone with Mr. Smith?

　　(A) discussing a bulk order

(B) negotiated with him about the discount.

(C) informed him that they were out of stock

(D) offered him a discount

2. What will the woman do next?

(A) tells her coworkers how.

(B) schedules a business lunch with Mr. Smith.

(C) makes a bulk order work.

(D) meets with her boss.

解析

1. 題目是問為什麼女子剛與史密斯先生通話呢？

‧選項 B，根據對話極有可能是仍在與對方談關於折扣的部分故可以得知答案為選項 B。

2. 題目是問女子接下來會做什麼？

‧選項 D，對話中有提到「喔…老闆想要見我。我稍後再與你們見面。」，此為同義表達，所以可以得知女子接下來會與老闆會面，答案為選項 D。

Unit 12

有人挖角，
其他事都要讓道

Instructions

❶ 請播放音檔聽下列對話，並完成試題。 🎧 MP3 069+MP3 070

❷ 「跟述」練習：寫完試題後請跟著音檔同步跟漸進式做「跟述」練習，提升聽力專注力。

❸ 加碼題：完成❶＋❷步驟後，請再播放音檔寫浣熊試題，掌握其他可能的出題考點，強化應考實力。 🎧 MP3 069+MP3 071

34. Why is the woman not in the annual budget meeting?

(A) She is not well prepared for the meeting.

(B) She cannot make it on time.

(C) The meeting was rescheduled to tomorrow.

(D) The meeting was called off.

 35. Why does the woman say, "I'm afraid not"?

(A) She is afraid to attend the budget meeting.

(B) She is not afraid to apply for a position in G&XM.

(C) She is unable to go through some reports.

(D) She is unable to talk to the shareholders.

36. **When might the woman help with the reports conducted by Accounting Department?**

(A) tomorrow afternoon

(B) tomorrow morning

(C) this evening

(D) right after they finish the conversation

中譯與聽力原文

Questions 34-36 refer to the following conversation
問題 34-36，請參考以下對話內容

Mark: Why are you still here? Don't you have an annual budget meeting with bosses and shareholders?

馬克：為什麼你仍在這裡？你不是與老闆們和股東們有個年度預算會議嗎？

Jane: They rescheduled it to tomorrow morning yesterday.

簡：昨天他們將它重新安排至明天早上。

Mary: That means you'll have time to go through the reports conducted by the Accounting Department, right?

瑪莉：這意味著你將有時間看完由會計部門的報告，對吧？

Jane: I'm afraid not. G&XM just called. They're going to offer

簡：恐怕不能。G&XM 剛來電。他們要提供我一份

me a job. Isn't that wild? The interview is in the afternoon at 3 p.m. I've got some paper work to prepare. I do have time tomorrow afternoon. Don't worry about those reports. Gotta run.

工作。是不是很瘋狂？面試是下午三點鐘。我有些文件資料要準備。我明天下午有時間。別擔心那些報告。該走囉。

 選項中譯與解析

34. 為何女子不參加年度預算會議？
(A) 她沒有做好準備。
(B) 她不能按時完成。
(C) 重新安排至明天。
(D) 會議被取消了。

35. 為何女子說「恐怕不能」？
(A) 她怕參加預算會議。
(B) 她不怕在 G&XM 申請工作。
(C) 她看不完一些報告。
(D) 她不能和股東交談。

36. 女子什麼時候可以幫會計部門處理報告？
(A) 明天下午。
(B) 明天早上。
(C) 今天晚上。
(D) 對話結束後。

獵豹

34.

‧ 聽到對話，直接鎖定 annual budget meeting 來定位問題點。根據對話，They rescheduled it to tomorrow morning yesterday.可知會議被改期至明天早上，故此題答案為 C。

35.

‧ 聽到對話，直接鎖定 I'm afraid not 來回推問題點。根據上一句 That means you'll have time to go through the reports conducted by Accounting Department, right?。但此人回答的是：I'm afraid I don't have time to go through the reports.，表達婉轉拒絕對方的要求，故答案為 C。

36.

‧ 聽到對話馬上鎖定 the reports conducted by Accounting Department 來定位問題點。根據對話，I do have time tomorrow afternoon.可知他明天下午有空，故此題答案為 A。

貓頭鷹

34.

‧ 此題為細節題，測試考生是否理解對話內容，可以對照選項，配合刪去法解題。根據對話，They rescheduled it to tomorrow morning yesterday.可知答案為 C 選項：The meeting was rescheduled to tomorrow.：reschedule，動詞「改期」。(A) 她沒有準備好；(B)她趕不上；(D)會議取消了。

35.

· 此題為細節題及推測題，根據對話問答，轉折句 I'm afraid not 是針對「have time to go through the reports conducted by Accounting Department」的否定，接著她馬上解釋否定的原因：G&XM just called. They're going to offer me a job. ...I've got some paper work to prepare，所以此人沒辦法看完會計部的報告，故此題答案為 C。

36.

· 此題為細節題，題目關鍵在於 the reports conducted by Accounting Department；也可視為 35 題的延伸，測試考生是否知道此人目前無法讀完的會計報告，會在什麼時候讀完。根據對話， The interview is in the afternoon 3 p.m. I've got some paper work to prepare.，可知她今天下午 3 點前要準備資料，然後 3 點開始面試；但是 I do have time tomorrow afternoon. Don't worry about those reports.可知她明天下午有空。

 浣熊 🎧 MP3 069+MP3 071

還可能怎麼問

NEW **1. Why does the woman say, "Gotta run"?**

    (A) because running is good for her career

    (B) because she runs for the chairman of the budget meeting

(C) because she is in a hurry

(D) because she wants some time alone

2. What will the woman do next?

(A) calls G&XM

(B) accepts the new job

(C) prepares some documents

(D) works on those reports

 解析

1. 題目是問為什麼女子說「該走囉」？

・選項 C，從對話中可以推測出她很趕著弄文件的資料，故可以得知答案為選項 C。

2. 題目是問女子接下來會做什麼？

・選項 C，對話中有提到「我有些文件資料要準備。」，paper work 和 documents 為同義表達，故可以得知答案為選項 C。

Unit 1 3

家庭跟工作只能二選一

 Instructions

❶ 請播放音檔聽下列對話，並完成試題。  MP3 072+MP3 073

❷ 「跟述」練習：寫完試題後請跟著音檔同步跟漸進式做「跟述」練習，提升聽力專注力。

❸ 加碼題：完成❶+❷步驟後，請再播放音檔寫浣熊試題，掌握其他可能的出題考點，強化應考實力。 MP3 072+MP3 074

37. Why does the woman say, "it's a long fall from the top"?

(A) The sales figures fell to a very low number.

(B) She is telling the others to be careful not to fall.

(C) She feels the fall season is too long.

(D) It's a long distance from the cafeteria to the meeting room.

38. Why does the woman ask everyone to grab a bagel or sandwich?

(A) Bagels and sandwiches are their favorite.

(B) She expects everyone to attend the meeting and have dinner there.

(C) The cafeteria is known for its bagels and sandwiches.

(D) She does not want her co-workers to eat at the cafeteria.

39. What is the purpose of mentioning a family obligation by one of the women?

(A) to show a family obligation should be a priority.

(B) to indicate that family should come first

(C) She is suggesting that she cannot attend the meeting because of family duty.

(D) She is telling the co-workers that family duty is more important than meetings.

 中譯與聽力原文

Questions 37-39 refer to the following conversation
問題 37-39，請參考以下對話內容

Mary: It's totally unacceptable... it's a long fall from the top.

瑪莉：這全然令人無法接受...從頂端跌至最底。

Jack: We've seen those sales figures. We're going to reposition our market place. Plus. We are launching a new feature next month. I'm pretty confident that we are gonna get back on track.

傑克：我們已經看的銷售數字。我們正重新定位我們的市場位置。再者，我們下個月會推出一個新的專題。我相當有信心我們會回到正軌的。

Mary: I want everyone to grab a

瑪莉：我想要每個人到自助

bagel or sandwich at the cafeteria and meet back here at 6 p.m.

餐拿個貝果或三明治然後下午六點在這裡會合。

Judy: I'm sorry. I've got a family obligation.

茱蒂：很抱歉。我有家庭義務要履行。

Mary: Excuse me? This is an important sales meeting. If the condition hasn't improved, a lot of you might as well have to dust off your resume and find another job.

瑪莉：不好意思？這是很重要的銷售會議。如果情況尚未改善的話，你們很多人都必須更新履歷另外找工作了。

選項中譯與解析

37. 為何女子說「從頂端跌至最底」？

(A) 銷售數字下跌到很低的數字。

(B) 她正告訴別人小心不要跌倒。

(C) 她覺得秋天太長了。

(D) 從自助餐廳到會議室距離很遠。

38. 為何女子要求大家拿個貝果或三明治？

(A) 貝果和三明治是他們的最愛。

(B) 她希望每個人都出席會議並在那吃晚餐。

(C) 自助餐廳以焙果和三明治而聞名。

(D) 她不希望同事在自助餐廳吃東西。

39. 其中一名女子提到家庭義務，其目的為何？

(A) 表示家庭義務應該要優先考慮。

(B) 表示家庭應優先考慮。

(C) 她暗示因家家庭義務而不能出席會議。

(D) 她告訴同事，家庭義務比會議更重要。

獵豹

37.

- 聽到對話，直接鎖定 it's a long fall from the top 來定位問題點，找出關鍵字 sales figures。 sales figures 指的是銷售數字；根據對話，We've seen those sales figures.可以推測這裡的 long fall from the top 是針對 sales figures，故此題答案 A。

38.

- 聽到對話，直接鎖定 grab a bagel or sandwich 來定位問題點。根據對話 grab a bagel or sandwich at the cafeteria and meet back here 和 This is an important sales meeting.，可以推測她希望大家能一邊吃飯一邊開會。

39.

- 聽到對話，直接鎖定 family obligation 來定位問題點；Obligation 是名詞「義務」。題目重點在於，詢問提起 family obligation「家庭義務」的目的，推測此人有私人因素不便參加會議，故答案為 C。

37.

· 此題屬於情境題及推測題，測試考生是否理解對話內容和討論主題，從而推測 It's a long fall 的指涉對象，也可由對話細節對照選項，配合刪去法解答。根據對話，從 it's a long fall from the top 到 we are gonna get back from tack 這幾句，可以確定 long fall 指涉的是對話主題字 sales figures 從頂端跌至最底的狀況，和 A 選項的敘述：「銷售數字下滑到非常嚴重」最為相近，故此題答案為 A。

38.

· 此題屬於情境題及推測題，根據對話 This is an important sales meeting. If the condition hasn't improved, a lot of you might as well have to dust your resume and find another job.可知目前的情況十分嚴重，有可能影響員工生計，強調了這個會議很緊急也非常重要，可以推測此人是希望大家能一起吃飯、一邊開會討論對策，故答案為 B。

39.

· 此題屬於推測題，family obligation 指的是家庭義務，與選項中的 family duty 同義。對照選項，A、B、D 敘述內容大同小異，認為家庭比工作重要；C 選項則強調無法參加會議，有請假的目的，最符合對話情境，故答案為 C。

浣熊 🎧 MP3 072+MP3 074

還可能怎麼問

1. Why does the woman say, "dust off your resume"? ?

(A) it means dumping your resume in the trash can

(B) it means filtering something that is not suitable

(C) it means updating or renewing the profile

(D) it means a lot to the company's sales meeting

2. Why does the man say, "we are gonna get back on track"?

(A) he thinks things will improve and get back to normal

(B) he thinks confidence is the key

(C) he has seen the worst sales figures

(D) he thinks they need to be back to where they were

 解析

1. 題目是問為什麼女子說「更新履歷」？

· dust off your resume，指的是更新或打掃履歷，有時候會搭 to find out what color is your parachute，故可以得知答案為選項 C。

2. 題目是問為什麼男子說「我們將會回到正軌」？

· 選項 A，對話中確實有提到「我們正重新定位我們的市場位置。再者，我們個月會推出一個新的專題。我相當有信心我們會回到正軌的。」，其實男子還是相信情況會有所改善，所以可以得知答案為選項 A。

Unit 14
廣告收益幾乎決定公司生死

Instructions

❶ 請播放音檔聽下列對話，並完成試題。 ▶ MP3 075+MP3 076

❷ 「跟述」練習：寫完試題後請跟著音檔同步跟漸進式做「跟述」練習，提升聽力專注力。

❸ 加碼題：完成❶+❷步驟後，請再播放音檔寫浣熊試題，掌握其他可能的出題考點，強化應考實力。 ▶ MP3 075+MP3 077

40. What are the speakers discussing?

(A) how awful the economy has become

(B) how to attract more sponsors

(C) how to stay positive

(D) how to increase earnings for the magazine

41. What is a possible solution to their problem?

(A) by marketing the magazine on social media

(B) by staying positive about the future

(C) by reducing the employees' salaries

(D) by doing business with ABC company

 42. What does the woman imply by saying "The economy has hit us all"?

(A) The economy will be better.

(B) She could not believe how devastating the economy is.

(C) The economic recession has affected everyone.

(D) Generating hits on the magazine's Facebook page will bring more ad revenues.

中譯與聽力原文

Questions 40-42 refer to the following conversation
問題 40-42，請參考以下對話內容

Jane: Did anyone call back?

簡：有任何人回電嗎？

Mark: no, why?

馬克：沒有，怎麼了？

Mary: The economy has hit us all. Apparently, no one wants to fund a magazine because they think that the magazine won't earn any money for them.

瑪莉：經濟不景氣衝擊到我們所有人。顯然沒有人想要注資雜誌，因為他們都認為雜誌不會替他們賺到錢。

Jane: Without ad revenues, there's no way we're gonna put our next issue on the stand.

簡：沒有廣告收入，我們不可能有辦法讓我們下期雜誌上架。

Mark: However, I do have a lunch meeting with ABC Company.

馬克：然而，我與 ABC 公司有午餐會議。我確信

I'm sure we'll find a way out.

我們會找到解決方法的。

Mary: We just have to be positive. I'm contacting our CFO to see if there are other things that we can do. We're gonna go through this.

瑪莉：我們只需要保持正向。我正聯繫我們的財務長看是否有其他事情是我們所能做的，我們能撐過這次的。

選項中譯與解析

40. 談話者正在討論什麼？

(A) 經濟變得有多糟。

(B) 如何吸引更多贊助商。

(C) 如何保持正向。

(D) 如何增加雜誌的收入。

41. 可能解決問題的方案是什麼？

(A) 在社交媒體上行銷雜誌。

(B) 對未來保持樂觀。

(C) 減少員工薪水〔減薪〕。

(D) 與 ABC 公司做生意。

NEW 42. 女子對話中說「經濟不景氣衝擊到我們所有人」，其暗示為何？

(A) 經濟會更好。

(B) 她不敢相信經濟有多慘。

(C) 經濟不景氣已經影響到每個人。

(D) 雜誌臉書頁面的點擊量將帶來更多廣告收入。

獵豹

40.

‧ 聽到對話，馬上鎖定 The economy has hit us all.，推測討論主題和經濟不景氣有關。根據對話，find a way out 和 go through this，判斷對話討論主題再找解決方案，所以 D 選項是最適合的答案。

41.

‧ 聽到對話，直接鎖定轉折詞 However，找到問題關鍵句：find a way out。根據對話，I do have a lunch meeting with ABC Company. I'm sure we'll find a way out.，可知和 ABC 公司做生意有可能解決困境，故答案為 D。

42.

‧ 聽到對話，直接鎖定 The economy has hit us all.，來定位題目問題點。根據對話，The economy has hit us all.，關鍵字 hit：動詞「打擊」，就字面解釋：經濟打擊所有人；可知答案即為選項 C。

貓頭鷹

40.

‧ 此題屬於情境題，測試考生是否理解對話主要內容，進而挑選出對話主

題，也可對照選項，搭配刪去法解題。根據對話，從 The economy has hit us all.開啟話題，提到目前雜誌的窘境，接著在轉折詞 However 之後提出可能解套的機會和動作；可以先刪除錯誤的 A、C 選項。對比 B、D 選項；B 選項較片面的針對討論「如何尋找贊助商」，所以 D 選項的「想辦法增加收入」會是較好的答案。

41.

· 此題屬於細節題，鎖定關鍵的轉折詞 However，從困境轉折到可能的解決機會。根據對話，I do have a lunch meeting with ABC Company. I'm sure we'll find a way out.，find a way out 表示「找到出路」，由此推測 D 選項 doing business with ABC company 會是解決問題的好機會，故此題答案為 D。

42.

· 此題屬於細節題及推測題，測試考生是否理解對話內容，運用換句話說，並通過對話細節對照選項，選出意思最接近 The economy has hit us all 的答案。根據對話內容，The economy has hit us all.以及雜誌面臨的危機，可以推測經濟帶來了不好的影響，最符合 C 選項「經濟蕭條影響所有人」的敘述，故答案為 C。(B) devastating，令人絕望的；(C) recession，不景氣。

 浣熊 🎧 MP3 075+MP3 077

還可能怎麼問

⭐NEW **1. Why does the woman say, "Did anyone call back"?**

  (A) she is waiting for a call from investors

(B) she is being paranoid about the phone call

(C) she is afraid that her colleagues will poach her major clients

(D) she is questioning her colleagues

 2. Why does the woman mention about "ad revenues"

(A) to fund another magazine

(B) to persuade investors

(C) to feel like a big shot

(D) to maintain the overall operation

解析

1. 題目是問為什麼女子說「有任何人回電嗎」？

‧選項 A，對話中有提到「顯然沒有人想要注資雜誌，因為他們都認為雜誌不會替他們賺到錢。」，其實可以從這句話中推斷她是在等投資客的電話，故可以得知答案為選項 A。

2. 題目是問為什麼女子提到關於「廣告收入」？

‧選項 D，對話中有提到「沒有廣告收入，我們不可能有辦法讓我們下期雜誌上架。」，此訊息與選項敘述一致，這是女子提到廣告收入的原因，這會影項到公司的整體營運，所以可以得知答案為選項 D。

Unit **15**
工作穩定性

Instructions

❶ 請播放音檔聽下列對話，並完成試題。 📀 MP3 078+MP3 079

❷ 「跟述」練習：寫完試題後請跟著音檔同步跟漸進式做「跟述」練習，提升聽力專注力。

❸ 加碼題：完成❶＋❷步驟後，請再播放音檔寫浣熊試題，掌握其他可能的出題考點，強化應考實力。 📀 MP3 078+MP3 080

 43. What does the term, "reality check" imply?

(A) checking the difference between the real world and the virtual world.

(B) an occasion causing someone to recognize the truth in reality by correcting his misconception

(C) a situation in which a person has to be realistic.

(D) a condition in which a person's perception of reality is far from the fact.

44. What is the main topic of the conversation?

(A) the best place to listen to music

(B) the woman's lack of long-term commitment to a job

(C) young people's lack of commitment to their jobs

(D) how taking a vacation enhances working performance

Unit 15　工作穩定性

1 照片描述

2 應答問題

3 簡短對話

4 簡短獨白

模擬試題

 45. Which of the following best describes "a job hop"?

(A) changing from one job to another frequently

(B) moving quickly in the office

(C) catching someone on the hop

(D) hopping during workout

 ## 中譯與聽力原文

Questions 43-45 refer to the following conversation
問題 43-45，請參考以下對話內容

Cindy: A reality check? What do you mean?

辛蒂：檢視現實？你是指什麼？

Jimmy: It's time to face the music. You can't commit to a job for at least three to five years.

吉米：是該面對現實的時候了。你不能對一份工作承諾至少 3-5 年。

Linda: That's the problem, my dear. You can't make a job hop every half a year. You seem pretty unstable.

琳達：這就是個問題，親愛的。你不能每半年就換工作。你似乎相當不穩定。

Cindy: From HR's perspective or from your opinion. It's just not the job I think I will be doing for the next five to ten

辛蒂：從人事專員的角度還是從你的意見來看。這只是不是我未來五到十年想要繼續做的

years.

Jimmy: Perhaps you should take a vacation, figuring out what really motivates you or what you really want to do.

工作。

吉米：或許你應該要休假，了解什麼真的能激勵你或你真的想要從事什麼？

選項中譯與解析

43.「現實檢視」這個詞含意為何？
(A) 檢視現實世界和虛擬世界的區別。
(B) 透過糾正錯誤觀念，使人們認識到事實真相
(C) 個人必須維持實際的情況。
(D) 個人對現實的看法與事實相差甚遠。

44. 本篇談話的主旨是什麼？
(A) 聽音樂的最佳場所。
(B) 這位女性缺乏對工作的長期承諾。
(C) 年輕人缺乏對工作的承諾。
(D) 度假如何提高工作表現。

45. 以下哪個選項最能描述"job hop"?
(A) 頻繁地換工作。
(B) 在辦公室動作快。
(C) 使某人措手不及。
(D) 健身時單腳跳。

 獵豹

43.

・聽到對話，直接鎖定關鍵字 reality check 來定位題目問題點。根據對話，figuring out what really motivates you or what you really want to do.可以推測 reality check 是對生活現況的檢討，此處特別針對工作和目標的選擇與達成，故此題答案為 B。

44.

・聽到對話，直接鎖定關鍵字 job hop 來定位題目問題點。根據對話，You can't commit to a job for at least three to five years.討論內容圍繞關鍵字 job hop，談論工作投入的時間長短和換工作的頻率，故此題答案為 B。

45.

・聽到對話，馬上鎖定關鍵字 job hop 來定位問題點。Hop，動詞「跳」，由字面的意思可以翻譯作「跳槽」。根據對話，You can't make a job hop every half a year. You seem pretty unstable.來推測，此處的 job hop 指的是頻繁的換工作。

 貓頭鷹

43.

・此題屬於細節題及推測題，測試考生是否理解對話內容，運用換句話說，並透過對話細節推測答案，同時以刪去法解題。根據對話，

figuring out what really motivates you or what you really want to do.，可知此處的 reality 指的是現實生活，特別針對工作目標；可以先刪除錯誤的 A、D 選項。而此處的 check，則有檢視、反省的意味，和 B 選項 recognize the truth：「認清現實」、correcting his misconception：「導正錯誤」等敘述相符，故此題答案為 B。

44.

· 此題屬於情境題，測試考生是否理解對話內容的主題，可以利用選項的刪去法來解題。根據對話，從 reality check 開始話題，內容圍繞 commit to a job、make a job hop；可以先刪除錯誤的 A、D 選項。對比 B、C 選項，兩者皆敘述無法投入工作，C 選項針對年輕人；而 B 選項強調「長期」的工作，更符合對話敘述，故答案為 B。

45.

· 此題屬於細節題及推測題，測試考生是否理解對話內容，運用換句話說，並透過對話細節推測答案，選出意思最接近 a job hop 的選項。直接鎖定關鍵字 job hop，根據對話，You can't make a job hop every half a year. You seem pretty unstable.，對照 A 選項 changing from one job to another frequently：頻繁地換工作，敘述最為相近，故答案為 A。

 浣熊 🎧 MP3 078+MP3 080

還可能怎麼問

1. How often does the woman switch her job?

(A) 3 years

(B) 5 years

(C) every year

(D) 6 months

2. What does the man suggest to the woman in the end?

(A) find the reality

(B) find her passions

(C) don't make a job hop ever again

(D) talk to another HR personnel

解析

1. 題目是問女子多久就換一次工作呢？

‧ 這題可以綜合一起看。對話中有提到「你不能每半年就換工作。你似乎相當不穩定。」可以得知 half a year 等同 six months。選項 D 六個月，此為對話中所表達的意思，故可以得知答案為選項 D。

2. 題目是問男子最後建議了女子什麼？

‧ 選項 B，對話末有提到「或許你應該要休假，了解什麼真的能激勵你或你真的想要從事什麼？」，這句其實說明了 find your passions，故可以得知答案為選項 B。

Unit 16
博物館暑期工讀申請

🔍 Instructions

❶ 請播放音檔聽下列對話，並完成試題。 🎧 MP3 081+MP3 082

❷ 「跟述」練習：寫完試題後請跟著音檔同步跟漸進式做「跟述」練習，提升聽力專注力。

❸ 加碼題：完成❶＋❷步驟後，請再播放音檔寫浣熊試題，掌握其他可能的出題考點，強化應考實力。 🎧 MP3 081+MP3 083

46. **Why does Jim tell the others to prepare the other documents?**
   (A) It is always better to be fully prepared.
   (B) The more documents, the better.
   (C) He wants to show off that he knows more than they do.
   (D) The museum might ask for an interview after receiving the applications.

47. **Why does Jim know how to apply for the position?**
   (A) He is a supervisor in the museum.
   (B) He designed the application process.
   (C) He was an intern in the museum last year.
   (D) He is the curator of the museum.

48. Which of the following is NOT mentioned as one of the application materials?

(A) recommendations

(B) proof of community service

(C) GPAs

(D) online application forms

中譯與聽力原文

Questions 46-48 refer to the following conversation
問題 46-48，請參考以下對話內容

Cindy: I really want to apply for a summer internship at Best Marine Museum, and I just don't know how. Should I just fill out on-line application forms?

辛蒂：我真的想要申請倍斯特海洋博物館的暑期實習，我不知道從哪開始。我應該只要填線上申請表格嗎？

Jim: That's right. But I do think you should prepare other things?

吉姆：對的。但是我認為你應該準備其他東西。

Mary: like what?

瑪莉：像是什麼？

Jim: For instance, recommendations, GPAs, and your senior project, in case there is a scheduled

吉姆：例如，推薦函、成績平均和你的大四專題，以防在你申請後

interview right after you apply.	有個面試安排。
Cindy: Should we prepare our passports, too?	辛蒂：我們也應該要準備護照嗎？
Jim: You should. In case you are assigned to an overseas museum.	吉姆：你應該要。以防你被分配到海外博物館。
Mary: How do you know all these?	瑪莉：你怎麼知道這些的？
Jim: I did it last year, and it's amazing.	吉姆：我去年申請的，這個機會很棒。

選項中譯與解析

46. 吉姆為何告訴其他人要準備其他文件？

(A) 準備充分總是比較好的。

(B) 文件越多越好。

(C) 他想炫耀他比他們知道得更多。

(D) 博物館收到申請後可能會要求面試。

47. 為何吉姆知道如何申請此職位？

(A) 他是博物館的主管。

(B) 他設計申請步驟。

(C) 去年他在博物館實習。

(D) 他是博物館館長。

48. 關於申請材料，下列選項中何者未被提及？

(A) 推薦函。

(B) 社區服務證明。

(C) 平均成績。

(D) 線上申請表格。

獵豹

46.

· 聽到對話，直接鎖定 in case there is a scheduled interview, right after you apply. 可知其他文件的事先準備，是為了以防萬一，申請後會馬上有面試要準備，故此題答案為 D。

47.

· 聽到對話，馬上鎖定 I did it last year。根據對話問答：How do you know all these?；I did it last year, and it's amazing.可知 Jim 去年申請過並通過了博物館實習，所以此題答案為 C。

48.

· 聽到對話，馬上鎖定關鍵字 application materials：申請資料。根據對話，application forms、recommendations、GPAs、senior project 和 passport 可知此題答案為 B。

46.

・此題屬於細節題，題目詢問準備資料的目的，可以直接鎖定連詞 in case：「萬一」，找到關鍵字 interview。根據對話 in case there is a scheduled interview, right after you apply.，最符合選項 D 的敘述：「博物館在收到申請後可能會要求面試」。故此題答案為 D。

47.

・此題屬於細節題，測試考生是否理解對話內容，並判斷說話者的身分。根據對話，由 apply for a summer internship 開始話題，可知對話關鍵在 internship：「實習」，所以此處的 I did it last year 表示他去年曾去實習過了，和 C 選項的敘述相符，故答案為 C。(A) supervisor：監督人；(C) intern：實習生；(D) curator：館長。

48.

・此題屬於細節題，考生須由題目一一對照對話，判斷選項是否正確。此題關鍵在 application materials，題目詢問對話「未」提及的申請資料。根據對話內容，答案為 B 選項社區服務證明。(A) recommendations，推薦函；(C) GPAs 平均成績；(D) online application forms 線上申請表。

浣熊　🎧 MP3 081+MP3 083

還可能怎麼問

1.　What are the speakers mainly discussing?

(A) apply for passports

(B) prepare for an interview

(C) discuss a summer study plan

(D) apply for a museum internship

2.　Where does the conversation probably take place?

(A) On campus

(B) At the airport

(C) At the museum

(D) At the Bureau of Foreign Affairs

解析

1.　題目是問說話者們主要在討論什麼？

· 選項 D，此為對話中所表達的意思，對話中有提到「申請倍斯特海洋博物館的暑期實習。」，故可以得知答案為選項 D。

2.　題目是問這個對話可能發生在哪裡？

· 選項 A，對話內容中可以推測，他們可能是在校園內討論這件事，所以可以得知答案為選項 A。

神經大條，
得罪大咖也不曉得

Instructions

❶ 請播放音檔聽下列對話，並完成試題。 MP3 084+MP3 085

❷ 「跟述」練習：寫完試題後請跟著音檔同步跟漸進式做「跟述」練習，提升聽力專注力。

❸ 加碼題：完成❶＋❷步驟後，請再播放音檔寫浣熊試題，掌握其他可能的出題考點，強化應考實力。 MP3 084+MP3 086

49. What is the woman's problem?

(A) She sat at the wrong table.

(B) She offended an important business partner.

(C) She ordered the wrong meal.

(D) She was rude to her co-worker.

50. Where might this conversation take place?

(A) in a restaurant

(B) in an airport

(C) in an airline company

(D) in a bank

51. Why is Best Airline the only airline their company is doing business with?

(A) Another airline the company used to do business with went bankrupt and their partnership was terminated.

(B) Best Airline gave the company the best deal.

(C) Best Airline specializes in transporting lightweight products.

(D) The company stopped doing business with another airline because of security breaches.

 中譯與聽力原文

Questions 49-51 refer to the following conversation
問題 49-51，請參考以下對話內容

Judy: You shouldn't be rude to him.

茱蒂：你不該對他這麼無禮。

Mary: Why?

瑪莉：為什麼？

Judy: He owns Best Airline. That's why. You're aware that most of our products are lightweight, and 90% of our products are heavily reliant on airplane to export.

茱蒂：他擁有倍斯特航空公司。這就是理由。你有查覺到大部分我們的產品都輕，且我們百分之九十的展品都仰賴飛機出口。

Mary: Oh... Crap... I have no idea. But

瑪莉：喔...糟了...我不知

he obviously has no idea who I am. I think we'll be fine. Relax.

道。但是他顯然不知道我是誰。我想我們會沒事。放輕鬆。

Jim: Based on the table we're sitting at and whom we are sitting with, I think he knows.

吉姆：根據我們坐的餐桌位子和我們跟誰坐，我想他知道。

Mary: Please tell me that Best Airline is not the only airline we've been having businesses with.

瑪莉：請告訴我倍斯特航空公司不是我們唯一有商業往來的航空公司。

Judy: After ABG Airline announced bankruptcy the other day, it's the only one.

茱蒂：在前幾天 ABG 航空公司宣告破產的後，這就是我們唯一合作的公司。

選項中譯與解析

49. 女子出了什麼問題？

(A)她坐錯位置。

(B) 她冒犯了重要的商業夥伴。

(C) 她點錯了餐。

(D) 她對同事無禮。

50.本篇對話可能發生的地點？

(A) 在餐廳。

(B) 在機場。

(C) 在航空公司。

(D) 在銀行。

 51. 為何倍斯特航空公司是他們公司唯一合作的航空公司？

(A) 曾和公司有業務往來的航空公司破產，因此合作關係終止。

(B) 倍斯特航空公司給這間公司的條件最好。

(C) 倍斯特航空公司專門運輸輕量產品。

(D) 因為安全漏洞，公司終止和另一家航空公司的生意。

49.

．聽到對話，馬上鎖定 You shouldn't be rude to him. 和 He owns Best Airline. 推測她可能得罪了 Best Airline 的老闆。以關鍵字 be rude to 和 having businesses with 配對選項的 offended：得罪以及 business partner，可知此題答案為 B。

50.

．聽到對話，直接鎖定 the table we're sitting at and and whom we are sitting with，來推測對話發生的情境。根據關鍵字 the table：餐桌，配對選項 a restaurant，可以推測最符合答案的選項即為 A。

51.

．聽到對話，直接鎖定關鍵字 bankruptcy：名詞，破產。根據對話，After ABG Airline announced bankruptcy the other day, it's the only one.可知在 ABG 航空公司宣告破產後，Best Airline 是他們唯一合作的公司。

貓頭鷹

49.

．此題為細節題，考生須先理解 be rude to Sb 的意思，表示對誰無禮；接著推測對話發生的情境。可以先排除較明顯錯誤的 A、C 選項，接著判斷人物關係。根據對話細節，be rude to him 接著延伸 He owns Best Airline、we've been having businesses with 推測她可能得罪了公司的合作對象。

50.

．此題為推測題，測試考生是否能透過對話細節，推測出對話發生的地點。根據對話：Based on the table we're sitting at and whom we are sitting with 來配對選項，從關鍵字 the table 來判斷，最適合的答案即為選項(A)restaurant：餐廳。(B) airport：機場；(C)airline company：航空公司；(D) bank：銀行。

51.

．此題為細節題，考生須先理解動詞片語 announced bankruptcy 的用法，接著找出他的相似詞來推測答案，也可以搭配刪去法解答。根據關鍵字 announced bankruptcy：宣告破產，配對選項 A 的 went bankrupt：破產，和 their partnership was terminated；terminated 在這句是過去分詞，和 be 動詞 was 搭配形成被動語態，表達「被終止」，可知答案即為 A。(B) gave the best deal：給最好的

折扣；(C)specializes in：專攻；(D)security breaches：安全漏洞。

  浣熊 MP3 084+MP3 086

還可能怎麼問

1. Why does the woman say, "Oh... Crap"?

(A) she shouldn't be rude to a customer

(B) she is just being casual with her colleagues

(C) she is joking around with a waiter

(D) she screws something up

2. What problem has the woman recognized when she say you shouldn't be rude to him?

(A) the bankruptcy of ABG

(B) the identity of the guy who owns Best Airline

(C) the wrong seating arrangement

(D) the lightweight product

 解析

1. 題目是問為什麼女子說「噢…糟了」？

・選項 D 她把事情搞砸了，此為對話中所表達的意思，因為她居然對一個公司有商業往來的老闆無禮，故可以得知答案為選項 D。

2. 題目是問當女子說你不該對他這麼無禮時，她發現了什麼問題？

・選項 B，這是她對同事講這句話時所想表達的部分，因為她知道對方身分，所以才會說不該對對方無禮，故可以得知答案為選項 B。

Unit 18
角逐西岸職缺

 Instructions

❶ 請播放音檔聽下列對話，並完成試題。 MP3 087+MP3 088

❷ 「跟述」練習：寫完試題後請跟著音檔同步跟漸進式做「跟述」練習，提升聽力專注力。

❸ 加碼題：完成❶＋❷步驟後，請再播放音檔寫浣熊試題，掌握其他可能的出題考點，強化應考實力。 MP3 087+MP3 089

52. What does the man mean when he says, "I was wondering if you could put in a few good words for me"?

(A) He wanted to know if the other man can give him some compliments.

(B) He wanted to know if the other man can show him how to give compliments.

(C) He wanted to know if the other man can say something nice about him to help with his application

(D) He wanted to know if the other man can teach him how to use good words in his application documents.

53. What does the man mean by saying, "But I don't have a say in this"?

(A) He does not want to give the other man the application

information
(B) He does not know how to explain the application process
(C) He does not have the power to decide who gets the new position
(D) He does not want to say good words about the other man

54. Which of the following is the closest in meaning to "Lots of people are eyeing that job"?
(A) Lots of people have good eyesight in this company.
(B) Lots of people are aiming to get that new position
(C) Many co-workers dislike their current jobs.
(D) Many co-workers are thinking about moving to the west coast.

 中譯與聽力原文

Questions 52-54 refer to the following conversation
問題 52-54，請參考以下對話內容

Mark: I didn't mean to eavesdrop, but I heard we're having a new position at our branch office.

馬克：我不是有意偷聽，但是我聽到分公司有個新的職缺。

Jim: Yep... the West Coast... you sound intrigued.

吉姆：是的…西岸…你看起來像對這很有興趣。

Mark: You got me. I'm thinking about moving to the West Coast. I

馬克：被你發現了。我正考慮要搬至西岸。我思

was wondering if you could put in a few good words for me.

考著是否你能替我美言幾句。

Jim: But I don't have a say in this. Why don't you ask Jane? She is our HR manager. She's been here since the company launched.

吉姆：但是關於這件事我沒有決定權。為什麼你不問簡呢？她是人事部門經理。從公司創立待到現在。

Mark: She doesn't seem like my big fan.

馬克：她似乎不太喜歡我。

Jim: But if you do want that job, you'd better talk to her right now. Lots of people are eyeing that job.

吉姆：但是如果你想要這份工作的話，你最好現在跟她說。許多人都覬覦那份工作。

選項中譯與解析

 52. 當男子說「我思考著是否你能替我美言幾句。」，其含意為何？

(A) 他想知道對方人是否讚美他幾句。

(B) 他想知道對方是否能教他如何讚美。

(C) 他想知道對方是否能美言幾句，以利於他的申請。

(D) 他想知道對方是否能教他如何在申請文件中用詞精煉。

 53. 對話中的男子說「但是關於這件事我沒有決定權」，其含意為何？

(A) 他不想提供申請資訊給對方。

(B) 他不知道如何解釋申請步驟。

(C) 他無權決定誰能獲得新職位。

(D) 他不想替其方説好話。

 54.下列選項中,何者最接近「許多人都覬覦那份工作」?

(A) 公司裡很多人視力良好。

(B) 很多人對新職缺躍躍欲試。

(C) 許多同事不喜歡目前的工作。

(D) 許多同事正考慮搬到西岸。

獵豹

52.

‧聽到對話,馬上鎖定 put in a few good words for me,推測是「替我説好話」的意思。用刪去法刪除選項(B)和(D)。之後比較選項(A)和(C)得知選項(C)較符合。

53.

‧聽到對話,馬上鎖定 don't have a say,由於 say 前面搭配動詞 have 及冠詞 a,由此得知 say 在此轉換成名詞,意思和 say 當動詞時「説」的意思不同。且整段對話沒提及 application information/process,所以先刪去(A)及(B)。have a say 這個慣用語是「有決定權」之意,又考慮對話第一句就有主題字 a new position,與(C)意思最接近。故正確選項是(C)。

54.

‧考慮主題是爭取新職位,只有(B)選項描述最貼近主題,故答案是(B)。

52.

· 此題屬於推測題，也同時測試考生對慣用語 "put in a few good words"的理解，考點引用句的另一線索字是 for me，所以 put in a few good words for me 是他希望另一位男士替他說好話，(C)選項完整句句意和此引用句最接近。選項(A)及(B)的 compliments 是陷阱字，雖然是「讚美」之意，似乎與 good words 意思類似，但這兩句的完整句句意都不符合考點的引用句。(D)也有句意不合的錯誤，而且引用句沒有牽涉到 application documents。

53.

· 此題屬於推測題，主要從慣用語 have a say，「有決定權」推測。且答案必須呼應主題。此對話主題是討論如何爭取新職位。(A)和(B)的 application information/process 是陷阱字，雖然申請職位或許需要獲得申請資訊，但整段對話完全沒有關於申請資訊或過程的描述。(D)選項敘述大意與 have a say 意思無關。唯一最貼切主題的選項是 (C)。

54.

· 此題屬於推測題，主要從慣用語 eye (for)...，「著眼於……，將目標放在……」推測。問句中 eye that job 的意思最接近的是(B)的動詞片語 aim to V.。(A)選項的 eyesight 是陷阱字，雖然此複合字有 eye，但和 eye for 的意思及詞性不同。且(A)及(C)敘述完全無關對話主題。(D)的 west coast 也是陷阱字，根據對話，新職位在西岸，但(D)大意是「許多同事正考慮搬到西岸」，若選擇(D)就犯下過度詮釋的錯誤。而且根據 I'm thinking about moving to the West Coast，我們能確

定的是只有講者一人正考慮搬到西岸。

 浣熊　MP3 087+MP3 089

還可能怎麼問

1. **Why is the man concerned?**

(A) because he is afraid of the competition with lots of people

(B) because he doesn't have a glowing recommendation

(C) because he has a feeling that the HR manager doesn't like him

(D) because he has to move to the West Coast

2. **What should the man do if he really wants the job?**

(A) he should talk to Jane

(B) he needs to persuade the boss

(C) he should bribe the HR manager

(D) he should speed up the application process

解析

1. **題目是問男子為什麼覺得擔心？**

· 對話中有提到「她似乎不太喜歡我。」，故可得知答案為選項 C。

2. **題目是問如果他真的想要這份工作，男子應該要？**

· 對話中另一名男子有回覆「但是關於這件事我沒有決定權。為什麼你不問簡呢？…」，所以可以得知此敘述與選項 A 相同，所以可以得知答案為選項 A。

Unit 19
換個角度想，有得必有失

🔍 Instructions

❶ 請播放音檔聽下列對話，並完成試題。 🔊 MP3 090+MP3 091

❷ 「跟述」練習：寫完試題後請跟著音檔同步跟漸進式做「跟述」練習，提升聽力專注力。

❸ 加碼題：完成❶＋❷步驟後，請再播放音檔寫浣熊試題，掌握其他可能的出題考點，強化應考實力。 🔊 MP3 090+MP3 092

55. Which of the following is the main factor that decides whether the man gets the job?

(A) talking to Jane

(B) filing for a new evaluation process

(C) moving to the west coast first

(D) the evaluation of his performance

56. Who are these speakers?

(A) HR agents

(B) co-workers

(C) accountants

(D) travel agents

57. Which of the following is the closest in meaning to "lucrative"?

(A) very valuable

(B) priceless

(C) worthwhile

(D) very profitable

 中譯與聽力原文

Questions 55-57 refer to the following conversation
問題 55-57，請參考以下對話內容

Mark: I think you're right about one thing... lots of people are eyeing that job. How can I get that job? I talked to Jane, apparently, she told me it will go according to the evaluation sheets and company procedures.

馬克：我認為你說對一件事了...許多人都覬覦那個工作。要怎樣才能拿到這份工作呢？我詢問過簡，她說一切都會照著評估表和公司流程走。

Jim: there is nothing I can do. But look on the bright side. You don't have to take a huge pay cut. The reason why other people are applying is because of the pay increase.

吉姆：我也無能為力。但是往好處想。你不用擔心大量的減薪。其他人會想申請的原因是因為薪資增加。

Mark: yep it seems lucrative to them. Perhaps I should rethink about moving to West Coast.

馬克：是的似乎對他們來説很有利可圖的。或許我應該要重新思考搬到西岸的事。

Jim: let's just watch the game and have some chicken wings.

吉姆：讓我們就只看場球賽然後來些雞翅吧。

選項中譯與解析

55.關於決定男子是否能得到這份工作，下列選項何者是主因？

(A) 和珍談談。

(B) 申請新的評估步驟。

(C) 先移居到西岸。

(D) 針對表現評估。

56.這些談話者是誰？

(A) 人資代表。

(B) 同事。

(C) 會計師。

(D) 旅行社員工。

57.下列選項中，何者最接近"lucrative"？

(A) 非常有價值的。

(B) 無價的。

(C) 值得做的。

(D) 非常有利可圖的。

獵豹

55.

· 聽到對話，馬上鎖定 it will go according to the evaluation sheets and company procedures，推測是「跟公司規定有關」的意思。選項(D)的針對表現評估是最符合的選項。

56.

· 聽到對話，馬上鎖定 job，evaluation sheets and company procedures，a huge pay cut，推測和「工作方面」有關。根據對話內容，談話者最可能是同事，故答案為選項(B)。

57.

· 聽到對話，馬上鎖定 because of the pay increase，因為薪資增加，推測是「利益」的意思。先刪去(B) & (C)，因為與薪資增加無直接關係，而(A) priceless 意思是無價的，所以(D) very profitable「非常有利可圖的」是最佳選項。

貓頭鷹

55.

· 此題屬於文意理解題，考點引用句的另一線索字是 evaluation sheets， 評估表和 company procedures，工作流程，照著評估表和流程來是否能得到工作。因此，可以推斷出工作表現很重要。而選項(A)talking to Jane，是用來混淆，因為此句話重點是簡後面說的話，

並非代表和她講完後，就能得到工作。選項(C)moving to the west coast first 則是馬克之後要考慮之事。

56.

· 此題屬於推測題，也同時測試考生對於對話理解程度，此題囊括所有內容，很容易被誤導。考點分析。對話中兩人提到幾個線索。(1) eyeing for that job ...，覬覦那個工作 (2) I talked to Jane...，我詢問過簡 (3) go according to the evaluation sheets and company procedures...，照著評估表 和公司流程走 (4) the reason why other people are applying is because of the pay increase...，其他人會想申請的原因是因為薪資增加， 因此推測出來兩人是同事關係。選項(A) HR agents，是陷阱選項。

57.

· 此題屬於單字理解題，"lucrative" 的意思為「有利可圖的」，假設不知道這單字的意思，仍然可以從四個選項中判斷出答案。通常此種單字考法，其中兩到三個選項的意思會類似，如：valuable 和 worthwhile， 因此可採刪去法，再來一一突破。

 浣熊 　🎧 MP3 090+MP3 092

還可能怎麼問

1. **Where does the conversation probably take place?**
   (A) in the office
   (B) at the restaurant
   (C) in the copy room

(D) at the lobby

2. **What is the downside if the man gets the job?**
    (A) he will have some chicken wings
    (B) he has to move to the West Coast
    (C) he will get pay increase
    (D) he will get a lower salary

解析

1. **題目是問這個對話可能發生在哪裡？**
・選項 A, C, D 所提到的地點均不像對話中的場景，所以可以排除這幾個選項。選項 B 在餐廳，對話中提到「讓我們就只看場球賽然後來些雞翅吧。」，很有可能是兩個人下班後約在美式餐廳聊工作的事，順便點了餐點和可以看看球賽，故可以得知答案為選項 B。

2. **題目是問男子拿到此份工作的缺點是什麼？**
・選項 D，對話中有提到「……其他人會想申請的原因是因為薪資增加。」，是對其他人來說薪資增加，對他本身來說其實是缺點，因為他會需要 take a huge pay cut，所以他本身又回覆了「是的，似乎對他們來說很有利可圖的。或許我應該要重新思考搬到西岸的事。」，所以可以得知答案為選項 D。

Unit **20**
事情辦得好，
升遷就有份

Instructions

❶ 請播放音檔聽下列對話，並完成試題。 🎧 MP3 093+MP3 094

❷ 「跟述」練習：寫完試題後請跟著音檔同步跟漸進式做「跟述」練習，提升聽力專注力。

❸ 加碼題：完成❶＋❷步驟後，請再播放音檔寫浣熊試題，掌握其他可能的出題考點，強化應考實力。 🎧 MP3 093+MP3 095

58. Who might this woman be?

    (A) the man's wife

    (B) the man's supervisor

    (C) the man's assistant

    (D) the man's girlfriend

 59. Why does the man say, "I'm considering giving you a promotion"?

    (A) He just thinks it's about time that the woman is promoted.

    (B) He is very satisfied with the woman's performance.

    (C) The woman has been asking for a promotion for several months.

    (D) Everyone is promoted except the woman.

60. Where will the man take a transfer?

(A) Hong Kong

(B) Dubai

(C) Los Angeles

(D) Singapore

中譯與聽力原文

Questions 58-60 refer to the following conversation
問題 58-60，請參考以下對話內容

Mary: I'm here to give you some update. I've booked your flight to Dubai. You're going to take a transfer at HK. I wrote a note to our sales manager that the weekly meeting will be postponed. I'm gonna get the dry cleaning for you.

瑪莉：我是要跟您報告最新狀況。我已經訂購您到杜拜的班機。您會要到香港轉機。我寫了字條給我們的銷售經理，每週會議會延期。我會替您拿好送洗衣物。

Jason: It seems that you handle things pretty well lately.

傑森：看來您最近處理事情都處理得相當妥善。

Mary: it's nothing, doing the usual routine, and I forgot to tell you about the financial reports. The accounting managers

瑪莉：這沒什麼，只是平常的例行事務，我忘了要跟您說財政報告的事。會計經理要到下

won't be able to give us those reports until next Monday.

Jason: You know what... if things keep going like this I'm considering giving you a promotion.

星期一才能將那些報告給我們。

傑森：你知道嗎？...如果事情都像這樣的話，我正考慮升遷妳。

選項中譯與解析

58. 女子可能的身分為何？

(A) 男子的老婆。

(B) 男子的主管。

(C) 男子的助理。

(D) 男子的女友。

59. 為何男子說「我正考慮升遷妳」？

(A) 他只是認為該是女子升遷的時候了。

(B) 他對女子的表現非常滿意。

(C) 女子一直要求升遷幾個月了。

(D) 除了女子外，每個人都已被升遷了。

60. 男子將在在哪裡轉機？

(A) 香港。

(B) 杜拜。

(C) 洛杉磯。

(D) 新加坡。

獵豹

58.

・聽到 who，馬上鎖定詢問關係，推測是此女子身分為何。選項(A)和 (D)列為一組，(B)和(C)列為另一組，因為前一組是私人關係，第二組是工作關係，再由第一句話：我是要跟您報告最新狀況。所以(A)(D)刪除，而報告是下屬對上級，因此答案(C) 男子的助理是最佳選項。

59.

・聽到對話，馬上鎖定，promotion 推測是「工作」方面。(A)just think 只是認為，(C) has been asking 一直要求， (D) Everyone is promoted ...，每個人都已經升遷，此三個選項在對話中，並無明顯提出，選項(B) very satisfied with the woman's performance，對女子的表現非常滿意，最接近主管想要表達之意，因此(B)是最佳選項。

60.

・聽到單字 transfer 馬上鎖定飛機或地點，注意聽之後的單字。

・首先，先瞭解四個地名的中文翻譯。(A) Hong Kong，香港 (B) Dubai，杜拜 (C) Los Angeles，洛杉磯 (D) Singapore，新加坡，這題是屬於單字題聽的時候，可以馬上得知答案。

貓頭鷹

58.

・此題屬於推測題，由前面第一句瑪莉說的話：我是要跟您報告最新狀況

和最後一句傑森説：我正考慮升遷妳，可推知答案。考點是supervisor，主管和 assistant，助理。女子跟男子報告例行事物，如：I'm here to give you some update. 和 tell you about the financial ...，財政報告的事，這些都提供非常有用的線索，可推測女子是助理。男子説：I'm considering giving you a promotion，我正考慮升遷妳，顯然他是上司或主管。

59.

· 此題屬於推測題，首先必須先懂得"considering giving you a promotion"的理解，考生必須先懂此句話的深層意思，再推測哪個選項描述的意思最接近此含意。be satisfied with Sb.，對某人感到滿意。上司對話中提到：It seems that you handle things pretty well lately.，看來妳最近處理事情都處理得相當妥善。以及：if things keep going like this ，如果事情都像這樣的話，後面提到升遷。因此推知，對於此女子的工作表現認可，故答案為選項為(B)。

60.

· 此題屬於地點考法，也同時測試考生對單字認識多寡。第一重點是transfer，轉機，第二重點是地點 Hong Kong，香港。考點引用句的另一線索字是 HK，HK 是香港縮寫，因此選項中並未用 HK，而是寫Hong Kong。聽力一個小技巧，先瀏覽過答案，可以加深對聽力的理解力。本題是很好的範例，如果先看地點，聽對話時，則對 transfer特別注意。

浣熊　🔊 MP3 093+MP3 095

還可能怎麼問

1. What is not included in the update?

(A) book a plane ticket

(B) get the clean clothe

(C) teach financial reports

(D) put off the weekly meeting

2. What are the speakers mainly discussing?

(A) An update of what has been assigned to an assistant

(B) Flight information

(C) how to write a financial report

(D) there's gonna be a huge promotion

解析

1. 題目是問工作項目的更新中哪個未包含在內？

· 選項 C 教授財政報告，對話中有提到財政報告，但未提到教授財政報告的部分，所以可以得知答案為選項 C。

2. 題目是問說話者們主要在討論什麼？

· 選項 A，對話中主要內容為助理向老闆報告所交辦的事項和進度，所以可以得知答案為選項 A。

Unit 21
醜陋牆還不如美麗牆

 Instructions

❶ 請播放音檔聽下列對話，並完成試題。 🎧 MP3 096+MP3 097

❷ 「跟述」練習：寫完試題後請跟著音檔同步跟漸進式做「跟述」練習，提升聽力專注力。

❸ 加碼題：完成❶＋❷步驟後，請再播放音檔寫浣熊試題，掌握其他可能的出題考點，強化應考實力。 🎧 MP3 096+MP3 098

 61. What does "an ugly wall" refer to in this context?

(A) a wall that is not painted well and ugly

(B) a wall that displays pictures of natural sceneries

(C) a wall that looks very shabby

(D) a wall that displays photos in which people don't look their best

62. Why does the man say, "It's so inappropriate"?

(A) He feels angry that he was humiliated.

(B) He doesn't think it's nice to feel good by mocking others.

(C) An ugly wall is not a proper name for this activity.

(D) A beauty wall is inappropriate.

63. What might the speakers do next?

(A) take away the photos on the ugly wall

(B) learn how to use photo editing APPs

(C) gather employees' photos in which they look good

(D) paint the ugly wall so that it will look better

🎄 中譯與聽力原文

Questions 61-63 refer to the following conversation
問題 61-63，請參考以下對話內容

Jason: I can't believe they're having an ugly wall.

傑森：我不敢相信我們有醜陋牆。

Mary: What's that? A wall that's ugly.

瑪莉：那是什麼？很醜的牆？

Jason: Putting a bunch of pictures, making fun of someone.

傑森：放些照片，取笑其他人為樂。

Jim: How did they get all of the employees' photos?

吉姆：他們怎麼有所有員工的照片呢？

Mary: Probably from annual meetings and casual Friday dinners.

瑪莉：可能是從年度會議和隨興的星期五晚餐。

Jim: It's so inappropriate. Humiliating someone in exchange for pleasure.

吉姆：這很不恰當。羞辱別人以換取樂趣。

Jason: Perhaps we can do a beauty wall, using photo editing devices.

傑森：或許我們可以弄個美貌牆，使用照片編輯裝置。

Mary: Why not everyone looks great, and it won't be hidden in some place we can't quite figure out.

瑪莉：為什麼不能？每個人看起來很棒，而且不會藏在我們無法找到的某些地方。

Jason: That rocks!

傑森：棒呆了。

選項中譯與解析

61. 根據對話，"an ugly wall" 是指什麼？

(A) 沒刷好又醜的牆

(B) 展示自然風景面的牆壁

(C) 看起來很破舊的牆

(D) 展出人們狀態不佳照的一道牆

62. 為何男子說「這很不恰當」？

(A) 他因被羞辱感到生氣。

(B) 他不認為羞辱別人感覺會有多好。

(C) 醜陋牆不適合這個活動名稱。

(D) 美貌牆不合適。

63. 談話者接下來可能會做何事？

(A) 把醜陋牆上的照片拿走

(B) 學習如何使用照片編輯裝置

(C) 收集員工看起來美美的照片

(D) 粉刷醜陋牆，如此看起來好多了

獵豹

61.

· 聽到對話，馬上鎖定 ugly wall 和 what's that 推測是真正意思。這四個選項中，只有選項(D)提到 photo，和對話中呼應。

62.

· 聽到對話，馬上鎖定 inappropriate 和其後面的對話 Humiliating someone in exchange of... ，推測是「不滿，不適合」的意思。看到 inappropriate，不適當，可推測談話者的想法不認同，根據後面解釋，可知道和 humiliating someone 有關，因此刪去不相關的主詞，推測出答案。

63.

· 聽到對話，馬上鎖定 對話最後的幾句，推測是進行「美貌牆」之事。最後幾句：Why not everyone looks great... ，that's rock 推測兩人達成共識。

61.

- 此題屬於推測題，此種推測題，考點引用句的另一線索字是 photo，四個選項中，只有選項(D)...displays photos ...出現。另外一個重點，ugly wall 直接翻譯是醜牆，通常答案不會是直翻，會有陷阱。因此，聽到女子問 What's that? 男子回答 Putting a bunch of pictures, making fun of someone. 可推測出來。

62.

- 此題屬於推測題，也同時測試考生對單字"humiliate"和"mock"的理解。考生必須先懂這個單字的意思，再推測哪個選項描述的意思最接近此意。考點引用句的另一線索字是 Humiliating someone ，羞辱別人，看到(A) ...that he was humiliated...，(D) A beauty wall...，刪去(A)&(D)，因為談話者並沒有被羞辱，以及 beauty wall 和主題不和。再比較(B) & (C)，刪去(C)，因為(C)a proper name... 意思是針對活動名稱，所以(B)He doesn't think it's nice...「他不認為…好」是最佳選項。

63.

- 此題屬於推測題，考點引用句的另一線索字是 do a beauty wall，所以有可能的答案，和此有關。本題有點弔詭，四個選項都和對話有連結。因此，必須用刪去法，選出最適合並最合理的答案。選項(A)不是接下來要做的，選項(B)文章中有提到所以表示已會使用軟體，選項(D)亦不符合，故答案為選項(C)。

浣熊 MP3 096+MP3 098

還可能怎麼問

1. What is the function of the ugly wall?

   (A) it's for an entertaining purpose.

   (B) it's about beautifying people.

   (C) it's for the annual meeting.

   (D) It's about photo editing.

NEW

2. Why does the man say, "that rocks"?

   (A) because no one can hide anymore.

   (B) because he gets to use some awesome software

   (C) because everyone gets to look great

   (D) because he is credited with the idea

 解析

1. 題目是問醜陋牆的功用是什麼？

‧選項 A，是用於娛樂用途，此為醜陋牆的功用，對話中亦有提到「放些照片，取笑其他人為樂」、「這很不恰當。羞辱別人以換取樂趣。」，可以知道這是用於消遣、娛樂用途，故可以得知答案為選項 A。

2. 題目是問為什麼男子說「棒呆了」？

‧選項 C，此為男子回應這句話的原因，故答案為選項 C。

Unit 22
銷售打賭，鹿死誰手還不曉得

Instructions

❶ 請播放音檔聽下列對話，並完成試題。 🎧 MP3 099+MP3 100

❷ 「跟述」練習：寫完試題後請跟著音檔同步跟漸進式做「跟述」練習，提升聽力專注力。

❸ 加碼題：完成❶+❷步驟後，請再播放音檔寫浣熊試題，掌握其他可能的出題考點，強化應考實力。 🎧 MP3 099+MP3 101

64. What is the main topic of the conversation?

(A) paying back mortgage and tuition

(B) booking a hotel

(C) making money in an exhibition

(D) printing pamphlets

65.What does the man mean by saying, "I'll have more incentives to do things"?

(A) He will feel more motivated.

(B) He feels the company should give him more incentives.

(C) The exhibition should offer more incentives to workers.

(D) He will have more bonuses.

66. Which of the followings is the place where they will make their earnings?

(A) a printing plant

(B) a booking center

(C) a construction site

(D) a computer exhibition

中譯與聽力原文

Questions 64-66 refer to the following conversation

問題 64-66，請參考以下對話內容

Jack: You are aware that we are working on a commission. The more we sell at a computer exhibition, the more we earn. The exhibition only opens for fourteen days. Why don't you grab this chance and earn as much as you can in half a month?

傑克：你有察覺到我們工作是抽成嗎？在電腦展，我們販售的越多，就賺越多。這個展覽僅開幕 14 天而已。為什麼你不抓住這機會，在半個月內盡可能地賺？

Mark: I get it. Sometimes it's hard to think that way. Perhaps I should think more about the mortgage and tuition fees, then I'll have more incentives

馬克：我懂了。有時候真的很難這樣思考。或許我應該要思考更多關於抵押貸款和學費，然後有更多的動機去

to do things.　　　　　　　　　　　做事。

Mary: That's a good start.　　　　瑪莉：這是個好的開始。

Jack: Let's have a bet. Who sells the most computers in fourteen days wins, and who sells the least gets punished.

傑克：讓我們來打賭。誰在 14 天裡賣最多的獲勝，而誰賣得最少的受到懲罰。

Mary: I've got to warn you that I've already sold more than you two combined.

瑪莉：我必須警告你們我已經賣出比你們兩個人加起來還多台了。

選項中譯與解析

64. 對話的主題為何？

(A) 償還抵押貸款和學費。

(B) 飯店預約。

(C) 在展覽中賺錢。

(D) 印刷小冊子。

65. 男子說「我會有更多的動機去做事」，其含意為何？

(A) 他會感覺更有動力。

(B) 他覺得公司應該給他更多的獎勵。

(C) 展覽應該提供員工更多獎勵。

(D) 他將獲得更多獎金。

66. 下列選項中，何者是他們賺錢之處？

(A) 印刷廠。

(B) 訂票中心。

(C) 建築工地。

(D) 電腦展。

獵豹

64.

· 聽到對話，馬上鎖定 main topic 兩字，為「主旨」的意思。主題的考法，是針對對話所有內容，因此將聽到的重要單字，進行連結，才能理解題意。如：computer exhibition，電腦展，The more we sell at ..., the more we earn.，我們販售的越多，就賺越多。

65.

· 聽到對話，馬上鎖定 mortgage and tuition fees，推測和「還貸款及學費」有關聯。先刪去(B) & (C)，因為和本身動機不同。再比較(A) & (D)，刪去(D)，因為(D)意思是獎金，所以(A)「更有動力」是最佳選項。

66.

· 本題重點是 place，推測「地點」之意。迅速瀏覽四個選項，其中(A) a printing plant，印刷廠，(D) a computer exhibition，電腦展，關係最接近，而(B) 訂票中心和(D) 建築工地，則無絕對關係。

貓頭鷹

1 照片描述

2 應答問題

3 簡短對話

4 簡短獨白

模擬試題

64.

- 此題屬於主旨考法，此種考法的好處為，即使單字並不全部理解，卻能從對話中，推測出談論之事。考點引用句的另一線索字是 grab this chance and earn as much as you can... ，所以 earn 這個單字非常重要。希望賺錢之意。(A)選項對話中有提到，不過是陷阱。選項(B)及(D)則和主題無關，針對 computer exhibition，電腦展，earn 和 sell 幾個字，推測之來他們討論在展覽中賺錢，答案為選項(D)。

65.

- 此題屬於單字推測題，考點引用句的另一線索字是 incentive，動力的，對話中女子提到貸款和學費，這兩點讓她有動機去電腦展銷售。選項(A)更有動力。選項(B) ...incentive 和題目單字一樣，然而意思不同。選項(C)incentive，在此是指獎勵。選項(D)bonus，在此指獎金或獎勵。因此，選項(B)(C)(D)皆出現陷阱字，請小心。

66.

- 此題屬於推測題，也同時測試考生對於對話的地點理解。此類型題目，對於整篇對話掌握度必須很強，因此通常答案不會「直接」出現在對話裡。考點引用句的重要線索句是 The more we sell at a computer exhibition, the more we earn. ，在電腦展，我們販售的越多，就賺越多。因此，推測出他們將在電腦展販售商品。 此類型考題有兩種考法，第一種，破題型：對話中直接講出地點。第二種：透過對話描述和暗示，讓考生推測出地點。本題是第一種考法，比較簡單，分數應該要掌握。

 浣熊 🔊 MP3 099+MP3 101

還可能怎麼問

 1. Why does the man say, "you are aware that we're working on a commission"?

(A) to show the importance of being committed to work.

(B) to boost the sales

(C) to point out something to his colleague

(D) to earn more money at the computer exhibition

 2. What can be inferred from what the woman says, "I've got to warn you that I've already sold more than you two combined"?

(A) she already won.

(B) she is just bluffing.

(C) she is giving a warning to her colleagues.

(D) she might have the best shot to win.

解析

1. 題目是問為什麼男子說「你有察覺到我們工作是抽成嗎」？

‧ 選項 C ，此敘述是男子為什會說這句話的原因，基於同事或朋友立場，好心跟對方說明一些作法的影響等等，算是提點他故可以得知答案為選項 C。

2. 題目是問可以從女子所說的「我必須提醒你們我已經賣出比你們兩個人加起來還多台了」推測出？

‧ 選項 D，對話中並未講述到結果，但以目前銷售來看確實可以推測女子是很有可能贏得打賭，所以可以得知答案為選項 D。

Unit 23
烤雞事業，東京也設點

Instructions

❶ 請播放音檔聽下列對話，並完成試題。 MP3 102+MP3 103
❷ 「跟述」練習：寫完試題後請跟著音檔同步跟漸進式做「跟述」練習，提升聽力專注力。
❸ 加碼題：完成❶+❷步驟後，請再播放音檔寫浣熊試題，掌握其他可能的出題考點，強化應考實力。 MP3 102+MP3 104

67. Where does the conversation take place?
(A) a chicken farm
(B) Tokyo
(C) a restaurant
(D) a coffee shop

68. Who is the woman?
(A) a chef
(B) a customer
(C) a writer
(D) an editor

69. What does the man mean by saying, "It's been ages"?
(A) It has been a long time.

(B) He is aging quickly.

(C) The recipe for the roast chicken is very old.

(D) Aging is unavoidable.

🌿 中譯與聽力原文

Questions 67-69 refer to the following conversation
問題 67-69，請參考以下對話內容

Jim: It's been ages. What brings you down here?

吉姆：已經好久了。是什麼風把你吹來這裡？

Mary: I haven't tasted your roast chicken for quite a bit, and the wine. It really is a perfect blend. Just out of curiosity, how can you do so well in both family and business?

瑪莉：我已經很久沒有嚐這裡的烤雞了，還有酒。這真是完美的組合。出於好奇心，你怎麼能在家庭跟事業上都做得這麼好？

Jim: It would be a lie, if I answered it's probably nothing. It takes efforts. By the way, would you like to come to our new opening in Tokyo. By then, we will be having another two special dishes. I suppose for a big fan of roast chicken like

吉姆：如果我回答這可能沒什麼，那我可能就是在說謊。是需要努力的。附帶一提的是，你會想要來我們東京的開幕嗎？到那時候我們會有另外兩個特別餐點。我想像你這

you, you certainly can't say "NO".

樣的烤雞迷，你確實無法說「不」。

Mary: Terrific. I'd love to.

瑪莉：棒極了。我會想去。

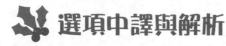 選項中譯與解析

67.本篇對話發生的地點？

(A) 養雞場。

(B) 東京。

(C) 餐廳。

(D) 咖啡店。

68. 女子職業為何？

(A) 廚師。

(B) 顧客。

(C) 作家。

(D) 編輯。

 69.男子說「已經好久了」，含意為何？

(A) 時間過了很久。

(B) 他老的很快。

(C) 烤雞食譜很古老。

(D) 老化是無法避免的。

Unit 23 烤雞事業，東京也設點

1 照片描述

2 應答問題

3 簡短對話

4 簡短獨白

模擬試題

 獵豹

67.

‧ 聽到對話，馬上鎖定 take place，是「發生」的意思，推測考地點。(A) a chicken farm 養雞場，(B) Tokyo 東京，(C) a restaurant 餐廳，(D) a coffee shop，咖啡廳，我們先將(A)和(B)刪除，因此對話是討論 roast chicken 和 new opening ，新開幕，故推知是他們在餐廳類的場所。

68.

‧ 聽到對話，馬上鎖定 who，推測是問「職業或關係」的意思。選項(C) a writer，作家和選項(D)an editor，編輯，和對話無關，可以先刪除。(A) a chef 和(B) a customer 兩者有關聯。由女子説：I haven't tasted your roast chicken 得知答案為(B)。

69.

‧ 聽到對話，馬上鎖定 ages，推測是「年紀，時間久」的意思。選項中，除了選項(A)(C)，均出現和 age 相關單字，如：aging。此為陷阱，讓考生再第一印象中，選出此錯誤答案。It's been ages. 是指時間已經好久了。

 貓頭鷹

67.

‧ 此題屬於推測題，也同時測試考生對片 take place 這個片語的理解。

從對話中，判斷出地點在哪裡。考點引用句的另一線索字是 our new opening，這裡的 new opening 是指「新開幕」，不是打開之一。選項(A) a chicken farm 只是誤導，因為對話中提到 roast chicken。選項(B) Tokyo，東京，對話中提到 new opening in Tokyo 是指在東京的開幕，因此不可能是此時談話之處。選項(D) a coffee shop，咖啡廳，也是類似的地點，不過對話中提到烤雞，因此餐廳較適合。

68.

· 此題屬於關聯題，考學生對於談話中的男女，兩者間有何關係。因此，先刪掉不相關的選項，再進行選擇。考點引用句的另一線索是 taste，品嚐和 roast chicken，烤雞，對話中，女子說「已經很久沒有嚐這裡的烤雞了，還有酒。」，以及詢問對方：how can you do so well in both family and business...「你怎麼能在家庭跟事業上都做得這麼好」，推知她是顧客，而男子是老闆，或是廚師。

69.

· 此題屬於推測題，也同時測試考生對慣用語 "It's been ages"的理解，考生必須先懂這個慣用語的深層意思，再推測哪個選項描述的意思最接近此慣用語。考點引用句的另一線索字是 for quite a bit，此句也有好久之意。age 意思多元，除了有年紀之意，還可指「很長時間」。選項(B)... aging quickly，是指老化得快。選項(C) The recipe ...is very old..是指「食譜古老」，選項(D) Aging is unavoidable.「老化是無可避免的。」此三字皆為引導錯誤方向，請小心選擇。

浣熊 MP3 102+MP3 104

還可能怎麼問

NEW **1. Why does the man say, "what brings you down here"?**

(A) he wants to bring down his friend.

(B) the smell of the chicken brings her here.

(C) he wants to bring down competitor's business.

(D) he is just wondering why his friend shows up.

NEW **2. Why does the man say, "you certainly can't say "NO" "?**

(A) he is not sure what his friend will respond.

(B) he knows she will say no.

(C) he knows she can't resist.

(D) he can't stand if his friend rejects him.

解析

1. 題目是問為什麼男子說「是什麼風把你吹來這裡」？

· 選項 D 他在想是什麼原因使他朋友現身，此為對話中所表達的意思，是在問候對方後常講的句子，故可以得知答案為選項 D。

2. 題目是問為什麼男子說「你確實無法說不」？

· 選項 C，對話中有提到「我想像你這樣的烤雞迷，你確實無法說「不」」，可以推斷他其實知道女子無法抗拒這個提議，故答案為選項 C。

1 照片描述

2 應答問題

3 簡短對話

4 簡短獨白

模擬試題

新人誤事，狀況連連

🔍 Instructions

❶ 請播放音檔聽下列對話，並完成試題。 ▶️ MP3 105+MP3 106

❷ 「跟述」練習：寫完試題後請跟著音檔同步跟漸進式做「跟述」練習，提升聽力專注力。

❸ 加碼題：完成❶＋❷步驟後，請再播放音檔寫浣熊試題，掌握其他可能的出題考點，強化應考實力。 🎧 MP3 105+MP3 107

70. Where does the conversation take place?

(A) a shopping mall

(B) an airplane

(C) an airline counter

(D) a travel agency

71. What company might these speakers work for?

(A) a cafeteria

(B) an airline

(C) a travel agency

(D) a restaurant

72. Why are meal tickets and coupons mentioned?

(A) The speakers are hungry.

(B) The speakers want to buy meals with coupons.

(C) The speakers are launching a marketing campaign by giving away meal tickets and coupons.

(D) The speakers try to appease the customers with meal tickets and coupons.

中譯與聽力原文

Questions 70-72 refer to the following conversation
問題 70-72，請參考以下對話內容

Linda: I just don't want to burden you with this.

琳達：我只是不想讓你感到負擔。

Tina: Excuse me? burden me? You have such a serious problem, and you don't come for help.

緹娜：不好意思？讓我感到負擔？你這問題嚴重了，而你卻不求助。

Linda: You guys are so busy... since I'm so new here. I just assumed things will turn out to be ok.

琳達：你們都很忙碌…既然我是這裡新來的。我只是設想成事情最後會沒事。

Tina: All flights are overbooked. I just don't know what to do.

緹娜：所有班機都超賣。我真的不知道該怎麼

Mark: I've checked with other ground crews. Customers are gonna lose it.

馬克：我已經與地勤人員確認過了。顧客要失控了。

Tina: I'm considering shutting down the system.

緹娜：我已經考慮到要先關閉系統。

Mark: Have Jack on line 2, and Cindy on line 3. Perhaps it's system errors.

馬克：傑克在 2 線，然後辛蒂在三線。或許是系統錯誤。

Tina: Prepare meal tickets and coupons to calm those passengers.

緹娜：準備餐卷和優惠券安撫那些乘客。

做。

選項中譯與解析

70 . 本篇對話發生的地點？

(A) 購物中心。

(B) 飛機上。

(C) 航空公司櫃檯。

(D) 旅行社。

71. 談話者可能在哪裡工作呢？

(A) 自助餐廳。

(B) 航空公司。

(C) 旅行社。

(D) 餐廳。

72. 為何提到餐券和優惠券？

(A) 談話者者肚子餓了。

(B) 談話者想用優惠券買餐點。

(C) 談話者正舉辦贈送餐券和優惠券的行銷活動。

(D) 談話者嘗試用餐券和優惠券安撫顧客。

獵豹

70.

・聽到對話，馬上鎖定 overbooked 和 ground crews，推測和「飛機或機場」有關。對話中提到，system errors，系統錯誤，all flights，所有班機，overbooked 超賣，這幾個字，因此可推論出地點是和飛機有關。由第一點鎖定地勤，因此選項(B)飛機上答案不符合，因此選項(C)，在航空公司櫃檯最有可能。

71.

・聽到對話，馬上鎖定 company，推測問「公司」。承上題，兩人討論超賣，顧客失控以及對話中有句：I'm so new here，我是新來的，推知她在航空公司工作。

72.

・聽到對話，馬上鎖定 meal tickets and coupons，推測是這些物品的

用途。由對話最後一句提到：calm those passengers，安撫顧客，所以(D)「用餐券和優惠券安撫顧客」是最佳選項。

貓頭鷹

70.

· 此題屬於推測題，考點引用句的另一線索字是，看到(A) a shopping mall，購物中心，先刪掉，因為是和航班方面有關。選項(D)a travel agency，旅行社，對話中提到 Customers are gonna lose it.，顧客要失控了。 gonna = going to，lose 在此為 lose control 指「失控」。綜合以上觀點，可以將飛機上的可能刪掉。

71.

· 此題屬於推測題，才能推測哪個選項描述的意思最接近此答案。考點引用句的另一線索字是 ...I'm new here.，已知單字和機場和票務方面有關，因此選項(B)an airline，航空公司，和(C)a travel agency 都有可能。另外一個重點為：單字 ground crews，地勤，因此推知選項(B)航空公司最佳。

72.

· 此題屬於細節及推測題，測試考生對動詞 calm 的理解，calm 和 appease 都有「安撫」之意。考點引用句的另一線索是：system errors，系統錯誤，和 lose，失去，由於航空公司失誤，導致問題，造成 Customers are gonna lost it.，顧客要失控了。因此採取某些措施來安撫他們。

浣熊　 MP3 105+MP3 107

還可能怎麼問

 1. What does the man mean when he says, "customers are gonna lose it"?

(A) customers lost their belongings.

(B) he offended major customers.

(C) he is considering shutting down the system.

(D) they will be so pissed off.

 2. Why does the woman say, "I just don't want to burden you with this "?

(A) because she feels this job is a heavy load.

(B) because she wants to lighten her colleagues' pressure.

(C) because she is new here.

(D) because she doesn't want to bother other colleagues.

 解析

1. 題目是問當男子說「顧客要失控了」他指的是什麼意思？

· 選項 D，此為對話中所表達的意思，顧客因為票超賣所以生氣，故可以得知答案為選項 D。

2. 題目是問為什麼女子說「我只是不想讓你感到負擔」？先從四個選項分別來看。

· 選項 D 因為她不想要打擾其他同事，此訊息與選項敘述一致，所以可以得知答案為選項 D。

Unit 25
休假，同事就是要多擔待

Instructions

❶ 請播放音檔聽下列對話，並完成試題。 🎧 MP3 108+MP3 109

❷ 「跟述」練習：寫完試題後請跟著音檔同步跟漸進式做「跟述」練習，提升聽力專注力。

❸ 加碼題：完成❶＋❷步驟後，請再播放音檔寫浣熊試題，掌握其他可能的出題考點，強化應考實力。 🎧 MP3 108+MP3 110

73. Why does the man say "sorry" to the other two speakers?
　(A) because the others have to cover for him
　(B) because he is sorry that he did a lousy job
　(C) because his work is a mess
　(D) because the vacation did not go well

74. Which of the following details is NOT mentioned regarding the work duties?
　(A) wire transfer
　(B) target customers
　(C) booking a flight
　(D) sending flowers

75. Why can't the man do the work by himself?

(A) He is going to quit his job.

(B) He is going to take a sick leave.

(C) He is going on a vacation.

(D) His mental condition is not stable.

中譯與聽力原文

Questions 73-75 refer to the following conversation

問題 73-75，請參考以下對話內容

Jack: I'm taking a vacation from Dec. 15 to Dec 25. Sorry that you have to do the job while I'm on a vacation.

傑克：我將於 12 月 15 日到 12 月 25 日休假。抱歉我休假時，你們要做我的工作。

Jim: We saw the note. Best Company only accepts a wire transfer. It has to be made on Dec. 16. We're targeting our customers on a younger viewer, a drastic change from the past. Send flowers to congratulate Sales Director of ABC, two days after you take the vacation.

吉姆：我們看到備註了。倍斯特公司款項僅收電匯。要在 12 月 16 日完成。我們目標顧客是年輕觀眾，與去年相對是極大的改變。你休假的兩天後，寄送花朵給 ABC 公司的銷售負責人。

Mary: I have two questions. You didn't write contact information of the flower shop. This is a credit card payment from the last business trip (Dec 17) you forgot to tell the accountant.

瑪莉：我有兩個問題。你沒寫到花店的連絡資訊。上次公差旅行的款項（12 月 17 日）你忘了告知會計。

選項中譯與解析

73. 為何男子向另外兩個人說「抱歉」呢？

(A) 因為其他人須替補他的工作。

(B) 因為他很抱歉工作表現不好。

(C) 因為他的工作一團糟。

(D) 因為假期不順利。

74. 關於工作細節，下列哪個選項沒提到？

(A) 電匯。

(B) 目標顧客。

(C) 預約航班。

(D) 送花。

75. 他為何不能自己做此工作呢？

(A) 他要辭職。

(B) 他要請病假。

(C) 他將去度假。

(D) 他精神狀況不穩。

 獵豹

73.

· 聽到對話，馬上鎖定 take a vacation，推測是和「度假」有關。看到 (B) ...lousy job ...，(C) ...work is a mess...，刪去(B)和(C)，因為對話是男子要休假，交代一些工作。比較(A) & (D)，刪去(D)，因為(A) 的意思是假期玩得不太好，在對話中未提及，所以(A) because the others have to cover for him 是最佳選項。

74.

· 重點是 work duties，指「工作職責」的意思。看到(A) wire transfer，(B) target customers， (D)sending flowers，在對話中都曾出現，所以(C) booking a flight「預定航班」是最佳選項。

75.

· 聽到對話，馬上鎖定，by himself ，自己來。對話第一句已經破題：I'm taking a vacation from Dec. 15 to Dec 25. ，我將於 12 月 15 日到 12 月 25 日休假，四個選項中，(C)答案最為符合。

 貓頭鷹

73.

· 此題屬於細節及推測題，也同時測試考生對慣用語 "take a vacation" 的理解，考生必須先懂這個慣用語的深層意思，再推測哪個選項描述與之有關。考點引用句的另一線索是 do the job ，所以 是他希望其他人

幫他做工作，當他度假時。(A)選項完整句句意和他要道歉的原因此符合。選項(A)及(B)的是陷阱字，雖然有 job 和 work，「工作」之意，但這兩句的完整句句意都不符合道歉的原因， 選項(D)尚未發生，因此不選。綜合所述，答案為(A)。

74.

· 此題屬於細節題，也同時測試考生針對對話中，記得幾個重點，再推測哪個選項描述，是對話中未曾提過的。考點引用句的另一線索字是 notes ，備註，對話中提過 notes 的幾點工作，包含電匯，目標顧客，送花等等。因此(A) wire transfer，(B) target customers，(D) sending flowers 都是正確，但並未提過選項(C) booking flight，可推知答案。

75.

· 此題屬於細節及推測題，也同時測試考生對慣用語 "by oneself"的理解，考生必須先懂這個慣用語的深層意思，再推測哪個選項描述的意思最接近此慣用語。考點引用句的另一線索字是 cover ，涵蓋，掩護，對話第一句說明原因：要度假，以及向同事道歉，因為他們必須做他的工作。而這些工作包含幾點，是第二題的考題。題目為 can't do himself ，不能自己做，因此可得知答案為(C)他將去度假。

 浣熊 🎧 MP3 108+MP3 110

還可能怎麼問

1. What are the speakers mainly discussing?

(A) a major holiday.

(B) a vacation.

(C) work duties.

(D) a business trip.

2. **What will happen on Dec 18?**

(A) a wire transfer will be made

(B) they'll eventually know the contact information of the flower shop

(C) accountants will ask for payment from last trip

(D) flowers will be delivered to ABC

解析

1. 題目是問說話者們主要在討論什麼？

‧選項 C 工作義務，對話中主要內容均與此有關，所以答案為選項 C。

2. 題目是問 12 月 18 日將會發生什麼事？先從四個選項分別來看。

‧選項 D，對話中有提到「休假的兩天後，寄送花朵給 ABC 公司的銷售負責人」，此訊息與選項敘述一致，所以可以得知答案為選項 D。

Unit 26
公司設立日間托孕中心，省下可觀的費用

 **Instructions**

❶ 請播放音檔聽下列對話，並完成試題。 🎧 MP3 111+MP3 112

❷ 「跟述」練習：寫完試題後請跟著音檔同步跟漸進式做「跟述」練習，提升聽力專注力。

❸ 加碼題：完成❶+❷步驟後，請再播放音檔寫浣熊試題，掌握其他可能的出題考點，強化應考實力。 🎧 MP3 111+MP3 113

76. What are the speakers discussing?
(A) how much nannies charge
(B) ordering takeout from the basement
(C) hiring nannies
(D) a change in the office building basement

 77. What does the woman mean when she says, "Plus, it can save some serious money"?
(A) Brewing coffee by themselves saves lots of money.
(B) The daycare center can save them a lot of money.
(C) Ordering takeout can save a little money.
(D) They need to think seriously about how to save money.

78. Which of the following is closest in meaning to "you win some, you lose some"?

(A) Winning and losing are part of life.

(B) Teaching children about winning and losing is important.

(C) You can't have the cake and eat it, too.

(D) Don't cry over spilt milk.

中譯與聽力原文

Questions 76-78 refer to the following conversation

問題 76-78，請參考以下對話內容

Mandy: Finally, we're having a daycare center in the office. B1. It can be officially used next month. Really can't wait. Plus, it can save us some serious money. You know how nannies charge these days.

曼蒂：終於，我們在辦公室要有自己的日間托育中心，在 B1。在下個月就能正式使用了。真的等不及了。再者，這可以省筆可觀的錢。你知道最近保母收費都不低。

Cindy: I've been waiting for this for three years, but with B1 being a daycare center, we won't be having a coffee shop. There's simply no room

辛蒂：我一直期待這個有三年了，但是隨著 B1 成了日間托育中心，我們就沒有咖啡店了。顯然沒有空間給

for a coffee shop. 咖啡店了。

Jack: So, from next month, we have to order a takeout or brew the coffee ourselves. I'm gonna miss those snacks, coffee, hand-made bagels, and tuna sandwiches.

傑克：所以從下個月，我們必須訂購外食或自己釀咖啡了。我真的會想念那些甜點、咖啡、人工製的貝果和鮪魚三明治。

Cindy: As the saying goes, you win some, you lose some.

辛蒂：有句俗諺說，你贏的同時，也輸掉了些東西。

選項中譯與解析

76. 談話者正在討論什麼？

(A) 保姆收多少費用

(B) 從地下室點餐

(C) 雇用保姆

(D) 辦公大樓地下室的改建

NEW 77. 當女子說「再者，這可以省筆可觀的錢」，其意為何？

(A) 自己煮咖啡可以省很多錢。

(B) 日間托育中心可以替他們省很多錢。

(C) 訂購外食可以省點錢。

(D) 他們需要認真思考如何省錢。

78. 下列選項何者最接近「你贏的同時，也輸掉了些東西」？

(A) 輸贏是生活的一部分。

(B) 教導兒童輸贏的重要性。

(C) 魚與熊掌無法兼得。

(D) 覆水難收。

獵豹

76.

・聽到對話，馬上鎖定 daycare center 和 B1，是「日間托育中心」和地下室一樓的意思。從對話中可以推知 B1 將會有所改變，故答案為 D。

77.

・聽到對話，馬上鎖定 serious money 推測是「~錢」的意思。先刪去 (A)，(C)因為沒提到煮咖啡和到訂購外食，跟省錢的關係為何。再比較 (B) & (D)，刪去(D)，對話中是針對托育中心。

78.

・聽到對話，馬上鎖定，win 和 lose 推測是「得失」方面的題目。本題答案出現兩句俚語，難度較高。you win some, you lose some，你贏的同時，也輸掉了些東西，可推知你不能兩者皆想要，有捨才有得。因此答案選(C)You can't have the cake and eat it, too. ，魚與熊掌無法兼得。

 貓頭鷹

76.

· 此題屬於推測題，考點引用句的另一線索是 no room for a coffee shop，由於第一句說道：要有自己的日間托育中心，在 B1。以及對話中：with B1 being a daycare center，隨著 B1 成了日間托育中心，因此可知道 B1 將會改造成托育中心。with 在此是指隨著。

77.

· 此題屬於推測題，也同時測試考生對慣用語 "can save us some serious money" 的理解，考點引用句的另一線索字是 save，省錢，在第一段對話中，提到托育中心，之後說了一句 plus，用意為補充說明。此句為：it can save us some serious money. 因此由前後對話，可推知因為托育中心的原故，省下很多錢。serious 是嚴肅，嚴重的，serious money 是片語，指一大筆錢。

78.

· 此題屬於推測題，也同時測試考生對慣用語 "you win some, you lose some" 的理解，本句考考生對慣用語的熟悉度。(A) Winning and losing are part of life.，輸贏是生活的一部分。(B) Teaching children about winning and losing is important.，教導兒童輸贏的重要性。winning 和 losing 是陷阱，讓考生誤以為最接近題意。(C) You can't have the cake and eat it, too.，魚與熊掌無法兼得。接近題目含意。(D) Don't cry over spilt milk.，覆水難收。毫無關係。考生如果無法理解所有選項描述，仍然有辦法破解，針對談話中，提到托嬰中心，省很多錢，但是卻沒有咖啡廳的空間等等內容，仍可判斷出答案。

浣熊　MP3 111+MP3 113

還可能怎麼問

1. According to the speakers, what will happen next month?

(A) nannies at a daycare center will charge less money.

(B) the office basement will be shut down.

(C) there will be a new opening of the coffee shop nearby.

(D) employees will have their own daycare center.

2. According to the woman, how long has she been waiting for a daycare center?

(A) A year

(B) 2 years

(C) 3 years

(D) 4 years

解析

1. 題目是問根據說話者們，下個月會發生什麼事？

‧ 選項 D 員工將有自己的日間托育中心，此為對話中所表達的意思，對話中曼蒂提到「終於，我們在辦公室要有自己的日間托育中心，在 B1。在下個月就能正式使用了。」，故可以得知答案為選項 D。

2. 題目是問根據女子，日間托育中心她等了多久呢？

‧ 這題可以綜合來看，辛蒂說了我一直期待這個有三年了，故可以得知答案為 3 年，答案為選項 C。

Unit 27
婚禮出問題

Instructions

❶ 請播放音檔聽下列對話，並完成試題。 🎧 MP3 114+MP3 115

❷ 「跟述」練習：寫完試題後請跟著音檔同步跟漸進式做「跟述」練習，提升聽力專注力。

❸ 加碼題：完成❶＋❷步驟後，請再播放音檔寫浣熊試題，掌握其他可能的出題考點，強化應考實力。 🎧 MP3 114+MP3 116

 79. Why does the man say, "we won't be able to set up the dreamy, romantic scene…"?

(A) because setting up the romantic scene will cost too much

(B) because the weather is too hot for a photoshoot outdoors

(C) because the weather is not good and they cannot set up the scene outdoors

(D) because the bride does not want a romantic scene

80. What company might these speakers work for?

(A) a photography studio

(B) a wedding planning company

(C) a hotel

(D) a travel agency

81. What is the solution that the speakers come up with?

(A) moving the photoshoot to a banquet hall

(B) canceling the photoshoot

(C) postponing the photoshoot date

(D) moving the photoshoot and the wedding to another location

中譯與聽力原文

Questions 79-81 refer to the following conversation
問題 **79-81**，請參考以下對話內容

Cindy: Is there something wrong with the wedding?

辛蒂：婚禮有什麼問題嗎？

Katie: Don't worry about it, but I'm afraid that we need to find you another stylist. The photographer is a pain in the ass. He has an attitude problem.

凱蒂：別擔心，但是我恐怕我們需要您找另一個時裝設計師。攝影師令人頭痛。他態度有問題。

Jack: Not only that... according to the weather forecast, we won't be able to set up the dreamy, romantic scene our customer wants.

傑克：不只這樣…根據氣象預測，我們無法架設客人想要的夢幻、浪漫的場景。

Cindy: Perhaps we should talk to the bride to see if we can do the shoot indoors, and schedule the wedding at a hotel, and of course, we are gonna compensate them by recalculating the fee.

辛蒂：或許我們應該跟新娘談談，看我們是否能在室內拍攝，然後將婚禮安排至旅館，當然我們要補償他們，重新計算婚禮費用。

選項中譯與解析

79. 為何男子說「我們無法架設客人想要的好夢幻、浪漫的場景」？

(A) 因為設置浪漫的場景所費不貲。

(B) 因為對戶外拍攝而言太熱。

(C) 天氣不佳，無法在戶外架設場景。

(D) 因為新娘不想浪漫場景。

80. 談話者可能在哪裡工作呢？

(A) 攝影工作室。

(B) 婚禮策劃公司。

(C) 飯店。

(D) 旅行社。

81. 談話者的解決方案是什麼？

(A) 移到宴會廳拍照。

(B) 取消拍攝。

(C) 延期拍攝日期。

(D) 將拍照和婚禮移到另一個地點。

獵豹

79.

・聽到對話，馬上鎖定 set up，推測是「架設」的意思。對話中提到，無架設夢幻、浪漫的場景，從中判斷原因。先刪除(A)，再刪去(B) & (C)，因為沒明顯提到。再比較(C) & (D)，刪去(D)，因為(C)「天氣不佳」才是無法架設的原因。

80.

・聽到對話，馬上鎖定 wedding，推測和「婚禮」有關。選項(A)a photography studio，攝影工作室，(C) a hotel，飯店，(D) a travel agency，旅行社，這些對話中都出現過，似乎都有關聯，不過，統合起來，以選項(B) a wedding planning company「婚禮策劃公司」最完整，因此(B)是最佳答案。

81.

・題目重點，馬上鎖定 solution，是「解決方案」的意思。解決方案通常會出現在對話最後，因為會提出結論。看到(A) moving the photoshoot to a banquet hall，(B)canceling the photoshoot，刪去(A)，(B)，因為沒提到要宴會廳，也沒說取消。再比較(C) & (D)，刪去(C)，因為對話中沒提到延後拍攝。(D) moving the photoshoot and the wedding to another location「將拍照和婚禮移到另一個地點」是最佳選項。

79.

· 此題屬於推測題，考點引用句的另一線索是 to weather forecast，天氣預測，根據天氣預測，解釋為何不能架設夢幻、浪漫的場景。選項 (A) 花費不貲。→沒提到費用問題。(B)因為對戶外拍攝而言太熱→沒提到。(C)因為天氣不佳造成。→對話中間有提到：according to weather forecast, we won't be able to set up the dreamy, romantic scene...，(D) 因為新娘不想浪漫場景→和顧客提出的要求相反。

80.

· 此題屬於推測題，考點引用句的另一線索是 recalculating the fee，重新計算費用，片語：a pain in the ass = 讓人頭痛。本題難度較高，對話中出現的單字，讓考生產生混淆，難以判斷。如：another stylist，photographer，hotel 等等。然而，最後一句，重新計算婚禮費用是重要之處，可以統籌這些事項者，以 a wedding planning company 最貼切。

81.

· 此題屬於推測題，也同時測試考生對於對話融會貫通的理解，考生必須先消化對話，再推測哪個選項描述的意思最適合解決方案。本題難度頗高。對話中並無明確說明，解決方案為何。但就幾點來看，歸納出最有可能的答案。(A) moving ...to a banquet hall，banquet hall 是指宴會廳，男子和女子對話說，並未提到。對話中的重點是：if we can do the shoot indoors，看我們是否能在室內拍攝，有此推測出要換地點。

浣熊　　MP3 114+MP3 116

還可能怎麼問

1. Why does the woman say, "a pain in the ass"?

(A) because the photographer has a headache.

(B) because the photographer is in pain.

(C) because the photographer is causing a scene.

(D) because the photographer is causing troubles for the shoot.

2. What is not mentioned as a problem for the shoot?

(A) photographer's attitude problem

(B) the need to find another stylist

(C) bad weather

(D) arrangement of the hotel

 解析

1. 題目是問為什麼女子說「令人感到頭痛」？

‧選項 D，此為對話中所表達的意思，因為攝影師的態度有問題，故可以得知答案為選項 D。

2. 題目是問關於造成拍攝問題，哪項並未提及？先從四個選項分別來看。

‧選項 D，文章中有提到「看我們是否能在室內拍攝，然後將婚禮安排至旅館」，此訊息與選項敘述一致，但這並非是造成拍攝問題的原因，所以可以得知答案為選項 D。

Unit 28
萬事俱足，
但當地居民反彈

🔍 Instructions

❶ 請播放音檔聽下列對話，並完成試題。 🎧 MP3 117+MP3 118

❷ 「跟述」練習：寫完試題後請跟著音檔同步跟漸進式做「跟述」練習，提升聽力專注力。

❸ 加碼題：完成❶＋❷步驟後，請再播放音檔寫浣熊試題，掌握其他可能的出題考點，強化應考實力。 🎧 MP3 117+MP3 119

82. What might the speakers do next right after the conversation?

(A) going to the airport

(B) starting an ad campaign

(C) talking about sanitation

(D) calling their foreign customers

83. What is the problem they are trying to solve?

(A) a political protest

(B) lowering sales of their drinks

(C) traffic jam

(D) doubts about their drinks

84. What does the woman mean when she says, "we can't go home with both hands empty"?

(A) It's not polite to visit our customers without bringing them gifts.

(B) We can't go home without any new ideas about the ad campaign.

(C) We had better keep ourselves busy.

(D) We had better go home with some good results

 中譯與聽力原文

Questions 82-84 refer to the following conversation
問題 82-84，請參考以下對話內容

Jack:	I guess you've gotta go. There's gonna be like two hours at traffic.	傑克：	我想你們該啟程了。會有兩小時的交通。
Cindy:	Why do we have a sales meeting at another country, and there is a protest. It's so jammed here.	辛蒂：	為什麼我們要在另一個國家開銷售會議，那有抗議遊行。這裡真擁擠。
Wendy:	If we can't convince local residents that our drinks are sanitary, all our previous efforts will be all gone. Is	溫蒂：	如果我們不能說服當地居民我們的飲品是衛生的，那我們先前的所有努力都會白

there any other thing that irritates them?

費。有任何什麼其他事情激怒到他們嗎？

Cindy: Oh! The ad campaign and billboard costs. So astonishing. We really need to pull this off. Perhaps we can come up with something in the car.

辛蒂：噢！廣告活動和廣告牌的花費。真是驚人。我們真的需要做好這件事。或許我們在車裡能想到些什麼。

Wendy: yep... we can't go home with both hands empty.

溫蒂：是的⋯我們不能回程時兩手空空的。

選項中譯與解析

82.對話結束後，談話者馬上會做什麼呢？

(A) 去機場。

(B) 開始廣告活動。

(C) 談論衛生。

(D) 致電給外國客戶。

83. 他們試圖解決什麼問題？

(A) 政治抗議。

(B) 降低飲料銷售量。

(C) 塞車問題。

(D) 飲料質疑一事。

84. 當女子說「我們不能回程時兩手空空的」，其含意為何？

(A) 拜訪顧客沒帶禮物是不禮貌的。

(B) 如果廣告活動沒有新主意，我們不能回家。

(C) 我們最好讓自己忙一點。

(D) 我們最好別無功而返。

82.

‧聽到對話，馬上鎖定 gotta go，推測是「要去某處」的意思。四個選項中，都和對話有關係，也有可能進行。不過，題目 do next right after the conversation，對話結束後，馬上，因此推測(A) going to the airport，去機場比較適合。

83.

‧聽到對話，馬上鎖定 sanitary，推測和「衛生」方面有關係。重點單字 get 後，對於作答方面非常有益。看到(A)和(B)先刪掉此兩個和衛生無關的選項。再比較(C) & (D)，刪去(C)，因為(C) traffic jam 意思是塞車，所以(D) doubts about their drinks「飲料質疑一事」是最佳選項。

84.

‧聽到對話，馬上鎖定 come up with something，推測是「想到些什麼」，不能無功而返的意思。看到(A)和(B)，刪去(A)和(B)，因為與本句慣用語意思有誤差，再比較(C) & (D)，刪去(C)，因為(A) ...keep ourselves busy 意思是讓自己忙一點，所以(D) ...with some good

1 照片描述

2 應答問題

3 簡短對話

4 簡短獨白

模擬試題

results 是最佳選項。

貓頭鷹

82.

· 此題屬於推測題，也同時測試考生對慣用語 "gotta go" 的理解，考點引用句的另一線索字是 another country ，所以推測必須搭飛機前往。再加上男子在對話一開始說道：I guess you've gotta go. ，我想你該啟程了，由以上兩點推知，前往機場可能性最大。two hours at traffic 是指「兩小時車程」。

83.

· 此題屬於推測題，對話中提到：If we can't convince local residents that our drinks are sanitary, all our previous efforts will be all gone. ，如果我們不能說服當地居民我們的飲品是衛生的，那我們先前的所有努力都會白費。local residents，當地居民，及 drinks ，飲料，是重點。previous effort 是先前的努力，因此推知，必須處理飲料衛生方面的事情。

84.

· 此題屬於推測題，也同時測試考生對慣用語 "with both hands empty" 的理解，考點引用句的另一線索片語是 pull it off ，這是非常關鍵的片語，如果理解，答題非常容易。不過，pull 這裡沒有拉或是停車之意，而是指「成功完成」，因此推知女子說：we can't go home with both hands empty 這句話，可以推知事情有好的結果，不能無功而返。

浣熊　　MP3 117+MP3 119

還可能怎麼問

1.　Who are the ones that they should persuade?

(A) investors.

(B) advertising companies.

(C) local residents.

(D) people at the sales meeting.

2. Why does the woman say, "so astonishing"?

(A) because it's so jammed there.

(B) because those drinks impressed local residents.

(C) because of the costs

(D) because ad companies did something astonishing.

解析

1.　題目是問誰是他們應該要說服的對象？

· 選項 C 當地居民，Wendy 有提到 If we can't convince local residents that our drinks are sanitary, all our previous efforts will be all gone.，所以可以得知他們必須要說服當地民眾飲品是衛生的，故答案為選項 C。

2.　題目是問為什麼女子說「真是驚人」？

· 選項 C 因為花費，講真為驚人的前一句，有提到廣告活動和廣告牌的花費，所以可以得知答案是選項 C。

265

有時候不只是聽懂細節和掌握聽力訊息就能
答對新制的題目，可以多注意星號的題型，
強化自己對推論、隱含句意、講者為什麼講
這句話題目的答題。此外，寫浣熊試題能大
幅強化應對靈活題目的能力，快來試試吧！

Part

4

簡短獨白

Unit 1
寵物店廣告：毛小孩最佳洗髮精和護髮液

Instructions

❶ 請播放音檔聽下列對話，並完成試題。  MP3 120+MP3 121

❷ 「跟述」練習：寫完試題後請跟著音檔同步跟漸進式做「跟述」練習，提升聽力專注力。

❸ 加碼題：完成❶+❷步驟後，請再播放音檔寫浣熊試題，掌握其他可能的出題考點，強化應考實力。 MP3 120+MP3122

1. **What products is this advertisement selling?**
   (A) toiletries for sensitive skin
   (B) toiletries for animal companions
   (C) shampoos made of organic ingredients
   (D) Skin infection treatment cream

2. **Who might be most likely interested in these products?**
   (A) people who have sensitive skin
   (B) people who have fur kids
   (C) people who have skin infection
   (D) people who walk their dogs regularly

3. What will happen in the shop this week?

(A) a discount on shampoos only

(B) giveaways

(C) an annual sale

(D) free pet grooming

聽力原文和中譯

Questions 1-3 refer to the following advertisement

If you're looking for shampoo and conditioner for your pets, Best Pet is the one for you. We used to diversify our products to different pets, pets, such as raccoons and rabbits, but now only focus on cats and dogs. With our products, you won't have to worry about the skin infection of your pets any more. We highly recommend you to visit our shop this week, since we will be having our annual sale. For the first one hundred customers, we're offering a special meal for you and your pets.

問題 1-3 請參閱下列廣告

如果你在替你的寵物尋找洗髮精和護髮液，倍斯特寵物公司是你的選擇。我們過去對於不同寵物有多樣化服務，例如像是浣熊和兔子這類的寵物，但我們現在僅將重心放在貓咪和狗身上。有我們的產品，你不用擔心你的寵物會在有皮膚感染。我們強烈推薦您這週拜訪我們的店，因為我們有年度銷售。對於前一百個顧客，我們會提供您和您的寵物一個特別餐。

答案：1. B 2. B 3.C

1. 此廣告賣什麼產品？

(A) 敏感性肌膚的洗護品。

(B) 動物的洗護品。

(C) 有機成分的洗髮精。

(D) 皮膚感染修護霜。

2. 關於這些產品，誰最可能感興趣？

　　(A) 敏感性肌膚者。

　　(B) 有毛皮孩子的人。

　　(C) 皮膚感染的人。

　　(D) 規律地遛狗的人。

3. 本星期店裡將舉辦什麼活動？

　　(A) 只有洗髮精打折。

　　(B) 贈品活動。

　　(C) 年度拍賣。

　　(D) 免費寵物美容。

 獵豹

1.

· 聽到對話，馬上鎖定 shampoo and conditioner for your pets，Best Pet is the one for you...。根據 shampoo, conditioner 馬上刪去(D) Skin infection treatment cream，(A) sensitive skin 及(C) organic ingredients 都未提及，因此(B) toiletries for animal companions（動物的洗護品）最佳答案。

2.

· 掃描(A)的關鍵字 sensitive skin（敏感性肌膚），(B)關鍵字 fur kids（毛小孩），掃描(C)的關鍵字 skin infection（皮膚感染），掃描(D)的關鍵字 walk their dogs（遛狗）。廣告和寵物有關，因此人類肌膚問題有關的選項(A)及(C)可先刪除，而(D)雖然和寵物有關，但遛狗的人和此廣告產品的消費族群沒有絕對關聯性，故也刪除(D)。

Unit 1 寵物店廣告：毛小孩最佳洗髮精和護髮液

1 照片描述

2 應答問題

3 簡短對話

4 簡短獨白

模擬試題

3.

· 聽到對話馬上鎖定在 happen in the shop。happen in the shop 是
「店裡有舉辦活動」的意思。聆聽時定位時間點 this week，在倒數第
二句出現: We highly recommend...（因為我們有年度銷售）， 所以
選(C) an annual sale。

貓頭鷹

1.

· 此題屬於單字題，由 pet 和 toiletries 判斷出答案。寵物除了 pet 一
字，現在也常以 animal companions，companion animals，fur
kids 等稱呼。正確選項(B)將 pet 換成 animal companions，測試考
生對類似字的理解。廣告一開始就說替寵物尋找洗髮精和護髮液，(A)
及(C)是陷阱選項。雖然(A)和(C)有可能是寵物盥洗用品的訴求，但廣
告都未提及。另外，(D) skin infection treatment cream 是針對皮膚
感染的修護霜，和一般洗護品不同，因此也可刪除。單字：toiletry 身
體及頭髮的洗護產品。另一快速解題技巧是: 最佳選項一定要密切呼應
主題，而只有(B)提到 animal companions 這一主題字。

2.

· 此題屬於推測題，要考生根據產品細節，推測出對產品最有興趣的人。
本題題目是誰感興趣，由 第一題可知道產品是關於寵物類。選項(B)有
毛小孩和(D)經常遛狗的人皆有可能，以主題切題度而言，選項(B)更符
合。

3.

· 此題是細節題。需要先理解片語 annual sale 是年度拍賣。四個選項
中，選項(A) a discount on shampoos only，比較有可能產生混淆，

問題是 only 一字。廣告並沒有明確指出只有洗髮精有折扣,所以(A)不能選。選項(B) giveaways 及(D) pet grooming 則未提到。注意(D) pet grooming 指寵物美容,雖然有 pet 一字,但廣告沒提及美容服務。考生要小心不要犯下過度延伸詮釋主題的思考錯誤。

 浣熊 🎧 MP3 120+MP3122

還可能怎麼問

1. **What type of business is being discussed?**

    (A) a cosmetics company

    (B) a gift shop

    (C) a shopping complex

    (D) a pet store

2. **Which products will no longer be provided?**

    (A) shampoo for golden retrievers

    (B) conditioner for Persian cats

    (C) shampoo for larger-than-normal dogs

    (D) shampoo for raccoons

中譯與解析

1. 正在敘述的是哪一種公司?

    (A) 化妝品公司。

    (B) 禮物店。

    (C) 購物中心。

    (D) 寵物店。

2. 哪項產品不在提供了？

(A) 黃金獵犬的洗髮精。

(B) 波斯貓的護髮液。

(C) 比一般狗體型較大的狗的洗髮精。

(D) 浣熊使用的洗髮精。

答案：1. D 2. D

1. 題目是問正在敘述的是哪一種公司？

‧選項 A，由首句 If you're..., Best Pet is the one for you，可以得知公司是間寵物公司，所以可以排除。選項 B, C，此篇聽力中未提到禮物店或購物中心相關敘述，所以可以排除此選項。選項 D，此篇聽力內容和相關敘述都是在描述寵物跟其用品，故可以得知答案為選項 D。

2. 題目是問哪項產品不在提供了？

‧選項 A，定位回段落可以得知公司推出的產品是狗和貓，黃金獵犬是狗，且洗髮精是公司推出的產品項目，故可以排除此選項。選項 B，同選項 A，題目跟聽力敘述常會有同義表達之間的轉換，同樣是名詞，只是一個是更精確的名詞項目，波斯貓包含在貓裡面，此為同義表達，加上護髮液是公司推出的產品，故可以排除此選項。選項 C，定位回段落，公司推出的產品是狗和貓，題目敘述「比一般狗體型較大的狗的洗髮精」其實等同「大型犬」，也是同義表達，別被較長的敘述干擾了，故可以排除此選項。 選項 D，定位回段落找到得知之前有推出包含浣熊和兔子的產品但現在沒有了，故可以得知答案為選項 D。

Unit 2
玩具公司廣告：填充玩偶，孩子最佳良伴

Instructions

❶ 請播放音檔聽下列對話，並完成試題。 MP3 123+MP3 124

❷ 「跟述」練習：寫完試題後請跟著音檔同步跟漸進式做「跟述」練習，提升聽力專注力。

❸ 加碼題：完成❶＋❷步驟後，請再播放音檔寫浣熊試題，掌握其他可能的出題考點，強化應考實力。 MP3 123+MP3 125

4. **Which of the following is NOT one of the functions of stuffed animals?**

   (A) helping kids to make friends

   (B) giving kids pleasure

   (C) keeping kids company

   (D) helping autistic kids

5. **What can be inferred about fidget toys based on this advertisement?**

   (A) They can stop children from fidgeting right away.

   (B) Fidget toys sell very well in America.

   (C) Stuffed animals are the most popular among fidget toys.

   (D) They serve soothing functions.

6. What does the term "role play" imply?

(A) playing with stuffed animals

(B) pretending to be an animal

(C) Being a role model for children

(D) pretending to be another person

聽力原文和中譯

Questions 4-6 refer to the following advertisement

Are you looking for stuffed animals for you kids? Best Toy Company has earned its reputation not by providing the durable and eye-catching toys, but by providing chemical-free toys. Best Toy Company has tons of fidget toys, including stuffed animals. Stuffed animals have lots of functions. They give kids pleasure if they're playing the role play. They keep the kids company so that they won't feel so lonely. For kids with autism, this is especially a great thing for them, since they can have a one-on-one talk with stuffed animals. Hugging stuffed animals gives them positive energies.

問題 4-6 請參閱下列廣告

你在替你的小孩找尋填充玩偶嗎？倍斯特玩具公司不是以提供耐用和誘人的玩具聞名，而是以無化學物質的玩具聞名，倍斯特公司有許多舒壓玩具，包含填充動物。填充動物有許多功能。它給予孩子們樂趣，如果他們玩角色扮演。他們讓小孩有伴所以小孩們不會感到寂寞。對自閉症小孩而言，這是特別棒的事，因為他們可以與填充玩偶有一對一的談話。與填充玩偶擁抱給予他們正向的能量。

答案：4. A　5. D　6. D

4. 下列選項何者不是填充玩偶的功能之一？

(A) 幫助孩子交友。

(B) 給予孩子樂趣。

(C) 陪伴孩子。

(D) 幫助自閉症的小孩。

5. 根據此廣告，關於舒壓玩具，我們能推測出什麼？

(A) 它們能阻止孩子坐立不安。

(B) 舒壓玩具在美國賣得很好。

(C) 填充玩偶是舒壓玩具中最受歡迎的。

(D) 它們提供安撫功能。

 6. 「角色扮演」這個詞的含意為何？

(A) 玩填充動物。

(B) 假裝自己是動物。

(C) 成為兒童榜樣。

(D) 假裝成其他人。

 獵豹

4

· 聽到對話，馬上鎖定 Stuffed animals have lots of functions. 後面所有的補充說明幾項功能。題目是問沒提到的功能，所以一邊聆聽，一邊將有提的功能刪除。(B)、(C)、(D)都有描述，所以選(A)。

5.

· 從第四題得知功能，能幫助解答此題。四個選項中，選項(B)和(C)於廣告中均未提及，因此可刪除。而選項(A) 阻止孩子坐立不安，並未明確指出，很多的功能都是關於安撫小孩，因此選項(D) 安撫功能最佳。

6.

· 首先判斷此題屬於片語題，單純測試考生是否理解 role play 一詞的定義。play 在此當名詞。role play 是指「角色扮演」，即使不懂字義也能從上下文做出判斷意思。。

貓頭鷹

4.

· 此題屬於細節題，廣告中的內容幾乎和本題有關聯，因此必須全部看完，才能融會貫通。廣告中有提到 pleasure（樂趣），keep the kids company（陪伴孩子），kids with autism（自閉症小孩）等等，kids with autism 換句話說是 autistic kids。但並未提到可以幫助孩子交友，因此答案為(A) helping kids to make friends。

5.

· 讀題時先定位關鍵字，可以讓解題速度變快，並且能夠歸納。此題是推測題。注意填充玩具的功能和線索字，得知這些功能都是正面的，最明確和正面影響有關的只有選項(D) They serve soothing functions. 考生也需具備足夠單字量，知道 soothing 是安撫的意思。才能將以上線索字和 soothing 做出聯想。

6.

· 選項(A)及(B)都用了 play，animal，是陷阱選項。(C) role model 是模範生，榜樣。注意 role 是多重意義字。必須理解 role model 片語的意思，而不能單從 role 一字就驟然決定(D)是答案。role play 本身是角色扮演。四個選項中，一一分析。(A) playing with stuffed animals（和填充玩具玩）此 play 是指玩耍，意思不同。(B) pretending to be an animal（假裝自己是動物）語意不同。(C) being a role model for children（成為兒童榜樣）跟角色扮演無關。(D) pretending to be another person（假裝成為其他人）答案符合。

浣熊  MP3 123+MP3 125

還可能怎麼問

1. What is Best Toy Company known for?

(A) making toys that contain positive energy

(B) making durable toys

(C) manufacturing eye-catching toys

(D) making toys that are healthy to users

2. Which of the following features of the toys designed by Best Toy Company is True?

(A) harmful substance detected in cotton of the stuffed animals

(B) toys that can endure for a really long time

(C) toys that are good companies for kids

(D) toys that contain lead

中譯與解析

1. 倍斯特玩具公司以什麼聞名？

(A) 製造包含正向能量的玩具。

(B) 製造耐用的玩具。

(C) 製造引人注目的玩具。

(D) 製造對使用者健康的玩具。

2. 下列哪個關於倍斯特玩具公司的所設計玩具特色是正確的？

(A) 填充玩具棉花中檢查出有害物質。

(B) 耐用度高的玩具。

(C) 對小孩來説是好伴侶的玩具。

(D) 包含鉛的玩具。

答案：1. D 2. C

1. 題目是問倍斯特玩具公司以什麼聞名？

· 選項 A，為干擾選項，且非題目所問的。選項 B，聽力訊息中 Best Toy Company has earned its reputation not by providing the durable and eye-catching toys, but by providing chemical-free toys.，注意「not...but」的表達，not 後的敘述不是公司聞名的原因，所以可以排除此選項。選項 C，同選項 B，所以可以排除此選項。選項 D，聽力訊息中 ...eye-catching toys, but by providing chemical-free toys.，注意「not...but」的表達，重點是在 but 後敘述，chemical-free 其實就是 healthy 的同義表達，故可以得知答案為選項 D。

2. 題目是問下列哪個關於倍斯特玩具公司的所設計玩具特色是正確的？

· 選項 A，聽力訊息中 ...but by providing chemical-free toys.，可以知道是不含化學物質的，且訊息中未提到「填充玩具棉花的敘述」，故可以排除。選項 B，同選項 A 提到的聽力訊息可以知道公司並非推出 durable 的玩具，故可以排除此選項。選項 C，聽力訊息中 give kids pleasure if they're playing the role play. ／keep the kids company ／have a one-on-one talk with stuffed animals.，都是關於玩具是小孩良伴的敘述，所以可以得知答案為選項 C。選項 D，公司推出的是 chemical free 的玩具，所以不可能含鉛，故可以排除。

Unit 3

渡假勝地廣告：堪稱最人性化人工馬服務，浪漫不減分

Instructions

❶ 請播放音檔聽下列對話，並完成試題。 🎧 MP3 126+MP3 127

❷ 「跟述」練習：寫完試題後請跟著音檔同步跟漸進式做「跟述」練習，提升聽力專注力。

❸ 加碼題：完成❶＋❷步驟後，請再播放音檔寫浣熊試題，掌握其他可能的出題考點，強化應考實力。 🎧 MP3 126+MP3 128

---

7. **What is this advertisement mainly about?**

   (A) lodging in Best Resort

   (B) horseback riding classes

   (C) horse-drawn carriage service

   (D) riding artificial horses

 8. **Why does the speaker say, "it's totally humane"?**

   (A) The horses have lots of rest.

   (B) Customers feel more at ease with artificial horses.

   (C) Artificial horses are used instead of real horses.

   (D) The horses receive very humane treatment.

9. When can customers use the service for free?

(A) during lunch hours

(B) on Valentine's Day

(C) in the evening

(D) on Christmas

聽力原文和中譯

Questions 7-9 refer to the following advertisement

Are you looking for a fresh and romantic way of starting your day while traveling? Best Resort is having a horse-drawn carriage service for anyone who comes to our place. You won't feel like it's inhuman because it's totally humane. We actually use artificial horses to mimic the performance of the real horses. Artificial horses are covered with real horse skin. We're offering the service for free during lunch hours. It'll be charged 120% at the romantic evening and 180% on Valentine's Day.

問題 7-9 請參閱下列廣告

你在找尋新鮮且浪漫的方式展開你在旅行期間的日子嗎？倍斯特渡假勝地有馬車服務，提供給任何來到這的遊客。你不會感到不人道，因為很人道。我們實際上使用的人工馬去模仿真實馬的表現。人工馬會覆蓋上真實馬的真皮。我們於中午時刻提供免費服務。在浪漫傍晚會收取 120%的費用，在情人節則是180%的費用。

答案：7. C 8. C 9. A

7. 這個廣告主要和何者有關？

(A) 入住倍斯特渡假村。

(B) 騎馬課。

(C) 馬車交通服務。

(D) 騎乘人工馬。

8. 為何敘述者說「很人道」？

(A) 馬匹有很多休息時間。

(B) 客戶坐人工馬比較自在。

(C) 使用人工馬代替真馬。

(D) 馬匹受到非常人道的待遇。

9. 客人在何時可以免費使用此服務？

(A) 午餐時間。

(B) 情人節。

(C) 傍晚。

(D) 聖誕節。

獵豹

7.

· 聽到對話，馬上鎖定 Best Resort is having a horse-drawn carriage service for anyone who comes to our place... horse-drawn carriage service 是馬車交通服務。根據 having a horse-drawn carriage service，推知和馬車交通服務方面有關。廣告中還提到 Best Resort（倍斯特度假村），artificial horses（人工馬）等等。

8.

· 首先判斷此題屬於單字題，首先先了解題目 humane 的意思。humane 是指「人道」，it's totally humane（很人道），從廣告中提出 humane 後面的句子開始，解釋為何說明很人道的原因。如：We actually use artificial horses to mimic the performance of the real horses.

9.

· 直接鎖定 use the service for free，for free 是「免費」的意思。free 除了當免費的，還有有空的之意。如:free time。when 是指「何時」，因此找出時間點，能判斷出答案，屬於單純細節題陷阱較少。

貓頭鷹

7.

· 此題屬於情境題，題目大意詢問廣告主題。廣告中提到度假村，馬車服務和人工馬，但未提及 horseback riding classes 騎馬課，選項(B)可先刪除。從廣告中重點都在馬車服務上，如馬匹用人工馬，費用如何收取，因此推知答案為(C) 馬車交通服務。

8.

· 考點關鍵字 humane 之後，馬上解釋 humane 的原因。「為何敘述者說很人道？」，鎖定 humane 後面那一句，We actually use artificial horses to mimic the performance of the real horses.（我們實際上使用的人工馬去模仿真實馬的表現。），因此答案選(C)。事實上，考生只要理解 artificial 是「人工的」意思，馬上可刪除(A) The horses have lots of rest.及(D) The horses receive very humane treatment。因為(A)，(D)都是指真馬獲得的待遇。而(B) Customers feel more at ease with artificial horses 也可刪除，因為humane 一字在此短講是針對人類以外的動物，但(B)強調的是顧客的感覺。

9.

· 此題是時間題目。通常在廣告後方可以找到答案。這題則是多加其他時間，增加困難度。倒數幾句提到：We're offering the service for free during lunch hours.（我們於中午時刻提供免費服務。）It'll be charged 120% at the romantic evening and 180% on Valentine's Day.（在浪漫傍晚會收取 120%的費用，在情人節則是 180%的費用。）選項中提到情人節和傍晚就是混淆功能。

 浣熊 🎧 MP3 126+MP3 128

還可能怎麼問

1. How is Best Resort's service different from others?

(A) It uses real horses

(B) It uses artificial horses

(C) It uses artificial skins to mimic real horses

(D) Its service does not contain any real horse materials

2. What is the purpose of using man-made horses?

(A) to make customers feel welcomed

(B) to reduce the overall cost

(C) to differentiate itself from competitors

(D) to provide service that is humane

中譯與解析

1. 倍斯特渡假勝地的服務與其他度假勝地的差別有何不同？

(A) 它使用真實馬。

(B) 它使用人工馬。

(C) 它使用人工皮去模仿真實馬。

(D) 它的服務不包含任何真實馬的材料。

2.　使用人造馬的目的是什麼呢？

(A) 讓顧客覺得更受歡迎。

(B) 降低整體成本。

(C) 與競爭對手們做出區隔化。

(D) 提供人道的服務。

答案：1. B 2. D

1.　題目是問倍斯特渡假勝地的服務與其他度假勝地的差別有何不同？

・選項 A，聽力訊息中 We actually use artificial horses to mimic the performance of the real horses.，可以得知公司並非使用真實馬，而是人工馬，所以可以排除此選項。選項 B，公司是使用人工馬仿製真實馬，故可以得知答案為選項 B。選項 C 它使用人工皮去模仿真實馬，聽力訊息中 Artificial horses are covered with real-skin of horses.，人工馬會覆蓋上真實馬的真皮，而非使用人工皮去模仿真實馬，所以可以排除此選項。選項 D，此敘述不完全對，聽力訊息中 Artificial horses are covered with real-skin of horses.，人工馬會覆蓋上真實馬的真皮，皮的部分還是有部分使用到真實馬，所以可以排除此選項。

2.　題目是問使用人造馬的目的是什麼呢？先從四個選項分別來看。

・A, B, C 選項，聽力訊息中均未提及，故可以排除。選項 D 提供人道的服務，聽力訊息中 You won't feel like it's inhuman because it's totally humane.可以得知是更符合人性的，humane 即人道的，故可以得知答案為選項 B。

285

Unit 4

動物園廣告：提供更多人和動物互動體驗、廚藝競賽

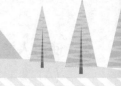

🔍 Instructions

❶ 請播放音檔聽下列對話，並完成試題。 🎧 MP3 129+MP3 130

❷ 「跟述」練習：寫完試題後請跟著音檔同步跟漸進式做「跟述」練習，提升聽力專注力。

❸ 加碼題：完成❶＋❷步驟後，請再播放音檔寫浣熊試題，掌握其他可能的出題考點，強化應考實力。 🎧 MP3 129+MP3 131

10. **Which of the following is NOT mentioned as one of the interactions with animals?**

(A) taking photos with them

(B) handling cotton candy to racoons

(C) preparing food for them

(D) grooming them

11. **How much does a visitor have to pay for interacting with animals?**

(A) the admission fee

(B) 5 dollars

(C) zero

(D) 10 dollars

12. Which animal is NOT mentioned?

(A) pandas

(B) koalas

(C) racoons

(D) monkeys

聽力原文和中譯

Questions 10-12 refer to the following advertisement

Are you feeling a little bit tired of going to the zoo? Best Zoo is offering a great one-on-one interaction between visitors and animals. You can get close to the animals without any fees. You are able to take photos with animals, such as koalas and pandas. Have an actual contact with them, such as handing cotton candy to raccoons, while filming how they end up ruining it. You also get to prepare food for them in the Zoo kitchen. In the afternoon, we're having a contest of prepared foods by attendees. Of course, animals will be the judge to decide which is more delicious.

問題 10-12 請參閱下列廣告

對於去動物園，你會感到有點累嗎？倍斯特動物園將提供參觀者和動物一對一的互動。你能夠與動物近距離接觸卻不用花費任何費用。你能與像是無尾熊和貓熊這樣的動物拍照。實際與他們接觸，例如遞棉花糖給浣熊，而攝影他們如何毀了棉花糖。你可以在動物園廚房準備食物給他們。在下午，我們會有替參加者準備好的食材做為競賽。當然，動物會是評判哪道料理比較美味。

答案：10. D　11. C　12. D

10. 關於動物一對一的互動，不包括下列哪個選項？

(A) 與牠們拍照。

(B) 遞棉花糖給浣熊。

(C) 為牠們準備食物。

(D) 梳理牠們。

11. 參觀者需要花多少錢才能和動物互動？

(A) 入場費。

(B) 5 元。

(C) 免費。

(D) 10 元。

12. 對話中沒被提到哪種動物？

(A) 熊貓。

(B) 無尾熊。

(C) 浣熊。

(D) 猴子。

獵豹

10.

・聽到對話，馬上鎖定 Best Zoo is offering a great one-on-one interaction between visitors and animals...。not mentioned（沒提到、不包括），找出廣告中沒提到的部分，注意題目是「沒有」，考生很容易看到答案見獵心喜，而粗心犯錯。

11.

・本題詢問價格。how much，多少錢，visitor，參觀者。詢問價格通常是比較簡易的題型，屬於問與答。第三句提到: without any fee<不需要費用>，就是免費之意。

12.

・首先判斷此題屬於細節題，掃描四個選項的答案，再進行下一步判斷。選項皆是動物，從廣告中的敘述，有提到貓熊，無尾熊和浣熊，並未提

到選項(D)猴子。

 貓頭鷹

10.

· 此題屬於細節題，必須看過完整廣告才能判斷，再加上是否定，因此更加困難。廣告中提到，可以和動物互動的內容如下：You can get close to the animals without any fees... You are able to take photos with animals... handing cotton candy to raccoons... prepare food for them，因此答案並不包括梳理牠們，因此選項(D)正確。

11.

· 讀題時先定位關鍵字是重要的解題技巧，如本題是 how much ，先從數字著手，另外的答案有可能是 free（免費）或是 without any fees（不用付費）。有可能以不同型式出現。選項(A)admission fee（入場費），許多地方都需要入場費，因此選項(A)用入場費，是個陷阱。考生務必讀完全部選項，再進行作答。

12.

· 細節題的選項通常同類相比。以本題為例，都是動物。從廣告敘述中，得知提到以下幾種動物：You are able to take photos with animals, such as koalas and pandas... such as handing cotton candy to raccoons...，因此可推知廣告中並無提到猴子。

 浣熊　🎧 MP3 129+MP3 131

還可能怎麼問

1. **What type of event will be held this afternoon?**
   (A) a film contest
   (B) a private session between animals and visitors
   (C) an interview for new recruits
   (D) a cooking competition

2. **Why does Best Zoo provide a one-on-one interaction between visitors and animals?**
   (A) to allure lots of crowds
   (B) to avoid complaints from visitors
   (C) to make animals feel energetic
   (D) to earn more money

中譯與解析

1. 下午會舉行什麼類型的活動？
   (A) 電影比賽。
   (B) 動物和參觀者的私人會面。
   (C) 招募新僱員的面試。
   (D) 廚藝競賽。

2. 倍斯特動物園為何提供動物和參觀者一對一的互動？
   (A) 吸引許多群眾。
   (B) 避免參觀者的抱怨。
   (C) 讓動物覺得更有活力。
   (D) 賺取更多錢。

答案：1. D 2. A

1. 題目是問下午會舉行什麼類型的活動？先從四個選項分別來看。

- 選項 A, B, C，聽力訊息中均未提到這部分，故可以排除此選項。選項 D 廚藝競賽，聽力訊息中前面有提到你可以在動物園廚房準備食物給他們。加上後來的敘述 In the afternoon, we're having a contest of prepared foods by attendees.，可以推斷將有美食大賽或廚藝比賽之類的，故可以得知答案為選項 D。

2. 題目是問倍斯特動物園為何提供動物和參觀者一對一的互動？先從四個選項分別來看。

- 選項 A 吸引許多群眾，聽力訊息中 Are you feeling a little bit tired of going to the zoo? Best Zoo is offering a great one-on-one interaction between visitors and animals.，和後面聽力訊息的敘述，都是在廣告一些特色要吸引群眾來動物園，所以可以得知答案為選項 A。選項 B, C, D 選項，聽力訊息中均未提及，故可以排除。

糖果公司廣告：萬聖節收服頑皮孩子就靠這款棒棒糖

❶ 請播放音檔聽下列對話，並完成試題。 🎧 MP3 132+MP3 133

❷ 「跟述」練習：寫完試題後請跟著音檔同步跟漸進式做「跟述」練習，提升聽力專注力。

❸ 加碼題：完成❶＋❷步驟後，請再播放音檔寫浣熊試題，掌握其他可能的出題考點，強化應考實力。 🎧 MP3 132+MP3 134

13. What occasion does the advertisement target at?

    (A) Thanksgiving

    (B) Halloween

    (C) Easter

    (D) Christmas

14. What is the product particularly designed for greedy children?

    (A) a huge piece of candy

    (B) a colorful lollipop

    (C) a giant chocolate bar

    (D) a big bag

15. Why does the advertisement mention "win-win"?

    (A) People who celebrate Halloween want to compete for the winner title for the best outfit.

(B) The child who gets the most candies wins the game on Halloween.

(C) Both chocolates and candies are children's favorite on Halloween.

(D) Both the people who give candies and those who receive them will feel glad.

聽力原文和中譯

Questions 13-15 refer to the following advertisement

Still can't figure out how to be a great contributor to the Halloween gala? Come to Best Candy. We have a dazzling array of candies and chocolates. Totally suits your needs, if kids are coming to your house for "trick or treat". Plus, this year we have a giant lollipop, specifically designed for the naughty kids or greedy kids. A giant lollipop is just enough, totally filling their bags. You won't have a feeling from looking at their faces that they're not satisfied or you're being too stingy. Win-win.

問題 13-15 請參閱下列廣告

仍不知道要如何在萬聖節慶當最棒的貢獻者嗎？來倍斯特糖果公司。我們有一系列令人暈眩的糖果和巧克力。全然能滿足你的需求，如果小孩到你們家「不給糖就搗蛋」。再者，今年我們有大型的棒棒糖，特別為頑皮的孩子或貪心的孩子所量身訂作的。小孩子裝糖袋剛好夠裝大型棒棒糖。你不用有種看著他們的臉龐卻感到他們不滿足的神情或是覺得你太過於小氣。雙贏。

答案：13. B　14. A　15. D

13. 此廣告的主題是何者？

(A) 感恩節。

(B) 萬聖節。

(C) 復活節。

(D) 聖誕節。

1 照片描述

2 應答問題

3 簡短對話

4 簡短獨白

模擬試題

14. 何種是專門為貪心的孩子所設計的產品？

(A) 大型的棒棒糖。

(B) 五顏六色的棒棒糖。

(C) 大型的巧克力棒。

(D) 一個大袋子。

15. 為何廣告提到 **"win-win"**（雙贏）？

(A) 人們慶祝萬聖節想爭取最佳裝扮的冠軍頭銜。

(B) 得到最多醣果的孩子在萬聖節比賽中獲勝。

(C) 萬聖節時，巧克力和糖果是兒童的最愛。

(D) 給糖果的人和得到糖果的人都會很高興。

獵豹

13.

· 聽到對話，馬上鎖定 Still can't figure out how to be a great contributor to the Halloween gala?... 重點單字 Halloween 萬聖節。根據第一句：仍不知道要如何在萬聖節慶當最棒的貢獻者嗎？可推知答案為(B)Halloween。

14.

· 首先判斷此題屬於細節題，product（產品）和 greedy kids（貪心的小孩）是重點。先找出 greedy kids，通常之後會補充說明。greedy kids 後面接：A giant lollipop is just enough... 此產品即為專門為貪心的孩子所設計。

15.

· 看到題目目光直接鎖定在 win-win，win-win 是「雙贏」的意思。

win-win 是正面之意。由廣告中找出正面的答案，再考慮細節敘述：You won't have a feeling... that they're not satisfied or you're being too stingy。推測出給貪心的孩子大型棒棒糖，自己也會開心，故推知答案為(D)。

貓頭鷹

13.

・此題屬於情境題，題目大意詢問文章是和哪方面有關。因為廣告第一句就提到萬聖節，之後內容也是敘述關於萬聖節的一二事，如："trick or treat"（不給糖就搗蛋）因此得知答案為(C)Halloween（萬聖節）。

14.

・細節題的選項會以同性質的答案出現，增加判斷難度。四個選項的答案，都跟甜食有關，如: (A) a huge piece of candy（大型的棒棒糖）(B) a colorful lollipop（五顏六色的棒棒糖）(C) a giant chocolate bar（大型的巧克力棒）(D) a big bag（一個大袋子）。

15.

・此題是推測題。需要先理解片語 win-win 的意思，再搜尋其造成雙贏的句子。因此，照之前教過的技巧，在此單字前後搜尋：You won't have a feeling from looking at their faces that they're not satisfied or you're being too stingy.（你不用有種看著他們的臉龐卻感到他們不滿足的神情或是覺得你太過於小氣。）正確選項(D)glad 有高興之意。而 be satisfied 是指「滿意」，都是正面情緒。選項(A) compete 是陷阱。選項(B) win the game（獲勝），和雙贏無關，透過單字 win，來混淆考生。

浣熊 🎧 MP3 132+MP3 134

還可能怎麼問

1. **What type of business is being discussed?**

    (A) a home appliance store

    (B) a Halloween flower shop

    (C) a shopping complex

    (D) a candy store

2. **What is mentioned about Best Candy?**

    (A) it provide specifically designed large bags for candies

    (B) it does not welcome naughty kids to its shop

    (C) it only provides candies during Halloween

    (D) it provides all kinds of candies

中譯與解析

1. 正在敘述的是哪一種公司？

    (A) 家庭用品店。

    (B) 萬聖節花店。

    (C) 購物中心。

    (D) 糖果公司。

2. 關於倍斯特糖果公司提到了什麼？

    (A) 它提供量身訂做裝糖果的較大袋子。

    (B) 它不歡迎頑皮的小孩到他們的店裡。

(C) 它僅於萬聖節期間提供糖果。

(D) 它提供各式各樣的糖果。

答案：1. D 2. D

1. 題目是問正在敘述的是哪一種公司？

‧選項 A，聽力訊息中都是關於糖果跟萬聖節等，所以可以排除此選項。選項 B，聽力訊息中有提到萬聖節，但是沒有跟花或花店有關的敘述，所以可以排除此選項。選項 C，聽力訊息中都是關於糖果跟萬聖節等，且沒有訊息是關於因為萬聖節所以到購物中心購物的敘述，所以可以排除此選項。選項 D，此為聽力訊息中所表達的意思，廣告一間糖果公司提供得糖果等，故可以得知答案為選項 D。

2. 題目是問關於倍斯特糖果公司提到了什麼？

‧選項 A，聽力訊息中 Plus, this year we have a giant lollipop, specifically designed for the naughty kids or greedy kids. A giant lollipop is just enough, totally filling their bags.，可以得知大的棒棒糖可以滿足頑皮的孩子，而非題目敘述的糖果公司有提供大袋子，故可以排除此選項。選項 B，聽力訊息中有提到「今年我們有大型的棒棒糖，特別為頑皮的孩子或貪心的孩子所量身訂作的。」，但沒有說不歡迎頑皮小孩到店裡，此為干擾選項，所以可以排除。選項 C，聽力訊息中有提到提供各式的糖果等，但沒有提到僅於萬聖節才提供，加 only 的選項其實過於絕對，大多時候是錯誤選項，故可以排除此選項。選項 D，此為此篇所表達的意思，所以可以得知答案為選項 D。

Unit **6**
超市公告：超良心酪農場，牛奶出問題不避責

🔍 Instructions

❶ 請播放音檔聽下列對話，並完成試題。 🎧 MP3 135+MP3 136

❷ 「跟述」練習：寫完試題後請跟著音檔同步跟漸進式做「跟述」練習，提升聽力專注力。

❸ 加碼題：完成❶＋❷步驟後，請再播放音檔寫浣熊試題，掌握其他可能的出題考點，強化應考實力。 🎧 MP3 135+MP3 137

16. Where might this announcement be made?

    (A) in a bookstore

    (B) in a call center

    (C) in a supermarket

    (D) on a dairy farm

17. What is the announcement about?

    (A) product recall

    (B) the benefit of drinking milk

    (C) the manufacturing process of milk

    (D) where to buy milk

18. What is the problem with ABC milk?

(A) The manufacturing process of ABC milk went wrong.

(B) The speaker does not like the taste of ABC milk.

(C) The manufacture and expiration dates are not correct.

(D) ABC milk cannot be returned at the checkout.

聽力原文和中譯

Questions 16-18 refer to the following announcement

Attention shoppers. We'd like you to know that there's been an oversight about ABC milk. We just got the phone call from ABC Diary, informing us that the manufacture date and expiration date are wrong. For those of you who have ABC milk, please return it at the supermarket checkout. For those who have purchased it, we will be having a news release with major media, so consumers are able to return the expired milk. Consumers are able to get their money back or in exchange for the same size of the purchased milk. We do hope you enjoy your afternoon shopping.

問題 16-18 請參閱下列公告

購物者注意了。我想讓你們知道關於 ABC 牛奶有了些疏忽。我剛與 ABC 酪農公司通話，製造日期和過期日都是錯誤的。對於那些手中有 ABC 牛奶的買家，請在超市結帳台退回商品。對於已經購買者，我們將與主要媒體有新聞發佈，所以消費者可以知道那些過期牛奶的退還日期。消費者也可以拿回退款或更換相等容量的牛奶商品。希望你們都能享受這個下午的購物。

答案：16. C 17. A 18. C

16. 此公告可能會在哪裡發布？

(A) 在書店裡。

(B) 在客服中心。

(C) 在超市。

(D) 在酪農公司。

17. 公告內容是關於哪方面？

(A) 產品回收。

(B) 喝牛奶的好處。

(C) 牛奶的製造過程。

(D) 買牛奶的地方。

18. ABC 牛奶出了什麼問題？

(A) ABC 牛奶的製造過程有問題。

(B) 敘述者不喜歡 ABC 牛奶的味道。

(C) 製造日期和過期日不對。

(D) ABC 牛奶不能在結帳櫃檯退貨。

 獵豹

16.

‧看到題目，目光直接鎖定在 We just got the phone call from ABC Diary...。根據 ABC Diary，milk，馬上刪掉(A) a bookstore 及(B) a call center。又根據 attention shopper（購物者注意了），推知在商店裡，因此(D)a daily farm 不符合目前場所。因此 選項(C) 超市最適合。

17.

‧四個選項都提到 milk，根據公告中提到製造日期有誤，可以推知產品有問題。從公告中，Consumers are able to get their money back or in exchange for the same size of the purchased milk. 推知選項(A) 產品回收是正確答案。

18.

．公告提到：製造日期和過期日有誤，可以退貨，或是更換箱等容量的商品。首先判斷此題屬於細節題，掃描公告中的重點原因：the manufacture date and expiration date are wrong（製造日期和過期日都是錯誤的），因此可推知答案是(A)。

貓頭鷹

16.

．此題屬於情境題，題目大意詢問地點或是出處。本題由 ABC Milk 推知 (C) in a supermarket 和 (D) on a dairy farm 皆有關聯，不過，透過 enjoy your afternoon shopping，則可推知超市更恰當。

17.

．此題屬於情境題，詢問公告的主題為何。讀題時先定位關鍵字很重要。milk（牛奶），return（退貨），checkout（結帳台）等等，都是本公告重要關鍵。

18.

．what's the problem...? 是常見題目。通常此類型題目，無法迅速判斷，必須歸納其他點，才能得出結論。「ABC 牛奶出了什麼問題？」，我們可以分析四個選項，究竟陷阱在哪裡。(A) ABC 牛奶的製造過程有問題。沒特別說明這項。(B) 談話者不喜歡 ABC 牛奶的味道。沒提到。(C) 製造日期和過期日不對。公告第二行提到。(D) ABC 牛奶不能在結帳櫃檯退貨。錯，可以退貨或更換牛奶。

浣熊　MP3 135+MP3 137

還可能怎麼問

1. How can listeners who have purchased ABC milk get further information?

　　(A) by telephoning ABC Diary

　　(B) by asking staff at the checkout

　　(C) by following the news release

　　(D) by contacting supermarket managers

2. What is NOT mentioned as the compensation for purchased milk?

　　(A) milk of larger volume

　　(B) the same size of the purchased milk

　　(C) an equivalent volume of milk

　　(D) a full refund

中譯與解析

1. 已經購買 ABC 牛奶的聽者如何取得進一步資訊呢？

　　(A) 藉由打電話給 ABC 酪農公司。

　　(B) 藉由詢問在收銀台的職員。

　　(C) 藉由追蹤新聞發佈。

　　(D) 藉由聯繫超市經理。

2. 下列哪項不是購買牛奶的補償？

　　(A) 較大量的牛奶。

　　(B) 與購買時同型號的牛奶。

　　(C) 相等容量的牛奶。

(D) 全額退費。

答案：1. C 2. A

1. 題目是問已經購買 ABC 牛奶的聽者如何取得進一步資訊呢？

‧選項 A，聽力訊息中有提到與 ABC 酪農公司通電話，但這是超市人員與該公司通電話，並非消費者/聽者，所以可以排除此選項。選項 B，這並非聽到這段話的聽者取得進一步資訊的方式，所以可以排除此選項。選項 C，聽力訊息中 For those who have purchased it, we will be having a news release with major media, so consumers are able to return the expired milk.，所以可以得知透過新聞發佈可以得知進一步訊息，故可以得知答案為選項 C。選項 D 藉由聯繫超市經理，聽力訊息中未提到超市經理且這並非取得的方式，所以可以排除此選項。

2. 題目是問下列哪項不是購買牛奶的補償？

‧選項 A，聽力訊息中 Consumers are able to get their money back or in exchange for the same size of the purchased milk.，可以得知是 same size 而非 larger，題目問的是「不是」所以可以得知答案為選項 A。選項 B，聽力訊息中 Consumers are able to get their money back or in exchange for the same size of the purchased milk.，故可以排除此選項。選項 C，聽力訊息中 Consumers are able to get their money back or in exchange for the same size of the purchased milk.，same size 即 an equivalent volume 此為同義表達，故可以排除此選項。 選項 D，聽力訊息中 Consumers are able to get their money back or in exchange for the same size of the purchased milk.，to get their money back 等同 a full refund，故可以排除此選項。

Unit 7
超市公告：書展之沒咖啡真的不行

 **Instructions**

❶ 請播放音檔聽下列對話，並完成試題。 🎧 MP3 138+MP3 139

❷ 「跟述」練習：寫完試題後請跟著音檔同步跟漸進式做「跟述」練習，提升聽力專注力。

❸ 加碼題：完成❶+❷步驟後，請再播放音檔寫浣熊試題，掌握其他可能的出題考點，強化應考實力。 🎧 MP3 138+MP3 140

19. How can a consumer get a coupon?
(A) by going to the Book Fair
(B) by purchasing 300 dollars worth of products at Best supermarket
(C) by buying books worthy of 550 dollars
(D) by buying coffee and biscuits

20. What is happening on B1?
(A) a Book Fair
(B) Coffee giveaway
(C) the opening of a supermarket
(D) the opening of a bookstore

21. What can consumers exchange with the coupons?

(A) cakes and coffee

(B) a free book

(C) a ticket to a lecture

(D) cookies and coffee

聽力原文和中譯

Questions 19-21 refer to the following announcement

Attention shoppers. Since we are having a Book Fair on B1, we have collaborated with several publishers to give consumers who have purchased over 500 dollars at Best supermarket or bought books worthy of 550 dollars a coupon. You get to use the coupon at our coffee shop to exchange for cookies and a cup of coffee. All coupons will expire on Dec. 12. Bring those biscuits with you while enjoying the lecture of a major author at the Book Fair. The lecture is about physics and earth science. You certainly need the coffee.

問題 19-21 請參閱下列公告

購物者注意了。因為我們在地下室一樓有書展，我們與其他出版商有合作，給予在倍斯特超市消費超過 500 元者或購書價值 550 元者優惠券。你可以在我們的咖啡店使用此優惠券換餅乾和一杯咖啡。所有的優惠券都會於 12 月 12 日過期。可以帶著這些餅乾一邊享用一邊到書展聽主要作者演講。這個演講是關於物理和地球科學。你確實需要咖啡。

答案：19. C 20. A 21. D

19. 購物者要如何才能得到優惠券？

(A) 去書展。

(B) 在倍斯特超市消費 300 元。

(C) 購買 550 元的書籍。

(D) 購買咖啡和餅乾。

20. 地下一樓有什麼活動嗎？

　　(A) 書展。

　　(B) 咖啡贈品。

　　(C) 超市開張。

　　(D) 書店開張。

21. 購物者能用優惠券兌換何物呢？

　　(A) 蛋糕和咖啡。

　　(B) 免費書籍。

　　(C) 演講門票。

　　(D) 餅乾和咖啡。

 獵豹

19.

・ 聽到對話，馬上鎖定 give consumers who have purchased over 500 dollars at Best supermarket or bought books worthy of 550 dollars a coupon...。有兩種方式，第一種是在超市購物，第二種是在書局購物，因此重點馬上鎖定此兩處，當然，購買金額分別為 500 元和 550 元，也是重點。

20.

・ what is happening 是問發生何事，或是活動。定位關鍵字，basement（地下室），再進行解題。

21.

・ exchange（交換、兌換），先定位關鍵字 coupon，可推知兌換何物。cookies，coffee，lecture 在廣告中都有提及，尤其咖啡出現兩

次，容易混淆判斷力。根據 You get to use the coupon at our coffee shop to exchange for cookies and a cup of coffee，馬上選(D)。

貓頭鷹

19.

・此題屬於細節題，通常問與答之間，前後可找到線索或答案。先定位關鍵字 coupon（優惠券），其後補充說明為(1)bought books worthy of 550 dollars (2) purchased over 500 dollars at Best supermarket。purchase=buy，相當於之意。在超市購買 500 元，在書店購買 550 員都是方法之一。選項(B)在超市購買三百元，是陷阱答案，請粗心的考生入甕。

20.

・讀題時關鍵字，是非常重要的解題技巧。本題屬於開門見山。短講第一句提到：Since we are having a Book Fair on B1...（因為我們在地下一樓有書展），Book Fair（書展），giveaways（贈品活動），都是常見單字。

21.

・細節題的選項描述會以類似詞或是片語出現在選項中，有時觀念不正確，或是理解度不夠，很容易判斷錯誤。「購物者能用優惠券兌換何物呢？」的題目須定位選項描述的關鍵字，同時掃描內文是否有類似字。關鍵字常是表達條件的名詞，例如(A) cakes and coffee (D)cookies and coffee 這兩個答案類似，然而廣告中提到的是 cookie 和 coffee，因此選項(A)是個陷阱。

1　照片描述

2　應答問題

3　簡短對話

4　簡短獨白

模擬試題

浣熊  MP3 138+MP3 140

還可能怎麼問

1. What does the speaker mean when he says "you certainly need the coffee"?

(A) because the Book Fair provides free coffee

(B) because drinking coffee makes you energetic

(C) because the topic is physics and earth science

(D) because you get to exchange the coffee by using the coupon

2. What will happen on Dec 13?

(A) the supermarket will be shut down

(B) B1 will be used for other purposes

(C) major authors won't show up

(D) coupons will expire

中譯與解析

1. 當他說「你確實需要咖啡」，說話者指的是？

(A) 因為書展會提供免費咖啡。

(B) 因為飲用咖啡使你有活力。

(C) 因為主題是物理和地球科學。

(D) 因為你能藉由優惠卷換取咖啡。

2. 12 月 13 日會發生什麼事？

　　(A) 超市將關閉。

　　(B) 地下室 1 樓將用於其他用途。

　　(C) 主要作者將不現身。

　　(D) 優惠卷會失效。

答案：1. C 2. D

1. 題目是當他說「你確實需要咖啡」，說話者指的是？

‧ 選項 A，聽力訊息中未提到提供免費咖啡的訊息，僅提到消費超過某個金額可以以優惠卷兌換咖啡，且這並非題目所問的部分，所以可以排除此選項。選項 B，但聽力訊息中未提到這部分，且這並非題目所問的部分，所以可以排除此選項。選項 C 因為主題是物理和地球科學，此為說話者講這句話的原因，故可以得知答案為選項 C。選項 D，聽力訊息中有提到消費超過某個金額可以以優惠卷兌換咖啡，但這並非題目所問的部分，所以可以排除此選項。

2. 題目是問 12 月 13 日會發生什麼事？

‧ 選項 A, B, C，聽力訊息中未提及，故可以排除。選項 D 優惠卷會失效，聽力訊息中有提到 All coupons will expire on Dec. 12.，故可以得知答案為選項 D。

智慧型手機公司內部談話：電子平台拓銷售

Instructions

❶ 請播放音檔聽下列對話，並完成試題。  MP3 141+MP3 142

❷ 「跟述」練習：寫完試題後請跟著音檔同步跟漸進式做「跟述」練習，提升聽力專注力。

❸ 加碼題：完成❶＋❷步驟後，請再播放音檔寫浣熊試題，掌握其他可能的出題考點，強化應考實力。 MP3 141+MP3 143

22. What do most shareholders feel about Q2 and Q3?

    (A) optimistic

    (B) pessimistic

    (C) excited

    (D) thrilled

23. How has this company been promoting their smartphones?

    (A) on Facebook

    (B) via bestsellers and magazines

    (C) on Twitter

    (D) on newspapers

24. Which of the following might the company do next?

(A) doing research on digital platforms

(B) promoting their products on magazine covers

(C) abandoning smartphone productions

(D) working with a new P.R. company

聽力原文和中譯

Questions 22-24 refer to the following talk

Let me begin today's sales meeting by announcing some feedback from our shareholders. 8 out of 10 shareholders are not optimistic about Q2 and Q3 sales. We need to come up with other ways to promote smartphone sales. Our research team has written a report on whether or not we should continue promoting our smartphones through magazines and bestsellers. It brings little profit for us since most consumers receive information on other digital platforms. We might consider other alternatives, such as Facebook, Twitter, and Instagram.

問題 22-24 請參閱下列談話

讓我為今天的銷售會議做的開頭，藉由公告一些我們股東的回饋。10 位股東中有 8 位對於第二季和第三季的銷售感到不樂觀。我們需要想出其他方法來促銷智慧型手機。我們的研究團隊已經寫了一份報告，關於我們是否該透過我們的雜誌和暢銷書繼續促銷智慧型手機。這替我們帶來很少的利潤，因為大部分的顧客是由其他電子平台收到資訊。我們可能要考慮其他替代方案，例如臉書、推特和 Instagram。

答案：22. B 23. B 24. A

22.大多數股東對 Q2 和 Q3 抱持什麼看法？

(A) 樂觀的。

(B) 悲觀的。

(C) 興奮的。

(D) 激動的。

23.這家公司如何推廣自家的智慧型手機？

(A) 在臉書上。

(B) 透過暢銷書和雜誌。

(C) 在推特上。

(D) 在報紙上。

24.公司下一步可能會做什麼呢？

(A) 在數位平台上進行研究。

(B) 在雜誌封面宣傳產品。

(C) 放棄製造智慧型手機。

(D) 和新的 P.R.公司合作。

 獵豹

22.

· 聽到對話，馬上鎖定 8 out of 10 shareholders are not optimistic about Q2 and Q3 sales... 十個中有八個的寫法為: 8 out of 10。根據 feel <感覺>，得知第一句就提出 10 位股東中有 8 位對於第二季和第三季銷售感到不樂觀(not optimistic)。因此，選項(B)悲觀的，和是不樂觀的類似單字，答案選(B)。

23.

· 首先判斷此題屬於細節題，how 是如何，常考的方式是詢問對方健康狀態，用何種方法，或是搭乘何種交通工具。how 的片語有:how long 多久，how often 多久一次。

會議中提到： We need to come up with other ways to promote smartphone sales. 之後說明：continue promoting our

Unit 8　智慧型手機公司內部談話：電子平台拓銷售

1 照片描述

2 應答問題

3 簡短對話

4 簡短獨白

模擬試題

smartphones through magazines and bestsellers，因此得知目前的推銷方式是(C)via bestsellers and magazines。

24.

・看到題目目光直接鎖定在 We might consider other alternatives...這句話的含意。alternative 是「替代」的意思。掃描替代雜誌行銷的類似詞，定位在最後一句的 Facebook，Twitter 等等平台，可以推知下一步即將進行跟此有關之事，會進行研究，看是否有利宣傳。

貓頭鷹

22.

・此題屬於單字題，題目中出現的單字，選項中以類似字呈現。第一句最後一個幾個字：not optimistic about Q2 and Q3 sales，not optimistic about，對…感到不樂觀。pessimistic 是指「悲觀」，因此語意最接近，故選(B) pessimistic。

23.

・細節題的選項描述會以類似詞在文章中出現。細節題須先注意描述裡的關鍵字。例如：magazines 雜誌、Facebook 臉書、Twitter 推特，and Instagram 這幾種都是會議中提到的宣傳方式。重點是文章的中間提到：whether or not we should continue promoting our smartphones through magazines and bestsellers，表示對於目前的行銷方式有疑問，想進行改變。

24.

・此題是推測題。需要先理解目前公司的宣傳方式，由於不滿意，推知想改變。此題和宣傳有關，分析以下選項的錯誤原因為何：（B）promoting their products on magazine covers 是目前的宣傳，所

以錯誤 (C) abandoning smartphone productions 目前仍製造手機，未放棄。(D) working with a new P.R. company 沒提過，因此建議不選。

 浣熊  MP3 141+MP3 143

還可能怎麼問

1. What type of business is being discussed?

(A) a smartphone startup

(B) an on-line publishing

(C) a research center

(D) an advertising company

2. Which is NOT mentioned as a replacement to boost sales?

(A) facebook

(B) twitter

(C) instagram

(D) magazine

中譯與解析

1. 正在敘述的是哪一種公司？

(A) 智慧型手機新創公司。

(B) 線上出版商。

(C) 研究中心。

(D) 廣告公司。

2. 關於提高銷售的替代方案，下列哪個未提及？

(A) 臉書。

(B) 推特。

(C) instagram。

(D) 雜誌。

答案：1. A 2. D

1. 題目是問正在敘述的是哪一種公司？先從四個選項分別來看。

· 選項 A，聽力訊息中有提到 We need to come up with other ways to promote smartphone sales.，這句和其他聽力訊息都在講關於智慧型手機的討論，故可以得知答案為選項 A。選項 B，聽力訊息中未提到這部分，所以可以排除此選項。選項 C，聽力訊息中有提到研究團隊，但所有敘述並沒有關於公司是研究中心，所以可以排除此選項。選項 D，聽力訊息中有提到「因為大部分的顧客是由其他電子平台收到資訊。我們可能要考慮其他替代方案，例如臉書、推特和 Instagram。」，但這是以廣告等增加利潤的方式，公司並非廣告公司，故可以排除。

2. 題目是問關於提高銷售的替代方案，下列哪個未提及？先從四個選項分別來看。

· 選項 A, B, C，聽力訊息中有提到，題目是問未提及，故可以排除。選項 D，聽力訊息中未提到，故可以得知答案為選項 D。

公司談話：三十週年慶
之這次沒魚可吃

🔍 Instructions

❶ 請播放音檔聽下列對話，並完成試題。 🎧 MP3 144+MP3 145

❷ 「跟述」練習：寫完試題後請跟著音檔同步跟漸進式做「跟述」練習，提升聽力專注力。

❸ 加碼題：完成❶+❷步驟後，請再播放音檔寫浣熊試題，掌握其他可能的出題考點，強化應考實力。 🎧 MP3 144+MP3 146

25. What is Linda in charge of?

(A) warehouse and distribution

(B) catering service

(C) barbecue equipment

(D) making beverages

26. What will Ken do according to the speaker?

(A) He will give everyone the direction to Best Park.

(B) He will prepare and send the beverages and barbecue materials.

(C) He will order foods and beverages from outside.

(D) He will drive his co-workers to Best Park.

27. Which of the followings is NOT TRUE about the barbecue?

(A) The barbecue materials come from the company products.

(B) It will be held in a park.

(C) Fish will be provided.

(D) It will be held on the company's 30th anniversary.

聽力原文和中譯

Questions 25-27 refer to the following talk

Hello everyone, my name is Linda. I'm in charge of the company warehouse and distribution. You all know tomorrow is our annual barbecue, and it's our 30th anniversary. This year, we are not ordering foods and beverages from outside. I was told that we will use our company products at the barbecue tomorrow. I will have Ken, who is our supermarket chain manager, prepare meat, beverages, wine and other related stuff, and ship them to Best Park. However, this year we won't be having fish. It's sort of in short supply, just wanted you to know that.

問題 25-27 請參閱下列談話

各位您好，我的名字是琳達。我們掌管了公司倉庫和配送。你們都知道明天會是我們的年度烤肉，而且這是我們 30 周年紀念日。今年我們不會再從外面訂購食物和飲料了。我被告知我們明天烤肉會用公司產品。我會請肯，我們的超市連鎖經理準備肉品、飲品、酒類和其他相關的物品，然後運送至倍斯特公園。然而，今年我們不會有魚。只是想要你們知道，它有點短缺。

答案：25. A 26. B 27 C

25. 琳達負責哪方面？

(A) 倉庫和配送。

(B) 餐飲服務。

(C) 烤肉設備。

(D) 製作飲料。

26. 根據說話者，肯將被分配做什麼事？

(A) 他將指引大家到倍斯特公園。

(B) 他將準備運送飲料和烤肉材料。

(C) 他會從外面訂購食物和飲料。

(D) 他會開車送同事到倍斯特公園。

27. 關於烤肉，下列選項何者有誤？

(A) 烤肉材料來自公司產品。

(B) 將在公園舉辦。

(C) 將供應魚類。

(D) 將在公司成立 30 週年之際舉辦。

獵豹

25.

．聽到對話，馬上鎖定 my name is Linda. I'm in charge of the company warehouse and distribution...。 根據自我介紹，馬上抓住後面的重點，是倉庫和配送。

26.

．從 Ken 這個名字，定位重點句。最後兩句說明: I will have Ken... prepare meat, beverages, wine and other related stuff，因此 Ken 負責飲料和肉類等方面的運送。

27.

．首先判斷此題屬於細節題，一邊聽一邊對照選項的關鍵字，(A) from the company products，(B) held in a park，(C) Fish... (D) held on the company's 30th anniversary.。其中魚類表示不供應，因此答案

為(C) Fish will be provided.。鎖定重點句：this year we won't be having fish.（今年我們不會有魚）。

貓頭鷹

25.

· 此題屬於細節題，在 Linda 的自我介紹開頭馬上有交代她負責的是 warehouse and distribution。be in charge of 是指「負責…」是常見片語。考生請掌握這個片語，非常實用。charge 還可當<索費>之意，是很常見的單字。warehouse（倉庫）， distribution（配送）。

26.

· 讀題時先定位重點人事物，人名是解題關鍵字。此題是細節題。肯負責的工作是準備肉類，飲料，酒類和相關物品，因此推知是 beverages and barbecue materials，因為 meat 是屬於烤肉的重要物品，故答案為(B) He will prepare and send the beverages and barbecue materials. 他將準備運送飲料和烤肉材料。

27.

· 選出正確或錯誤選項的題目，通常範圍比較大，描述會分布在文章各處。「下列何者為真或錯」的細節題須先定位選項描述裡的關鍵字，同時掃描文章裡是出現。本題沒有陷阱，因此判斷時可以很清楚。再加上答案出現在文章中，請考生把握。be held 是「舉辦」，舉辦派對或是活動之意。

浣熊 MP3 144+MP3 146

還可能怎麼問

1. **Who most likely are the listeners?**

   (A) local residents who like barbecue

   (B) staff from Marketing and Sales Division

   (C) park rangers who hates fish

   (D) corporate investors who enjoy wine

2. **Which products will not be provided during the barbecue this year?**

   (A) tuna and salmon

   (B) coke and soda

   (C) beer and vodka

   (D) meat and wine

中譯與解析

1. 誰最有可能是聽者？

   (A) 喜歡烤肉的當地居民。

   (B) 行銷和銷售部門的職員們。

   (C) 討厭魚的公園管理者。

   (D) 喜愛飲酒的公司投資者。

2. 今年哪項產品在烤肉期間不會提供？

   (A) 鮪魚和鮭魚。

   (B) 可樂和蘇打。

   (C) 啤酒和伏特加。

(D) 肉和酒。

答案：1. B 2. A

1. 題目是問誰最有可能是聽者？

· 選項 A，聽力訊息中有提到烤肉且這是主要聽力訊息，但未提到「當地居民」，所以可以排除此選項。選項 B，聽力訊息中其實是某間公司在講述公司所辦的活動，即有可能是琳達對這個部門講得一段談話，所以可以得知答案為選項 B。選項 C，聽力訊息中有提到魚，但未提到「討厭魚」和「公園管理者」，所以可以排除此選項。選項 D，聽力訊息中有提到酒，但未提到「公司投資客」和「喜愛飲酒」的訊息，所以可以排除此選項。

2. 題目是問今年哪項產品在烤肉期間不會提供？先從四個選項分別來看。

· 選項 A，聽力訊息中有提到 However, this year we won't be having fish. It's sort of in short supply，鮪魚和鮭魚即魚的同義表達，而題目是問不會提供，所以可以得知答案為選項 A。選項 B，聽力訊息中有提到飲料，可樂和蘇打即飲料的同義表達，而題目是問不會提供，故可以排除此選項。選項 C，聽力訊息中有提到酒，啤酒和伏特加即酒的同義表達，而題目是問不會提供，故可以排除此選項。選項 D，聽力訊息中有提到肉跟酒，題目是問不會提供，故可以排除此選項。

Unit 10
公司談話：新人剛做幾天就被叫去法務部門，被嚇得不要不要的

Instructions

❶ 請播放音檔聽下列對話，並完成試題。 ⊙ MP3 147＋MP3 148

❷ 「跟述」練習：寫完試題後請跟著音檔同步跟漸進式做「跟述」練習，提升聽力專注力。

❸ 加碼題：完成❶＋❷步驟後，請再播放音檔寫浣熊試題，掌握其他可能的出題考點，強化應考實力。 ⊙ MP3 147＋MP3 149

28. **Why does the speaker ask these people to go to the Legal Department?**

　　(A) to seek legal consultation

　　(B) to talk to the new lawyer

　　(C) to go under a legal investigation

　　(D) to get their bonuses

29. **What does the man mean by saying, "you all have pretty well settled in here"?**

　　(A) You look pretty.

　　(B) You make this place pretty.

　　(C) You adjust to this place well.

　　(D) This place does not look pretty.

30. Who might be the speaker?

(A) a supervisor

(B) a lawyer

(C) an attorney

(D) an accountant

聽力原文和中譯

Questions 28-30 refer to the following talk

Hello everyone. How's everything going around here? It seems that you all have pretty well settled in here. All of you smiling. But here is other news. You all need to go to the Legal Department right now. Shocked and amazed? Don't worry it's your signing bonuses. I've accountants ready for all signing bonuses. You'll see that it's in your envelope with your names on the cover of the envelope. I do need you to double check the money before you leave the Legal Department. After signing on the computer screen, we do need your fingerprints as well. That's all.

問題 28-30 請參閱下列談話

各位你好。這裡的每件事都還好吧？似乎你們都適應下來了。你們都在微笑。但是這是另一件事了。你們現在都需要到法務部門。感到震驚且驚訝嗎？別擔心這是你們的簽約獎金。我有請會計師們將所有簽約金準備好了。你可以看到它在你們的信封裡，有你們的名字在每個信封上。我需要你們離開法務部門前再確認下金額。在電腦螢幕上簽名後，我們也需要你們的指紋。大概是這樣。

答案：28. D 29. C 30. A

28. 發言者為何要求這些人去法律部門？

(A) 尋求法律諮詢。

(B) 與新律師對話。

(C) 進行法律調查。

(D) 獲得簽約金。

29. 男子表示"**all have pretty well settled**"，其含意為何？

(A) 你們看起來很漂亮。

(B) 你們讓此地變美。

(C) 你們很適應這個地方。

(D) 這個地方看起來不太漂亮。

30. 發言者的身分可能為何？？

(A) 主管。

(B) 律師。

(C) 律師。

(D) 會計師。

 獵豹

28.

．聽到對話，馬上鎖定 You all need to go to the Legal Department right now...。根據 bonus（獎金），可以推知是好事，到法務部門應該是不是負面的原因。signing bonus 是簽約金。

29.

．首先判斷此題考片語。看到題目，目光直接鎖定 pretty settle，是指「相當適應」。pretty 在此是副詞，指「相當，非常」修飾 settle。四個選項中，除了答案(C)，其他三個選項的 pretty 都是陷阱字，讓題目增加難度。

30.

．who 是詢問某人關係，職稱，或身分。因此，通常這種題目不會直接表明，需從短講中的敘述，聽到蛛絲馬跡。目光直接鎖定在 After

Unit 10　公司談話：新人剛做幾天就被叫去法務部門，被嚇得不要不要的

1 照片描述

2 應答問題

3 簡短對話

4 簡短獨白

模擬試題

signing on the computer screen, we do need your fingerprints as well. 在電腦螢幕上簽名後，我們也需要你們的指紋。That's all. 最「大概是這樣」。從以上的線索，推測此人身分應該是主管或上司。

 貓頭鷹

28.

・此題屬於細節題。why 用來詢問原因，因此從文章中，找出真正原因為何。此類型題目，難以猜測，必須先對整段文意理解。因為提到 Legal Department right（法務部），通常的答案都和律師有關。因此，很容易選錯。本題在法務部後，馬上說明原因：it's your signing bonuses. I've accountants ready for all signing bonuses.（這是你們的簽約獎金。我有請會計師們將所有簽約金準備好了。）

29.

・此題考點較複雜，測試 pretty 當形容詞和副詞時的意思，也測試 settle，適應的類似詞，adjust 的意思。請看看四個選項。(A) You look pretty. pretty 當形容詞，漂亮。(B) You make this place pretty. pretty 是形容詞，漂亮。(C) You adjust to this place well. 適應。(D) This place does not look pretty. pretty 形容詞，漂亮。

30.

・此題是細節題。需要從整篇文章中歸納出來，才能推測出身分。文章中他提出：You all need to go to the Legal Department right now.; Don't worry it's your signing bonuses. I've accountants ready for all signing bonuses. I do need you to double check the money before you leave the Legal Department. 根據這幾句話判斷，此人有一定地位，比起律師，主管機率更大。

浣熊 🎧 MP3 147+MP3 149

還可能怎麼問

1. Who most likely are the listeners?

(A) accountants

(B) attorneys

(C) interviewees

(D) new recruits

2. What will listeners most likely do next?

(A) talk to accountants

(B) ask for more singing bonuses

(C) sign their name and press their thumbs on the screen

(D) forge a signature

中譯與解析

1. 誰最有可能是聽者？

(A) 會計師。

(B) 律師。

(C) 面試者。

(D) 新僱人員。

2. 聽者接下來最有可能做什麼？

(A) 與會計師談話。

(B) 要求更多的簽約獎金。

(C) 簽他們的名字且將他們的拇指壓在螢幕上。

(D) 偽造簽名。

答案：1. D 2. C

1. 題目是問誰最有可能是聽者？先從四個選項分別來看。

・選項 A，聽力訊息中有提到 I've accountants ready for all signing bonuses.，但這並非是對會計師講的話，也要注意不要被 accountants 干擾了，所以可以排除此選項。選項 B，聽力訊息中有提到 You all need to go to the Legal Department right now. 和 before you leave the Legal Department，Legal Department 出現兩次，但是這不是對 attorney 說的話，訊息中也未提到 attorney，所以可以排除此選項。 選項 C，signing bonuses 跟聽力訊息 It seems that you all have pretty well settled in here.等等都表示了，這是對公司已經錄取的人講的話，所以不可能是面試者，所以可以排除此選項。選項 D，此為聽力訊息中所表達的意思，公司在錄取後所發簽約獎金，故可以得知答案為選項 D。

2. 題目是問聽者接下來最有可能做什麼？

・選項 A，聽力訊息中有提到 I've accountants ready for all signing bonuses.，其實後面沒有訊息指出會再跟會計師進一步的談話，故可以排除此選項。選項 B，這也不太可能是接下來聽者會做得部分，故可以排除此選項。選項 C，聽力訊息中有提到 After signing on the computer screen, we do need your fingerprints as well.，這極可能是接下來聽者會做得事，所以可以得知答案為選項 C。選項 D，聽力訊息中有提到 signing 但未提到偽造或偽造簽名，且不太可能是接下來會發生得事，故可以排除此選項。

Unit 11
新聞報導：颱風來真的不是做科學專題的好時候

 **Instructions**

❶ 請播放音檔聽下列對話，並完成試題。 🎧 MP3 150+MP3 151

❷ 「跟述」練習：寫完試題後請跟著音檔同步跟漸進式做「跟述」練習，提升聽力專注力。

❸ 加碼題：完成❶+❷步驟後，請再播放音檔寫浣熊試題，掌握其他可能的出題考點，強化應考實力 🎧 MP3 150+MP3 152

 31. Why does the speaker say, "For those who are at this sandy beach, you probably need to leave"?

(A) because the beach is not clean

(B) because the beach is closed by the government

(C) because a typhoon is approaching the beach

(D) because it's harmful to one's health if one stays at a sandy place

 32. Which of the following is most likely the reason that the speaker says, "I guess I've got another excuse to buy a new one"?

(A) She wants to buy a new swimming suit.

(B) Her umbrella was broken.

(C) She forgot to bring her umbrella.

(D) Her raincoat was broken.

33. Which of the followings is most likely happening as the speaker speaks?

(A) They are having torrential rain.

(B) Many people are swimming in the ocean.

(C) Umbrellas are on sale.

(D) Raincoats are in high demand.

聽力原文和中譯

Questions 31-33 refer to the following news report

I don't understand why we're having an early typhoon in March. As you can see, with the typhoon coming soon, it's pretty windy out there. My umbrella is... oops... I guess I've got another excuse to buy a new one. It's really pouring here. I really need to get my raincoat. For those who are at the sandy beach, you probably need to leave, since most residents are evacuating according to our early report. It really is not the time to do your science project. For the safety's sake, stay indoors probably in the basement, and this is Jane at Best beach. Now back to our news anchor Cindy Chen.

問題 31-33 請參閱下列新聞報導

我不知道為什麼我們在三月會有早颱。你可以看到，隨著颱風逼近，這裡風超大。我的雨傘…糟了…我想我有理由可以買隻新的了。這裡真的雨降好大。我真的需要拿我的雨衣了。對於在沙灘的你們，可能需要離開了，因為根據我們稍早的報導，大部分的居民正在撤離了。這真的不是做科學專題的時刻。由於安全的考量，待在室內，盡可能像是地下室，這是簡在倍斯特海灘的播報。現在把新聞還給新聞主播辛蒂·陳。

答案：31. C 32. B 33. A

31. 新聞報導說「對於在沙灘的你們,可能需要離開了」,是什麼原因?

(A) 因為沙灘不乾淨。

(B) 因為沙灘被政府關閉。

(C) 因為颱風正逼近沙灘。

(D) 因為如果人待在沙地上,對身體有害。

 32. 談話者說「我想我有理由可以買把新的了」,下列那個選項是最有可能的原因?

(A) 她想買件新的泳衣。

(B) 她的雨傘壞了。

(C) 她忘了帶傘。

(D) 她的雨衣破了。

33. 下列選項何者最有可能發生在談話者發言時?

(A) 他們遭受暴雨侵襲。

(B) 很多人在海裡游泳。

(C) 雨傘正在特價。

(D) 雨衣需求量很大。

31.

· 聽到對話,馬上鎖定 As you can see, with typhoon coming soon, it's pretty windy out there...。

· 根據 typhoon is coming(颱風來了),以及風很大,推知不適合戶

外運動，會有危險性，故推知 you probably need to leave?是因為颱風接近的關係。

32.

· 從 My umbrella is... oops，短短幾個字，可以推測出答案。oops 有糟糕之意，因此推測出雨傘負面的結果。從第三句 My umbrella is... oops，後面接 I guess I've another excuse to buy a new one（我想我有理由可以買把新的了）這句話推知雨傘可能無法使用，壞掉機率比較大。

33.

· 首先判斷此題屬於細節及推測題，發言者説颱風逼近，風很大，希望大家遠離海灘，根據此段話推測，大雨最有可能，再找出選項中表達大雨的單字或片語。It's really pouring here.是下大雨之意。torrential rain 是類似詞，故正確選項是(A)。

貓頭鷹

31.

· 此題屬於推測題，題目會透過暗示，讓考生推測出答案。題目：For those who are at this sandy beach, you probably need to leave? who 是關係代名詞，those 是指在沙灘的那些人。前面提到，with typhoon coming soon（隨著颱風逼近），因此希望那些人離開沙灘。

32.

· 讀題時先定位關鍵字詞是重要的解題技巧，因為關鍵字後常有解題線索，如 oops 就是解題重點。選項中(B) Her umbrella was broken. (D) Her raincoat was broken. 兩個類似考法，不過由於提到

umbrella，因此得知答案是(B) Her umbrella was broken.。

33.

· 推測題的答案，通常不會重複短講內一樣的單字，常以同義字替換短講的關鍵字。

· 「下列最有可能發生」的題目，通常須要先理解細節，再以換句話說的技巧，找出選項中最接近對話細節的詞彙。另外也可用刪去法將可能是正確選項的範圍縮小。如： (B) Many people are swimming in the ocean.已經通知大家離開，沒人游泳。(C) Umbrellas are on sale.只提到雨傘壞了，沒提到是否特價。(D) Raincoats are in high demand. 雨衣需求量沒提到。

 浣熊 ⊙ MP3 150+MP3 152

還可能怎麼問

1. **What is the tone of the reporter when she says "I've another excuse to buy a new one"?**

(A) half-joking

(B) miserable

(C) angry

(D) sad

2. **According to the reporter, what are listeners able to do?**

(A) do the science project by calculating rainfall

(B) capture a phenomenal view at the beach

(C) seize the moment to sell umbrellas

(D) stay indoors, probably underground

中譯與解析

1. 當她說「我有另一個理由買新的了」，播報者的語調是？

(A) 半開玩笑的。

(B) 悲慘的。

(C) 生氣的。

(D) 傷心的。

2. 根據播報員，聽者們可以做什麼？

(A) 藉由計算降雨量來做科學計劃。

(B) 捕捉海灘驚人的畫面。

(C) 抓住販賣雨傘的時刻。

(D) 待在室內，可能是待在地下室。

答案：1. A 2. D

1. 題目是問當她說「我有另一個理由買新的了」，播報者的語調是？

· 選項 A 半開玩笑的，這個題目需要更多的推論跟語感來做答，其實播報者是屬於比較幽默類型的人，所以是半調侃說這樣自己就能有藉口來買隻傘，所以是半開玩笑的語調，故可以得知答案為選項 A。

2. 題目是問根據播報員，聽者們可以做什麼？

· 選項 A，聽力訊息中有提到 It really is not the time to do your science project.，但未提到降雨量，且這不是聽到播報員播報後會做的事，故可以排除此選項。選項 B，聽力訊息中未提到這部分，故可以排除此選項。 選項 C，聽力訊息中未提到這部分，故可以排除此選項。選項 D，可能是待在地下室，聽力訊息中有提到 For safety's sake, stay indoors probably in the basement，basement 即 underground 的同義表達，所以可以得知答案為選項 D。

Unit 12
新聞報導：千鈞一髮，鯨魚差點成為棕熊的餐點

structions

❶ 請播放音檔聽下列對話，並完成試題。 🎧 MP3 153+MP3 154

❷ 「跟述」練習：寫完試題後請跟著音檔同步跟漸進式做「跟述」練習，提升聽力專注力。

❸ 加碼題：完成❶＋❷步驟後，請再播放音檔寫浣熊試題，掌握其他可能的出題考點，強化應考實力。 🎧 MP3 153+MP3 155

34. **Which of the following is NOT covered by the news report?**

    (A) a huge machine

    (B) a whale

    (C) water sport

    (D) the video about saving a whale

35. **Which of the following is the closest in meaning to "exhilarating"?**

    (A) very terrifying

    (B) very excited

    (C) very disappointing

    (D) very exciting

36. **What might happen this weekend?**

(A) There might be a show at the department store.

(B) The saved whale might be returned to the ocean.

(C) A typhoon might hit the place.

(D) It might rain.

聽力原文和中譯

Questions 34-36 refer to the following news report

I'm Mary Cheng and this is Jane Chen. First, we're going to give you an update on some exhilarating news. The whale that was found in shallow water has been saved. At least, he won't be the meal for brown bears. Let's see the video. Now back to domestic news. There is a giant automatic machine at Best Department. Wow, that certainly arouses lots of crowds. That's usually how things go. Coming up, the weather report will tell you whether we will have rainfall this weekend.

問題 34-36 請參閱下列新聞報導

我是馬克·鄭。首先我們將給你關於最令人感到興奮的新聞的更新。被發現在淺水水域擱淺的鯨魚已被救了。至少他不會是棕熊的食物了。讓我們看下視頻。現在回到國內新聞。在倍斯特百貨公司有個巨型販售機器。哇！這真的引來不少人潮。事情發展通常是這樣。接下來是，我們的天氣預測會告訴你這週是否會有降雨。

答案：34. C 35. D 36. D

34. 關於新聞報導內容，下列何者不包括在內？

　　(A) 巨型機器。

　　(B) 鯨魚。

　　(C) 水上運動。

　　(D) 拯救鯨魚的影片。

35.下列哪項，何者與**"exhilarating"**的含意最接近？

　　(A) 非常恐怖的。

(B) 非常興奮的。

(C) 令人非常失望的。

(D) 令人非常興奮的、刺激的。

36. 本週末將會發生何事？

(A) 百貨公司可能會有表演。

(B) 被救回的鯨魚可能會回到海洋。

(C) 可能會有颱風。

(D) 可能會降雨。

 獵豹

34.

・news report（新聞報導），cover （包含）。題目為 Which of the followings is NOT...，注意是否定。根據 news，找出新聞中的重點：whale，giant automatic machine，video，因此選項(C) 水上運動，並沒提到。

35.

・聽到短講，馬上鎖定 First, we're going to give you an update on some exhilarating news.。First, we're going to give you an update on some exhilarating news. 後面出現鯨魚獲救的消息，推知此新聞偏向激勵人心方面。

36.

・聽到短講，馬上鎖定 Coming up, the weather report will tell you whether we will have rainfall this weekend.。根據時間點 this weekend 及 rainfall，降雨，馬上選(D) It might rain，可能會下雨。

Unit 12 新聞報導：千鈞一髮，鯨魚差點成為棕熊的餐點

1 照片描述

2 應答問題

3 簡短對話

4 簡短獨白

模擬試題

貓頭鷹

34.

· 此題屬於細節題，詢問新聞沒報導的部分。新聞中提 The whale that was found in shallow water has been saved. 被發現在淺水水域擱淺的鯨魚已被救了。Let's see the video. 讓我們看下視頻。There is a giant automatic machine at Best Department. 在倍斯特百貨公司有個巨型販售機器。內容沒有提到水上運動。

35.

· 本題考單字題。可以由前後文，推知此單字的意思。exhilarating 是（令人興奮的）。題目中，選項(A)恐怖的，選項(C)失望的，可先刪除。選項(B)excited，本身有「興奮」的意思。不過通常主詞為人，表示某人感到興奮，振奮。選項(D)exciting 指「有興奮的，刺激的」，通常用來形容事或物。如:the game is exciting 這場比賽很刺激。

36.

· 本題考細節題。天氣預報是多益聽力的必考主題，考生只要熟悉常用的氣候現象的單字，並掃描哪個選項有類似描述，極容易得分。注意此篇先報導關於鯨魚，接著提及巨型機器的新聞，直到 Coming up，接下來，這一轉折詞才暗示考生記者要轉換話題，除了轉折詞很重要，the weather report 也是關鍵線索字。(A)及(B)是陷阱選項，雖然whale，department store 都是新聞提及的單字，但不符合題目問的時間點 this weekend。(C)的 typhoon，颱風，全篇未提。

浣熊  MP3 153+MP3 155

還可能怎麼問

 1. What does the reporter mean when he says "At least, he won't be the meal for brown bears."?

(A) because he is also a marine biologist

(B) because the whale will be immune from being eaten by brown bears

(C) because those bears will have to find another food resources

(D) because those bears can't be opportunistic all the time

 2. Which of the following is the international news?

(A) brown bears eating the whale carcass

(B) a crowd of people at the department store

(C) a rescued whale at shallow water

(D) weather report

中譯與解析

1. 當播報員說「至少他不會是棕熊的食物了」他指的是什麼？

(A) 因為他也是海洋生物學者。

(B) 因為鯨魚將免於被棕熊食用。

(C) 因為那些熊將會尋找其他食物來源。

(D) 因為那些熊無法總是當機會主義者。

2. 下列哪個項目是國際新聞？

(A) 棕熊吃鯨魚屍體。

(B) 在百貨公司的一群人。

(C) 在淺水水域獲救的鯨魚。

(D) 天氣預報。

答案：1. B 2. C

1. **題目是問當播報員說「至少他不會是棕熊的食物了」他指的是什麼？**

· 選項 A，聽力訊息中未提到播報員是海洋生物學者，所以可以排除此選項。

· 選項 B 因為鯨魚將免於被棕熊食用，聽力訊息中有提到 The whale that was found in shallow water has been saved. At least, he won't be the meal for brown bears.，won't be the meal for brown bears 即 will be immune from being eaten by brown bears 的同義表達，故可以得知答案為選項 B。選項 C，聽力訊息中未提到那些熊將會尋找其他食物來源，所以可以排除此選項。選項 D，聽力訊息中未提到那些熊無法總是當機會主義者，所以可以排除此選項。

2. **題目是問下列哪個項目是國際新聞？**

· 從 Now get back to domestic news 聽力訊息作區隔，可以得知在這之前的鯨魚擱淺獲救的新聞最可能是國際新聞，而接下來的幾則都是國內新聞了，可以得知答案為選項 C。

Unit 13
新聞報導：雨季一來，路況百出

Instructions

❶ 請播放音檔聽下列對話，並完成試題。 🎧 MP3 156+MP3 157

❷ 「跟述」練習：寫完試題後請跟著音檔同步跟漸進式做「跟述」練習，提升聽力專注力。

❸ 加碼題：完成❶＋❷步驟後，請再播放音檔寫浣熊試題，掌握其他可能的出題考點，強化應考實力。 🎧 MP3 156+MP3 158

37. What happened in tunnel A?

　　(A) Some car accidents happened.

　　(B) It was too foggy in tunnel A.

　　(C) It was heavily jammed.

　　(D) Some landslides occurred.

38. What are car drivers advised to do?

　　(A) to take the bus

　　(B) to take a different route

　　(C) to join a carpool

　　(D) to take the subway

39. What is wrong with the airport?

　　(A) It's shot down permanently.

(B) There are not enough runways to accommodate incoming flights.

(C) It's too old and needs refurbishment.

(D) It's shut down due to the weather condition.

聽力原文和中譯

Questions 37-39 refer to the following news report

Morning it's the morning news. First, the important news about tunnel A. There've been several landsides happening, so it's officially closed. Car drivers are suggested to take tunnel B instead or take Road 555 through the super high way. This problem won't be fixed until weather is more stable, which according to our newsman it's gonna last until next Friday, and of course it's our rainy season. Next is also related to our transportation. Due to heavy rain and fog, the airport will be temporarily shut down for a while. For more flight information please visit our website. Front page.

問題 37-39 請參閱下列新聞報導

早安，這是早間新聞。首先，最重要的新聞是關於隧道 A。持續有幾個山崩的狀況發生。所以隧道正式關閉了。建議開車的駕駛透過高速公路行駛隧道 B 或公路 555 號。根據我們新聞播報人員，此問題在天氣較穩定前不會修復好，且情況會持續到下週五，當然這是我們的雨季。下則報導是有關於我們的交通運輸。由於大雨傾盆，機場會暫時關閉。更多航班資訊，請瀏覽我們的網站。首頁。

答案：37. D 38. B 39. D

37. 隧道 A 發生什麼事？

(A) 發生車禍。

(B) 隧道 A 內濃霧瀰漫。

(C) 塞車嚴重。

(D) 發生山崩的狀況。

38. 汽車駕駛被建議做何事？

(A) 搭公車。

(B) 開不同路線。

(C) 加入共乘。

(D) 搭地鐵。

39. 機場發生什麼事？

(A) 永久關閉。

(B) 跑道不夠安排航班。

(C) 太老舊需要翻新。

(D) 由於天氣狀況而關閉。

獵豹

37.

· 聽到對話，馬上鎖定 First, the important news about tunnel A. There's been several landsides happening,...。根據第一句，可得知答案。tunnel 是指隧道，本題的核心單字。landside 是指山崩。

38.

· 從 advise（建議），來判斷答案。新聞中有提到：Car drivers are suggested to take tunnel B instead or take Road 555...（建議開車的駕駛透過高速公路行駛隧道 B 或公路 555 號...）。advise 的同義字是 suggest，雖然新聞中沒提到 advise，但由 suggest 來判斷建議事項。

39.

· 首先判斷主題是 airport，找出新聞中和機場相關的事件。倒數第二句

提到：Due to heavy rain and fog, the airport will be temporarily shut down for a while. 因此推知答案為(D) 由於天氣狀況(不佳)而關閉。due to 是指由於，for a while 是指一段時間。

貓頭鷹

37.

・此題屬於開門見山題，題目的答案通常在文章中的第一二句。看到 tunnel A，後面句子會補充說明此發生之 事。landside（山崩），由於山崩，所以決定 closed（關閉），因此答案為(D)Some landslides occurred.發生山崩的狀況。

38.

・讀題時先定位關鍵字詞是重要的解題技巧，因為關鍵字後常有解題線索，如 take tunnel B instead 就是解題重點。此題是細節題。Car drivers are suggested: (1) take tunnel B instead (2) take Road 555 through super high way. 建議走其他隧道，以及開到高速公路，雖然沒直接說搭不同路線，然而可以判斷出來答案為(B)。

39.

・細節題的選項描述會以不同句型或單字將意思敘述重述。新聞中提到：Due to heavy rain and fog... 因此機場暫時關閉。due to，由於，後面接原因。heavy rain and fog 指「傾盆大雨和霧」。選項中未出現此單字。因此找出最接近的原因是 the weather（天氣）問題。

1 照片描述

2 應答問題

3 簡短對話

4 簡短獨白

模擬試題

浣熊 🎧 MP3 156+MP3 158

還可能怎麼問

1. **According to the reporter, what are car drivers who take Tunnel A able to do?**

   (A) wait until the weather is more stable

   (B) inform other drivers that there're several landsides

   (C) take Road 555 if necessary

   (D) take tunnel B through super high way

2. **When will the tunnel A problem be fixed?**

   (A) after the rainy season

   (B) after the fog is clear

   (C) after the removal of rocks and stones

   (D) probably next Friday when the weather is more steady

中譯與解析

1. **根據播報員，行駛隧道 A 的開車駕駛可以做什麼？**

   (A) 等直到天氣較穩定。

   (B) 通知其他駕駛有幾個山崩發生。

   (C) 如果必要的話行駛公路 555 號。

   (D) 透過高速公路行駛隧道 B。

2. **隧道 A 的問題何時會修復呢？**

   (A) 在雨季後。

   (B) 在霧散去時。

(C) 在岩石和石頭移除後。

(D) 可能是下週五，當天氣較穩定後。

答案：1. D 2. D

1.　題目是問根據播報員，行駛隧道 A 的開車駕駛可以做什麼？

· 選項 A，聽力訊息中有提到 This problem won't be fixed until weather is more stable，但這指的是問題修復，題目是問在行駛隧道 A 的開車駕駛可以做什麼，所以別被干擾到，且行駛的駕駛不可能等到修復，而是必須改道等等的，所以可以排除此選項。選項 B，聽力訊息中有提到 several landsides happening 但沒有提到要通知其他駕駛，所以別被 several landsides 干擾到，所以可以排除此選項。選項 C，聽力訊息中有提到 take Road 555 through super high way 是解決辦法之一，但題目選項多了 if necessary，已經公布無法通行了不可能是如果必要的話要改道，所以可以排除此選項。選項 D，聽力訊息中有提到 take tunnel B instead or take Road 555 through super high way.此選項為其中的解決辦法之一，故可以得知答案為選項 D。

2.　題目是問隧道 A 的問題何時會修復呢？

· 選項 A，聽力訊息中有提到 of course it's our rainy season，也有提到修復的可能日期，但是無法推斷出雨季有多長和修復日即是雨季後，故可以排除此選項。選項 B，聽力訊息中有提到 Due to heavy rain and fog, the airport will be temporarily shut down for a while，但未表明說霧何時會散去，故可以排除此選項。 選項 C，聽力訊息中有提到 several landsides，但沒有提到岩石和石頭和移除等的訊息，僅有何時會修復可以通行的訊息，故可以排除此選項。選項 D，當天氣較穩定後，且非女子所擔心的部分，所以可以得知答案為選項 D。

1
照片描述

2
應答問題

3
簡短對話

4
簡短獨白

模擬試題

航空公司公告：
班次大亂，好險有補償

🔍 Instructions

❶ 請播放音檔聽下列對話，並完成試題。 🎧 MP3 159+MP3 160

❷ 「跟述」練習：寫完試題後請跟著音檔同步跟漸進式做「跟述」練習，提升聽力專注力。

❸ 加碼題：完成❶＋❷步驟後，請再播放音檔寫浣熊試題，掌握其他可能的出題考點，強化應考實力。 🎧 MP3 159+MP3 161

40. What is the problem with flight CX1098 from Frankfurt to Holland?

(A) It is cancelled.

(B) It is delayed.

(C) It is under maintenance.

(D) It is overbooked.

41. What happened to CV2687 and CW1098?

(A) They are overbooked.

(B) They are delayed.

(C) They are cancelled.

(D) They are under maintenance.

42. Why is the word "coupons" mentioned?

(A) It is mentioned as a promotion strategy.

(B) It is mentioned because the airline is generous.

(C) It is mentioned as a compensation to consumers.

(D) It is mentioned because consumers asked for them.

聽力原文和中譯

Questions 40-42 refer to the following announcement

Attention please. Due to some mechanical problems, flight CX1098 from Frankfurt to Holland has been cancelled. Again... flight CX1098 from Frankfurt to Holland has been cancelled. Also, there seems to be some problems with the left wings of CV2687 and CW1098, so they're delayed. There's going to be another announcement for whether or not CX1098 will be able to depart tomorrow morning, and now it's our final boarding call for CX2687. For the overbooked problems of CV1098, we're going to compensate you by giving coupons for a 50% discount. For safety concerns, please wait patiently. We sincerely apologize for any inconvenience caused.

問題 40-42 請參閱下列公告

請注意。由於一些機械問題，從法蘭克福到荷蘭的 CX1098 班機已經取消。重複…從法蘭克福到荷蘭的 CX1098 班機已經取消。而且 CV2687 和 CW1098 飛機左翼有些問題。所以他們延遲了。對於 CX1098 在明早是否能起飛將會有另外的公告。現在是我們對 CX2687 的最後登機呼叫。對於 CV1098 超賣的問題，我們將補償顧客 5 折優惠卷。由於安全的考量，請耐心等待。我們誠摯地對於任何引起的不便感到抱歉。

答案：40. A 41. B 42. C

40. 從法蘭克福到荷蘭的 **CX1098** 班機出了什麼問題？

(A) 飛機被取消了。

(B) 飛機誤點了。

(C) 飛機正在維修。

(D) 飛機超賣。

41. CV2687 和 CW1098 航班有什麼問題？

(A) 它們超賣。

(B) 它們誤點了。

(C) 它們被取消了。

(D) 它們正在維修。

 42. 為何會提到「優惠券」這個單字？

(A) 被提到因為宣傳策略。

(B) 被提及是因為航空公司很大方。

(C) 被提及是因為對消費者進行補償。

(D) 被提到是因為消費者要求。

40.

・聽到對話，馬上鎖定 flight CX1098 from Frankfurt to Holland has been cancelled...。根據 what's the problem 可知詢問班機出現某些問題，因此根據後面文字敘述，可推知答案為(A) It is cancelled.

41.

・由 what happened 得知是細節題，和第一道題目 What is the problem，問法類似。聽到對話，馬上鎖定 there seems to be some problems with the left wings of CV2687 and CW1098, so they're delayed...（CV2687 和 CW1098 飛機左翼有些問題。所以他們延遲了）。

42.

‧聽到對話直接鎖定在 coupons，coupons 是「優惠券」的意思。掃描 coupon 出現的原因。答案通常就在此單字的前後，會加以補充敘述。因此，聽到關鍵字，馬上注意前後文。

貓頭鷹

40.

‧此題屬於細節題，題目詢問 CX1098 班機出了什麼問題。牽涉到數字的題目，考生須眼耳並用，以數字當定位字，同時掃描選項，答案常出現在數字之後的細節。flight CX1098 from Frankfurt to Holland has been cancelled... 從法蘭克福到荷蘭的 CX1098 班機已經被取消，動詞時態是現在完成式，再搭配被動語態 have/has been +過去分詞，已經被…。另外，從 A 處到 B 處的片語: from A to B。

41.

‧本題關鍵字為 delay（延遲、誤點）。公告中提到兩架飛機因為某些原因而誤點。此題沒有陷阱，可直接判斷。選項中的細節題須先定選項描述裡的關鍵字。(A) They are overbooked. 超賣是班機 CV1098 的問題。(B) They are delayed. 公告中有提到。(C) They are cancelled. 取消班機是另外一架。(D) They are under maintenance. 並未提到此狀況

42.

‧此題是細節題。公告中提到： For the overbooked problems of CV1098, we're going to compensate you by giving coupons for a 50% discount. （對於 CV1098 超賣的問題，我們將補償 5 折優惠券）。compensate 是（補償）之意。compensate Sb. by...，用…補

償某人。

浣熊 ⓢ MP3 159+MP3 161

還可能怎麼問

1. Which of the following flights is overbooked?

(A) CX1098

(B) CV2687

(C) CW1098

(D) CV1098

2. When will fight CX1098 depart?

(A) right after the departure of flight CX2687

(B) after left wing problems are fixed

(C) should wait until further announcement

(D) after the announcement tomorrow morning

中譯與解析

1. 下列哪個班機超賣？

(A) CX1098。

(B) CV2687。

(C) CW1098。

(D) CV1098。

2. CX1098 班機會於何時起飛呢？

(A) 在 CX2687 班機起飛後。

(B) 在飛機左翼問題修復後。

(C) 應該要等到進一步的公告。

(D) 在明天早晨公告後。

答案：1. D 2. C

1. 題目是問下列哪個班機超賣？

· 聽力訊息中有提到 For the overbooked problems of CV1098, we're going to compensate you by giving coupons for a 50% discount.，而且聽力訊息中只有此班次是超賣，所以可以排除 A,B,C 選項。選項 D 是 CV1098，此班次是超賣的班次，故可以得知答案為選項 D。

2. 題目是問 CX1098 班機會於何時起飛呢？先從四個選項分別來看。

· 選項 A，聽力訊息中有提到 There's going to be another announcement for whether or not CX1098 will be able to depart tomorrow morning，所以可以推斷不知道是何時才公告起飛時間，只有提到稍後公告，聽力訊息中也有出現 now it's our final boarding call for CX2687，要小心別被干擾到，故可以排除此選項。選項 B，聽力訊息中有提到 there seems to be some problems with the left wings of CV2687 and CW1098, so they're delayed，這是提到飛機左翼的部分，但與題目所問的班次無關，故可以排除此選項。選項 C，此為正確選項，所以可以得知答案為選項 C。選項 D，聽力訊息中有提到 There's going to be another announcement for whether or not CX1098 will be able to depart tomorrow morning，所以可以推斷不知道是何時才公告起飛時間，只有提到稍後公告，別將聽力訊息的 depart tomorrow morning 和 after the announcement tomorrow morning 搞混或干擾到，因為不是明早才公告，故可以排除此選項。

Unit **15**
航空公司公告：邁向最佳航空公司，巧妙化解班次突然取消的問題

 **Instructions**

❶ 請播放音檔聽下列對話，並完成試題。 🎧 MP3 162+MP3 163

❷ 「跟述」練習：寫完試題後請跟著音檔同步跟漸進式做「跟述」練習，提升聽力專注力。

❸ 加碼題：完成❶＋❷步驟後，請再播放音檔寫浣熊試題，掌握其他可能的出題考點，強化應考實力。 🎧 MP3 162+MP3 164

43. What will passengers taking CZ1088 probably do after the announcement?

(A) receive a compensation

(B) talk to the ground crew

(C) wait for the plane to be repaired

(D) see the bulletin board

44. How does the airline solve the problem with CZ1088?

(A) by giving passengers coupons

(B) by arranging a new flight

(C) by giving each passenger 50 dollars

(D) by refunding

45. Which of the following is TRUE regarding flight CZ1089?

(A) It's from Dubai to Taiwan.

(B) It's an indirect flight.

(C) Passengers taking CZ1089 will be compensated.

(D) It is going to land in 20 minutes.

聽力原文和中譯

Questions 43-45 refer to the following announcement

Passengers taking CZ1088 from Taiwan to Dubai are cancelled. Passengers please contact our ground crew as soon as you can. They'll arrange another flight CZ1089, also from Taiwan to Dubai. The difference is that it's a direct flight, so you won't have to take a transfer through HK. There won't be any compensation. Since it's a direct flight, it'll take less time to arrive at Dubai Airport. Please be ready, CZ1089 is about to land in twenty minutes. For other flight information, please see our bulletin board.

問題 43-45 請參閱下列公告

搭乘 CZ1088 從杜拜到台灣的班機取消了。乘客請盡早聯繫我們的地勤人員。他們將安排另一個班機 CZ1089，也是從台灣到杜拜。差別在於這是直航航班，所以你不用在香港轉機。將不會有任何補償，且既然這是直航航班，會花較少時間就能抵達杜拜機場。請準備好 CZ1089 會於 20 分鐘左右降落。關於更多班機資訊請看我們的公告欄。

答案：43. B 44. B 45. D

---

43. 聽完通知後，搭乘 CZ1088 班機的乘客可能會做什麼？

(A) 獲得賠償。

(B) 跟地勤人員說話。

(C) 等待飛機維修。

(D) 去看公告欄。

44. 航空公司如何解決 **CZ1088** 班機的問題？

(A) 給旅客優惠券。

(B) 安排新航班。

(C) 給每位乘客 50 元。

(D) 退款。

45. 關於 **CZ1089** 航班，下列敘述何者為真？

(A) 從杜拜飛到台灣。

(B) 轉機。

(C) 乘坐 CZ1089 的乘客將獲得賠償。

(D) 將在 20 分鐘內降落。

 獵豹

43.

· 聽到短講，馬上鎖定 Passengers please contact out ground crew as soon as you can...。根據公告，由於班機取消，於是告知與地勤人員聯絡。故乘客下一個步可能會和地勤人員談話。

44.

· 從 how，推知詢問「方法、身分、感覺」等等問題。在此是詢問解決方式。又從第三句的 They'll arrange another flight CZ1089...，因此得知是安排另外一架飛機。

45.

· 聽到短講馬上鎖定在 Which of the followings is TRUE，是「下列敘述何者為真」的意思。regarding 是「對於、關於」之意。首先找到 CZ1089 航班，根據前後文，可理解出它的敘述有哪幾項，再進行下一

Unit 15　航空公司公告：邁向最佳航空公司，巧妙化解班次突然取消的問題

1 照片描述

2 應答問題

3 簡短對話

4 簡短獨白

模擬試題

355

步判斷。

 貓頭鷹

43.

・此題是細節題。公告一開始就說明原因，因此找到 cancelled（取消），從前後文，可以得知蛛絲馬跡。讀題時先定位關鍵字是重要的解題技巧，和某人說話時，除了 talk，還有 contact（聯繫），discuss（討論）和 communicate（溝通），這些單字都是可能選項。

44.

・此題需要先理解 solve the problem 的意思，再搜尋其解決方式。公告內文多，然而定位關鍵片語，答案呼之欲出。文中提到:They'll arrange another flight CZ1089, also from Taiwan to Dubai.和選項 (B) by arranging a new flight（安排新航班）意思相符，因此答案為 (B)。

45.

・細節題的選項描述會以類似詞或不同句型將短講敘述重述。「下列何者為真或錯」的細節題須先定位位每個選項描述裡的關鍵字，同時搜尋短講裡是否有類似關鍵字的單字。關於 CZ1089 航班，短講中指出：CZ1089 is about to land in twenty minutes，因此推知答案為(D) It is going to land in 20 minutes.。

 浣熊　🎧 MP3 162+MP3 164

還可能怎麼問

1. **What does the speaker mean when she says "The difference is that it's a direct flight"?**
   (A) it takes longer to arrive the destination than indirect flights
   (B) she wants to ensure that every passenger knows that
   (C) it means you won't have a layover at other places
   (D) it means you won't get any compensation

2. **What happened to this indirect flight?**
   (A) it's overbooked.
   (B) it's delayed.
   (C) it's cancelled.
   (D) it's going to land in around 20 minutes

中譯與解析

1. 當她說「差別在於這是直航航班」，說話者指的是什麼？
   (A) 它比起非直航航班花費較長的時間抵達目的地。
   (B) 她想要確保每個乘客都知道這件事。
   (C) 它意謂著不會於其他地方中途停留。
   (D) 它意謂著你不會獲得任何補償。

2. 此非直航航班發生了什麼問題？
   (A) 它超賣了。
   (B) 它延遲了。
   (C) 它取消了。
   (D) 它將於 20 分鐘左右降落。

答案：1. C 2. C

1. 題目是問當她說「差別在於這是直航航班」，說話者指的是什麼？

・選項 A，這部分是錯誤的，因為直航航班會比非直航航班所需要的時間更短，且聽力訊息中有 Since it's a direct flight, it'll take less time to arrive at Dubai Airport.，更可以推斷會花費較少的時間就到杜拜，所以可以排除。選項 B，聽力訊息中未提及且這並非她說這句話所表達的，所以可以排除。選項 C，聽力訊息中提到 The difference is that it's a direct flight, so you won't have to take a transfer through HK.，選項並沒有直接用 take a transfer，而是做了改寫，改成了 you won't have a layover at other places，layover 即中途停留或短暫滯留，won't have to take a transfer 即 won't have a layover at other places 的同義表達，故可以得知答案為選項 C。選項 D，聽力訊息中提到不會有補償，但這與題目所問的無關，所以可以排除。

2. 題目是問此「非直航」航班發生了什麼問題？先從四個選項分別來看。

・選項 A，這題需要更多的推斷能力，聽力訊息中未提到非直航航班但題目卻問非直航航班，但其實可以從 Passengers taking CZ1088 from Taiwan to Dubai are cancelled. Passengers please contact our ground crew as soon as you can. They'll arrange another flight CZ1089, also from Taiwan to Dubai. The difference is that it's a direct flight，這些訊息中推斷出 CZ1089 和 CZ1088 同為飛往杜拜的班機，但是 CZ1089 是直航航班，所以不用像 CZ1088 一樣要轉機，得知 CZ1088 是非直航航班，此班次是 cancelled 所以可以排除此選項。選項 B，解說同上，故可以排除此選項。選項 C，此為正確選項，所以可以得知答案為選項 C。 選項 D，CZ1089 才是 20 分鐘後降落的選項，故可以排除。

Unit 16
體育場公告：娛樂性「親吻鏡頭」，人人都有機會

Instructions

1. 請播放音檔聽下列對話，並完成試題。 🎧 MP3 165+MP3 166
2. 「跟述」練習：寫完試題後請跟著音檔同步跟漸進式做「跟述」練習，提升聽力專注力。
3. 加碼題：完成❶+❷步驟後，請再播放音檔寫浣熊試題，掌握其他可能的出題考點，強化應考實力。 🎧 MP3 165+MP3 167

46. Where might this announcement be heard?

    (A) on a sports field

    (B) in an aquarium

    (C) in a shopping mall

    (D) in a restaurant

 47. Which of the following is the closest in meaning to "intrigued"?

    (A) very scared

    (B) very excited

    (C) very interested

    (D) very attractive

48. Which of the following is NOT mentioned?

(A) hot dogs

(B) diet soda

(C) hamburgers

(D) cokes

聽力原文和中譯

Questions 46-48 refer to the following announcement

Welcome to Best City Field. It's a clear, sunny morning. Our hot dogs are just as fresh as you might think, and it's "buy one get one free". Our diet soda and coke are also on discount. In addition to foods and beverages, we are having a whole new scoreboard, with the Kiss Cam in the middle. Don't be afraid of showing some love to your loved one. Here I mean, not just among couples. Kissing your kids can also be shown on the big screen. Anyone that makes our photographers intrigued, you'll see your face up there.

問題 46-48 請參閱下列公告

歡迎來到倍斯特體育場。這是無雲且陽光普照的早晨。我們的熱狗就像你所能想到那樣新鮮，而且它「買一送一」。我們的健怡蘇打和可樂也在折扣中。除了食物和飲品，我們也有一整個新的計分板，有親吻鏡頭在中間。別害怕對自己喜愛的人展示些愛。對此我指的是不只是夫妻間。親吻你的小孩也可能被展示到大螢幕上喔。任何人使得攝影師感到興趣者，你都會在那看到你的臉龐在上面喔。

答案：46. A 47. C 48. C

46. 哪裡可以看到這個公告？

(A) 在運動場。

(B) 在水族館。

(C) 在購物中心。

(D) 在餐廳。

47. 下列哪個選項最接近「興趣」一字？

(A) 非常害怕的。

(B) 非常興奮的。

(C) 非常感興趣的。

(D) 非常有吸引力的。

48. 下列選項何者沒提到？

(A) 熱狗。

(B) 健怡蘇打。

(C) 漢堡。

(D) 可樂。

獵豹

46.

· 聽到對話，馬上鎖定 Welcome to Best City Field. It's a clear, sunny morning..。根據 field，可推知是田野，或是球場。因此選項(A) on a sports field 適合。

47.

· 本題考單字題，直接詢問單字的意義。單字 intrigued 本身的意思是很感興趣。選項(C)very interested <非常感興趣>，常見片語：be interested in...，對……感興趣的，其他選項語意不合。

48.

· 首先判斷此題屬於細節題，掃描選項的單字，有印象後，可從公告中推知答案。第三句提到 hot dogs，diet soda，cokes，直到公告結束，並沒有提到漢堡，因此答案為(C)hamburgers 漢堡。

 貓頭鷹

46.

・此題屬於開門見山題，公告第一句，通常會先聲明場地的名稱。

・休閒地點除了 sports field，還有 swimming pool 游泳池、court 球場、playing ground 操場等等，都是常見的地方。

47.

・讀題時先定位關鍵字是重要的解題技巧，如本題單字題，如果考生本身不瞭解此單字，可以從前後文來判斷出意思。此題可從後文或句子判斷出意思。Anyone that makes our photographers intrigued, you'll see your face up there.如果臉被看到上面，表示他吸引了攝影師的注意，讓其感興趣，因此推知答案為選項(C) very interested。

48.

・細節題的選項常列出屬性一樣的名詞。Our hot dogs are just as fresh...我們的熱狗就像你所能想到那樣新鮮 Our diet soda and coke are also on discount.我們的健怡蘇打和可樂也在折扣中。，公告中提

・了幾項食物和飲料，但並沒有 hamburger。

 浣熊　🎧 MP3 165+MP3 167

還可能怎麼問

1.　What is kiss cam?

(A) it's designed for couples only.

(B) it's designed for parents with kids.

(C) it's designed to increase the profits of the Best City Field

(D) it's designed for an entertainment purpose

2. **Who are the most likely to show up on the kiss cam?**
   (A) athletes who score the most out of the entire contest
   (B) designers who design the cam
   (C) photographers who win the award
   (D) kids who want to calm their pet, but accidentally spill their coke

中譯與解析

1. **親吻鏡頭是什麼？**
   (A) 針對夫妻所設計的。
   (B) 設計給有小孩陪同的父母。
   (C) 設計以增加倍斯特體育場的利潤。
   (D) 設計用於娛樂用途。

2. **誰最有可能出現在親吻鏡頭上？**
   (A) 在整場比賽得最多分的運動員。
   (B) 設計此鏡頭的設計師。
   (C) 得獎的攝影師。
   (D) 想要安撫他們寵物，但卻不小心灑出他們可樂的小孩們。

1. **題目是問親吻鏡頭是什麼？**

· 選項 A，聽力訊息中有提到出現在親吻鏡頭上的並非僅有夫妻之間，但這不是親吻鏡頭設計的目的，且僅設計給夫妻太絕對，所以可以排除此選項。選項 B，聽力訊息中有提到小孩即親吻小孩也能出現在鏡頭上，但這不是親吻鏡頭設計的目的，所以可以排除此選項。選項 C，聽力訊

息中未提到利潤，所以可以排除此選項。選項 D，這題需要更多的推斷能力，其實親吻鏡頭的設計就是增加觀賽者的樂趣，而非傳統只有球賽，故可以得知答案為選項 D。

2.　題目是問誰最有可能出現在親吻鏡頭上？

‧選項 A，聽力訊息中未提到運動員，也沒有提到分數等，故可以排除此選項。選項 B，聽力訊息中未提到設計此鏡頭的設計師等，故可以排除此選項。選項 C，聽力訊息中未提到得獎，僅提到攝影師會捕捉那些畫面，故可以排除此選項。選項 D，聽力訊息中有提到好幾個會出現在畫面上的舉例項目，可是答案是較隱含的，可以從 Anyone that makes our photographers intrigued, you'll see your face up there.推斷這就是指選項的 kids who want to calm their pet, but accidentally spill their coke，讓攝影師感興趣而被放上去的，所以可以得知答案為選項 D。

Unit 17
錄製訊息：前往新加坡
進行公司收購

Instructions

❶ 請播放音檔聽下列對話，並完成試題。 🎧 MP3 168+MP3 169

❷ 「跟述」練習：寫完試題後請跟著音檔同步跟漸進式做「跟述」練習，提升聽力專注力。

❸ 加碼題：完成❶＋❷步驟後，請再播放音檔寫浣熊試題，掌握其他可能的出題考點，強化應考實力。 🎧 MP3 168+MP3 170

---

49. Why does the speaker want the colleagues to cover up his/ her duty?

(A) He/She needs to take a sick leave.

(B) He/She needs to go abroad to find another investor.

(C) He/She will take a personal leave.

(D) He/She will be on a business trip abroad.

50. Which of the following is NOT mentioned by the speaker?

(A) inviting investors

(B) a list of investors

(C) a new project

(D) having lunch with investors

51. When will the company driver pick investors up?

(A) Dec. 1st

(B) Dec. 9th

(C) Dec. 5th

(D) Dec. 2nd

聽力原文和中譯

Questions 49-51 refer to the following recorded message

Dear fellow colleagues, since I'll be at Singapore for company acquisition from Dec. 1st to Dec. 9th, I'm recording messages for you to cover up my duty while I'm in Singapore. I need you to find another investor for our new project. I have a list of investors on my desk, and their contact information of course. Invite them to our hotel annual meeting and have dinners with them all. Be sure to give them the wonderful treatment. The boss has granted us to use the company limo. You can have our driver pick them up at Dec. 5th, 2018, 2 p.m. Thanks.

問題 49-51 請參閱下列錄製訊息

我親愛的同事們，既然我在 12 月 1 日到 12 月 9 日會到新加坡進行公司收購。我錄製了訊息，讓你們能在我在新加坡時，完成我的工作。我需要你們找另一個我們新專案的投資者。我已經列出了一列的投資者清單，而且當然有他們的聯繫資訊。邀請他們到我們旅館參加年度會議且與他們共進晚餐。保證給他們美好的待遇。老闆已經允許我們使用公司豪華車。你可以用我們的司機在 2018 年 12 月 5 日下午兩點接送他們。謝謝。

答案：49. D 50. D 51. C

49. 為何敘述者（敘述者）希望同事幫忙做他／她的工作？

(A) 他／她需請病假。

(B) 他／她需出國尋找另一名投資者。

(C) 他／她將休假。

(D) 他／她將到國外出差。

50. 下列選項，何者敘述者未提到？

(A) 邀請投資者。

(B) 投資者名單。

(C) 一個新專案。

(D) 與投資者共進午餐。

51. 公司司機何時會去接送投資者？

(A) 12 月 1 日。

(B) 12 月 9 日。

(C) 12 月 5 日。

(D) 12 月 2 日。

獵豹

49.

・聽到對話，馬上鎖定 since I'll be at Singapore for company acquisition from Dec. 1st to Dec. 9th, I'm recording messages for you to cover up my duty...。根據第一行提到此人要到新加坡出差，因此需要同事幫忙：cover up my duty。duty 是「責任，職責」。

50.

・首先判斷此題屬於細節題。先歸納出留言的幾個重點，再進行判斷。此類考法比較全面性，相對難度較高。留言簡單包括幾項，其中一項是和投資者共進晚餐，不是午餐： have dinners with all.。此為陷阱題，請小心作答。

51.

・看到題目目光直接鎖定在 when 和 pick up，pick up 是「接送某人」

的意思。掃描 when 可能出現的答案。留言中出現的日期有三項，前兩項是出差日期，最後一項是接送日期： Dec. 5th, 2018，故答案為 (C) Dec. 5th。

 貓頭鷹

49.

‧ 此題屬於因果題，詢問原因或是結果。因為此人要在新加坡 for company acquisition（進行公司收購），這是公事，因此選項(D) business trip（出差）比較適合。其他請假說法如下：take a sick leave 病假，take a personal leave 休假、事假。

50.

‧ 細節題的選項描述會以類似詞或不同句型將文章敘述重述。「下列何者為不包括」的細節題，需快速整理全文。我們將所需項目簡單化：company acquisition， cover up my duty， find another investor for our new project.，I have a list of investors，have dinners with an investor，因此選項(D) having lunch with investors 有誤。

51.

‧ 此題是考時間。通常時間有年月日，日期或是幾點。選項中除了選項 (D)，其他均有出現。(A) Dec. 1st → 出差日 (B) Dec. 9th → 回國日 (C) Dec. 5th → 接送投資者(D) Dec. 2nd → 在新加坡出差。

 浣熊 MP3 168+MP3 170

還可能怎麼問

1. **Where does the speaker work?**

   (A) at a Singapore startup

   (B) at an investment bank

   (C) at Mergers and Acquisitions

   (D) at overseas hotel chains

2. **When will the speaker return to his workplace?**

   (A) on Dec 1

   (B) on Dec 5

   (C) on Dec 9

   (D) on Dec 11

中譯與解析

1. 說話者在哪裡工作？

   (A) 在新加坡新創公司。

   (B) 在投資銀行。

   (C) 在合併和收購公司。

   (D) 在國外旅館連鎖。

2. 說話者何時會回到他的工作地點呢？

   (A) 12 月 1 日。

   (B) 12 月 5 日。

   (C) 12 月 9 日。

   (D) 12 月 11 日。

答案：1. C 2. D

1.　題目是問說話者在哪裡工作？

．選項 A，聽力訊息中有提到要到新加坡進行公司收購，但公司不在新加坡，所以可以排除此選項。選項 B，聽力訊息中有提到我需要你們找另一個我們新專案的投資者，但沒辦法推斷出這是投資銀行，所以可以排除此選項。選項 C，聽力訊息中有提到要到新加坡進行公司收購，公司很有可能是合併和收購公司，故可以得知答案為選項 C。選項 D，有可能是海外或國外跨國公司，但是訊息多了旅館連鎖，所以可以排除此選項。

2.　題目是問說話者何時會回到他的工作地點呢？

．選項 A，聽力訊息中有提到 since I'll be at Singapore for company acquisition from Dec. 1st to Dec. 9th，所以不可能是 1 號回工作地點，故可以排除此選項。選項 B，You can have our driver pick them up at Dec. 5th, 2018, 2 p.m.，這是接送客戶的時間，故可以排除此選項。選項 C，聽力訊息中有提到 since I'll be at Singapore for company acquisition from Dec. 1st to Dec. 9th，所以不可能是 9 號回工作地點，故可以排除此選項。選項 D，可以從聽力訊息中得知放假日其實到 9 號，所以可以推斷 11 日他應該回到工作地點了，所以可以得知答案為選項 D。

Unit 18
錄製訊息：助理就是要認命些，接貓、衣物送洗樣樣要做

Instructions

❶ 請播放音檔聽下列對話，並完成試題。 🎧 MP3 171+MP3 172

❷ 「跟述」練習：寫完試題後請跟著音檔同步跟漸進式做「跟述」練習，提升聽力專注力。

❸ 加碼題：完成❶＋❷步驟後，請再播放音檔寫浣熊試題，掌握其他可能的出題考點，強化應考實力。 🎧 MP3 171+MP3 173

52. To whom is the message addressed?

(A) the speaker's assistant

(B) the speaker's friend

(C) the speaker's boss

(D) the speaker's child

53. Why does the cat need to be dressed up?

(A) The speaker will arrange a photoshoot for the cat.

(B) The speaker will take the cat to a party.

(C) The speaker just wants to make his/her cat look gorgeous.

(D) The speaker will take the cat to a masquerade.

54. Which of the following is NOT included in the tasks assigned by the speaker?

(A) grooming his/her pet

(B) moving his/her car

(C) picking up his/her pet

(D) sending his/her clothes to dry cleaning

1 照片描述

2 應答問題

3 簡短對話

4 簡短獨白

模擬試題

聽力原文和中譯

Questions 52-54 refer to the following recorded message

My Dear assistant, I do need you to pick up my cat at Best Pet at 3 p.m., and have our house maid dress him up. I'll be taking him to my friend's party tonight, and I forgot to tell you my car is still at C lot. My friends gave me a ride to the company, so I don't have time to move it to A lot. Please do that before I finish my meeting at 2:30 p.m. Send my clothes to dry cleaning at 3:30 p.m, since they only accept clothes before 4 p.m.

問題 52-54 請參閱下列錄製的訊息

我親愛的助理，我需要你在下午三點時在倍斯特寵物店接我的貓咪，然後叫我的傭人將它打扮好。晚上我會帶它到我朋友的派對，而且我忘了告訴你我的車還在 C 停車場。我的朋友載我到公司了，所以要請你將車移到 A 停車場。請在我下午兩點半會議結束前完成這些。將我的的衣物在下午 3 點 30 送洗，因為他們只在下午四點前受理衣物。

答案：52. A 53. B 54. A

52. 這封訊息是給誰呢？

(A) 留言者的助理。

(B) 留言者的朋友。

(C) 留言者的老闆。

(D) 留言者的小孩。

53. 貓咪為何需要打扮？

(A) 留言者將為貓安排照片拍攝。

(B) 留言者將帶貓帶到派對上。

(C) 留言者只是想讓他／她的貓看起來亮眼。

(D) 留言者將帶貓到化裝舞會。

54. 留言者指定的任務中，下列選項何者不包括？

(A) 梳理他／她的寵物。

(B) 移動他／她的車。

(C) 接送他／她的寵物。

(D) 把他／她的衣服送去乾洗。

獵豹

52.

・聽到對話，馬上鎖定 My Dear assistant, I do need you to pick up my cat at Best Pet at 3 p.m....。根據訊息一開始的收件者是： Dear my assistant（親愛的助理），推知答案為(A)留言者的助理。

53.

・be dressed up 是「被打扮」之意。本題 why 開頭，詢問原因，因此先定位關鍵字 cat 和 dress up。又從第三句 I'll be taking him to my friend's party tonight... 晚上我會帶它到我朋友的派對。推知原因。him 是指 cat，因為要去派對，所以需要打扮。

54.

・首先判斷此題屬於細節題，掃描關鍵字 task（任務），從留言中找出幾項交代事項。 將留言中線索字以更精簡的方式重述： pick up my cat... dress him up... move it to A lot... Send my clothes to dry cleaning。所以正確選項是(A) grooming his/her pet。

貓頭鷹

52.

· 此題屬於開門見山題，題目通常在第一句出現，抓到技巧後，考生可以節省很多時間搜尋。assistant 是「助理」，boss 是「老闆」。即使開頭未說明給誰，訊息中交代的事情，亦可推知叮嚀給助理或秘書的工作。

53.

· 讀題時先定位關鍵字是重要的解題技巧，因為關鍵字前後常有解題線索，例如本題: pick up my cat at Best Pet at 3 p.m., and have our house maid dress him up. I'll be taking him to my friend's party tonight。have Sb.+原型動詞，要某人去做某事情。have 在此片語是使役動詞，常表達命令，這句 have our house maid dress him up 是祈使句。

54.

· 細節題的選項描述會以類似詞或不同句型將文章敘述重述。「下列何者沒被提及」的細節題，每個選項描述裡的關鍵字，同時掃描文章裡是否有類似的關鍵字。(A) grooming his/her pet → 訊息中沒提到。(B) moving his/her car → 移車到 A 停車場。(C) picking up his/her pet → 第一句提到。(D) sending his/her clothes to dry cleaning → 三點半前送洗。

浣熊  MP3 171+MP3 173

還可能怎麼問

1. **Where most likely does the speaker work?**

   (A) at Best Pet

   (B) at a dry cleaning store

   (C) at a parking lot

   (D) at an architecture firm

2. **According to the speaker, what will happen after 4 p.m.?**

   (A) her cat will be all dressed up, ready for the party

   (B) the party is about to start

   (C) she will be having a presentation in the meeting

   (D) the dry cleaning store won't accept any clothes

中譯與解析

1. 說話者最有可能在哪裡工作？

   (A) 在倍斯特寵物店。

   (B) 在乾洗店。

   (C) 在停車場。

   (D) 在建築事務所。

2. 根據說話者，下午四點後會發生什麼事？

   (A) 她的貓將盛裝打扮好，準備好參加宴會。

   (B) 宴會正要開始。

   (C) 她將於會議中做簡報。

   (D) 乾洗店不會接受任何衣物。

1. 題目是問說話者最有可能在哪裡工作？

- 選項 A，聽力訊息中有提到 I do need you to pick up my cat at Best Pet at 3 p.m.，但是說話者並不是在寵物店工作，僅是交代助理要完成這件事，所以可以排除此選項。選項 B，聽力訊息中有提到 Send my clothes to dry cleaning at 3:30 p.m, since they only accept clothes before 4 p.m.，但是說話者並不是在乾洗店工作，僅是交代助理要完成這件事，所以可以排除此選項。選項 C，聽力訊息中有提到停車場跟移車，但是說話者並不是在乾洗店工作，僅是交代助理要完成這件事，所以可以排除此選項。選項 D，說話者很可能是在此工作交代助理去做這件事，且可以明確知道不可能是在 A-C 這三個選項的地方工作，故可以得知答案為選項 D。

2. 題目是問根據說話者，下午四點後會發生什麼事？

- 選項 A，聽力訊息中有提到 I do need you to pick up my cat at Best Pet at 3 p.m.，and have our house maid to dress him up.，但是無法推斷出何時會將貓盛裝打扮好，故可以排除此選項。選項 B，聽力訊息中關於宴會的部分僅有 I'll be taking him to my friend's party tonight，得知是晚上，但確切時間不知道，也不可能於四點開始，故可以排除此選項。選項 C，聽力訊息中有提到 Please do that before I finish my meeting at 2:30 p.m.，故可以排除此選項。選項 D，聽力訊息中有 Send my clothes to dry cleaning at 3:30 p.m, since they only accept clothes before 4 p.m.，所以可以得知答案為選項 D。

Unit 19

公司談話：工會大勝，牙齒保健納入保險

 Instructions

❶ 請播放音檔聽下列對話，並完成試題。 🎧 MP3 174+MP3 175

❷ 「跟述」練習：寫完試題後請跟著音檔同步跟漸進式做「跟述」練習，提升聽力專注力。

❸ 加碼題：完成❶＋❷步驟後，請再播放音檔寫浣熊試題，掌握其他可能的出題考點，強化應考實力。 🎧 MP3 174+MP3 176

55. What does the speaker mean by saying, "sorry to cut your afternoon short"?

(A) sorry that no afternoon tea will be served

(B) sorry to interrupt your afternoon

(C) sorry that you cannot order pizza this afternoon

(D) sorry that the afternoon break will shortened

56. What does the triumph refer to in this talk?

(A) free pizza and chicken wings

(B) dental insurance

(C) free biscuits

(D) longer afternoon break

57. Where might this talk be given?

(A) in a dentist's clinic

(B) in a cafeteria

(C) in a company

(D) in an insurance company

聽力原文和中譯

Questions 55-57 refer to the following talk

Good afternoon, sorry to cut your afternoon short, but I do have good news to tell you. It's not that we're gonna order pizzas and chicken wings or get free biscuits and cakes from our manufacturers. This is actually another triumph for our employees. The Labor Union has convinced the board to include dental in our insurance. That means starting next Monday, you can do your dental for free. It's covered. Even I can't wait to do the teeth whitening myself. So congratulations guys.

問題 55-57 請參閱下列廣告

下午好，抱歉打斷你們下午，但是我有幾個好消息要告訴你們。不是關於我們要訂購比薩和雞翅或從製造商那裡拿到免費的餅乾和蛋糕。實際上這是員工另一個勝利。工會已經說服董事會將牙齒保健納入保險。這意味著下週一，你可以免費做牙齒。費用包含在內了。連我都等不及要替自己做個牙齒美白了。所以恭喜各位。

答案：55. B　56. B　57. C

55. 發言者說「抱歉打斷你們下午」，意思為何？

(A) 抱歉沒有下午茶。

(B) 抱歉打斷你們的下午。

(C) 抱歉今天下午你不能點披薩。

(D) 抱歉午休會縮短。

56. 發言者所指的勝利是指什麼？

　　(A) 免費披薩和雞翅。

　　(B) 牙齒保險。

　　(C) 免費餅乾。

　　(D) 午休時間較長。

57. 這段發言的可能地點在哪裡？

　　(A) 在牙科診所。

　　(B) 在自助餐廳。

　　(C) 在某家公司。

　　(D) 在保險公司。

 獵豹

55.

・聽到對話，馬上鎖定 sorry to cut your afternoon short, but I do have good news to tell you...。根據 sorry to cut your afternoon short，後面接的子句： but I do have good news to tell you... 表示中斷對方的下午的時間。cut 有「切斷、打斷」之意。

56.

・首先判斷此題屬於細節題，搜尋 triumph 出現的位置。triumph（勝利），但此談話在辦公室，和戰爭無關，因此，透過 triumph 前後文來判斷出所指為何。從第二句 This is actually another triumph for our employees.，關注後面提到的：include dental in our insurance（牙齒保健納入保險）。

57.

- 首先判斷此題屬推測題。將談話所有內容，找出重要關鍵，推測出真正適合的答案。這裡有個小陷阱是 dental（牙齒保健）和 do the teeth whitening（牙齒美白）。乍聽之下，第一個反應是選牙科診所，因為內容都圍繞牙齒方面。然而，仔細思考，納入保險只是公司的福利，並非一定是牙醫診所。

貓頭鷹

55.

- 此題屬於釋義題，題目通常用俚語或片語來出題。因為(B) interrupt 有「打斷」之意，因此推知此答案較為接近。選項(A)抱歉沒有下午茶，談話中並未提到。選項(D) shortened（縮短），是因為 short 這個字，容易造成考生認為意思接近。Sorry to + V....，很抱歉做出⋯動作。

56.

- 讀題時先定位關鍵字是重要的解題技巧，本談話的關鍵字是：include dental in our insurance（牙齒保健納入保險）。此題是細節題。先鎖定 triumph 這個單字，下一句馬上聽到答案：This is actually another triumph for our employees. The Labor Union has convinced the board to include dental to our insurance. 相關單字：Labor Union（工會），insurance（保險）。

57.

- 此為細節題和推測題的綜合題型。
  首先，先來理解四個選項：(A) in a dentist's clinic（在牙科診所）→ 提到牙齒保健問題，但無直接關聯。(B) in a cafeteria（在自助餐廳）→ 談話提到餅乾、蛋糕和雞翅，但和餐廳無直接關係。(C) in a

右側邊欄：
1 照片描述
2 應答問題
3 簡短對話
4 簡短獨白
模擬試題

company（在某家公司）→ 提到工會和保險，可能性最大。(D) in an insurance company（在保險公司）→雖然提到 insurance，但和保險公司無直接關係。

 浣熊 🎧 MP3 174+MP3 176

還可能怎麼問

1. **Who most likely is the speaker?**
    (A) a pizza delivery man
    (B) a guy who convinced the board
    (C) a manufacturer who offers free afternoon snack
    (D) an executive of the company

2. **What will the listeners probably do next?**
    (A) convince the board for another benefit
    (B) schedule the time for family members to do the teeth whitening
    (C) cheer and arrange teeth cleaning time
    (D) calculate fees of doing teeth whitening

中譯與解析

1. 誰最有可能是說話者？
    (A) 披薩遞送員。
    (B) 說服董事會的人員。
    (C) 提供下午茶點心的製造商。
    (D) 公司的高階主管。

2. 聽者接下來可能會做什麼？

(A) 說服董事會另外的福利。

(B) 安排家庭成員做牙齒美白的時間。

(C) 歡慶且安排牙齒美白的時間。

(D) 計算牙齒美白的費用。

答案：1. D 2. C

1. 題目是問誰最有可能是說話者？

‧ 選項 A，聽力訊息中有提到披薩，It's not that we're gonna order pizzas and chicken wings or get free biscuits and cakes from our manufacturers.，但是說話者不是披薩遞送員，所以可以排除此選項。選項 B，聽力訊息中有提到 The Labor Union has convinced the board to include dental to our insurance.，說服者是工會而非說話者，且不能推斷出說話者代表工會，所以可以排除此選項。選項 C，聽力訊息中有提到 It's not that we're gonna order pizzas and chicken wings or get free biscuits and cakes from our manufacturers. 但說話者不是提供下午茶點心的製造商，所以可以排除此選項。選項 D，從聽力訊息中可以推斷極有可能是公司的高階主管得知消息後來通知其他人，故可以得知答案為選項 D。

2. 題目是問聽者接下來可能會做什麼？

‧ 選項 A，聽力訊息中未包含此訊息，故可以排除此選項。選項 B，員工極有可能聽到後想要安排做牙齒美白的時間，但是聽力訊息中未提到此福利有提供給家庭成員，故可以排除此選項。選項 C，員工極有可能聽到後想要很高興且想要安排做牙齒美白的時間，所以可以得知答案為選項 C。選項 D，聽力訊息中未包含此訊息，故可以排除此選項。

Unit 20
公司談話：食品檢查不合格率高，員工們繃緊神經

Instructions

❶ 請播放音檔聽下列對話，並完成試題。 MP3 177+MP3 178

❷ 「跟述」練習：寫完試題後請跟著音檔同步跟漸進式做「跟述」練習，提升聽力專注力。

❸ 加碼題：完成❶＋❷步驟後，請再播放音檔寫浣熊試題，掌握其他可能的出題考點，強化應考實力。 MP3 177+MP3 179

58. How does the speaker feel about the result of the examination by the Food and Drug Administration?

(A) glad

(B) interested

(C) disappointed

(D) encouraged

59. What might the speaker do next?

(A) call Food and Drug Administration

(B) spray pesticide in all of the shops

(C) survey the company's shops

(D) read the examination result again

60. What kind of company does the speaker most likely work for?

(A) a restaurant franchise

(B) a tea shop

(C) a hostel

(D) a school cafeteria

聽力原文和中譯

Questions 58-60 refer to the following talk

Good morning everyone. I just got a call from Food and Drug Administration. 26 out of 60 shops did not pass the examination. We're a company dedicated to producing high-quality and healthy foods to our customer. I don't see why this is happening. Cockroaches are rampant in several shops, and some major ingredients are expired. Totally unacceptable. I wanna you to prepare all forms here because I'm going to check with your guys per shop today. Grab your documents and meet me in the hall, right now.

問題 58-60 請參閱下列談話

各位午安。我剛收到食物藥品管理局的來電。60 間店有 26 間沒有通過檢驗。我們是間致力於產出高品質和健康食品給我們顧客的公司。我不知道為什這種事會發生。蟑螂蔓延在幾間店裡，而且有些主要的原料成分是過期的。這真的無法令人接受。我想要你們在此準備所有的表格，因為我今天要到每間店逐一與你們檢視。現在拿著你們的文件到大廳等我。

答案：58. C 59. C 60. A

58. 說話者對食物藥品管理局審查的結果，反應如何？

(A) 高興的。

(B) 興趣的。

(C) 失望的。

(D) 鼓舞的。

59. 說話者接下來會做什麼？

　　(A) 致電美國食品藥物管理局。

　　(B) 在所有店裡噴灑殺蟲劑。

　　(C) 檢查公司的商店。

　　(D) 再次閱讀審查結果。

60. 說話者最有可能在哪間公司任職？

　　(A) 連鎖店。

　　(B) 茶店。

　　(C) 旅館。

　　(D) 學校自助餐廳。

獵豹

58.

‧ 聽到對話，馬上鎖定 26 out of 60 shops did not pass the examination... 以及 I don't see why this is happening...。根據 I don't see why this is happening. 由這麼多店檢驗沒通過，推知心情不佳，刪去(A)及(B)。談話者對於沒通過檢驗比例之高，產生疑惑和沮喪。因此(C) disappointed 最適合。

59.

‧ 首先判斷此題屬於細節題，掃描(A)call Food and Drug Administration，致電美國食品藥物管理局(B) spray pesticide（噴灑殺蟲劑），(C) survey 檢測，(D) read the examination result（閱讀審查結果）。線索字以更精簡的方式重述：prepare all forms 準備所有的表格，check with your guys per shop today 因為我今天要到每

間店逐一與你們檢視。由此句得知說話者要檢查商店，所以正確選項是 (C) survey the company's shops。

60.

· 看到題目目光直接鎖定在 work for，work for 是「任職」的意思。

· 掃描說話者闡述的幾個重點如下：

(1) 26 out of 60 shops did not pass the examination.

(2) We're a company dedicated to producing high-quality and healthy foods to our customer.

(3) I'm going to check with your guys per shop today. 由 60 間店有 26 間沒有通過檢驗，到每一間店去檢視，推知應該是連鎖餐廳或加盟餐廳，所以答案選(A)。

貓頭鷹

58.

· 此題屬於推理題，題目大意是由於檢驗結果，26 間沒通過： 26 out of 60 shops，根據結果來推測說話者感受。談話中有句提到：Totally unacceptable.（無法令人接受）。由於太多商店沒通過檢測，因此可推知說話者，無法接受，甚至 disappointed（失望的）。glad, interested 和 encouraged 都是正面之意，和本題不符合，故答案選 (C)。

59.

· 推測題的選項，通常都是歸納出談話中的結論。「說話者接下來會做什麼」發言中可能直接或者間接表達出答案為何，通常會先敘述其他事項，最後提出結論。如本題，說話者表達了檢驗結果、失望的感覺、蟑螂蔓延，等等問題。然而，他接下來做什麼，是依據這些問題而產生。

因此推知：survey the company's shops。

60.

· 此題是推測題。需要幾個聽力訊息的整合後作出推斷，最後選出最佳答案。訊息有提到致力於產出高品質和健康食品，因此(B)茶飲店比較不恰當。訊息還提到產出高品質和健康食品，所以(C)旅館不適合。由聽力訊息最後一句和到每間店檢視，相較之下，(A)連鎖餐廳更加正確。

 浣熊   🎧 MP3 177+MP3 179

還可能怎麼問

1. **Who most likely is the speaker?**

 (A) an employee of FDA

 (B) a manufacturer responsible for major ingredients

 (C) a clerical worker in charge of all forms

 (D) the boss

2. **What will the listeners probably do next?**

 (A) telephone FDA

 (B) write an apology note to their boss

 (C) hold a press conference to prove their shops are hygienic

 (D) have documents ready

中譯與解析

1. **誰最有可能是說話者？**

 (A) 食品藥物管理局的員工。

(B) 負責主要原物料的製造商。

(C) 負責所有表格的文書人員。

(D) 老闆。

2. 聽者們接下來可能會做什麼？

(A) 致電食品藥物管理局。

(B) 寫道歉註給他們老闆。

(C) 開新聞會議證明他們的店是衛生的。

(D) 準備好文件。

答案：1. D 2. D

1　照片描述

2　應答問題

3　簡短對話

4　簡短獨白

模擬試題

1. 題目是問誰最有可能是說話者？先從四個選項分別來看。

· 選項 A，聽力訊息中提到接到食品藥物管理局的電話，可以推斷出說話者本身不是該管理局的員工。選項 B，聽力訊息中提到 ...and some major ingredients are expired.，但是是說明主要原料過期，沒有其他訊息是說明說話者是製造商。選項 C，聽力訊息中提到 I wanna you to prepare all forms here because I'm going to check with your guys per shop today. Grab your documents and meet me in the hall, right now.，此部分是涉及表格和文件的部份，但沒有提到 clerical worker 且聽者是負責其他業務的人員，所以可以排除。選項 D，聽者最有可能的是準備好文件和表格，故可以得知答案為選項 D。

2. 題目是問聽者們接下來可能會做什麼？

· 選項 A、B 和 C，聽力訊息中未提及。選項 D，此部分為聽力訊息表達出的意思，故可以得知答案為選項 D。

Unit 21

錄製 line 訊息：員工被挖角，大老闆的反擊

 Instructions

❶ 請播放音檔聽下列對話，並完成試題。 🎧 MP3 180+MP3 181

❷ 「跟述」練習：寫完試題後請跟著音檔同步跟漸進式做「跟述」練習，提升聽力專注力。

❸ 加碼題：完成❶＋❷步驟後，請再播放音檔寫浣熊試題，掌握其他可能的出題考點，強化應考實力。 🎧 MP3 180+MP3 182

NEW

61. Which of the following is the closest in meaning to "steal" as in "to steal our Marketing Director"?

(A) to hide

(B) to fire

(C) to flatter

(D) to recruit

62. What is the purpose of this talk?

(A) to give directions about what Bob should do

(B) to prevent an important employee from flying to L.A.

(C) to ask Tina to arrange flights and a hotel

(D) to prevent an important employee from being hired by another company

63. What will Bob probably do after this talk?

(A) to ask Tina to arrange flights and boarding

(B) to take over the Marketing Directors' job

(C) to take over the duty of his co-workers who will fly to L.A.

(D) to seal a contract

聽力原文和中譯

Questions 61-63 refer to the following recorded line message

I heard that Best TV is trying to steal our Marketing Director. They are offering twice the pay. They're scheduling a lunch meeting with him, probably talking about other benefits. I want you to fly to L.A. and convince him to stay before he signs the contract. As a CEO, I won't let this happen. Shareholders are gonna be so pissed if they find out our Marketing Director is being poached. Talk to my assistant, Tina, she will arrange flights and a hotel for you. I'll have Bob do your work while you are not here.

問題 61-63 請參閱下列錄製的 line 訊息

我聽説倍斯特電視試圖要挖角我們的行銷總監。他們提供了兩倍的薪資。他們安排了與他的午餐會議，可能要談論其他的福利。我想要你飛往洛杉磯且在他簽約前説服他留下。作為 CEO，我不會讓這種事發生。股東們會很生氣如果他們發現我們的行銷總監被挖走。跟我們的助理 Tina 説下，她會替你安排班機和旅館。我會要求 Bob 在你離開這段時間完成你的工作即可。

答案：61. D 62. D 63. C

---

61. 以下哪一項與「獵取我們的行銷總監」中的「獵取」最接近？

(A) 偷竊。

(B) 炒魷魚。

(C) 奉承。

(D) 招聘。

62. 訊息的目的為何？

(A) 指導 Bob 應該做什麼。

(B) 防止重要員工飛往洛杉磯。

(C) 要求 Tina 安排班機和旅館。

(D) 防止重要員工被其他公司任用。

63. 看完訊息後，Bob 可能會做什麼？

(A) 要求 Tina 安排班機和登機。

(B) 交接行銷總監的工作。

(C) 和將飛往洛杉磯同事的交接工作。

(D) 簽訂合約。

獵豹

61.

· 聽到對話，馬上鎖定 Best TV is trying to seal our Marketing Director...。根據 They are offering twice the pay. talking about other benefits. 這兩句，推知和提供工作有關，seal 本身有適合獵取之意，在此為獵人頭，因此答案為(D) recruit（雇用、招聘）。

62.

· 本題考主旨，無法從一個句子中判斷出答案，必須融會貫通整個談話內容，答題時才不會游移不定。幾個重點單字，需要理解，助於答題。seal our Marketing Director, offer...（提供…薪資），benefit（員工福利），sign the contract （簽約），由這幾個重要單字，推知本文主旨和防止行銷總監跳槽，故答案選(D)。

63.

· 首先判斷此題屬於推測題，CEO 要求某人去阻止行銷總監簽約，因此談話結束後，此人有可能去完成任務。此人不是 Bob，這是小小的設計，第一個想法會將 Bob 帶入，而做出錯誤的判斷。此人將和 Bob 交接工作，將飛往 LA。

貓頭鷹

61.

· 此題屬於單字題，由談話中的大意，來推測出單字的含意。有些單字意思很多元，不同地方，可能含意相差甚遠。本題的 seal，有「密封、獵取、海豹、確認、蓋章」之意。不過如果將此單字用在工作上面，則有招聘其他家公司的優秀領袖之意。

62.

· 主旨題目是基本考題。題目常見寫法為：main pint，purpose，theme 等等。此題是推測題。必須全文看過，才能理解答案為何。請見選項的盲點。 (B) to prevent an important employee from flying to L.A. →不是防止員工飛洛杉磯，而是要求對方去洛杉磯勸總監留下。(C) to ask Tina to arrange flights and a hotel → 這不是主旨。(D) to prevent an important employee from being hired by another company → CEO 安排。這麼多事情，就是要防止總監被挖角，故答案為(D)。

63.

· 推測題看似簡單，容易掉落陷阱。從四個選項來進行篩選答案。 (A) to ask Tina to arrange flights and boarding→這和 Bob 無關。(B) to take over the Marketing Directors' job → 錯，CEO 希望行銷總監不要離職。(C) to take over the duty of his co-workers who will fly to L.A. →正確，他是職務代理人。(D) to seal a contract→錯誤，只是透過 contract 來引導考生。

 浣熊 MP3 180+MP3 182

還可能怎麼問

1. **What is the benefit that other company offers to Marketing Director?**
   (A) stock options
   (B) access to the company's jet
   (C) double the salary
   (D) a bogus title

2. **What does the man mean when he says "find out our Marketing Director is being poached"?**
   (A) he knows it's just a sooner-or-later phenomenon.
   (B) he totally gets why Marketing Director is notorious for poaching things.
   (C) He knows Marketing Director value things, such as ivory and animal skin
   (D) he is worried Marketing Director will take that job

中譯與解析

1. 其他公司所提供給行銷總監的福利是？
   (A) 股票選擇。

(B) 使用公司噴射機的機會。

(C) 兩倍的薪資。

(D) 贗造的頭銜。

2. 當男子說「發現我們的行銷總監被獵走」，他指的是什麼？

(A) 他知道這是遲早的現象。

(B) 他全然理解為什麼行銷總監因為盜獵的事情而惡名昭彰。

(C) 他知道行銷總監重視，例如象牙和動物皮。

(D) 他擔心行銷總監會接受那份工作。

答案：1. C 2. D

1. 題目是問其他公司所提供給行銷總監的福利是？

‧ 選項 A 股票選擇，聽力訊息中未提及。選項 B，聽力訊息中未提到這部分，所以可以排除。選項 C 兩倍的薪資，聽力訊息中提到 They are offering twice the pay.，twice the pay 即 double the salary 此為同義表達，故可以得知答案為選項 C。選項 D 贗造的頭銜，聽力訊息中未提到這部分，所以可以排除。

2. 題目是問當男子說「發現我們的行銷總監被獵走」，他指的是什麼？

‧ 選項 A，聽力訊息中未提到這部分且其實男子是擔憂的，故可以排除。選項 B，聽力訊息中有提到 I heard that Best TV is trying to steal our Marketing Director.，雖然 steal 和 poach 為同義字，但與選項所表達的 poaching things 無關，且這部是男子講這句話的原因，故可以排除。選項 C，聽力訊息中未提到這部分，僅說 Marketing Director is being poached 沒有提到盜獵和象牙和動物皮，故可以排除。選項 D，此為聽力訊息中所表達的，所以可以得知答案為選項 D。

電影公司公告：看電影順道
玩玩挖寶遊戲、電腦遊戲

🔍 Instructions

❶ 請播放音檔聽下列對話，並完成試題。 🎧 MP3 183+MP3 184

❷ 「跟述」練習：寫完試題後請跟著音檔同步跟漸進式做「跟述」練習，提升聽力專注力。

❸ 加碼題：完成❶＋❷步驟後，請再播放音檔寫浣熊試題，掌握其他可能的出題考點，強化應考實力。 🎧 MP3 183+MP3 185

---

64. Where might you hear this announcement?

(A) in a zoo

(B) at a movie premiere

(C) at a cinema

(D) in a school

---

65. How will people gain the opportunity to join the treasure hunt?

(A) by hugging the cartoon characters

(B) by posting photos of themselves and the cartoon characters on Facebook

(C) by leaving nice comments about the movies on Facebook

(D) by posting their selfies taken in front of the theater on Facebook

66. How can a person get a stuffed animal?

(A) by playing a computer game

(B) by buying the ticket to see Zootopia

(C) by leaving comments on Facebook about Zootopia

(D) by playing with the cartoon characters at the entrance

聽力原文和中譯

Questions 64-66 refer to the following announcement

Welcome to Best Cinema. We have cartoon characters at the entrance. Some of you probably have noticed that. Taking a photo with them after watching the film and posting photos on Facebook will get you the chance to join the treasure hunt with us. You'll be getting three free tickets of your choice. If you don't get anything, don't feel discouraged yet. If you match all cartoon characters of Zootopia through the computer screen, and get all of them correct, you will get a stuffed animal of your choice.

問題 64-66 請參閱下列公告

歡迎歡迎到倍斯特電影。我們在入口有卡通人物。你們有些人可能已經注意到了。在觀看電影後與他們拍張照且上傳到臉書將讓你有機會與我們一同參加尋寶。你會得到你所想看的電影的三張免費票卷。如果你沒有得到任何東西，也別為此感到失望。如果你透過電腦螢幕配對動物方城市的所有卡通角色，且全部答對，你將獲得你喜愛的填充娃娃。

答案：64. B 65. B 66. A

64.在哪裡能看到此廣告？

(A) 在動物園裡。

(B) 在電影首映會。

(C) 在戲院。

(D) 在學校。

65. 人們如何能獲得參與尋寶的機會？

(A) 透過擁抱漫畫人物。

(B) 在臉書張貼自己和卡通人物合照。

(C) 在臉書留下好評。

(D) 在臉書上張貼電影院前拍的照片。

66. 如何才能得到填充娃娃？

(A) 玩電腦遊戲。

(B) 透過買票看動物方城市。

(C) 在臉書評論動物方城市。

(D) 在門口和卡通人物玩。

獵豹

64.

·聽到對話，馬上鎖定 Welcome to Best Cinema .We have cartoon characters at the entrance...。根據 cinema（電影院、戲院），可得知答案跟電影院有關。選項中有兩個電影院選項：(B) at a movie premiere 在電影首映會，(C) at a cinema 在電影院必須從細節中，推知何者最為適合。

65.

·how 是詢問用「方法、工具、交通和感受」等等。本題是考用何種方法，因此由 join the treasure hunt（尋寶機會）前後子句，可以得知方法。又從第二句的得知 Taking a photo with them after watching the film and posting photos on Facebook will get you the chance...（在觀看電影後與他們拍張照且上傳到臉書將讓你有機

會⋯）。

66.

・首先判斷此題屬於細節題，公告中敘述許多活動。定位關鍵字 stuffed animal（填充玩偶）。最後一句 If you match all cartoon characters of Zootopia through the computer screen 就明白地告知聽眾利用 computer 可獲得玩偶。

貓頭鷹

64.

・此題屬於情境題，題目大意詢問對話在哪種媒體或地方出現。因為一開始說：Welcome to Best Cinema. 推知可能電影院聽到此對話。再經過其他公告內容，可以得知更確切的答案。如：我們在入口有卡通人物。Taking a photo with them after watching the film and posting photos on Facebook will get you the chance to join the treasure hunt with us.這些可推測出是電影首映會。

65.

・讀題時定位重要的疑問詞是解題技巧之一。w-的疑問詞有：who（誰），how（如何），where（哪裡），when（何時），what（什麼）。此題是細節題。通常要得到答案，先找出關鍵字。本題關鍵字是 join the treasure hunt，因此找出這個片語，再即使不瞭解意思，從前後文來判斷，亦可以判斷出答案。

66.

・此細節題需要稍微以換句話說的技巧，推測最佳選項。最後一句 If you match all cartoon characters of Zootopia through the computer screen 換言之就是某種電腦遊戲，所以選 (A) by playing a computer game。注意(C) by leaving comments on Facebook about Zootopia 和(D) by playing with the cartoon characters at the entrance 是陷阱選項，雖然有提及 Facebook 和 cartoon characters，但和獲得填充玩偶都沒有直接的因果關係。

 浣熊 🎧 MP3 183+MP3 185

還可能怎麼問

1. **Why is the announcement being made?**

   (A) to inform moviegoers about activities related to the film

   (B) to increase moviegoers' chance of getting the prize

   (C) to elevate the difficulty of the computer game

   (D) to encourage people to buy three movie tickets

2. **What is the speaker mainly discussing?**

   (A) cartoon characters

   (B) an innovative computer game

   (C) a Zootopia craze

   (D) activities that make moviegoers feel enjoyable

中譯與解析

1. 為什麼會發布公告？

(A) 告知電影愛好者有關與電影相關的活動。

(B) 增加電影愛好者得獎的機會。

(C) 提升電腦遊戲的難度。

(D) 鼓勵人們購買三張電影票。

2. 說話者主要在討論什麼？

(A) 卡通人物。

(B) 創新的電視遊戲。

(C) 動物方城市狂熱。

(D) 讓電影愛好者感到享受的活動。

答案：1. A 2. D

1. 題目是問為什麼會發布公告？先從四個選項分別來看。

· 選項 A 告知電影愛好者有關與電影相關的活動，此為聽力訊息中所傳達的意思，故可以得知答案為選項 A。

· 選項 B 增加電影愛好者得獎的機會，聽力訊息中未提到此訊息，所以可以排除此選項。

· 選項 C 提升電腦遊戲的難度，聽力訊息中未提到此訊息僅提到尋寶未獲獎者還能玩電腦遊戲，所以可以排除此選項。

· 選項 D 鼓勵人們購買三張電影票，聽力訊息中提到參加尋寶則你會得到你所想看的電影的三張免費票卷，但未提到鼓勵購買，所以可以排除此選項。

2. 題目是問說話者主要在討論什麼？先從四個選項分別來看。

· 選項 A，聽力訊息中有提到入口有卡通人物但主要講述內容不是這個，故可以排除此選項。選項 B，聽力訊息中有提到電腦遊戲但是未提到創新，故可以排除此選項。選項 C，聽力訊息中未提到此訊息，故可以排除此選項。選項 D，此為電影公司發佈此公告的原因，所以可以得知答案為選項 D。

Unit 23

電視節目公告：獎金雙倍讓人躍躍欲試

Instructions

❶ 請播放音檔聽下列對話，並完成試題。 🎧 MP3 186+MP3 187

❷ 「跟述」練習：寫完試題後請跟著音檔同步跟漸進式做「跟述」練習，提升聽力專注力。

❸ 加碼題：完成❶+❷步驟後，請再播放音檔寫浣熊試題，掌握其他可能的出題考點，強化應考實力。 🎧 MP3 186+MP3 188

67. How will the candidates be selected to participate in the race?

(A) by submitting their videos and resumes

(B) by proving that they are 20 years old

(C) by submitting their diplomas

(D) by cooperating with others

68. What does the speaker mean by "we're gonna pair you at random"?

(A) We are going to pay you.

(B) The candidates will be picked randomly.

(C) We are going to assign a partner to you by chance.

(D) We're going to pair you with the person you like.

69. How much was last year's award?

(A) 2 million dollars

(B) 1 million dollars

(C) 20 million dollars

(D) 3 million dollars

聽力原文和中譯

Questions 67-69 refer to the following recorded footage

Best Race is going to pick our candidates for the next season. All candidates have to submit their resumes and videos to our website before July 3rd, 2018, and the age limit is 20. You should be at least 20 years old to apply. For this season, we're gonna pair you at random, so this really tests your ability to cooperate with another person in order to win. I highly recommend chosen candidates stay positive during the entire race. For this season, the winner will get an award of two million dollars, twice that of last year's. Are you ready?

問題 67-69 請參閱下列錄製的影片片段

倍斯特競賽要替下季選角。所有候選人必須在 2018 年 7 月 3 日之前遞交他們的履歷和視頻，而且年齡限制是 20 歲。你應該要至少滿 20 歲才符合申請資格。對於這季，我們會隨意配對參賽者，所以這真地考驗你與其他人合作而獲勝的能力。對於這季，贏家會獲得 200 萬元的獎金，是去年的兩倍。你準備好了嗎？

答案：67. A. 68. C 69 B

67. 候選人如何才能被選中參加比賽？

(A) 遞交他們的視頻和履歷。

(B) 證明他們滿 20 歲。

(C) 遞交畢業證書。

(D) 與他人合作。

68. 廣告中的談話者說「我們會隨意配對參賽者」，其含意為何？

(A) 我們要付錢給你。

(B) 候選人將被隨機挑選。

(C) 我們將隨意指派夥伴給你。

(D) 我們要把你和喜歡的人配對。

69. 去年的獎金有多少？

(A) 200 萬元。

(B) 100 萬元。

(C) 2000 萬元。

(D) 300 萬元。

獵豹

67.

·聽到聽力訊息，馬上鎖定 All candidates have to submit their resumes and videos to our website... 遞交他們的履歷和視頻。根據 candidate，找出被選中參賽資格是 submitting their videos and resumes，因此答案為(A) by submitting their videos and resumes。

68.

·聽到聽力訊息直接鎖定在 pair you at random，pair you at random 是「隨意配對參賽者」的意思。掃描 pair you at random 的類似詞，pair 在此是動詞，指「配對」，random「隨意」，因此推知並非和自己選擇的人當夥伴，而是隨意配對，故答案為(C) We are going to assign a partner to you by chance..., by chance 意指「隨機」，為

at random 類似詞。

69.

· 首先判斷此題屬於細節題，掃描 award（獎金，獎項）的關鍵字。
How much，多少錢。注意是問去年的獎金，因此還要從今年的獎金
推測答案。短講快結束時提到，今年的獎金是去年的兩倍，今年是
two million dollars，兩百萬元。因此推知答案為(B)one million
dollars。

貓頭鷹

67.

· 此題是詢問管道和方式。此種問與答的模式，是獲取分數的好機會。
candidate（候選人），submit（遞交），resume（履歷表）。這
些重點單字，在多益考題中很常見，請熟背。

68.

· 此題是細節題。需要先理解動詞片語 pair you at random 的意思，再
搜尋其類似詞。cooperate with another person 是指「與其他合
作」，這也是隨機配對的用意之一。本題答案選項，容易混淆，請小
心。(A) We are going to pay you. → pay 是付錢，和 pair 沒有關
係。(B) The candidates will be picked randomly. → 是隨意配對。
(C) We are going to assign a partner to you by chance. → by
chance 是重要片語。(D) We're going to pair you with the person
you like. → 不能自己選擇。

69.

· 本題乍看之下是細節題型，但因為講者沒有明講去年的獎金，所以仍需
要運用推測能力，才不會落入陷阱。(A) 2 million dollars 就是陷阱選

項。本公告到數第二句提到：the winner will get the award of two million dollars, twice as last year's. ，今年獎金是 two million dollars，是去年的兩倍，因此去年是一百萬。twice as last year's 是指「去年獎金的兩倍」，請注意此細節。

 浣熊 🎧 MP3 186+MP3 188

還可能怎麼問

1. Who might the speaker be?

　　(A) a chosen candidate

　　(B) a super star

　　(C) a receptionist

　　(D) a TV host

2. What does the speaker strongly encourage?

　　(A) teenagers should find ways for them to look like 20

　　(B) forge your resume to make it more appealing

　　(C) don't split your winning money with your partner

　　(D) avoid negativity

中譯與解析

1. 說話者可能是誰？

　　(A) 獲選的候選人。

　　(B) 巨星。

　　(C) 接待員。

　　(D) 電視主持人。

2. 說話者強烈建議什麼？

(A) 青少年應該要找辦法讓他們看起來像 20 歲。

(B) 偽造你的履歷讓它更吸引人。

(C) 別將贏得的獎金分給你的夥伴。

(D) 避免負面。

答案：1. D 2. D

1. 題目是問說話者可能是誰？

．選項 A，廣告是在說「要替下季選角」，但選項確有 chosen 的訊息，且說話者不可能是已獲選者，比賽並未開始，所以可以排除此選項。選項 B，聽力訊息中未提到巨星，且無法推測出是巨星，所以可以排除此選項。選項 C，聽力訊息中未提到接待員且不符論述，所以可以排除此選項。選項 D，極有可能是電視主持人針對下次選角所拍的廣告，故可以得知答案為選項 D。

2. 題目是說話者強烈建議什麼？

．選項 A，聽力訊息中有提到「而且年齡限制是 20 歲。你應該要至少滿 20 歲才符合申請資格。」，但是沒有要他們偽造資格，故可以排除此選項。選項 B，聽力訊息中有提到要遞交履歷但沒有提到偽造的部分，故可以排除此選項。選項 C，聽力訊息中僅提到「對於這季，贏家會獲得 200 萬元的獎金，比去年多兩倍。你準備好了嗎？」，沒有提到分享獎金等訊息，故可以排除此選項。選項 D，聽力訊息中有提到 I highly recommend chosen candidates stay positive during the entire race.，highly recommend 即題目的 strongly encourage 此為同義表達，聽力訊息中的 stay positive 即選項中的 avoid negativity 此為同義表達所以可以得知答案為選項 D。

Unit 24

醫院公告：Ａ 型跟 AB 型血之情況大逆轉

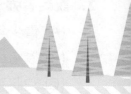

Instructions

❶ 請播放音檔聽下列對話，並完成試題。 🎧 MP3 189+MP3 190

❷ 「跟述」練習：寫完試題後請跟著音檔同步跟漸進式做「跟述」練習，提升聽力專注力。

❸ 加碼題：完成❶＋❷步驟後，請再播放音檔寫浣熊試題，掌握其他可能的出題考點，強化應考實力。 🎧 MP3 189+MP3 191

70. What is the purpose of the announcement?

(A) introducing the benefit of blood donation

(B) talking about a collision on the highway

(C) asking people to donate blood

(D) describing the process of blood donation

71. What does the sentence, "people with type A are so accident prone", imply?

(A) People with type A are prone to depression.

(B) People with type A blood get involved in accidents often.

(C) People with type A are usually careless.

(D) Blood types have nothing to do with car accidents.

72. **Why does the speaker say "We're gonna need type AB donors"?**

(A) A hospital just announced that type AB blood is running out.

(B) He thinks type AB blood is rare.

(C) Everyone who is injured in the collision has type AB blood.

(D) Some serious car crashes might cause the demand of type AB blood.

聽力原文和中譯

Questions 70-72 refer to the following announcement

One behalf of Best Memorial Center, I'd like you to know there's gonna be a blood donation booth outside our building from 9 a.m. to 6 p.m. We're totally running out of blood. We're in desperate need of type A blood donors. Type B and type O are also below the norm. I don't think we should joke about it that why people with type A are so accident prone, whereas people with type AB are in the paradise. Oh my phone just vibrated... there's a series of collisions on the highway. We're gonna need type AB donors.

問題 70-72 請參閱下列公告

代表倍斯特紀念中心，我想讓你了解在早上九點到下午六點，將有捐血站在我們的建築物外頭。我們幾乎用光了血量。我們迫切地需要 A 型血的捐贈者。B 型血和 O 型血也在標準值下。我不認為我們應該要拿這個來開玩笑，為什麼 A 型血這麼易於受到意外傷害，而 AB 型血的卻活在天堂。噢我的手機震動了…在高速公路上發生連環車禍。我們需要 AB 型的血液捐贈者。

答案：70. C 71. B 72. D

70. 此公告的目為何？

(A) 介紹捐血的好處。

(B) 談論高速公路上的連環車禍。

(C) 要求人們捐血。

(D) 描述捐血的過程。

 71. 句子「A 型血這麼易於受到意外傷害」是什麼意思？

(A)A 型的人容易憂鬱。

(B)A 型的人經常遇到傷害。

(C)A 型的人通常很粗心的。

(D)血型與車禍無關。

 72. 發言人為何說「我們迫切地需要 A 型血的捐贈者」？

(A)醫院剛剛宣布 AB 型血即將用光。

(B)他認為 AB 型血是罕見的。

(C)車禍受傷的每個人都是 AB 型血。

(D) 一些連環車禍。我們需要 AB 型的血液捐贈者。

 獵豹

70.

· 聽到聽力訊息，馬上鎖定 there's gonna be a blood donation booth outside... We're totally running out of blood...。根據 run out of blood 得知用光血量，因此推知需要眾人捐血。廣告一開始提到: 早上九點到下午六點，將有捐血站在我們的建築物外頭。答案非常清楚。

71.

· 聽到聽力訊息，馬上鎖定 I don't think we should joke about it that why people with type A are so accident prone...。從句子描述中，發現 A 型的人容易受到意外傷害。accident 意外，是重點單字，有此

推知答案(B) People with type A blood get involved in accidents often.正確。

72.

· 首先判斷此題屬於細節題，掃描(A)的關鍵字提到 AB 型，和 A 型不同。 選項(B)AB 型沒提到是否罕見。選項是(C)關於車禍都是 AB 型的人，不見得，選項(D) 一些連環車禍。我們需要 AB 型的血液捐贈者，則在公告的最後一行提到。

貓頭鷹

70.

· 此題屬於主旨題，題目大意詢問目的或是主旨為何。將廣告簡化出幾個單字，加強理解。如：a blood donation booth，running out of blood， type A blood donors， need type AB donors... 等等。

71.

· 本題的細節題，廣告中說到各血型的特點，以及血庫嚴重不足的情況。accident prone 容易遇到意外傷害。accident 本身有意外之意。選項(A)depression（憂鬱），選項(B)意外(C)粗心，選項(D)車禍。

72.

· 找出 need type AB donors 原因，請注意本句的前後子句。「我們迫切地需要 A 型血的捐贈者」的原因，請見最後一行：there's a series of collisions on the highway. We're gonna need type AB donors. 因為發生連環車禍的因素，才會有大量需求。

還可能怎麼問

NEW **1. What does the speaker mean when he says "Type B and type O are also below the norm"?**

(A) these types need to most attention.

(B) these types are within the standard.

(C) these types have fewer donors.

(D) these types are also in a short supply.

2. What type of business is being discussed?

(A) The Cosmetic Surgery Clinic.

(B) a cosmetic company.

(C) a pharmacy store.

(D) a hospital.

 中譯與解析

NEW **1. 當她說「B 型血和 O 型血也在標準值下」，說話者指的是什麼？**

(A) 那些類型的血型需要最多關注。

(B) 那些類型的血型在標準值內。

(C) 那些類型的血型有較少的捐贈者。

(D) 那些類型的血型也短缺。

2. 正在敘述的是哪一種公司？

(A) 美容整形外科診所。

(B) 化妝品公司。

(C) 藥品店。

(D) 醫院。

答案：1. D 2. D

1. **題目是問當他說「B 型血和 O 型血也在標準值下」，說話者指的是什麼？**

· 選項 A，血液庫存量不足可能會引起關注，但題目是需要最多關注，目前需要最多關注的是 A 型血，且這不是她講這句話的目的，所以可以排除此選項。選項 B，題目是説「在標準值下」與「在標準值內」意思不同，所以可以排除此選項。 選項 C，無法從聽力訊息中推斷血液在標準值下是因為捐贈者少或是因為使用量大，所以可以排除此選項。選項 D，此為聽力訊息中表達的意思，故可以得知答案為選項 D。

2. **題目是問正在敘述的是哪一種公司？**

· 選項 A，外科診所也有可能需要臨時輸血等，但更適合的選項比較是輸血中心、捐血中心或醫院，故可以排除此選項。選項 B，不太可能是化妝品公司，故可以排除此選項。選項 C，藥品店不太符合，故可以排除此選項。選項 D，由 Best Memorial Center 等可以推斷極有可能是醫院，所以可以得知答案為選項 D。

Unit 25
電影工作室公告：解壓有道，讓員工玩玩水晶球、算個塔羅牌也無妨

Instructions

❶ 請播放音檔聽下列對話，並完成試題。 📣 MP3 192+MP3 193

❷ 「跟述」練習：寫完試題後請跟著音檔同步跟漸進式做「跟述」練習，提升聽力專注力。

❸ 加碼題：完成❶＋❷步驟後，請再播放音檔寫浣熊試題，掌握其他可能的出題考點，強化應考實力。 📣 MP3 192+MP3 194

73. According to the speaker, which of the following topics are the sessions about?

(A) astronomy

(B) making crystal balls

(C) fortune telling

(D) health problems

74. Why does the speaker say, "I benefited from that"?

(A) Studying astrology allowed him to find out his health problems.

(B) The palm reading gave him a chance to find out his health problems.

(C) He made some money from palm reading.

(D) Reading tarot cards has many benefits.

75. **Which of the following is the closest in meaning to the phrase, "drag you down there", as in "It's really not my business to tell you to come to afternoon's sessions, and drag you down there"?**

(A) make you come down to the basement

(B) The sessions really drag.

(C) drag something out of you

(D) make you go somewhere you might not want to go

聽力原文和中譯

Questions 73-75 refer to the following talk

I know you probably work overtime lately, rewriting stories. It's really not my business to tell you to come to the afternoon's sessions, and drag you down there. They include knowing astrology, crystal ball learning, palm reading, and tarot cards. Definitely, don't get so obsessed with those things, but it won't cause a harm to get to know them. Last year, I did the palm reading and I found out my health problems. I benefited from that. Reading tarot cards allows you to get to know your career path or your relationship problems, and it's free.

問題 73-75 請參閱下列談話

我知道你們近期都加班，改寫故事。告知你們要來下午的會議和把你們拖到這來不是我的職務範圍。他們包括了了解星相、讀水晶球、看手相和塔羅牌。沒有必要那麼沉迷那些東西，但了解下其實也無傷大雅。去年我透過讀手相發現自己的健康問題。我從中獲益。解讀塔羅牌能讓你了解你的職涯走向或感情問題，而且是免費的。

答案：73. C　74. B　75. D

---

73. 根據談話者敘述，下列哪些話題和會議有關？

(A) 天文學。

(B) 製作水晶球。

(C) 算命。

(D) 健康問題。

74. 談話者說「我從中受益」，其含意為何？

(A) 學習占星術使他能找出自己的健康問題。

(B) 看手相讓他有機會找出他的健康問題。

(C) 他從看手相中賺了一些錢。

(D) 閱讀塔羅牌有很多好處。

75. 在「告知你們要來下午的會議和把你們拖到這來不在我的職務範圍。」句子中，下列哪個選項和片語「把你們拖到這來」意思最接近？

(A) 讓你到地下室。

(B) 會議真的拖延。

(C) 迫使你交代某事。

(D) 讓你去可能不想去的地方。

73.

・聽到對話，馬上鎖定 They include knowing astrology, crystal ball learning, palm reading, and tarot cards...。根據第三句，會議和星相、水晶球、塔羅牌有關，綜合以上，可推知為算命(fortune telling)。

74.

・首先判斷此題屬於細節題，I benefited from that... benefit 在此當動

詞，受到好處。聽到對話，馬上鎖定 Last year, I did the palm reading and I found out my health problems. 去年我透過掌紋閱覽了解了自己的健康問題。因此得知是健康問題。

75.

- 本題考片語，鎖定 drag you down there，drag you down there 是「把你拖來這裡」的意思。這是屬於不情願的行為，因此答案是(D)。選項(B)的 drag 是拖延之意，是屬於混淆作用。

貓頭鷹

73.

- 此題是屬於單字理解部分。一個句子有許多類似的技能，很容易因此搞混了其中的意思，請考生小心。注意這題的 topics 是指會議主題，不是詢問整篇短講的主題。考生要小心不要將此題和整篇主題題型搞混。首先定位題目的關鍵字 sessions，會議。關鍵字在第二句出現，下一句就交代會議內容：They include knowing astrology, crystal ball learning, palm reading, and tarot cards.統整這句細節，都是算命方式，故選(C) fortune telling。

74.

- 理解題通常需要很多資料，或許無法直接得知答案。palm reading 是指「手相」，說話者提到看手相時，發現了健康問題。這點讓他從中受益。health problem（健康問題）。選項(A)不是占星數，是手相。選項(B)正確，選項(C)沒提到金錢部分，選項(D)跟受益沒有直接關連。

75.

- 此題是單字題。需要先理解動詞片語 drag you down there 的意思。

(A) make you come down to the basement 讓你到地下室(B) The sessions really drag.會議真的拖延。(C) drag something out of you 迫使你交代某事(D) make you go somewhere you might not want to go 讓你去可能不想去的地方，選項(D)和此片語意思最接近。

 浣熊 MP3 192+MP3 194

還可能怎麼問

1. **What type of business is being discussed?**
   (A) a fortune-telling company
   (B) a health insurance company
   (C) a Head Hunter
   (D) a Movie Studio

2. **What will the listeners probably do next?**
   (A) teach others tarot cards
   (B) use crystal balls to increase profits
   (C) make a career move
   (D) relax for a while by joining the session

中譯與解析

1. 正在敘述的是哪一種公司？
   (A) 一間算命公司。
   (B) 一間健康保險公司。
   (C) 一間獵人頭公司。

(D) 一間電影工作室。

2. 聽者們接下來可能會做什麼？

(A) 教導其他人塔羅牌。

(B) 使用水晶球增加利潤。

(C) 採取職涯動作。

(D) 藉由參加下午的活動講習放鬆一回兒。

答案：1. D 2. D

1. 題目是問正在敘述的是哪一種公司？

· 選項 A，聽力訊息中有提到算命，但是是公司請人來讓員工解壓，而非公司是算命公司，所以可以排除此選項。選項 B，聽力訊息中有提到 I did the palm reading and I found out my health problems，這部分提到健康，但沒有提到保險，且無法推測出公司是間保險公司，所以可以排除此選項。選項 C，聽力訊息中未提及獵人頭且不符合，所以可以排除此選項。選項 D，聽力訊息中有提到 I know you probably work overtime lately, rewriting stories.，所以極有可能是電影工作室，故可以得知答案為選項 D。

2. 題目是問聽者們接下來可能會做什麼？

· 選項 A，有提到塔羅牌但是未提到教導的訊息，故可以排除此選項。選項 B，有提到水晶球但是未提到使用水晶球增加利潤的訊息，所以可以得知答案為選項 B。選項 C，聽力訊息中未提到這部分，故可以排除此選項。選項 D，確實是公司舉辦讓大家來解壓的活動，所以可以得知答案為選項 D。

1 照片描述

2 應答問題

3 簡短對話

4 簡短獨白

模擬試題

Unit 26
公司公告：幾個分公司裁撤，打道回洛杉磯總部

🔍 Instructions

❶ 請播放音檔聽下列對話，並完成試題。 🎧 MP3 195+MP3 196

❷ 「跟述」練習：寫完試題後請跟著音檔同步跟漸進式做「跟述」練習，提升聽力專注力。

❸ 加碼題：完成❶＋❷步驟後，請再播放音檔寫浣熊試題，掌握其他可能的出題考點，強化應考實力。 🎧 MP3 195+MP3 197

76. What does "a brutal battle" refer to in this announcement?

(A) bidding on a shopping website

(B) fighting with co-workers

(C) the takeover bid

(D) the takeover of the HR department

77. What does the new owner want?

(A) moving to L.A.

(B) building a new headquarters

(C) reading every worker's resume

(D) reducing human power cost

78. Which of the following is the closest in meaning to the phrase, "dust off your resume"?

(A) renew your resume

(B) print out your resume

(C) send your resume

(D) check your resume

聽力原文和中譯

Questions 76-78 refer to the following announcement

This morning the takeover bid was just as crazy. It was a brutal battle. Unfortunately, we lost. Several branch offices are gonna get cut. Apparently, the new owner wants to reduce the cost of human power. We won't get the exact information until HR managers contact me. I don't even know whether I will keep my position. Oh, HR managers are here. It seems that our jobs are safe, but we all need to move to the L.A. headquarters. For those who can't move to the headquarters, you probably have to dust off your resume to see where your parachute is.

問題 76-78 請參閱下列公告

今天早上收購競標如往常一樣瘋狂。競爭嚴峻。不幸的是，我們輸了。幾個分公司會被裁撤。顯然地，新的雇主想要減少人事成本。直到人事部經理們告知我時，才得知確切的消息。我甚至不知道為什麼我的職務未更動。噢人事部經理來了。似乎我們的工作都受到保障，但是我們都需要搬至洛杉磯總部。對於那些不能搬至總部者，你可能需要更新履歷看自己下的落腳處在哪了。

答案：76. C 77. D 78. A

---

76. 此公告中「競爭嚴峻」是指什麼？

(A) 在購物網站上競標。

(B) 與同事打架。

(C) 收購競標。

(D) 收購人力資源部。

77. 新的雇主想要什麼呢？

(A) 搬到洛杉磯。

(B) 成立新總部。

(C) 看每個員工的履歷。

(D) 減少人事成本。

 78. 下列選項，何者的意思與「更新履歷」最接近？

(A) 更新你的履歷。

(B) 列印你的履歷。

(C) 寄出你的履歷。

(D) 檢查你的履歷。

 獵豹

76.

・聽到對話，馬上鎖定第一句 This morning the takeover bid was just as crazy。It was a brutal battle，競爭嚴峻，延續第一句，可推測 It 指的是第一句的 takeover bid。

77.

・what 是詢問什麼，題目越短，必須吸收的可能更多。從第五句： the new owner wants to reduce the cost of human power. 這是前因後果，因為收購競標失利，造成公司裁撤，因此需要減少人力成本。

78.

・聽到對話，馬上鎖定 have to dust your resume to see where your parachute is...。dust one's resume 是更新履歷之意。由於減少人力成本，加上要搬到洛杉磯總部，因此有人無法前往的，就會被裁員。此

Unit 26　公司公告：幾個分公司裁撤，打道回洛杉磯總部

1 照片描述

2 應答問題

3 簡短對話

4 簡短獨白

模擬試題

時，更新履歷是最重要之事。

貓頭鷹

76.

· 此題屬於推測題，題目考點的 brutal battle 和字面意思不同，不是指真的戰役，考生須具備代名詞的文法觀念，及熟悉 bid 這個單字有「競標」之意，才能推測出 brutal battle 的深層意思。是比較難的推測題。brutal 指「嚴峻的、殘酷的」。從第一句得知： takeover bid... It was a brutal battle，因此可以推知在此指的是 the takeover bid（收購競標）。

77.

· 讀題時先找出關鍵字:want（想要）和 what（何者）。原因有很多，如： we lost. Several branch offices are gonna get cut. Apparently, the new owner wants to reduce the cost of human power. 由於競標失利，造成後續的損失，因此減少成本是可以推測得知的答案。

78.

· 單字題和用不同單字，表達相同意思。考生平常準備的單字充足與否，此時就能見真章。where your parachute is 是指「何處是落角處」，換句話說，亦即下一分工作在哪間公司。dust off one's resume 是「更新某人履歷」，因此選項(A) renew your resume 為正確答案。

浣熊 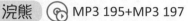 MP3 195+MP3 197

還可能怎麼問

1. **Why is the announcement being made?**

   (A) to inform employees that they've acquired another L.A. company

   (B) to inform employees that the speaker's job will remain unchanged

   (C) to protect employee's job security

   (D) to inform employees that there're going to be layoffs

2. **Where are the listeners?**

   (A) at an L.A. headquarter

   (B) at an HR managers' office

   (C) at a branch office

   (D) at a stockholder meeting room

中譯與解析

1. 為什麼會發佈公告？

   (A) 告知員工們他們已經收購另一間洛杉磯公司。

   (B) 告知員工說話者的工作會維持不變。

   (C) 保護員工們的工作穩定。

   (D) 告知員工們將會有裁員。

2. 聽者們在什麼地方？

   (A) 在洛杉磯總部。

   (B) 在人事經理的辦公室。

(C) 在分公司辦公室。

(D) 在股東會議室。

答案：1. D 2. C

1. **題目是問為什麼會發佈公告？**

・選項 A，聽力訊息中有提到 This morning the takeover bid was just as crazy. It was a brutal battle. Unfortunately, we lost.，代表收購失敗了，而且洛杉磯的部分是公司的總部，公司要整併，所以可以排除此選項。選項 B，聽力訊息中有提到 It seems that our jobs are safe, but we all need to move to the L.A. headquarters.，代表工作會維持不變，但沒主因，所以可以排除此選項。選項 C，聽力訊息中未提到此訊息，所以可以排除此選項。選項 D，主要公告是要告知員工人事異動，故可以得知答案為選項 D。

2. **題目是問聽者們在什麼地方？**

・選項 A，從聽力訊息中可以得知他們目前不在總部，是要搬過去，故可以排除此選項。選項 B，聽力訊息中有提到人事經理，但是他們不在人事經理的辦公室，故可以排除此選項。選項 C，此為他們即可能待的地點，所以可以得知答案為選項 C。 選項 D，聽力訊息中未提到這部分，故可以排除此選項。

本書所附的模擬試題包含了多樣化的類型、融入道地慣用語和現實實況，除了寫一回試題練習檢視自我學習成果外，可以使用分拆的音檔，特別練習聽 part 3 和 part 4，熟悉聽這樣長度的聽力訊息，並做數次的影子跟讀練習，提升聽力專注力。此外，請務必也將解析看完了解自己是否都理解了還是剛好猜對答案喔！

模擬試題

▶ **Listening Test** 🎧 MP3 198

In the Listening test, you must demonstrate your ability to understand spoken English. This section is divided into four parts and will take approximately 45 minutes to complete. Do not mark the answers in your test book. Use the answer sheet that is provided separately.

▶ **PART 1**

Directions: For each question, you will listen to four short statements about a picture in your test book. These statements will not be printed and will only be spoken one time. Select the statement that best describes what is happening in the picture and mark the corresponding letter (A), (B), (C), (D) on the answer sheet.

Example   Sample Answer
                                             A ● C D

Statement (B), "Some people are wearing backpacks", is the best description of the picture. So you should select answer (B) and mark it on your answer sheet.

1.

(A)   (B)   (C)   (D)

2.

(A)   (B)   (C)   (D)

3.

(A)   (B)   (C)   (D)

4.

(A)   (B)   (C)   (D)

5.

(A)　(B)　(C)　(D)

6.

(A)　(B)　(C)　(D)

Directions: For each question, you will listen to a statement or a question followed by three possible responses spoken in English. They will not be printed and will only be spoken one time. Select the best response and mark the corresponding letter (A), (B), or (C) on your answer sheet.

7. Mark your answer on your answer sheet.

8. Mark your answer on your answer sheet.

9. Mark your answer on your answer sheet.

10. Mark your answer on your answer sheet.

11. Mark your answer on your answer sheet.

12. Mark your answer on your answer sheet.

13. Mark your answer on your answer sheet.

14. Mark your answer on your answer sheet.

15. Mark your answer on your answer sheet.

16. Mark your answer on your answer sheet.

17. Mark your answer on your answer sheet.

18. Mark your answer on your answer sheet.

19. Mark your answer on your answer sheet.

20. Mark your answer on your answer sheet.

21. Mark your answer on your answer sheet.

22. Mark your answer on your answer sheet.

23. Mark your answer on your answer sheet.

24. Mark your answer on your answer sheet.

25. Mark your answer on your answer sheet.

26. Mark your answer on your answer sheet.

27. Mark your answer on your answer sheet.

28. Mark your answer on your answer sheet.

29. Mark your answer on your answer sheet.

30. Mark your answer on your answer sheet.

31. Mark your answer on your answer sheet.

▶ **PART 3** 🎧 MP3 200

Directions: In this part, you will listen to several conversations between two or more speakers. These conversations will not be printed and will only be spoken one time. For each conversation, you will be asked to answer three questions. Select the best response and mark the corresponding letter (A), (B), (C), (D) on the answer sheet.

32. Which of the following best explains the term "photo credit"?
(A) the way for photographers to make money
(B) the acknowledgement of the source of photos
(C) the way for photographers to build their credibility
(D) the acknowledgement that the photo is beautiful

33. Why did the man say, "ouch!"?
(A) He was bitten by a deer.
(B) He was chased by a deer.
(C) He did not like the photo.
(D) A deer stepped on his foot.

34. Why did the woman say, "that deer…?
(A) The deer looks very funny.
(B) The man looks ridiculous in pink.
(C) The situation of the deer biting the man is really funny.
(D) The situation of the deer chasing the man is hilarious.

35. Why did the man say, "perhaps... not that close to them"?
   (A) Because those monkeys were pushing him
   (B) He wanted the others to follow the rule not to get close to the monkeys.
   (C) Because he did not want the others to frighten the monkeys
   (D) He's trying to persuade the others to stay away from the monkeys.

36. Which of the following is the closest to "agitated"?
   (A) excited
   (B) disturbed and upset
   (C) adorable and sweet
   (D) frightened

37. According to the context of the conversation, why did the woman say, "can't we just have some sushi and seafood"?
   (A) She heard that sushi and seafood in Arashiyama are delicious.
   (B) Arashiyama is famous for sushi and seafood.
   (C) She is not interested in seeing monkeys, and would rather do something else.
   (D) Seeing those monkeys eating reminds her it's dinner time.

Donor Name	number
Nick	BF-1007
Jack	BY-1007
Chris	CF-1006
Jimmy	CY-1007

38. Which of the following is the closest in meaning to "my hands are tied"?
(A) There's nothing else I can do.
(B) Someone tied my hands.
(C) I am too busy.
(D) I cannot pick one for you.

 39. Who does the phrase "four candidates" refer to in this conversation?
(A) sperm donors
(B) blood donors
(C) candidates for an election
(D) candidates for the admission to Ivy League schools

 40. What does the sentence "they all graduated from Ivy League schools" imply?
(A) Having a university degree is not important in the speakers' criteria.
(B) Ivy League school graduates are more competitive in general.
(C) They are highly educated.
(D) Having an Ivy League university degree is enviable.

Name	Price
Jack	US 7 million dollars
Tim	US 8 million dollars
Jim	US 8 million dollars
Derek	US 10 million dollars

41. What does "we just have to think outside the box" imply?
(A) We have to think according to the rules.
(B) It's better for us to bribe the basketball player.
(C) We have to come up with more creative ways.
(D) We need to see what's printed on the box.

42. What is the solution that these speakers come up with to sign Derek?
(A) paying him cash under the table
(B) negotiating with him
(C) making him look like a big shot
(D) bribing him

43. Which of the following is the closest in meaning to "a big shot" in the sentence "invite him to the dinner, making him look like a big shot or something"?
(A) someone who looks nice on camera
(B) someone good at taking photos
(C) a good basketball player
(D) a VIP

proposal	Budget
A	20 million dollars
B	2 billion dollars
C	20,000,000 dollars

44. Who might these speakers be?
(A) construction workers
(B) bank investors
(C) construction company employees
(D) students studying architecture

45. What is the special situation regarding proposal A?
   (A) It did not pass the evaluation by the Department of Environmental Protection
   (B) It is being assessed by the Department of Environmental Protection.
   (C) The government does not allow construction in that place in proposal A.
   (D) Proposal A will cost too much money.

46. What does the woman mean by saying "we haven't reached a consensus..."?
   (A) We still need to reach an agreement.
   (B) We still need to do more research.
   (C) We have reached a conclusion.
   (D) We need to carry out more surveys.

Item
Old chair
Picasso painting
Monet painting
museums

47. Who is Rick Chen?
   (A) a child
   (B) a father
   (C) an auctioneer
   (D) a salesman

48. What is the main topic of the conversation?
   (A) auctioning the possessions of a person who passed away
   (B) mourning a person who passed away
   (C) selling things from an antique shop
   (D) how to buy a chair

49. Why are Rick Chen's possessions sold?

(A) His children want them sold.

(B) because his family is bankrupt

(C) because his wife wants them sold.

(D) They are sold according to his will.

Movie	Rating
A	PG
B	PG-13
C	R
D	G

50. What is the purpose of the conversation?

(A) purchasing the tickets to a movie

(B) deciding who will go see movies

(C) asking for the suggestions about a movie

(D) asking how much the tickets will cost

51. Why does the woman recommend movie B or D?

(A) The content of movie B or D is more appropriate for children.

(B) Movie B and D are both animations.

(C) The tickets to movie B or D are on discount.

(D) Both movie B and D receive high accolades.

52. Why is movie C not recommended?

(A) It has lots of violence.

(B) Some scenes are not proper for children.

(C) The tickets to movie C were sold out.

(D) It received horrible reviews.

53. What does 'hiring freeze" imply?

(A) The weather was freezing cold when they got hired.

(B) Companies have stopped hiring more people.

(C) Companies are hiring more people.

(D) They don't have much information about the employment.

54. Why does the man say to the woman "you're such a workaholic"?

(A) because the woman is very demanding

(B) because the woman wants more overtime hours

(C) because he wants to compliment the woman

(D) because he wished he were a workaholic, too

55. What does the woman think about the other woman's home-baked cookies?

(A) She thinks those cookies taste better with chocolate milk shake.

(B) She does not like those cookies.

(C) She thinks highly of those home-baked cookies.

(D) She does not like having those cookies with coffee.

56. What does "a fuzzy" refer to?

(A) a fuzzy picture

(B) a humanities major

(C) a warm feeling

(D) an engineering major

57. What does "a techie" refer to?

(A) a science major

(B) a technician

(C) a Chinese major

(D) a repairman

58. Which of the following is the closest in meaning to "You guys complement each other"?
(A) You give each other compliments often.
(B) You have been dating for a long time.
(C) Giving compliments is important in your relationship.
(D) You make each other a better person.

Candidate	photo
A	High fashion
B	commercial
C	commercial
D	High fashion

59. What are the speakers talking about?
(A) a catwalk
(B) models' performances
(C) a fashion show
(D) which model is prettier

60. According to the speaker, what is wrong with candidate B?
(A) Her walk is terrible.
(B) Her photos are not stunning.
(C) She has an attitude problem.
(D) She's too short.

 61. Which of the followings best explains, "her photos are stunning"?
(A) Her photos are breathtakingly beautiful.
(B) Her photos are very shocking.
(C) She does not perform well in photoshoots.
(D) She works well with photographers.

62. **What does the man think about the offer?**
   (A) He is confused.
   (B) He is disappointed.
   (C) He is very curious.
   (D) He is very interested.

63. **According to the woman, what are the responsibilities of the spokesperson?**
   (A) taking campaign photos
   (B) shooting commercials for the Medical Center
   (C) building a healthy image of the Medical Center
   (D) going through a surgery

64. **What is the man probably going to do after the conversation?**
   (A) registering for a surgery
   (B) revising the contract
   (C) taking campaign photos
   (D) signing the contract

65. **Why does Jack Collins make this phone call?**
   (A) He wants to place a new order.
   (B) He wants to clarify a misunderstanding.
   (C) He wants to know where Linda is.
   (D) He wants to file some complaints.

66. **Who is Jack Collins?**
   (A) a pharmacist
   (B) a travel agent
   (C) a customer who wants to place orders with a pharmaceutical company
   (D) a sales representative from a pharmaceutical company

67. Why is Linda not available to answer the call?
   (A) She is on a business trip.
   (B) She went on a personal trip in Paris.
   (C) She is in a meeting with her boss.
   (D) She does not want to answer the call.

68. What is the problem with the sample?
   (A) It is smaller than expected.
   (B) It was not produced under the SOP guidelines.
   (C) It does not meet the lab standard.
   (D) It is contaminated.

69. Which of the followings is the closest in meaning to "negligence" as in "it could be negligence on our part"?
   (A) not paying enough attention
   (B) finishing the production too fast
   (C) abiding by the guidelines
   (D) not cooperating with FDA

70. What will the speakers probably do after the conversation?
   (A) talking to FDA
   (B) talking to lab employees
   (C) examining the sample again
   (D) devising more scrupulous rules

▶ **PART 4** 🎧 MP3 201

   Directions: In this part, you will listen to several talks by one or two speakers. These talks will not be printed and will only be spoken one time. For each talk, you will be asked to answer three questions. Select the best response and mark the corresponding letter (A), (B), (C), or (D) on your answer sheet.

71. Where might you hear this advertisement?

(A) a shopping mall
(B) a Hello Kitty amusement park
(C) a cartoon amusement park
(D) a zoo

72. According to this advertisement, what might personal shoppers do for consumers?

(A) renew membership
(B) line up
(C) go shopping
(D) buying rabbits

73. What does Black Friday imply in the advertisement?

(A) the day Jesus died
(B) a major shopping day
(C) the day before Christmas
(D) Easter

74. Which of the following is the closest to "a computer glitch"?

(A) a discount on computers
(B) a computer bug
(C) a poster shown on computer
(D) a weather forecast software

75. What kind of disaster will hit Florida during the weather forecast?

(A) a hurricane
(B) a typhoon
(C) a tornado
(D) an earthquake

76. Why does the weatherman say, "I guess people in Miami will feel so relieved..."?
(A) because the tornado might not strike Miami
(B) because people at Miami are quite used to tornadoes
(C) because people at Miami are already evacuated
(D) because people at Miami are not afraid of any disaster

77. Why does the speaker say, "Oops... My office glass wall just shattered"?
(A) The glass was not bulletproof.
(B) The glass was shot by bullets.
(C) The police officers shot the glass.
(D) The glass was destroyed by the crocodiles.

78. What are the visitors told to do when they see the crocodiles?
(A) start panicking.
(B) remain calm.
(C) call the police.
(D) call animal specialists.

79. How is the weather on the day of this announcement?
(A) very hot
(B) warm
(C) very cold
(D) cool

80. Where might you hear these instructions?
(A) a department store
(B) a cooking school
(C) a Thanksgiving party
(D) a weapon store

81. Who might the speaker address?
(A) gourmets
(B) recipe writers
(C) people interested in learning cooking
(D) people interested in kitchenware

82. Why does the speaker say, "I'd like to show you my personal weapon... don't be afraid"?
(A) He is trying to display his weapons.
(B) He knows some people are scared by weapons.
(C) When he says weapon, he's not referring to a real weapon.
(D) He knows some people dislike guns.

83. What do cheerleaders do in this activity?
(A) They perform gymnastics.
(B) They donate money.
(C) They give kisses.
(D) They dance

84. What is the main topic of the news report?
(A) a charity event
(B) an amusement park
(C) cheerleading
(D) kissing skills

85. Why does the speaker say, "Too bad, I'm a reporter"?
(A) He does not enjoy his job.
(B) He does not think the quality of the report is excellent.
(C) He thinks the charity is being held badly.
(D) He cannot participate in the activity because of his identity.

86. **Which of the followings is the most likely to put on this advertisement?**
(A) tailors
(B) an online shopping site
(C) a diaper manufacturer
(D) a convenience store

 87. **Why does the speaker quote this line, "The diapers just magically appear at our door"?**
(A) to show the high quality of the diapers
(B) to advertise that they offer magic shows
(C) to show how convenient the service is
(D) to target consumers who need diapers

88. **What kind of people is the most likely to use the service in this advertisement?**
(A) career women who have children
(B) tailors
(C) single men
(D) young students

 89. **Which of the following is the closest to the word "spots" as in "we still have two spots left"?**
(A) dots
(B) sightseeing spots
(C) vacancies
(D) spotlights

90. **Why does the speaker mention that they are short of funds for their new computer lab?**
(A) to hold a fundraiser
(B) to imply a way to draw applications
(C) to ask for the donation of new computers
(D) to ask for advice from parents

91. If parents want to ensure their children will be accepted by the Academy, what might they do?
(A) They might talk to the principal directly.
(B) They might train their children to have more talents.
(C) They might donate funds to the Academy.
(D) They might train their children to become bilingual.

92. Who might the speaker be talking to?
(A) his father's friends
(B) his family members
(C) tourists
(D) vintners

93. Why does the speaker's father buy the cellar?
(A) to develop his hobby
(B) for investment
(C) to make more money
(D) to store things he does not need

 94. What does "such a perfect blend" refer to?
(A) great taste of coffee
(B) mixing cocktails
(C) blending in the party
(D) great taste of wine

 95. According to the speaker, what is the effect of "a light brown shadow"?
(A) to highlight your eyes
(B) to reduce puffiness around the eyes
(C) to make you look thinner
(D) to make your skin darker

96. Why does the speaker mention "orange and grape flavors"?
(A) They are her favorite flavors.
(B) The auction provides desserts of orange and grape flavors.
(C) The company aims to sell more lipsticks of these two flavors.
(D) She does not wear lipsticks of these two flavors.

97. If a customer buy 6 lipsticks, what will she receive?
(A) free samples
(B) lipsticks of strawberry flavor
(C) lipsticks of grape flavor
(D) a beautiful handbag

98. What does the speaker mean by "It's gonna wow you"?
(A) It will amaze you.
(B) It will frighten you.
(C) It will make you feel shocked.
(D) It will make you relaxed.

99. Where is this talk given?
(A) a castle
(B) a haunted house
(C) a cinema
(D) a department store

100. Which of the following is the closest to "It's just insider information"?
(A) information about movies
(B) the speaker's secret
(C) information not known to the public
(D) information about the new facilities

新多益 模擬試題解析

 Part 1 照片描述

聽力原文與中譯	
1. (A) There are no traffic lights on the street. (B) There are three cars on the street. (C) The façade of the building is covered by trees (D) There are many taxis on this street.	**1.** (A) 路上沒有紅綠燈。 (B) 路上有三台車。 (C) 這棟建築的正面都被樹覆蓋。 (D) 路上有許多計程車。
答案：(B)	

 解析

依據圖片下方三台轎車，再確認背景沒有其它轎車，故選(B)。注意(C)是陷阱選項，左側雖然有樹，但沒有完全覆蓋建築物正面，所以不能選。

聽力原文與中譯	
2. (A) The storefront is decorated with a huge shrimp. (B) There are few pedestrians. (C) The storefront is decorated with a huge crab. (D) All of the pedestrians are wearing short sleeve shirts.	**2.** (A) 臨街店面用一隻超大蝦子裝飾。 (B) 幾乎沒有路人。 (C) 臨街店面用一隻超大螃蟹裝飾。 (D) 所有的路人都穿短袖上衣。

答案：(C)

解析

Storefront 指臨街店面，明顯可見有一隻巨大螃蟹的裝飾品，所以選(C)。

聽力原文與中譯	
3. (A) There are tall buildings everywhere. (B) The streets are lined with flowers on both sides. (C) There are more bicycles than cars. (D) A festival is being held.	3. (A) 到處都是高樓。 (B) 馬路兩邊都是花。 (C) 腳踏車比汽車多。 (D) 一場慶典正被舉辦。

答案：(A)

解析

圖片特色是大部份空間都被高樓佔據，因此最適合的選項是 (A)。(B)，(C)提及的 flowers，bicycles 在圖片都沒出現，(D) A festival 完全與圖片主題無關。

聽力原文與中譯	
4. (A) Two men are trying to pull the rickshaws. (B) None of the men is wearing glasses. (C) The woman in the rickshaw is weeping. (D) The passengers are children.	4. (A) 兩個男人正試著拉人力車。 (B) 沒有人戴眼鏡。 (C) 人力車裡的女生正在哭泣。 (D) 乘客是小孩。

答案：(A)

解析

人力車是 rickshaw。(A)選項的主詞：Two men 及動作 pulling the rickshaws 完全符合圖片的主題。

聽力原文與中譯	
5. (A) A spoon and a fork are on the table. (B) A dessert and a cup of coffee are served. (C) There is no napkin on the tray. (D) The table is occupied.	**5.** (A) 一個湯匙和叉子在桌上。 (B) 有甜點和咖啡。 (C) 托盤上沒有紙巾。 (D) 桌子邊坐滿人。

答案：(B)

解析

此題考餐桌上物品的細節，由一份甜點及一杯飲料判斷，(B)是細節準確度最高的選項。

聽力原文與中譯	
6. (A) It is raining heavily. (B) The street is barren. (C) There is no queue near the store. (D) People are lining up.	**6.** (A) 正下傾盆大雨。 (B) 馬路很荒涼。 (C) 商店旁沒有隊伍。 (D) 人們正在排隊。

答案：(D)

解析

由排隊人潮的穿著，可判斷沒有下雨，排除(A)，根據人潮，也排除(B)。排隊的名詞及動詞有 queue 和 line，故選(D)。

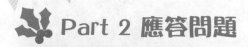 **Part 2 應答問題**

聽力原文與中譯	
7. The weather forecast is quite accurate, isn't it? (A) I like the weather here. (B) Yes, it is. (C) The weatherman seems confident.	**7. 這場氣象預報很準確，不是嗎？** (A) 我喜歡這裡的天氣。 (B) 是的。 (C) 氣象主播似乎有信心。

答案：(B)

解析

此題的疑問句型是附加問句，正確的回答方式和回答 Yes or No 是非疑問句方式相同。因此(B) Yes, it is 表達贊同疑問句提出的看法：「氣象預報很準確」是最佳答案。

聽力原文與中譯	
8. We need to order some office supplies. (A) I'll get right on it. (B) The office supplies are expensive. (C) Who will order office supplies?	**8. 我們需要訂購一些辦公室用品。** (A) 我馬上處理。 (B) 辦公室用品是昂貴的。 (C) 誰將訂購辦公室用品？

答案：(A)

解析

此題是肯定句，說話者表達需要訂購一些辦公室用品。合理的應答是呼應需求，(A) I'll get right on it. 在口語表達「馬上處理」。

聽力原文與中譯

9. Let's grab a bite, and then hurry back to the office.
(A) Where did you eat out?
(B) You should hurry up.
(C) I agree with you.

9. 我們去吃一下東西，然後趕快回辦公室。
(A) 你去哪裡吃？
(B) 你要趕快。
(C) 我同意你。

答案：(C)

 解析

此題是肯定句，說話者表示要和對方一起行動，因此合理的應答是表達贊同或反對，(C) I agree with you.是最佳選項。注意(B) You should hurry up.是陷阱選項，雖然和題目都使用動詞 hurry，但句意不符合雙方一起行動的意思。

聽力原文與中譯

10. How was your business trip?
(A) I look forward to the trip.
(B) Business is going well.
(C) It went pretty well.

10. 你出差的狀況如何？
(A) 我期待這場旅行。
(B) 生意不錯。
(C) 蠻順利的。

答案：(C)

 解析

此題屬於 WH-疑問句，用 How 詢問狀況，注意動詞 was 的時態是過去式，因此馬上排除(A)，(B)。正確選項(C) It went pretty well.意為「事情或狀況進行蠻順利的」。

聽力原文與中譯

11. Have you reserved the table for our clients?
(A) The clients are visiting us today.
(B) No, I haven't.
(C) Yes, I have reserved the rooms.

11. 你已經替我們的顧客預定餐桌了嗎？
(A) 顧客今天正拜訪我們。
(B) 不，還沒有。
(C) 是的，我已經訂好房間了。

答案：(B)

解析

此題以現在完成式的助動詞 have 開頭，助動詞導引的疑問句屬於 Yes or No 是非疑問句，由此可判斷(B)No, I haven't.是最佳答案。(A)文不對題，(C) ...have reserved... 是陷阱選項。

聽力原文與中譯	
12. Wasn't it fun to go skydiving? (A) It was a real blast! (B) Skydiving is dangerous. (C) I would rather not.	**12. 去跳傘很好玩吧？** (A) 超棒的！ (B) 跳傘是危險的。 (C) 我寧可不要。

答案：(A)

 解析

此題是過去式 be 動詞 was 導引的疑問句，屬於 Yes or No 是非疑問句，此題型的應答有時比較靈活，不一定有 Yes 或 No 一字。(A) It was a real blast! 過去式的動詞時態呼應題目，a blast 指很好玩或有趣的活動，表達贊同題目的看法。

聽力原文與中譯	
13. When should we pick up the clients? (A) 3 o'clock sharp (B) Let's pick them up. (C) We always put clients first.	**13. 我們應該幾點去接顧客？** (A) 三點整 (B) 讓我們去接他們。 (C) 我們總是顧客至上。

答案：(A)

解析

此題聽到疑問詞 When，何時，比較三個選項，(A) 3 o'clock sharp，三點整，是最佳答案。

聽力原文與中譯

14. Is it possible to hand in the proposal by next Friday?
(A) I'll need someone to give me a hand.
(B) Let me review the proposal.
(C) It's very likely.

14. 有可能星期五前交出企劃案嗎？
(A) 我將需要人幫我。
(B) 讓我研讀企劃案。
(C) 很有可能。

答案：(C)

此題是現在式 be 動詞 is 導引的疑問句，屬於 Yes or No 是非疑問句，possible 詢問可能性，(C) It's very likely.的 likely 也是「可能的」，贊同題目的句意。

聽力原文與中譯

15. Did the accountant reimburse you for the trip?
(A) The sooner, the better.
(B) I might have to check with the accounting department.
(C) Filing for the reimbursement is complicated.

15. 會計師有把旅行的費用補償給你了嗎？
(A) 越快越好。
(B) 我可能需要和會計部門確認。
(C) 申請補償是複雜的。

答案：(B)

此題以過去式助動詞 did 開頭，主要動詞 reimburse 是「償清」，(B) 選項是比較靈活的應答，沒有直接肯定或否定，而是表達另一種可能性：需要和會計部門確認。

16. **Who will be our new team leader?** (A) The team leader did a great job. (B) It has not been announced. (C) Leadership is a rare trait.	16. **誰將是我們新的團隊領袖？** (A) 這位團隊領袖做得不錯。 (B) 還沒被宣布。 (C) 領袖特質是少見的特質。

答案：(B)

根據疑問詞 Who 及未來式助動詞 will，預測合理應答可能提及人名或職稱，而(B) It has not been announced.也是符合邏輯的應答，以現在完成式表達「還沒被宣布」。

17. **Do you think our mortgage will come through?** (A) It will take many years to pay off the mortgage. (B) I don't see why it won't be approved. (C) She should arrive here any minute.	17. **你認為我們的房貸會被批准嗎？** (A) 付清房貸將會花費很多年。 (B) 我想不出有什麼原因不會被批准。 (C) 她應該隨時會抵達這裡。

答案：(B)

此疑問句以現在式助動詞 do 引導，屬於 Yes or No 是非疑問句，Do you think... 詢問對方意見，動詞片語 come through 意為「通過或批准」，approve 是「批准，贊同」，是類似字，故正確選項是(B)。

聽力原文與中譯

18. Where should we hold our annual convention?
(A) probably the World Trade Center
(B) The convention is held annually.
(C) We ought to meet at the convention.

18. 我們應該在哪裡舉辦年度大會?
(A) 可能在世貿中心。
(B) 大會每年舉辦。
(C) 我們應該在大會碰面。

答案:(A)

解析

根據疑問詞 Where,有提到明確地點 the World Trade Center 的 (A) 是最適合的答案。(B) 描述大會每年舉辦,文不對題。(C) 亦答非所問。

聽力原文與中譯

19. Why is the flight delayed?
(A) The flight attendants are ready.
(B) I hate flying.
(C) due to the blizzard

19. 為何這班機延誤了?
(A) 空服員準備好了。
(B) 我討厭飛行。
(C) 因為暴風雪。

答案:(C)

解析

根據疑問詞 Why,推測答案應該提出原因。(C) due to... 是「因為」,接名詞。blizzard,暴風雪。

聽力原文與中譯

20. What is your opinion on the merger?
(A) It will bring more profits for sure.
(B) I value his opinion.
(C) I don't remember anything about it.

20. 你對這場合併案的看法是什麼?
(A) 它一定會帶來更多利潤。
(B) 我重視他的意見。
(C) 關於它我不記得任何事。

答案：(A)

解析

根據疑問詞 What 及名詞 your opinion，知道詢問對方意見。以切題度而言，(A)……帶來更多利潤最切題，能呼應題目另一關鍵字 merger，合併案。

聽力原文與中譯	
21. They pulled off the negotiation pretty well, didn't they? (A) Yep, that's a success. (B) Please pull over the car. (C) Negotiation takes many skills.	**21.** 他們這場談判進行蠻成功的，不是嗎？ (A) 是的，是場成功。 (B) 請把車停在路邊。 (C) 談判需要許多技巧。

答案：(A)

解析

此題須知道動詞片語 pull off Sth.是「成功完成某事」。此題的疑問句型是附加問句，正確的回答方式和回答 Yes or No 是非疑問句方式相同。(A) Yep, that's a success.以「成功」的名詞: success 表達贊同疑問句提出的看法，所以是最佳答案。

聽力原文與中譯	
22. Which is your preferable form of transport, trains or buses? (A) I have taken both transportations. (B) I prefer trains. (C) Buses are quite convenient downtown.	**22.** 哪一個是你偏好的交通，火車或巴士？ (A) 兩個我都搭過。 (B) 我偏好火車。 (C) 市中心巴士很方便。

答案：(B)

解析

疑問詞 Which 詢問兩者以上的選擇，此題詢問火車或巴士。preferable，「較好的，偏好的」。(B) I prefer trains. 以「偏好」的動詞 prefer 明確回答。

聽力原文與中譯	
23. **The new employee is very accommodating.** (A) Great to know that! (B) We'll have to arrange new accommodation for her. (C) The new policy does not accommodate the employees.	23. 那位新員工配合度蠻高的。 (A) 知道這件事真是太好了！ (B) 我們需要幫她安排新住宿。 (C) 新政策對員工不方便。

答案：(A)

解析

形容詞 accommodating 意思是「樂於助人的，通融的」。題目是肯定句，表達稱讚新員工。合理的答案也表示認同，故正確選項是(A) Great to know that! (B) 和 (C) 分別以 accommodation 和 accommodate 發音類似的字混淆考生。

聽力原文與中譯	
24. **Would you close the door on your way out?** (A) I'm on my way out. (B) There's no way out. (C) No problem.	24. 你出去時可以順便關門嗎？ (A) 我正要出去。 (B) 沒有出路。 (C) 沒問題。

答案：(C)

解析

此題以助動詞 Would 詢問對方出去時是否能關門，屬於 Yes or No 是非疑問句，但真正目的是表達請求。(A) 及 (B) 雖然都有 way out，但答非所問，是陷阱選項。(C) 沒問題最合理。

25. Can we try to take a neutral stand on this issue?
(A) I hope you can stand by me.
(B) The issue has been solved.
(C) We could try to achieve that.

25. 關於這議題，我們可以試著採取中立的立場嗎？
(A) 我希望你能支持我。
(B) 這問題已經被解決了。
(C) 我們可以試著做到。

答案：(C)

解析

根據 Can we try...? 句首三個字得知詢問嘗試某事的可能性，(C) We could try to achieve that.句首的 We could try 是最明顯的線索，代名詞 that 指的是「採取中立立場」一事。

26. I heard they were snowed in in New York.
(A) Snowy scenery is beautiful.
(B) Yes, they had to stay in the airport because of the blizzard.
(C) No, it is not hot in New York.

26. 我聽說他們在紐約被雪困住了。
(A) 雪景是美麗的。
(B) 是的，由於暴風雪，他們必須待在機場。
(C) 沒有，紐約不熱。

答案：(B)

解析

題目是肯定句，以動詞過去式及被動語態 were snowed in 表示「被雪困住」，in 在此片語是副詞。in New York 的 in 是介系詞。根據題目句意，可判斷 (B)...because of the blizzard，由於暴風雪，是正解。

27. The Xerox is running out of toner.
(A) Call the repairman.
(B) We'd better order it.
(C) We're running out of paper.

27. 影印機的碳粉快沒了。
(A) 打電話給維修人員。
(B) 我們最好訂購（碳粉）。
(C) 我們快沒紙了。

答案：(B)

解析

題目是使用動詞現在進行式 is running out of... 表達「快用完，快耗盡……」。針對「碳粉快用完了」的合理應答是「訂購碳粉」，所以正解是 (B)。(A) Call the repairman 是陷阱選項，因為題目並不是描述影印機壞掉。

聽力原文與中譯	
28. Can you finalize the itinerary by the end of the week? (A) Why don't you go on a trip? (B) We had fun on the weekend. (C) I'll do my best.	**28.** 在週末前能將旅行行程表定案嗎？ (A) 你為何不去旅行？ (B) 我們上個週末玩得很高興。 (C) 我會盡力。

答案：(C)

解析

此題以助動詞 Can 開頭，詢問對方能否完成某事。動詞 finalize 有「終結，定案」之意。(C) I'll do my best.，我會盡力，最能呼應疑問句句意。

聽力原文與中譯	
29. How did the orientation go? (A) When was the orientation held? (B) We need more workers for the orientation. (C) It went smoothly.	**29.** 新生訓練進行得如何？ (A) 新生訓練何時舉辦？ (B) 新生訓練我們需要更多員工。 (C) 進行順利地。

答案：(C)

解析

此題屬於 WH-疑問句，用 How 詢問狀況，注意過去式助動詞 did，排除 (B)，因為動詞 need 是現在式。(C) It went smoothly.以過去式動詞 went 表達進行，副詞 smoothly，順利地，所以是正解。

30. When will the refurbishment be wrapped up?

(A) It should be finished by next Wednesday.

(B) They should wrap up the gifts.

(C) It's challenging to decorate the house.

30. 裝潢何時會結束?

(A) 下星期三之前應該會結束。

(B) 他們應該包裝禮物。

(C) 裝潢房子是充滿挑戰的。

答案：(A)

解析

根據疑問詞 When 搭配未來式助動詞 will，判斷合理應答可能包含時間點，主詞 refurbishment 是「裝潢，裝修」，搭配主詞字意，可知動詞片語 wrap up 在此是「結束」。綜合以上分析，(A)...finished，結束，...by next Wednesday，下週三之前，(A) 是正解。

31. Who is in charge of the task?

(A) Olivia is the one.

(B) They did not charge me anything.

(C) It's a challenging task.

31. 誰負責這任務?

(A) 是奧麗薇雅。

(B) 他們沒跟我收任何錢。

(C) 它是個有挑戰的任務。

答案：(A)

解析

根據疑問詞 Who，預測合理應答可能提及人名或職稱，(A) Olivia is the one. 有人名，明顯是正解。慣用語 beV in charge of Sth.是意思是「掌控或負責……」。

Part 3 簡短對話

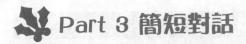

聽力原文和對話

32-34 refer to the following conversation

Mary: I do think they're gonna be so impressed... those couple of frames look stunning.

Cindy: Thanks... you know something about "photo credit"? It really belongs to the photographer, capturing a really fine moment of me. Plus, Nara looks so beautiful.

Chris: My pleasure... Ouch!

Cindy: What's going on?

Chris: he bit me. Oh my butt... that hurts.

Mary: that deer...? Too hilarious... I told you not to wear pink. Perhaps he has some obsessions or fantasy about pink... or maybe he happens not to be a vegetarian.

Cindy: if the editor-in-chief were here, she would be laughed out of the room.

問題 32-34，請參考以下對話內容

瑪莉：我真的認為他們會對此留下深刻印象⋯那幾張照片看起來很美。

辛蒂：謝謝⋯你知道有關於「照片來源」嗎？這真的要歸功於攝影師，捕捉到我真的很美的時刻。再者，奈良看起來真的很美。

克里斯：我的榮幸⋯哎喲！

辛蒂：發生什麼事了？

克里斯：他咬我。嗚我的屁股⋯真的痛。

瑪莉：那隻鹿⋯嗎？太好笑了吧⋯我早告訴你別穿粉紅色了。或許他對粉紅色有著迷戀或幻想⋯或是或許他可能剛好不是素食者。

辛蒂：如果總編在這的話，她會笑掉牙吧。

32. Which of the following best explains the term "photo credit"? (A) the way for photographers to make money (B) the acknowledgement of the source of photos (C) the way for photographers to build their credibility (D) the acknowledgement that the photo is beautiful	32. 下列何者最能解釋「照片來源」？ (A) 攝影師賺錢的方式。 (B) 照片來源的認可。 (C) 攝影師建立可信度的方式。 (D) 認可照片是美麗的。
33. Why did the man say, "ouch!"? (A) He was bitten by a deer. (B) He was chased by a deer. (C) He did not like the photo. (D) A deer stepped on his foot.	33. 為何男士說「哎呦！」？ (A) 他被鹿咬了。 (B) 他被鹿追。 (C) 他不喜歡這張照片。 (D) 一隻鹿踩在他的腳上。
34. Why did the woman say, "that deer...? Too hilarious"? (A) The deer looks very funny. (B) The man looks ridiculous in pink. (C) The situation of the deer biting the man is really funny. (D) The situation of the deer chasing the man is hilarious.	34. 為何女士說「那隻鹿……？太好笑了」？ (A) 那隻鹿看起來很好玩。 (B) 那位男士穿粉紅色很滑稽。 (C) 那隻鹿咬那位男士的狀況真是好笑的。 (D) 那隻鹿追那位男士的狀況是好笑的。

答案：32. B 33. A 34. C

解析

32. 根據 photo credit 的下一句: 這真的要屬於攝影師，推測 photo credit 的意思是照片歸功於攝影師，即照片最初來源，所以答案是(B)。

33. 根據男生喊了"Ouch!"之後的兩句對話，他解釋: He bit me.，牠咬我。換句話說是:他被鹿咬了。故選(A)。

34. Too hilarious 是男生被鹿咬了之後，女生發表的看法，可推測是她認為這個情況很好笑，故選(C)。

聽力原文和對話

Question 35-37 refer to the following conversation

Chris: relax... this tour package includes a day at Arashiyama. Plus, everyone visiting Japan would love to see these lovely creatures... as you tour guide... it really is my job to bring you guys here.

Cindy: can't we just have some sushi and seafood? Perhaps some wine. I'm not really a big fan of monkeys... and they seem agitated.

Chris: they... are adorable and sweet, aren't they? Wow... they don't usually act this way... I think they are a bit out of control... perhaps... not that close to them.

Jimmy: Ha... perhaps they think of you as a piece of meat... Tasty... and they are hungry.

Chris: haha... True.

問題 **35-37**，請參考以下對話內容

克里斯：放輕鬆…這個旅遊組合包含在嵐山一天。再者，每個來日本玩的遊客都喜愛看到這些討喜的生物…作為你們的導遊…帶你們來這裡真的是我的工作。

辛蒂：我們就不能吃些壽司和海產嗎？或許一些酒。我真的不是很喜歡猴子…而且他們看起來很躁動。

克里斯：他們…是可愛而且體貼的，對吧？哇…他們通常不會有這樣的舉動…我認為他們有點失控了…或許…別這麼靠近他們。

吉米：哈…或許他們把你當作一塊肉…可口…而且他們感到飢餓。

克里斯：哈哈…真的。

35. Why did the man say, "perhaps... not that close to them"? (A) Because those monkeys were pushing him (B) He wanted the others to follow the rule not to get close to the monkeys. (C) Because he did not want the others to frighten the monkeys (D) He's trying to persuade the others to stay away from the monkeys.	35. 為何這位男士説「或許……不要那麼靠近他們」? (A) 因為那些猴子在推他們。 (B) 他想要其他人遵守規則不要靠近猴子。 (C) 因為他不想要其他人嚇到猴子 (D) 他正試著説服別人遠離猴子。
36. Which of the following is the closest to "agitated"? (A) excited (B) disturbed and upset (C) adorable and sweet (D) frightened	36. 下列何者最接近「躁動的」? (A) 興奮的。 (B) 看來困擾且不悦的。 (C) 可愛且甜美的。 (D) 害怕的。
37. According to the context of the conversation, why did the woman say, "can't we just have some sushi and seafood"? (A) She heard that sushi and seafood in Arashiyama are delicious. (B) Arashiyama is famous for sushi and seafood. (C) She is not interested in seeing monkeys, and would rather do something else. (D) Seeing those monkeys eating reminds her it's dinner time.	37. 根據對話情境,為何那位女士説「我們就不能吃些壽司和海產嗎」? (A) 她聽説嵐山的壽司和海產是美味的。 (B) 嵐山以壽司和海產出名。 (C) 她對看猴子沒興趣,寧可做別的事。 (D) 看到那些猴子吃東西提醒她晚餐時間到了。

答案:35. D 36. B 37. C

解析

35. 使用刪去法，(A) 因為那些猴子在推他們，(B) ……遵守規則不要靠近猴子，(C) 因為他不想要其他人嚇到猴子，這些細節都沒提及，故選(D)。
36. 根據對話，知道 agitated 形容猴子，又根據「他們有點失控了」，可判斷 agitated 是負面意涵的單字，比較四個選項，最有負面意涵的選項是 (B)。
37. 在"can't we just have some sushi and seafood"隨後，女生說:我真的不是很喜歡猴子。換言之，她對猴子沒興趣。故選(C)。

聽力原文和對話

Question 38-40 refer to the following conversation

Donor Name	number
Nick	BF-1007
Jack	BY-1007
Chris	CF-1006
Jimmy	CY-1007

Jack: I've narrowed the donors down to four candidates. If you still can't pick one, then my hands are tied.

Mary: it's really hard to decide. They seem so perfect.

Linda: picking the right sperm donor is harder than I thought. BY-1007 is married.

Mary: what about BF-1007? He's handsome and he has a master's degree from Harvard.

Linda: they all graduated from Ivy League schools. I do need to look at other criteria.

Mary: CF-1006. He is a model... OMG he is in the oatmeal commercial.

Linda: but he is 35 years old.

Mary: CY-1007. He is a pilot and an athlete.

Linda: OMG he is perfect. That guy for the sperm donor ad campaign.

Jack: Oh... him... but he won't be available until 2025. I guess someone's egg can't wait that long.

捐贈者姓名	號碼
尼克	BF-1007
傑克	BY-1007
克里斯	CF-1006
吉米	CY-1007

傑克：我已經把人選縮小到剩四個了。如果你仍選不出來，那我真的束手無策了。

瑪莉：真的很難決定。他們似乎都很完美。

琳達：選個合適的精子捐贈者比我想像中難多了。BY-1007 結婚了。

瑪莉：那 BF-1007 呢？他英俊且他有哈佛的碩士學位。

琳達：他們都從常春藤盟校畢業。我想我需要看其他的條件。

瑪莉：CF-1006。他是模特兒…天啊他是燕麥粥廣告的那個人。

琳達：可是他 35 歲了。

瑪莉：CY-1007。他是飛行員也是運動員。

琳達：天啊他很完美。那個精子捐贈者廣告宣傳的那個男的。

傑克：喔…他…但是他在 2025 年前都沒空。我想有人的卵子可能等不了這麼久。

試題中譯與解析

38. Which of the following is the closest in meaning to "my hands are tied"?
(A) There's nothing else I can do.
(B) Someone tied my hands.
(C) I am too busy.
(D) I cannot pick one for you.

38. 下列何者意思最接近「我真的束手無策了」？
(A) 我無能為力。
(B) 有人綁住我的手。
(C) 我太忙。
(D) 我無法替你選擇。

39. Who does the phrase "four candidates" refer to in this conversation? (A) sperm donors (B) blood donors (C) candidates for an election (D) candidates for the admission to Ivy League schools	39.「四個人選」在對話中指誰？ (A) 精子捐贈者。 (B) 捐血者。 (C) 選舉候選人。 (D) 常春藤聯盟學校的入學人選。
40. What does the sentence "they all graduated from Ivy League schools" imply? (A) Having a university degree is not important in the speakers' criteria. (B) Ivy League school graduates are more competitive in general. (C) They are highly educated. (D) Having an Ivy League university degree is enviable.	40.「他們都從常春藤盟校畢業」這句暗示什麼？ (A) 有大學文憑在說話者的標準裡不重要。 (B) 常春藤聯盟學校的畢業生普遍比較有競爭優勢。 (C) 他們受過高等教育。 (D) 有常春藤聯盟學校的文憑是讓人羨慕的。

答案：38. A 39. A 40. C

解析

38. my hands are tied 這句是延伸 If you still can't pick one，考慮搭配「如果你仍選不出來」的連貫性，(A) There's nothing else I can do. 最通順。

39. 對話中段明確指出主題是 picking the right sperm donor，因此 four candidates 指的是 sperm donors。

40. Ivy League schools 指的是美國名校常春藤聯盟大學，換言之暗示的是他們都受過高等教育。

1 照片描述

2 應答問題

3 簡短對話

4 簡短獨白

模擬試題

Question 41-43 refer to the following conversation

Name	Price
Jack	US 7 million dollars
Tim	US 8 million dollars
Jim	US 8 million dollars
Derek	US 10 million dollars

Chris: we have to sign two potential basketball stars on a very tight budget. And there is no way that we can sign Derek under the law. He wants 10 million dollars, not 8.

Jimmy: that's right. Legitimately, we can only sign him at 8 million dollars, but we can still get him... we just have to think outside the box.

Chris: how? Bribe him?

Jimmy: absolutely not... we can sign Jack but cut his pay from 7 million dollars to 5, and we can assure Derek that we're gonna pay him the extra 2 in private. It's in cash... no one knows.

Chris: brilliant... but how to persuade Jack to sign at 5 million dollars.

Jimmy: invite him to the dinner, making him look like a big shot or something.

Chris: problem solved.

問題 44-46，請參考以下對話內容

名字	價格
傑克	7 百萬美元
提姆	8 百萬美元
吉姆	8 百萬美元
德瑞克	1 千萬美元

克里斯：我們必需以非常緊縮的預算簽兩個有潛力的籃球球星。根據現在法條的規定我們不可能簽下德瑞克。他想要 1 千萬美元，而不是 8 百萬美元。

吉米：對的。法律上我們只能夠以 8 百萬美元簽下他，但是我們仍可以簽下他…我們只是需要跳出框架思考。

克里斯：如何？賄絡他嗎？

吉米：當然不是…我們可以簽下傑克但是將他的費用從 7 百萬美元砍到 5 百萬美元，而且我們可以向德瑞克保證我們會私底下付他另外的兩百萬美元。是付現…沒有人會知道。

克里斯：真高明…但是要如何說服傑克以 5 百萬美元簽下呢？

吉米：邀請他來晚餐，服侍他讓他像個大咖或什麼的。

克里斯：問題解決了。

試題中譯與解析

41. What does "we just have to think outside the box" imply?
(A) We have to think according to the rules.
(B) It's better for us to bribe the basketball player.
(C) We have to come up with more creative ways.
(D) We need to see what's printed on the box.

41.「我們只是需要跳出框架思考」暗示什麼？
(A) 我們必須按照規則思考。
(B) 匯率那位籃球選手對我們比較好。
(C) 我們要想出比較有創意的方式。
(D) 我們需要看盒子上印的是什麼。

42. What is the solution that these speakers come up with to sign Derek? (A) paying him cash under the table (B) negotiating with him (C) making him look like a big shot (D) bribing him	42. 這些說話者想出簽下德瑞克的解決方式是什麼？ (A) 私下付他現金。 (B) 跟他談判。 (C) 讓他看似大人物。 (D) 賄賂他。
43. Which of the following is the closest in meaning to "a big shot" in the sentence "invite him to the dinner, making him look like a big shot or something"? (A) someone who looks nice on camera (B) someone good at taking photos (C) a good basketball player (D) a VIP	43. 下列何者的意思最接近「邀請他來晚餐，讓他像個大咖或什麼的」這句裡的「大咖」？ (A) 很上鏡頭的人。 (B) 擅長拍照的人。 (C) 好的籃球選手。 (D) 大人物。

答案：41. C 42. A 43. D

解析

16. 此題考 think outside the box 這個慣用語的意思，是「跳出框架或常規思考」之意。選項中與此慣用語最接近的是(C)我們要想出比較有創意的方式。

17. 先以人名 Derek 當定位字，根據 we can assure Derek that we're gonna pay him the extra 2 in private. It's in cash... no one knows. 關鍵字是 in private/ in cash，故選(A)私下付他現金。

18. 以對話情境判斷 a big shot 的意思，invite him to the dinner 是解題線索，暗示要給對方好處，a big shot 意思是大人物，類似字是 VIP。

聽力原文和對話

Question 44-46 refer to the following conversation

proposal	Budget
A	20 million dollars
B	2 billion dollars
C	20,000,000 dollars

Linda: we should begin today's meeting by discussing the construction sites.

Mary: that's right... we haven't reached a consensus since Dec 12th, 2016.

Jack: B proposal is the most costly, but mansions can be built in two years.

Mary: C proposal takes around 5 years... we can't wait for that long.

Linda: but it's actually the money we can afford.

Jack: how about proposal A?

Linda: the place is still under evaluation by the Department of Environmental Protection.

Mary: we should leave board members to decide... we don't even have a vote.

Linda: let's vote...by raising your hands...

Jack: I'm counting the vote... 15 to B, 12 to C, and 13 to A.

問題 44-46，請參考以下對話內容

提案	預算
A	2 千萬美元
B	200 億美元
C	2 千萬美元

琳達：我們應該開始今日的會議以討論建築位址開始。

瑪莉：對的…從 2016 年 12 月 12 日，我們尚未達到共識。

傑克：B 提案是花費最貴的，但是豪宅能在兩年內建好。

瑪莉：C 提案花費大約五年的時間…我們無法等那麼久。

琳達：但這其實是我們所能負擔的金額。

傑克：那提案 A 呢？

琳達：那地方還在環境保護部門的評估中。

瑪莉：我們應該要留給董事會成員去決定…我們根本沒有投票權。

琳達：我們開始投票吧…由舉手表示…。

傑克：我來數下投票…B 提案 15 票、C 提案 12 票和 A 提案 13 票。

試題中譯	
44. Who might these speakers be? (A) construction workers (B) bank investors (C) construction company employees (D) students studying architecture	44. 這些說話者可能是誰？ (A) 建築工人。 (B) 銀行投資人。 (C) 建設公司員工。 (D) 建築系學生。

45. What is the special situation regarding proposal A? (A) It did not pass the evaluation by the Department of Environmental Protection (B) It is being assessed by the Department of Environmental Protection. (C) The government does not allow construction in that place in proposal A. (D) Proposal A will cost too much money.	45. 企劃 A 的特殊狀況為何？ (A) 它沒通過環保部門的評量。 (B) 它正被環保部門評量。 (C) 政府不准許在企劃 A 的地點建設。 (D) 企劃 A 會花太多錢。
46. What does the woman mean by saying "we haven't reached a consensus..."? (A) We still need to reach an agreement. (B) We still need to do more research. (C) We have reached a conclusion. (D) We need to carry out more surveys.	46. 女生說「我們還沒達到共識……」的意思為何？ (A) 我們仍需要達成同意。 (B) 我們仍需要做更多研究。 (C) 我們已經達成結論。 (D) 我們需要進行更多調查。
答案：44. C 45. B 46. A	

1 照片描述

2 應答問題

3 簡短對話

4 簡短獨白

模擬試題

44. 由對話第一句 we should begin today's meeting by discussing the construction sites. ，得知說話者是在會議中討論建案地點，之後提及三個企劃案，綜合以上線索，最佳選項是(C)建設公司員工。

45. 疑問句 how about proposal A?是定位線索，回答是 The place is still under evaluation by the Department of Environmental Protection. ，Sth. is under evaluation 類似講法是 Sth. is being assessed，某事正被評量/評估，故選(B)。

46. 此題考與 we haven't reached a consensus... 大意最接近的選項，關鍵字 consensus，共識。換言之是我們還沒同意某事，故選(A)我們仍需要達成同意。

聽力原文和對話

Question 47-49 refer to the following conversation

Item
Old chair
Picasso painting
Monet painting
museums

Nick: this is not the annual auction. I'm here on behalf of the owner of antique shop and hotel chains to arrange this auction... and announce Rick Chen's will...his money will be given to five kids evenly. So today we will auction something in his office and other things.

Jack: Old chair... are you kidding me...

Linda: why didn't dad just give us these paintings... I don't have that much money in my bank account let alone buying them.

Nick: old chair for 500 dollars... ok... old chair for 300 dollars... do any of the family members want a chair for 300 dollars. The chair actually represents your father... Since there is none... the auction is over. All his shares of hotel chains and listed items will be donated to charity... thank you guys.

問題 47-49，請參考以下對話內容

尼克：這不是年度拍賣。我代表古董店和旅館連鎖店的擁有者安排這個銷售會…和宣布瑞克陳的遺囑…他的金錢將會平均分配給五個孩子。所以今天我們會拍賣他辦公室的東西和其他東西。

傑克：舊椅子…你在跟我開玩笑嗎…

琳達：為什麼老爸就不給我們那些畫呢…我銀行存款也沒有那個多現金，更別說要購買了。

尼克：舊椅子五百美元…好的…舊椅子 300 美元…有任何家庭成員想要以 300 美元購買椅子嗎？這椅子實際上代表著你的父親…既然沒有的話…這個拍賣會結束了。所有他的旅館連店股份和列表的項目都會捐贈給慈善機構…謝謝各位。

試題中譯

47. Who is Rick Chen?
(A) a child
(B) a father
(C) an auctioneer
(D) a salesman

47. 瑞克‧陳是誰？
(A) 一個孩子。
(B) 一位父親。
(C) 一位拍賣官。
(D) 一位銷售員

48. What is the main topic of the conversation?
(A) auctioning the possessions of a person who passed away
(B) mourning a person who passed away
(C) selling things from an antique shop
(D) how to buy a chair

48. 此對話主題為何？
(A) 拍賣過世者的財產。
(B) 哀悼過世者。
(C) 賣古董店的東西。
(D) 如何買椅子。

49. Why are Rick Chen's possessions sold?
(A) His children want them sold.
(B) because his family is bankrupt
(C) because his wife wants them sold.
(D) They are sold according to his will.

49. 瑞克‧陳的財產為何被賣？
(A) 他的孩子想把財產賣掉。
(B) 因為他的家庭破產了。
(C) 因為他的老婆想把財產賣掉。
(D) 依照他的遺囑把財產賣掉。

答案：47. B 48. A 49. D

解析

47. 由對話開頭的 ...and announce Rick Chen's will...his money will be given to five kids evenly.可知道兩個重要線索：(1)此說話者要宣布瑞克·陳的遺囑，(2)瑞克·陳是位父親，故選(B)一位父親。

48. 由對話開頭的 I'm on behalf of the owner of antique shop and hotel chains to arrange this auction... So today we will auction something in his office and other things.，得知主題關於往生者的物品拍賣，關鍵字 auction，拍賣，possessions 指財產或所有物，故選(A)。

49. 第一位說話者表示他代表瑞克·陳宣布他的遺囑，可推測此拍賣是在他的遺囑規劃好的，I'm on behalf of ...，我代表…，announce Rick Chen's will，宣布瑞克·陳的遺囑，故選(D)。

聽力原文和對話

Question 50-52 refer to the following conversation

Movie	Rating
A	PG
B	PG-13
C	R
D	G

Linda: Best Cinema... how can I help you?

Mary: I'd like to book two tickets?

Linda: which movie?

Mary: please hold on just a second.

Mary: do they want to go to see the movie as well?

Jack: yep.

Mary: Sorry... my boyfriends' two little sisters would like to see the movie with us... so that means four tickets to be exact.

Linda: In that case, I do recommend you to choose Movie B or D. Movie C contains a lot of nude scenes, and PG films include some violence that is somewhat inappropriate.

Mary: in that case, four tickets for Movie B.

問題 50-52，請參考以下對話內容

電影	評制
A	家長指導級
B	家長指導級-13 歲
C	限制級
D	普遍級

琳達：倍斯特電影...有什麼我能替您服務的嗎？

瑪莉：我想要訂兩張票。

琳達：哪個電影？

瑪莉：請等一下。

瑪莉：她們也想要去看電影嗎？

傑克：是的。

瑪莉：抱歉…我的男朋友的兩個小妹也想要跟我們一起看電影…所以正好是四張票。

琳達：那樣的話，我想推薦你們看電影 B 或電影 D。電影 C 有很多裸露的場景，而且家長指導級電影包含一些暴力，有點不太恰當。

瑪莉：那樣的話，電影 B 四張票。

試題中譯

50. What is the purpose of the conversation?
(A) purchasing the tickets to a movie
(B) deciding who will go see movies
(C) asking for the suggestions about a movie
(D) asking how much the tickets will cost

50. 此對話的目的為何？
(A) 購買電影票。
(B) 決定誰要去看電影。
(C) 詢問關於電影的建議。
(D) 詢問票價多少。

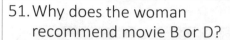

51. Why does the woman recommend movie B or D? (A) The content of movie B or D is more appropriate for children. (B) Movie B and D are both animations. (C) The tickets to movie B or D are on discount. (D) Both movie B and D receive high accolades.	51. 為何女士推薦電影 B 或 D？ (A) 電影 B 或 D 的內容比較適合小孩。 (B) 電影 B 和 D 都是動畫。 (C) 電影 B 或 D 的票有折扣。 (D) 電影 B 和 D 都受到高度讚賞。
52. Why is movie C not recommended? (A) It has lots of violence. (B) Some scenes are not proper for children. (C) The tickets to movie C were sold out. (D) It received horrible reviews.	52. 電影 C 為何不被推薦？ (A) 它包含很多暴力。 (B) 有些場景不適合小孩。 (C) 電影 C 的票賣完了。 (D) 它的評語很糟糕。

答案：50. A 51. A 52. B

解析

50. 根據對話開始兩句:Best Cinema... how can I help you? I'd like to book two tickets，得知主題是透過電話訂電影票。

51. 女生提到有兩位小妹妹會一起去看電影，接著售票員推薦電影 B 或 D，並提到電影 C 有裸露和暴力場景。換言之，電影 C 是不適合兒童的。即電影 B 或 D 比較適合兒童。

52. 根據售票員說的: Movie C contains a lot of nude scenes,... violence... ，許多裸露場景……暴力，推測出電影 C 是不適合兒童的。

聽力原文和對話

Question 53-55 refer to the following conversation

Cindy: why do people complain about overtime? I'm begging for more. I need lots of money.

Jack: only to you... you're such a... workaholic.

Mary: since there is a hiring freeze and a lack of orders... I don't think your overtime dream is gonna come true.

Cindy: too bad... I guess I will just sell some home-baked cookies during the weekends.

Jack: I'm missing the chocolate chips with hazelnuts.

Mary: just a perfect blend with coffee. Perhaps you can make some serious money by opening your own shop someday.

問題 53-55，請參考以下對話內容

辛蒂：為什麼人們都抱怨加班呢？我還乞求更多。我需要更多的錢。

傑克：只有你這樣想吧…你真是個…工作狂。

瑪莉：既然有雇用冷凍期和缺乏訂單…我不覺得你的加班夢會成真。

辛蒂：真不巧…我想我只好在週末時販賣一些家庭烘培餅乾。

傑克：我還真想唸有著榛子的巧克力餅乾。

瑪莉：搭咖啡真的是完美的組合。或許你可以真的賺進一筆錢，有天開了你自己的店。

試題中譯

53. What does 'hiring freeze" imply?
(A) The weather was freezing cold when they got hired.
(B) Companies have stopped hiring more people.
(C) Companies are hiring more people.
(D) They don't have much information about the employment.

53.「雇用冷凍期」暗示什麼？
(A) 他們被雇用時，天氣很冷。
(B) 公司已經停止雇用更多人。
(C) 公司正雇用更多人。
(D) 他們沒有很多關於雇用的資訊。

54. Why does the man say to the woman "you're such a workaholic"? (A) because the woman is very demanding (B) because the woman wants more overtime hours (C) because he wants to compliment the woman (D) because he wished he were a workaholic, too	54. 為何男生對女生說「你真是個工作狂」？ (A) 因為女生要求很高。 (B) 因為女生想要更多加班時數。 (C) 因為他想要讚美女生。 (D) 因為他但願他也是工作狂。
55. What does the woman think about the other woman's home-baked cookies? (A) She thinks those cookies taste better with chocolate milk shake. (B) She does not like those cookies. (C) She thinks highly of those home-baked cookies. (D) She does not like having those cookies with coffee.	55. 女生對另一位女生的手工餅乾看法如何？ (A) 她認為那些餅乾和巧克力奶昔一起吃比較美味。 (B) 她不喜歡那些餅乾。 (C) 她對那些手工餅乾評價很高。 (D) 她不喜歡吃餅乾配咖啡。

答案：53. B 54. B 55. C

解析

53. 根據 since there is a hiring freeze and a lack of orders...，得知 hiring 形容 freeze，freeze 這裡是名詞，指「凍結」，引申為企業不再雇用新人，故選(B)。

54. 對話開頭女生說 why do people complain about overtime? I'm begging for more.，她渴求更多加班時數，男生回應: 你真是個工作狂，所以選(B)。

55. 第一位女生說她要販賣一些家庭烘培餅乾之後，另一位女生說: 或許你可以真的賺進一筆錢，有天開自己的店。由此句推測她對那些餅乾看法不錯，故選(C)。

聽力原文和對話

Question 56-58 refer to the following conversation

Jack: Relax... they're in a meeting. So are you a techie or a fuzzy?

Cindy: what do you mean?

Jack: the fuzzies refer to students of the humanities and social sciences, whereas the techies refer to students of the engineering or hard science. It's the categorization from Stanford.

Cindy: I see... then I'm a techie... I majored in Chemistry.

Jack: I prefer to call myself a techie... but I'm actually a fuzzy... it's funnier. What about you husband?

Cindy: a fuzzy. He was a Chinese major.

Jack: You guys complement each other. Normally a fuzzy dates a techie... that's how things normally go.

問題 56-58，請參考以下對話內容

傑克：放輕鬆…他們在開會。所以你是科技人還是社科人呢？

辛蒂：你指的是什麼呢？

傑克：模糊性指的是人文社會科學學系的學生，而技術專家指的是工程或純科學學系的學生。這是史丹佛的分類。

辛蒂：我懂了…那麼我是技術專家…我主修是化學。

傑克：我偏好將自己稱作技術專家…但我實際上是人文社會科學學系學生…只是有趣些。那你丈夫呢？

辛蒂：人文社會科學學系學生。他是中文系主修。

傑克：你們真的彼此互補。通常人文科系學生跟理工科系學生約會…事情通常都是這樣走。

試題中譯	
56. What does "a fuzzy" refer to? (A) a fuzzy picture (B) a humanities major (C) a warm feeling (D) an engineering major	56. 社科人指的是什麼？ (A) 一張模糊的照片。 (B) 一位主修社會人文學科的人。 (C) 一種溫暖的感覺。 (D) 一位主修機械工程的人。
57. What does "a techie" refer to? (A) a science major (B) a technician (C) a Chinese major (D) a repairman	57. 科技人指的是什麼？ (A) 主修科學的人。 (B) 維修人員。 (C) 主修中文的人。 (D) 維修人員。
58. Which of the following is the closest in meaning to "You guys complement each other"? (A) You give each other compliments often. (B) You have been dating for a long time. (C) Giving compliments is important in your relationship. (D) You make each other a better person.	58. 下列何者和「你們彼此互補」意思最接近？ (A) 你們常彼此讚美。 (B) 你們已經約會很久了。 (C) 在你們的關係裡給讚美是重要的。 (D) 你們讓彼此成為更好的人。

答案：56. B 57. A 58. D

 解析

56. 對話中男生解釋:Fuzzies 指的是人文社會學科的學生，而 techies 指的是工程或純科學的學生。從關鍵字 humanities，人文學科，選擇(B)。註：Techie= 科技族 / 理工派，Fuzzy= 人文族 / 社會課派。

57. 解題線索同 25 題，此題考 techies 的定義，根據男生的解釋，選擇(A)。

58. 動詞 complement 是補充的意思，題目考的 You guys complement each other.意思是「你們彼此互補」。(A) 及 (C) 使用 compliment，讚美，是陷阱選項。和考點句意最接近的是(D) 你們讓彼此成為更好的人。

聽力原文和對話

Question 59-61 refer to the following conversation

Candidate	photo
A	High fashion
B	commercial
C	commercial
D	High fashion

Jack: what do you think about four candidates' performance?

Linda: I do love candidate A. She looks great and her photos are stunning.

Ken: what about other candidates?

Linda: I love candidate D, but her walk is terrible.

Linda: I think I'll book candidate A for an ad campaign and candidate C for a catwalk of our swimsuits during Fashion Week.

Ken: What's wrong with candidate B? She is pretty and she has a strong walk.

Linda: she is too cocky and she really needs to work on her personality.

Jack: thanks for your time...

問題 **59-61**，請參考以下對話內容

候選人	照片
A	高端時尚
B	商業廣告
C	商業廣告
D	高端時尚

傑克：你覺得這四位候選人的表現如何呢？

琳達：我真的喜愛候選人 A。她看起來很棒而且她的照片很美。

肯：那其他候選人呢？

琳達：我喜愛候選人 D 但是她的台步糟透了。

琳達：我認為我會簽候選人 A 作為廣告活動然後候選人 C 在時尚週期間時替我們的泳裝走台步。

肯：候選人 B 有什麼問題嗎？她很漂亮，而且她台步走的很強。

琳達：她太自負了而且她真的需要在個性上多作努力。

傑克：謝謝妳的時間。

試題中譯

59. What are the speakers talking about? (A) a catwalk (B) models' performances (C) a fashion show (D) which model is prettier	59. 這些說話者在討論什麼？ (A) 伸展台 (B) 模特兒的表現 (C) 時尚展 (D) 哪個模特兒比較漂亮
60. According to the speaker, what is wrong with candidate B? (A) Her walk is terrible. (B) Her photos are not stunning. (C) She has an attitude problem. (D) She's too short.	60. 依照說話者，候選人 B 的問題是什麼？ (A) 她走路的樣子很糟。 (B) 她的照片不漂亮。 (C) 她有態度方面的問題。 (D) 她太矮了。

61. Which of the following best explains, "her photos are stunning"? (A) Her photos are breathtakingly beautiful. (B) Her photos are very shocking. (C) She does not perform well in photoshoots. (D) She works well with photographers.	61. 下列何者最能解釋「她的照片很漂亮」? (A) 她的照片超級美麗的。 (B) 她的照片讓人驚嚇。 (C) 她在拍照時表現不好。 (D) 她和攝影師合作地不錯。

答案:59. B 60. C 61. A

解析

59. 綜合第一句提及的 our candidates' performance 及對話細節 photos,catwalk,the Fashion Week 等線索,推測出主題是討論模特兒的表現。

60. 以 candidate B 當定位詞,說話者對她的評語是:she is too cocky and she really needs to work on her personality. cocky 是俚語的形容詞,意為「傲慢的」,由此可推測 candidate B 是態度有問題。

61. 考點句子裡的形容詞 stunning 意為「極漂亮的」,由此可推測(A) Her photos are breathtakingly beautiful.意思和考點句子最接近。

1 照片描述

2 應答問題

3 簡短對話

4 簡短獨白

模擬試題

Question 62-64 refer to the following conversation

Jack: you look handsome... so if you're willing to be the spokesperson for our Medical Center... We'd like to give you a 50% discount on the surgery.

Derek: wow... that's an intriguing offer. With that kind of reduction in costs... I might be able to afford a surgery without getting into debt. So what does your spokesman do? Taking the campaign photos or?

Mary: helping us build a healthy image. Letting others know that a surgery can transform how the world perceives you. Appearance still matters when you go to interviews and dates. People love to be around good-looking people.

Derek: Is this a revised version of the contract... and where do I need to sign?

問題 62-64，請參考以下對話內容

傑克：你看起來英俊…所以如果你願意替我們醫療中心作代言人的話…我們會給你外科手術 5 折折扣。

德瑞克：哇…這提議真的吸引人。以如此的費用折扣…我可能可以負擔起外科手術費用又不用負債。所以你們的代言人都做些甚麼呢？替活動拍攝照片嗎？

瑪莉：幫助我們建立健康的形象。讓其他人知道外科手術可以改變世界是如何看待你的。外表仍在你參加面試或約會時至關重要。人們喜愛周遭環繞著好看的人。

德瑞克：這是修改後的合約版本嗎？…我需要在哪裡簽名呢？

試題中譯

62. What does the man think about the offer?	62. 這位男士對提議的看法如何？
(A) He is confused.	(A) 他感覺困惑。
(B) He is disappointed.	(B) 他感覺失望。
(C) He is very curious.	(C) 他很好奇。
(D) He is very interested.	(D) 他很有興趣。

63. According to the woman, what are the responsibilities of the spokesperson? (A) taking campaign photos (B) shooting commercials for the Medical Center (C) building a healthy image of the Medical Center (D) going through a surgery	63. 依照女生，發言人的責任是什麼？ (A) 拍攝活動照片。 (B) 替醫療中心拍廣告。 (C) 替醫療中心建立健康形象。 (D) 動手術。
64. What is the man probably going to do after the conversation? (A) registering for a surgery (B) revising the contract (C) taking campaign photos (D) signing the contract	64. 對話之後男生可能做什麼？ (A) 掛號動手術。 (B) 修改合約。 (C) 拍攝活動照片。 (D) 簽署合約。

答案：62. D 63. C 64. D

解析

62. 以 offer 當定位字，男生說：wow... that's an intriguing offer.。intriguing，形容詞，令人著迷的，由此字可推測男生對這項提議很感興趣，故選(D) He is very interested.。

63. 在男生詢問 So what does spokesperson do?之後，女生回答：helping us to build a healthy image，因此正確選項為(C) building a healthy image of the Medical Center。

64. 此題要考生推測對話之後男生可能做什麼，此題型線索偏向對話快結束時，對話最後男生問：Is this a revised version of the contract... and where do I need to sign?由此可推測接下來的動作是簽署合約。

1 照片描述

2 應答問題

3 簡短對話

4 簡短獨白

模擬試題

Question 65-67 refer to the following conversation

Mary: how may I direct your call?

Jack: this is Jack Collins... a sales rep of Best pharmaceuticals... is Linda available? I'd like to discuss the orders with her. There seems to be a terrible misunderstanding.

Mary: I see... but she is having a business meeting in Paris. Or do you wanna to talk to the other sales reps... I can direct the call for you.

Jack: No thanks... when will she be back from the trip?

Mary: July 14, 2018...

Jack: I think I can call back later... thanks again.

問題 65-67，請參考以下對話內容

瑪莉：我要幫您轉接給誰呢？

傑克：這是傑克‧柯林斯…倍斯特藥品的銷售業務代表…琳達目前有空嗎？我想與她討論關於訂單的事。似乎有個嚴重的誤會。

瑪莉：我懂了…但是她正在巴黎開商務會議。或是你可以跟其他銷售代表談談…我可以替您轉接電話。

傑克：不，謝謝…她什麼時候會回來呢？

瑪莉：2018 年 7 月 14 日…

傑克：我想我可以稍後再撥…謝謝了。

試題中譯

65. Why does Jack Collins make this phone call? (A) He wants to place a new order. (B) He wants to clarify a misunderstanding. (C) He wants to know where Linda is. (D) He wants to file some complaints.	65. 傑克‧柯林斯為什麼打這通電話？ (A) 他想下新訂單。 (B) 他想澄清一個誤會。 (C) 他想知道琳達在哪裡。 (D) 他想提出一些申訴。

66. Who is Jack Collins?	66. 傑克・柯林斯是誰？
(A) a pharmacist	(A) 一位藥劑師。
(B) a travel agent	(B) 一位旅行社人員。
(C) a customer who wants to place orders with a pharmaceutical company	(C) 一位想向藥廠下訂單的客戶。
(D) a sales representative from a pharmaceutical company	(D) 一位藥廠的業務代表。
67. Why is Linda not available to answer the call?	67. 琳達為什麼沒空接電話？
(A) She is on a business trip.	(A) 她正在出差。
(B) She went on a personal trip in Paris.	(B) 她去巴黎進行個人旅遊。
(C) She is in a meeting with her boss.	(C) 她正和老闆開會。
(D) She does not want to answer the call.	(D) 她不想接電話。

答案：65. B 66. D 67. A

解析

65. Jack Collins 簡短表明他的身份後，他說：is Linda available? I'd like to discuss the orders with her. There seems to be a terrible misunderstanding.，根據 misunderstanding，誤會，推測出他打電話的目的是想澄清一個誤會。

66. 對話開頭 Jack Collins 簡短表明身份：a sales rep of Best pharmaceuticals，rep 是 representative，代表，的縮寫，故選(D)。

67. 根據女生說的：but she is having a business meeting in Paris.，解釋為何琳達無法接電話的原因，將此句換句話說，就是(A) She is on a business trip.。

Question 68-70 refer to the following conversation

Mary: they detected contamination in our sample.

Jack: who?

Cindy: FDA and Department of Health.

Jack: but how? Our lab report shows that all results are within the standard.

Mary: I hate to bring this up... but it could be negligence on our part. Sometimes I don't think they're actually following the SOPs and executing all the procedures as they should've.

Cindy: I think they'll be here in a minute. The press is gonna make a big deal about it.

Jack: I do think we should enforce a stricter guideline for the staff of the product line.

問題 68-70，請參考以下對話內容

瑪莉：他們從我們的樣本中察覺到有汙染。

傑克：誰？

辛蒂：食品藥物管理局和衛生部門。

傑克：但是怎麼會？我們的實驗報告顯示所有結果都在標準值內。

瑪莉：我討厭提出這個…但是可能是我們這邊的疏忽。有時候我不認為他們實際上照著 SOP 程序走，而且執行所有應該要走的程序。

辛蒂：我認為他們可能幾分鐘就會到了。新聞記者又會大做文章了。

試題中譯

68. 樣本的問題是什麼？ (A) 它比預期的小。 (B) 它沒按照 SOP 準則製造。 (C) 它沒達到實驗室標準。 (D) 它被汙染了。	68. What is the problem with the sample? (A) It is smaller than expected. (B) It was not produced under the SOP guidelines. (C) It does not meet the lab standard. (D) It is contaminated.

69. 下列何者意思和「可能是我們這邊的疏忽」這句裡「疏忽」的意思最接近？ (A) 沒有給與足夠的注意力。 (B) 產品太快完成。 (C) 遵守規則。 (D) 不和食品藥物管理局合作。	69. Which of the following is the closest in meaning to "negligence" as in "it could be negligence on our part"? (A) not paying enough attention (B) finishing the production too fast (C) abiding by the guidelines (D) not cooperating with FDA
70. 對話後說話者可能做什麼？ (A) 和食品藥物管理局談話。 (B) 和實驗室員工談話。 (C) 再檢查一次樣本。 (D) 制定更嚴謹的規則。	70. What will the speakers probably do after the conversation? (A) talking to FDA (B) talking to lab employees (C) examining the sample again (D) devising more scrupulous rules

答案：68. D 69. A 70. D

 解析

根據對話第一句: they detected a contamination from our sample. ，「他們從我們的樣本中察覺到汙染」，(D) 選項: 它被汙染了，意思和此句相同。

68. 此題考 negligence 的字義，negligence 是「疏忽」的名詞。也能從考點句子的下一句: Sometimes I don't think they're actually following the SOPs and execute all the procedures as they should've. ，推測 negligence 是負面意義的字，故(A) 沒有給與足夠的注意力，是最佳選項。

69. 根據對話最後一句: I do think we should enforce a stricter guideline for the staff of the product line. ，關鍵字是 enforce a stricter guideline，選項(D) devising more scrupulous rules 和 enforce a stricter guideline 意思相同。

聽力原文與中譯

Questions 71-73 refer to the following advertisement

See the giant Hello Kitty and balloons of several cartoon characters... yep... it's Black Friday... Friddaaay. Come join us at our auction. For the first one hundred customers, there is a chance that you might get a renewed membership. For those whose shopping exceeds US 5000 dollars, you will be rewarded with line points and a gift bag. Also, we have our personal shoppers waiting for you. You won't feel that you are like a rabbit getting lost in the jungle... completely overwhelmed by tons of options. Tell our personal shoppers what you need... just that easy.

問題 71-73 請參閱下列廣告

看那巨大的 Hello Kitty 和幾個卡通人物的氣球⋯是的⋯這是黑色購物節⋯星期五五。加入我們的拍賣行列吧。對於前一百位顧客,你可能有機會獲得更新的會員資格。對於那些購物超過 5000 美元者,我們會獎勵您 line 的點數和禮物袋。而且我們有我們的個人購物員等著你們。你不用感到你像隻在叢林中迷失的小白兔⋯對於許多選擇感到全然不知所措。告訴我們的個人購物員你需要的⋯就是這樣簡單。

試題中譯與解析

| 71. Where might you hear this advertisement?
(A) a shopping mall
(B) a Hello Kitty amusement park
(C) a cartoon amusement park
(D) a zoo | 71. 你可能在哪裡聽到這個廣告?
(A) 購物中心。
(B) Hello Kitty 遊樂園。
(C) 卡通遊樂園。
(D) 動物園。 |

72. According to this advertisement, what might personal shoppers do for consumers? (A) renew membership (B) line up (C) go shopping (D) buying rabbits	72. 依照此廣告，個人購物員可能替消費者做什麼？ (A) 更新會員資格。 (B) 排隊。 (C) 購物。 (D) 買兔子。
73. What does Black Friday imply in the advertisement? (A) the day Jesus died (B) a major shopping day (C) the day before Christmas (D) Easter	73. 在廣告中黑色星期五暗示什麼？ (A) 耶穌過世那天。 (B) 主要購物日。 (C) 聖誕節前一天。 (D) 復活節。

答案：71. A 72. C 73. B

解析

71. 此題詢問廣告地點，對話開頭的 Hello Kitty 和 cartoon characters 是陷阱，綜合 Black Friday 和對話中段 For those whose shopping exceeds US 5000 dollars... personal shoppers 等線索，推測答案是(A) a shopping mall。

72. 根據對話最後一句 Tell our personal shoppers what you need，告訴我們的個人購物員你需要的，言下之意即消費者不用親自購物，個人購物員可以代勞，故選(C) go shopping。

73. 廣告提到 Black Friday 之後，有 auction，拍賣，及 shopping，personal shoppers 等線索字，依這些線索字推測 Black Friday 主要跟 shopping 有關。

Questions 74-76 refer to the following news report

Good afternoon it's afternoon news. I can feel Florida heat even if I'm not outside. Let's see if an approaching tornado is gonna affect our weekend. There seems to be a computer glitch... our weatherman is trying to fix that... he certainly has been working out...

Weatherman: thanks...we do have a poster here... let me show you... see the tornado doubles its size when it reaches here... and it's getting bigger... it's gonna be the biggest in history... we're predicting two different routes... first it's gonna hit the Bahamas and land at Daytona and the second route would be directly landing at palm beach... no... not palm beach but cocoa beach... I guess people in Miami will feel so relieved...

問題 74-76 請參閱下列新聞報導

下午好這是下午新聞。我能感受到佛羅里達州的熱即使我不在外頭。讓我們看即將逼近的颶風是否影響我們周末。似乎有些電腦小故障…我們的天氣播報男正在修復…看來他確實有在健身…

天氣播報男：謝謝…我們這裡有海報…讓我們向你展示…看這颶風當它抵達這裡時體型成了雙倍…它漸漸增大…將會成為史上最大…我們正預測兩個不同路徑…第一個是他們會先侵襲巴哈馬然後於蝶同那登陸，而第二個路徑是它可能直接在棕櫚海灘…不…不是棕櫚海灘而是可可亞海灘登陸…我想在邁阿密的人會感到如釋重負。

74. Which of the following is the closest to "a computer glitch"?	74. 下列何者和「電腦小故障」的意思最接近？
(A) a discount on computers	(A) 電腦折扣。
(B) a computer bug	(B) 電腦故障。
(C) a poster shown on computer	(C) 電腦顯示的海報。
(D) a weather forecast software	(D) 氣象預報軟體。

75. What kind of disaster will hit Florida during the weather forecast? (A) heavy rainfall (B) a typhoon (C) a tornado (D) an earthquake	75. 在天氣預報期間，哪種災難將襲擊佛羅里達州？ (A) 大雨。 (B) 颱風。 (C) 颶風。 (D) 地震。
76. Why does the weatherman say, "I guess people in Miami will feel so relieved..."? (A) because the tornado might not strike Miami (B) because people at Miami are quite used to tornadoes (C) because people at Miami are already evacuated (D) because people at Miami are not afraid of any disaster	76. 氣象播報員為何說「我想在邁阿密的人會感到如釋重負」？ (A) 因為龍捲風可能不會襲擊邁阿密。 (B) 因為邁阿密的人們非常習慣龍捲風。 (C) 因為邁阿密的人們已經撤離了。 (D) 因為邁阿密的人們不害怕任何災難。

答案：74. B　75. C　76. A

解析

74. 此題考 computer glitch 的類似字，glitch <n.> 小毛病、小故障，講者提到 a computer glitch 的下一句也是解題線索：that our weatherman is trying to fix that。從 fix，修理，一字能推測 glitch 有「故障」的意思。電腦故障的另一片語是 computer bug。

75. 此題問哪種災難將襲擊佛羅里達州，由短講提到的細節 see the tornado doubles its size when it reaches here，定位 tornado，颶風。

76. I guess people at Miami will feel so relieved，「我想在邁阿密的人會感到如釋重負」是短講最後一句，因此回溯倒數第二句以推測氣象播報員這麼說的原因。倒數第二句：the second route would be directly landing at Palm Beach... no... not Palm Beach but Cocoa Beach，雖然沒有明說龍捲風路線不會襲擊邁阿密，但是可從 no... not Palm Beach（不會襲擊 Palm Beach）推測 Palm Beach 位於邁阿密，氣象播報員才會延續說「我想在邁阿密的人會感到如釋重負」。

Questions 77-79 refer to the following announcement

Attention visitors! I do hope you enjoy your day in the zoo, and I'm here to inform you that our crocodiles seem to decide to have a day off or something. They're not in their compartments. But it's chilly out there. I'm not sure why they have to take a weekend getaway or something. I don't want you guys to panic. I've four animal specialists and police officers out there looking for them already. When you see them, just to keep calm... and you'll be fine... OMG what are they doing out there. Oops... My office glass wall just shattered. Apparently, I was fooled by Glass Company. It can't stand crocodile's punch.

問題 77-79 請參閱下列公告

觀光者們注意！我希望你們都能享受在動物園的時光，我在此是要告知你們我們的鱷魚們似乎決定想休息一天或幹嘛的。他們不在我們的隔間裡。但是外頭相當寒冷。我不知道為什麼他們想要上演個周末大逃亡或什麼的。我不想要你們感到驚嚇。我已經派四個動物專人和警察們找尋他們。當你們看到他們就保持冷靜…我想你們會沒事的…天啊他們在這幹嘛…糟了…我的辦公司玻璃牆剛碎掉了。顯然我被玻璃公司騙了。它無法承受鱷魚的撞擊。

77. Why does the speaker say, "Oops... My office glass wall just shattered"? (A) The glass was not bulletproof. (B) The glass was shot by bullets. (C) The police officers shot the glass. (D) The glass was destroyed by the crocodiles.	77. 為何講者說「糟了…我的辦公司玻璃牆剛碎掉了」？ (A) 玻璃牆不防彈。 (B) 玻璃牆被子彈射擊。 (C) 警官射擊玻璃牆。 (D) 玻璃牆被鱷魚破壞了。
78. What are the visitors told to do when they see the crocodiles? (A) start panicking. (B) remain calm. (C) call the police. (D) call animal specialists.	78. 訪客被告知看到鱷魚時該做什麼？ (A) 開始驚慌。 (B) 保持鎮定。 (C) 打電話給警察。 (D) 打電話給動物專家。

79. How is the weather on the day of this announcement?	79. 在此宣布當天天氣如何？
(A) very hot	(A) 很熱。
(B) warm	(B) 溫暖。
(C) very cold	(C) 很冷。
(D) cool	(D) 涼爽。

答案：77. D 78. B 79. C

解析

77. 綜合短講開頭描述「鱷魚們……不在我們的隔間裡」（our crocodiles... They're not in their compartments.）及考點句子的上一句:OMG what are they doing out there.，推測 they 指的是鱷魚，因此玻璃牆剛碎掉和鱷魚關係最密切，故選(D)。

78. 根據 When you see them, just to keep calm，知道講者告訴訪客保持鎮定。故選(B)。

79. 此細節題詢問天氣，根據 But it's chilly out there.，chilly，形容詞，寒冷的，故選(C)。

聽力原文與中譯

Questions 80-82 refer to the following instructions

Don't worry that you don't have any experience. Grab your apron and prepare all ingredients. Best kitchen will show you how. Before we start, I'd like to show you my personal weapon... don't be afraid..it's not a gun... it's a pot. It looks like it's new doesn't it, but I'm gonna tell you she is two years old... actually...it's been used for 23 months... that's almost two years... see just a few scratches here... and really perfect for cooking fish and meat. I do have a really good oven ideal for cooking Thanksgiving turkey... let me demonstrate it for you. First defrost the turkey... see? Put it in the oven and press defrost... how convenient...

問題 80-82 請參閱下列操作說明

別擔心你不具備任何經驗。拿起你的圍裙和準備所有成分。倍斯特廚房將向你展示如何製作。在我們開始之前，我想要向你展示我的個人武器…別害怕…這不是槍…這是鍋具。這看起來想是新的，對不對？但是我要告訴你她兩年了…實際上她已經使用了 23 個月…算成兩年…看這裡只有幾個刮痕…拿來煮魚和肉品真的很完美。我有很好的烤箱拿來煮感恩節的火雞是很理想的廚具…讓我向你展示我第一個去凍火雞…看放進烤箱然後按「去凍」鍵…多方便啊…。

試題中譯與解析

80. Where might you hear these instructions? (A) a department store (B) a cooking school (C) a Thanksgiving party (D) a weapon store	80. 你可能在哪裡會聽到這些指示？ (A) 百貨公司。 (B) 烹飪學校。 (C) 感恩節派對。 (D) 武器商店。
81. Who might the speaker address? (A) gourmets (B) recipe writers (C) people interested in learning cooking (D) people interested in kitchenware	81. 講者可能是針對誰說話？ (A) 美食家。 (B) 食譜作家。 (C) 對學習烹飪有興趣的人。 (D) 對廚具有興趣的人。
82. Why does the speaker say, "I'd like to show you my personal weapon... don't be afraid"? (A) He is trying to display his weapons. (B) He knows some people are scared by weapons. (C) When he says weapon, he's not referring to a real weapon. (D) He knows some people dislike guns.	82. 為何講者說「我想要向你展示我的個人武器…別害怕」？ (A) 他正試著展示他的武器。 (B) 他知道有些人害怕武器。 (C) 當他說武器，他指的不是真的武器。 (D) 他知道有些人不喜歡槍。

答案：80. B 81. C 82. C

解析

80. 依據 Best kitchen will show you how. 及 let me demonstrate it for you，這兩句表達講者要給聽眾一些指示及示範，即講者的身份類似老師，所以(B) a cooking school 最搭配此篇情境。

81. 綜合第 10 題的解題線索和第一句: Don't worry that you don't have any experience，「別擔心你不具備任何經驗」。推測聽眾最可能的身份是學生，最接近的選項是(C)。

82. 在題目考點句之後，講者馬上說: it's not a gun... it's a pot.，「這不是槍…這是大鍋」。可知他不是指真的武器。

聽力原文與中譯

Questions 83-85 refer to the following news report

See the kissing booth over there... it's is by far the greatest in Best amusement park. Every year there'll be numerous cheerleaders volunteering for this meaningful job. The money every guy pays goes totally to the charity. Too bad, I'm a reporter, or I will jump at the chance... they all look very gorgeous... there's a guy kissing a girl of my dream... I can't watch it... there's another girl... seems she is sending me a mixed signal... come join us...even if it's a long line here... but you might be able to kiss your dream girl... and this is Tim at Best amusement park.

問題 83-85 請參閱下列新聞報導

看親吻亭這裡…這是倍斯特遊樂園有史以來最大的。每年有許多啦啦隊員自願做這個有意義的工作。每個男子付的款項都全部捐給慈善機構。真不巧我是記者，否則我會抓住這好機會…他們看起來都很美…有個男子親了我夢想中女孩…我無法再看下去了…又有另一個女孩…似乎他正向我遞送混雜的訊號…來加入我們吧…即使這裡隊排的很長…但是你可能有機會能夠親到你夢想中的女孩…這是提姆於倍斯特遊樂園。

1 照片描述

2 應答問題

3 簡短對話

4 簡短獨白

模擬試題

83. What do cheerleaders do in this activity? (A) They perform gymnastics. (B) They donate money. (C) They give kisses. (D) They dance	83. 在這場活動中啦啦隊員要做什麼？ (A) 他們表演體操。 (B) 他們捐錢。 (C) 他們親吻。 (D) 他們跳舞。
84. What is the main topic of the news report? (A) a charity event (B) an amusement park (C) cheerleading (D) kissing skills	84. 此新聞報導主題為何？ (A) 慈善活動。 (B) 遊樂園。 (C) 啦啦隊活動。 (D) 親吻技巧。
85. Why does the speaker say, "Too bad, I'm a reporter"? (A) He does not enjoy his job. (B) He does not think the quality of the report is excellent. (C) He thinks the charity is being held badly. (D) He cannot participate in the activity because of his identity.	85. 講者為何說「真不巧我是記者」？ (A) 他不喜歡他的工作。 (B) 他不認為報導品質是優秀的。 (C) 他認為這場慈善活動舉辦得很糟。 (D) 因為他的身份他不能參與這場活動。

答案：83. C　84. A　85. D

解析

83. 第一句提到主題 kissing booth，接著講者說: there'll be numerous cheerleaders volunteering for this meaningful job.，綜合以上線索，推測啦啦隊員在這場活動提供親吻。

84. 依據 The money every guy pays goes totally to the charity.，尤其關鍵字 charity，確定正確選項是(A)。

85. 在題目考點句之後，講者馬上說: or I will jump at the chance，「否則我會抓住這好機會」，又考慮考點句只表明他的身份是記者，即不能參與的原因是身份，因此正確選項是(D)。

聽力原文與中譯

Questions 86-88 refer to the following advertisement

Still struggling to balance your life and work... especially after giving birth to a second child... feeling so tired... and there seems to be a lot of chores waiting to be done. Just can't squeeze some time in to shop? Come to our website. We have all the specifically tailored household items for you. Let us do the magic for you. I'm quoting a most frequently used line from our customers. The diapers just magically appear at our door... it really is a great relief... don't hesitate to contact us... and we run 24/7. Just contact us.

問題 86-88 請參閱下列廣告

仍在平衡你的生活和工作中掙扎嗎？…特別是特別是在生產第二個小孩過後…感到很疲憊…而這似乎有許多雜事等待你完成。就是無法擠出一些時間購物嗎？來我們的網站。我們有所有替您量身訂作的家庭用品。讓我們替您施展魔力吧。我來引述一個頻繁被我們顧客用的台詞。尿布就像是魔法般地出現在我們家門口…這真的是讓人鬆一口氣…別猶豫聯絡我們…我們 24 小時都有營運，就連絡我們就是了。

試題中譯與解析

86. Which of the followings is the most likely to put on this advertisement? (A) tailors (B) an online shopping site (C) a diaper manufacturer (D) a convenience store	86. 下列何者最有可能刊登這則廣告？ (A) 裁縫師。 (B) 購物網站。 (C) 尿布製造商。 (D) 便利商店。

87. Why does the speaker quote this line, "The diapers just magically appear at our door"? (A) to show the high quality of the diapers (B) to advertise that they offer magic shows (C) to show how convenient the service is (D) to target consumers who need diapers	87. 為何講者引用這句「尿布就像是魔法般地出現在我們家門口」？ (A) 顯示尿布的高品質。 (B) 廣告他們有提供魔術表演。 (C) 顯示這項服務有多方便。 (D) 針對需要尿布的消費者。
88. What kind of people is the most likely to use the service in this advertisement? (A) career women who have children (B) tailors (C) single men (D) young students	88. 哪種人最有可能使用廣告裡的服務？ (A) 有小孩的職業婦女。 (B) 裁縫師。 (C) 單身男士。 (D) 年輕學生。

答案：86. B 87. C 88. A

解析

86. 依據 Just can't squeeze some time to shop? Come to our website.，推測此篇是購物網站的廣告。

87. 題目考點句之後，講者馬上說: it really is a great relief，真是讓人鬆一口氣，也可回溯短講開頭幾句都是描述聽眾在生活和工作中的辛苦，換言之此網站的服務讓聽眾的生活更方便。

88. 短講開頭幾句都是描述聽眾在生活和工作中的辛苦，尤其是 especially after giving birth to a second child 這句，especially 這個副詞就暗示考生這句很重要，從此句推測答案是(A) career women who have children。

聽力原文與中譯

Questions 89-91 refer to the following line recordings

This is Linda... an admissions administrator of Best Academy... we still have two spots left. We're looking for kids with special talents. We will train them to outperform kids in other schools. We're welcoming kids with different backgrounds... like I always say we value diversity here at Best Academy... another thing that I would like to tell you is that we're short of funds for our new computer lab... so if anyone of you would like to go beyond that... I'll submit your paperwork directly to our principal... and there is an excellent chance... your kids might get far ahead of other candidates... you know how parents wanna send their kids to our school...

問題 89-91 請參閱下列 line 錄製訊息

這是琳達…倍斯特學院的招生行政人員…我們仍有兩個空缺。我們在找尋有特別才能的小孩。我們會訓練他們到勝過其他學校的小孩們。我們也歡迎不同背景的小孩…像是我總是說我們倍斯特學院這裡重視多樣性…另一件事我想讓你們知道的事我們對於新電腦實驗室仍資金短缺…所以如果你們任何人有想要做些超越那個的…我會將你的書面作業直接遞給我們校長…有很大的機會是…你的小孩會比其他候選人都還前面…你知道父母有多想要將小孩送到我們學校…

試題中譯與解析

89. Which of the followings is the closest to the word "spots" as in "we still have two spots left"? (A) dots (B) sightseeing spots (C) vacancies (D) spotlights	89. 下列何者和「我們仍有兩個空缺」的「空缺」意思最接近？ (A) 圓點。 (B) 觀光景點。 (C) 空缺。 (D) 焦點。
90. Why does the speaker mention that they are short of fund for their new computer lab? (A) to hold a fundraiser (B) to imply a way to draw applications (C) to ask for the donation of new computers (D) to ask for advice from parents	90. 為何講者提到他們新的電腦教室資金不夠？ (A) 為了舉辦募款會。 (B) 暗示一種吸引申請案件的方式。 (C) 要求捐新電腦。 (D) 向家長徵詢建議。

91. If parents want to ensure their children will be accepted by the Academy, what might they do?
(A) They might talk to the principal directly.
(B) They might train their children to have more talents.
(C) They might donate funds to the Academy.
(D) They might train their children to become bilingual.

91. 如果家長想確定他們的小孩能被學院接受，他們可能怎麼做？
(A) 他們可能和校長直接談話。
(B) 他們可能訓練小孩有更多才華。
(C) 他們可能捐款給學院。
(D) 他們可能訓練小孩會雙語。

答案：89. C 90. B 91. C

解析

89. spot 是多重意義字，因此一定要考慮題目考點句的情境，才能確定類似字。由第一句提及 an admission administrative of Best Academy，知道此篇是學校入學部門的宣佈，進而推測 spot 指的是「空缺」。

90. 講者提到「新電腦實驗室仍資金短缺」之後，馬上說「所以如果你們任何人有想要做些超越那個的…我會將你的書面作業直接遞給我們校長」，暗示家長可透過捐款，加快申請速度，即提供吸引申請案件的方式。

91. 考慮第 20 題的線索句，講者暗示家長捐款，及 your kids might get far ahead of other candidates 的句意類似「家長想確定他們的小孩能被學院接受」，故選(C)。

聽力原文與中譯

Questions 92-94 refer to the following talk

Welcome to our cellar. I'm your tour guide. My father bought this cellar in southern France a long time ago. This cellar mainly functions as a way to keep him from getting bored. As we all know about retirees... having nothing else to do but watch TV. He loves wine so one day it hit him... why not buy yourself a place where you can get to enjoy beautiful scenery and at the same time you can have time to do what you love... something you can only do when you retire. Have a taste for the chardonnay... such a perfect blend... just promise you won't drive after drinking...

問題 92-94 請參閱下列談話

歡迎來到我們的地窖。我是你們的導遊。我的父親在很久之前買了這南法國的地窖。這個地窖主要的功用是讓他免於無聊之苦。如同我們都知道關於所有退休者…無所事事只能看電視。他喜愛酒,所以有天他突然靈光一閃…想到為什麼不買個能讓你享受美麗風景且同時又能有時間做自己喜愛的事的地方呢?…一些你只能於退休後從事的事。嚐嚐夏多內白酒…如此完美的結合…答應我你不會在喝了之後開車。

試題中譯與解析

92. Who might the speaker be talking to? (A) his father's friends (B) his family members (C) tourists (D) vintners	92. 講者可能正向誰說話? (A) 他父親的朋友。 (B) 他的家人。 (C) 觀光客。 (D) 酒商。
93. Why does the speaker's father buy the cellar? (A) to develop his hobby (B) for investment (C) to make more money (D) to store things he does not need	93. 為何講者的父親買酒窖? (A) 發展他的嗜好。 (B) 為了投資。 (C) 為了賺更多錢。 (D) 為了儲藏他不需要的東西。
94. What does "such a perfect blend" refer to? (A) great taste of coffee (B) mixing cocktails (C) blending in the party (D) great taste of wine	94.「如此完美的結合」指的是什麼? (A) 咖啡的美好滋味。 (B) 調雞尾酒。 (C) 在派對交際。 (D) 酒的美好滋味。

答案:92. C 93. A 94. D

1 照片描述

2 應答問題

3 簡短對話

4 簡短獨白

模擬試題

92. 根據 I'm your tour guide.，馬上推測聽眾是觀光客，tourists。

93. 根據 This cellar mainly functions as a way to keep him from getting bored.及 you can have time to do what you love，推測當初購買酒窖的動機是發展喜歡的事物，換言之是(A) to develop his hobby。

94. 根據 such a perfect blend 的前後文: Have a taste for the chardonnay 及 just promise you won't drive after drinking，確定考點片語指的是酒的完美味道，換言之是(D) great taste of wine。

聽力原文與中譯

Questions 95-97 refer to the following advertisement

Hi everyone... Best cosmetics is having an annual auction. Try this. It really is perfect. A light brown shadow softens your puffiness. And our lipsticks. They have ten different flavors. See the shining color on my lip. It's orange flavor. I myself love the strawberry one... really sweet... but we're kind of promoting orange and grape flavors... so I picked orange. We're offering some samples for you, and with Christmas coming up, you can actually pick one as a present for your friends. We are gonna give customers purchasing more than four lipsticks an exquisite handbag.

問題 95-97 請參閱下列廣告

嗨，大家好…倍斯特化妝品將有年度販賣。試試這個。這真的很完美。淡淡的棕色眼影柔和了你的眼袋。看我唇上的亮澤眼色。這是柳橙口味。我自己則喜歡草莓的…真的甜甜的…但是我們有點在推銷柳橙和葡萄口味…所以我選了柳橙口味的。我們將提供樣品給你們，隨著聖誕節的到來，你可以實際挑選一個當作禮物贈送給你的朋友們。我們會給購買超過四個口紅的顧客精緻的手提袋。

試題中譯與解析

95. According to the speaker, what is the effect of "a light brown shadow"? (A) to highlight your eyes (B) to reduce puffiness around the eyes (C) to make you look thinner (D) to make your skin darker	95. 依據講者，「淡淡的棕色眼影」效果是什麼？ (A) 強調你的眼睛 (B) 減少眼周圍的浮腫 (C) 讓你看來更瘦 (D) 讓你的膚色更暗
96. Why does the speaker mention "orange and grape flavors"? (A) They are her favorite flavors. (B) The auction provides desserts of orange and grape flavors. (C) The company aims to sell more lipsticks of these two flavors. (D) She does not wear lipsticks of these two flavors.	96. 為何講者提到「柳橙和葡萄口味」？ (A) 它們是她最愛的口味。 (B) 拍賣會提供柳橙和葡萄口味的甜點。 (C) 公司的目標是賣更多這兩種口味的口紅。 (D) 她不塗這兩種口味的口紅。
97. If a customer buy 6 lipsticks, what will she receive? (A) free samples (B) lipsticks of strawberry flavor (C) lipsticks of grape flavor (D) a beautiful handbag	97. 如果顧客買六支口紅，她會收到什麼？ (A) 免費樣品 (B) 草莓口味的口紅。 (C) 葡萄口味的口紅。 (D) 一個漂亮的手提袋。

答案：95. B 96. C 97. D

解析

95. 講者提到 A light brown shadow 的同一句，她說 softens your puffiness，關鍵字 puffiness 是「浮腫」的名詞。

96 依據 we're kind of promoting orange and grape flavors，關鍵字 promote，促銷，換言之是(C) 公司的目標是賣更多這兩種口味的口紅。

97. 依據最後一句：「購買超過四個口紅的顧客能得到精緻的手提袋」。 exquisite，精美的，故選(D)。

聽力原文與中譯

Questions 98-100 refer to the following talk

Best cinema will be having a renovation from June 20 to July 28. We're really sorry for the inconvenience caused. Good news is that we are adding several facilities. It's gonna wow you when we reopen. I guess I'm gonna tell just a bit. For example, we are having a ghost castle. Whoever makes it to the end of the castle will get a free ticket, but whoever quits or not being able to make it to the end will get punished. It's just insider information... I hope I'm not revealing too much...

問題 98-100 請參閱下列談話

倍斯特電影將於 6 月 20 日到 7 月 28 日進行整修。我們對於引起的不便感到抱歉。好消息是我們將新增幾項設施。當我們重新開張時您會感到驚艷。我想我可以說一點點。例如，我們將有鬼屋城堡。不論誰達到城堡終點都將獲得免費的票，但任何放棄或無法抵達終點的將會受到懲罰。這只是內部消息…希望我沒有透露太多。

試題中譯與解析

98. What does the speaker mean by "It's gonna wow you"? (A) It will amaze you. (B) It will frighten you. (C) It will make you feel shocked. (D) It will make you relaxed.	98. 講者說「它會讓你感到驚艷」的意思是什麼？ (A) 它會讓你感到神奇。 (B) 它會讓你害怕。 (C) 它會讓你驚嚇。 (D) 它會讓你放鬆。
99. Where is this talk given? (A) a castle (B) a haunted house (C) a cinema (D) a department store	99. 此短講在哪裡發生？ (A) 城堡。 (B) 鬼屋。 (C) 電影院。 (D) 百貨公司。

100. Which of the following is the closest to "It's just insider information"? (A) information about movies (B) the speaker's secret (C) information not known to the public (D) information about the new facilities	100. 下列何者和「這只是內部消息」意思最接近？ (A) 關於電影的資訊。 (B) 講者的秘密。 (C) 大眾不知道的資訊。 (D) 關於新設施的資訊。

答案：98. A 99. C 100. C

解析

98. It's gonna wow you 是比較厘語的說法，wow 由感嘆語轉換成動詞，指「讓人驚訝」，通常使用於正面情境，(A) It will amaze you.最類似 It's gonna wow you 的意思。

99. 由開頭 Best cinema 馬上確定地點(C) 電影院，注意雖然短講有提到 a ghost castle，但(A) a castle 和(B) a haunted house 是陷阱選項，a ghost castle 只是戲院的設備之一。

100. insider information 是慣用語，指「機密資訊」或「內部消息」。換言之是大眾不知道的資訊，故選(C)。

新多益聽力模擬試題 答案表

PART 1									
1. B	2. C	3. A	4. A	5. B	6. D				

PART 2									
7. B	8. A	9. C	10.C	11.B	12.A	13.A	14.C	15.B	16.B
17.B	18.A	19.C	20.A	21.A	22.B	23.A	24.C	25.C	26.B
27.B	28.C	29.C	30.A	31.A					

PART 3									
32.B	33.A	34.C	35.D	36.B	37.C	38.A	39.A	40.C	41.C
42.A	43.D	44.C	45.B	46.A	47.B	48.A	49.D	50.A	51.A
52.B	53.B	54.B	55.C	56.B	57.A	58.D	59.B	60.C	61.A
62.D	63.C	64.D	65.B	66.D	67.A	68.D	69.A	70.D	

PART 4									
71.A	72.C	73.B	74.B	75.C	76.A	77.D	78.B	79.C	80.B
81.C	82.C	83.C	84.A	85.D	86.B	87.C	88.A	89.C	90.B
91.C	92.C	93.A	94.D	95.B	96.C	97.D	98.A	99.C	100. C

國家圖書館出版品預行編目(CIP)資料

全新制—新多益聽力：金色證書 / 莊琬君
、韋爾著. -- 初版. -- 臺北市：倍斯特, 2018
.7 面；　公分. --（考用英語系列；10）
ISBN 978-986-96309-2-4（平裝附光碟）
1.多益測驗

805.1895　　　　　　　　　　107009168

考用英語 010

全新制—新多益聽力：金色證書（附MP3）

初　　版	2018年7月
定　　價	新台幣499元

作　　者	莊琬君、韋爾
出　　版	倍斯特出版事業有限公司
發 行 人	周瑞德
電　　話	886-2-2351-2007
傳　　真	886-2-2351-0887
地　　址	100 台北市中正區福州街1號10樓之2
E - m a i l	best.books.service@gmail.com
官　　網	www.bestbookstw.com
執行總監	齊心瑀
行銷經理	楊景輝
企劃編輯	陳韋佑
執行編輯	曾品綺
內頁構成	菩薩蠻數位文化有限公司
印　　製	大亞彩色印刷製版股份有限公司

港澳地區總經銷	泛華發行代理有限公司
地　　址	香港新界將軍澳工業邨駿昌街7號2樓
電　　話	852-2798-2323
傳　　真	852-2796-5471

沒有冗長的文法解釋，降低學習負擔！用最簡單、濃縮的敘述引用耳熟能詳、的流行英文歌曲，串起學習連結！

◎ 引用歌曲中的共鳴/感動句強化大腦記憶，連結文法重點。
◎ 「富創意+趣味」的口訣和諧音激起學習文法的動力。
◎ 只給重點精闢解析，輕鬆找出文法脈絡、透徹理解文法核心概念。

定 價：NT$ 399元
規 格：352頁/18K/雙色印刷/平裝

獨家公開考官必問話題！用母語人士的思維，說出與眾不同的高分回答！

◎ 聽力講解篇：先說明概念，再由關鍵句＆小提點，
做「聽力」＋「跟讀」練習，奠定紮實的基礎。
◎ 每單元均有字彙輔助，特別規劃慣用語補充，
擴充個人字彙庫，面對考試更無往不利。
◎ 跟著講解、演練、實戰篇的順序學習並且多做練習，
一舉獲取理想成績。

定 價：NT$ 380元
規 格：288頁/18K/雙色印刷/平裝

運用中西諺語，搭配獨家規劃三大類議題，一次就考到雅思寫作6.5up！

◎ 濃縮式提點協助考生擬定作文大綱，**立即掌握**
作文中的起、承、轉、合。
◎ 收錄必學作文範例，寫出具說服力、論點清楚
、語句**通順且連貫**的句子或文章！

定 價：NT$ 380元
規 格：288頁/18K/雙色印刷/平裝